Through the dirty glass I saw a black Jeep Comanche pull into the parking area, followed by a sober gray Chrysler New Yorker. Doors were opening before the vehicles had come to a rest, disgorging men in dark clothes.

I thundered down the stairs. I decided to exit the house the way I'd come in, make a break for it, find somewhere to hide outside.

I bent, turned, stuck one leg through the window followed by the other one, and dropped out and down onto the grass. There were woods back there, but first there was a lawn and a field and—

"All right, freeze!"

I skidded to a stop and spread my arms out without turning. I said, "I'm not armed."

"I am. Go flat on the ground. Now."

I heard footsteps. A backup. I started to turn. "Look—"

The gunshot was deep and throaty and scared the hell out of the indigenous birds. It also scared the hell out of me. I dropped to the ground. More footsteps, a pair of new sneakers, and my hands were yanked hard to the small of my back. I heard the oily snick and felt the pinching embrace of cuffs.

"Up now," the voice grunted.

The man was a young dark-haired tough, shaved and groomed, wearing trousers and sport shirt and an orange hunting vest. His face was expressionless, almost bored; a killer face or a cop face, I couldn't tell which.

I had been afraid these were cops. Now I found myself hoping they were. . . .

Bantam Books offers the finest in classic and modern American murder mysteries
Ask your bookseller for the books you have missed

Rex Stout

Broken Vase
Death of a Dude
Death Times Three
Fer-de-Lance
The Final Deduction
Gambit
The Rubber Band
Too Many Cooks
The Black Mountain
Plot It Yourself
Three for the Chair

Max Allan Collins

The Dark City
Bullet Proof

A. E. Maxwell

Just Another Day in Paradise
Gatsby's Vineyard
The Frog and the Scorpion
Just Enough Light to Kill

Joseph Louis

Madelaine
The Trouble with Stephanie

Mary Jo Adamson

Not Till a Hot January
A February Face
Remember March
April When They Woo
May's Newfangled Mirth

P. M. Carlson

Murder Unrenovated
Rehearsal for Murder

Dick Lupoff

The Comic Book Killer

Margaret Maron

The Right Jack
Baby Doll Games
One Coffee With
coming soon: Corpus Christmas

Randy Russell

Hot Wire

Marilyn Wallace

Primary Target

William Murray

When The Fat Man Sings
coming soon: The King of the Nightcap

Robert Goldsborough

Murder in E Minor
Death on Deadline
The Bloodied Ivy
coming soon: The Last Coincidence

Sue Grafton

"A" Is for Alibi
"B" Is for Burglar
"C" Is for Corpse
"D" Is for Deadbeat
"E" Is for Evidence

Joseph Telushkin

The Unorthodox Murder of Rabbi Wahl
The Final Analysis of Doctor Stark

Richard Hilary

Snake in the Grasses
Pieces of Cream
Pillow of the Community
Behind the Fact

Carolyn G. Hart

Design for Murder
Death on Demand
Something Wicked
Honeymoon With Murder
coming soon: A Little Class on Murder

Annette Meyers

The Big Killing

Rob Kantner

Dirty Work
The Back-Door Man
Hell's Only Half Full

Robert Crais

The Monkey's Raincoat
coming soon: Falling Scarecrow

Keith Peterson

The Trapdoor
There Fell a Shadow
The Rain
coming soon: Rough Justice

David Handler

The Man Who Died Laughing
The Man Who Lived by Night

Jeffery Deaver

Manhattan Is My Beat

HELL'S ONLY HALF FULL

Rob Kantner

BANTAM BOOKS
NEW YORK · TORONTO · LONDON · SYDNEY · AUCKLAND

PUBLISHER'S NOTE

This book is a work of fiction. Names, characters, places and incidents either are the product of the author's imagination or are used fictitiously. Any resemblance to actual persons, living or dead, events, or locales is entirely coincidental.

HELL'S ONLY HALF FULL
A Bantam Book / October 1989

ISBN 0-553-28259-X

Published simultaneously in the United States and Canada

Bantam Books are published by Bantam Books, a division of Bantam Doubleday Dell Publishing Group, Inc. Its trademark, consisting of the words "Bantam Books" and the portrayal of a rooster, is Registered in U.S. Patent and Trademark Office and in other countries. Marca Registrada. Bantam Books, 666 Fifth Avenue, New York, New York 10103.

PRINTED IN THE UNITED STATES OF AMERICA

OPM   0 9 8 7 6 5 4 3 2 1

This one is for
Meaghan '78, John '79, and Robert '81,
with love and pride from their old man.

And also for Valerie,
who's put up with a lot.
I love you.

CHAPTER 1

AFTER TEN MINUTES of panhandling, I managed to bum a weed off a fellow defendant. He was an accused rapist, and the cigarette was a Kool, but who's complaining? I accepted a light, inhaled gratefully, and leaned against the yellow brick wall, staring out the window at the traffic barreling west on Michigan Avenue.

"Mr. Perkins?"

I turned warily. The middle-aged man was fleshy-faced, balding, dressed in mismatched coat, shirt, tie, and pants that looked like they'd fallen on him out the window of a Salvation Army depot. Well, I wasn't dressed all that sharp, myself. "Huh," I answered.

"Mr. Ben Perkins," he pressed, stepping closer.

The hallway, which functioned as a holding pen, was filled with perpetrators, attorneys, and gawkers, all under the watchful eye of a sleepy, heavily paunched city of Wayne policeman. This guy fit no category. "That's me," I said.

His smile looked like the grille of an old Mercedes. "Jim Gant, *Detroit Free Press*. Like to ask you a few questions about the, uh, incident."

Oh, God. "I'm getting ready to split, soon as my lawyer gets the paperwork done. Besides, I don't want to talk about it." I inhaled some smoke and squinted at him. "This must be one hell of a slow news day."

He stood beside me at the window, grinning. "Not really. And I normally don't mess around with district court stuff. Circuit court and Recorder's court are where the action is. But you have to admit your case is somewhat, uh, unique."

1

I looked back out the window. "As in, they're hammering *me* when all I did was save some lives, most likely. Two felonies. Jesus. But I don't want to talk about it."

He had a pad out and was standing very close to me. His voice was a brisk murmur. "Felonious assault and felonious driving." His eyes were on me. "Why do you suppose they're hitting you so hard?"

"You were in court there?" I growled. He nodded. "I didn't even get a chance to tell them my side. Just bing-bang, two charges, bail's at ten thousand, and here I am." I glared at him. "But I still don't want to talk about it."

Gant's eyebrows arched and he slipped his pad into his coat pocket. "Okay. I just thought maybe you'd like to get your side on the record."

I looked over my shoulder up the hallway. Carole was sure taking her sweet time at the clerk's office. I had the sudden dreadful thought that maybe she wouldn't be able to post bail for me. Now, that would be just dandy. I pictured myself being loaded on a bus and rendered to Wayne County Jail, and my hands curled into fists. I took a hard hit on the cigarette and said to the reporter, "You want to hear it?"

The pad came back out.

"I was coming east on Michigan Avenue. Yesterday afternoon. Saw a couple of cars in the ditch. One of them rolled over. Must have just happened, the people were still inside and everything."

"Is that when you saw the truck?" Gant asked.

"Yeah. Way ahead. I didn't know what was going on right that minute. I gained on the truck. A double-bottom gravel hauler, really moving, sixty-five at least."

"Over the limit," Gant murmured.

"What else is new?" I inhaled some more cigarette. It tasted flat, sweet, and stale. "He came up on a pickup truck, hogged the guy's bumper for a minute. Then he swung to the left, moved up beside him, swerved right and smacked him right off the road. Like a kid swatting a Matchbox toy off a table."

"That one's in the hospital," Gant observed. "He hit a tree. Go ahead."

"So anyway, I powered up and drew next to the truck. Ran

e by side with him for a minute. He tried to run me off,
t I dodged him. That's when I put him out of business."

"With your gun."

"I didn't shoot at the driver. All I did was shoot out his left
nt tire. He ran the light at Hannan, took out about a
ndred yards of cyclone fence by the drive-in, and jack-
ifed to a stop in front of Ford's Michigan Truck plant."

"What did you do then?" Gant asked, barely looking up
m his scribbling.

I took a last hit off the cigarette, dropped it on the floor, and
mped it out. "Well, I U-turned, came back. I didn't try to
n, for God's sake. I waited for the cops and I told them
at happened. So what do they do? They lock my ass up!
o felonies. Shit. If I hadn't 'a' done what I did, he probably
uld have killed somebody. Damn near did as it was."

Gant studied his notes, then looked at me. "Why do you
nk he was running all those people off the road?"

"I asked him that, while we were waiting for the cops.
ow what he said? He said, 'They were in my way.'"

The reporter stared sourly at his notes for a long moment.
Vhat do you do for a living, Ben?" he asked.

I opened my mouth, then closed it. I realized I'd been
nding here spilling my guts to this guy without even
alizing it. A night in jail will do that to you. "Public-spirited
izen," I answered. Close enough.

"Any prior offenses?"

"None that lived."

"Are you licensed to carry a concealed handgun?"

"Did they hit me with a weapons charge? You figure it
t."

Beyond the reporter I glimpsed Carole Somers striding
ward us. Gant said, "How about some personal details,
n?"

"Oh. Okay. I'm a Detroit Tigers fan whether it makes sense
not. I'm a Democrat and unashamed of it. I bowl and play
rds, drink beer and smoke cigars. I like rock and roll and
e blues. I have lots of friends, some of them women.
ostly, I'm just a plain working lug who tries to do the right
ing and usually gets hammered for it, like today, f'rinstance.
u put that in your story."

Carole reached us and gestured with the hand that did not
rry the attaché case. "Let's go."

"Nice talking to you," I said to Gant, and fell in step wi
Carole's long stride.

We burst out the double doors at the front of the sma
courthouse and walked along the sidewalk toward the parki
lot at the west end of the building. The sky was the gray
old library paste and there was a slight chill in the humid a
good old Michigan in early May, trying to decide betwee
spring and summer. Traffic whistled past us on the fo
westbound lanes of Michigan Avenue, and three massiv
diesels thundered slowly on the C & O Railroad overpass t
the road from us. An altogether unpleasant day, but aft
twenty-four hours in the can I felt like springing cartwheel
Sort of.

Carole looked at me as we walked, smiling with britt
brightness. "That certainly went well, don't you think?"

"Well, I'm back on the street." I jerked a thumb in th
direction of the courthouse. "Would you mind explaini
what happened in there?"

Carole was dressed in her trial-lawyer best: double-breaste
collarless jacket in tan over a matching skirt and a whi
high-collared blouse. The skirt had a side slit that allowed
peek of a gleaming knee as she walked in her sturdy pump
She still wore her blond hair in an effortless Princess Dia
cut, and she stood straight and strong, all long-limbed fi
feet nine of her. Clasping her attaché case under her arm, sh
groped in her pocketbook for keys. "You were arraigned," sh
answered. "The judge set bail. I posted it and you we
released."

"That much I gathered. But I didn't get to tell the judg
what happened. They didn't even ask for a plea or anything

Carole cruised around to the driver's side of her blu
Thumper station wagon and spoke to me over its roof as sh
fumbled the lock open. "We don't talk at an arraignment
she said patiently. "We don't enter a plea either. That come
when and if the case is handed up to circuit court, and eve
then we won't."

"I thought we had to."

"We stand mute," she said. "That protects our right t
complain about preliminary procedures, if it comes down t
that later."

"Oh, man. This sounds like it could drag on for months.

She ignored me. "At the arraignment hearing, all we do

ten. The prosecution had to convince the judge that a
me may have been committed and that there is probable
use to believe that you committed it."

"Which they did," I said.

She got in, reached across, unlocked the door. I got in and
mmed the tinny door shut. Carole fired up the whiny little
r-banger and shoved the shifter into drive. "Of course they
d," she answered. "Stop pouting. You did shoot at the truck
d it did crash."

"But he was—"

She held up a hand, wheeling the car with the other as we
lled out onto Michigan Avenue. "I know. Our turn will
me. We've demanded a preliminary hearing. The judge has
schedule it within twelve days. That's where we make our
oves."

"Such as?"

Carole wheeled the Thumper in a U-turn and pulled out
to the eastbound lanes. The engine whined and rasped
th a weak-kneed roar as it did its game best to pick up
eed. "All kinds of things," she said remotely. "The trucker's
nduct precipitated your action, of course. That's defense
mber one, and it just might fly. Failing that, there's
herent redundancy between the charges. We might be able
use that to have one of them thrown out. Preferably the
onious assault count; that's the heavier of the two, four
ars in state prison."

"Swell."

"Hey," she said sharply, "they could have hit you with
sault with intent to do great bodily harm less than murder.
at's ten years."

"Golly. I feel so lucky, somehow."

"You shot at the truck, Ben. However pure your heart is,
hich is another whole discussion, you did shoot at the
mned truck." She shook her head, annoyance clouding her
ce. "I just don't believe it sometimes, the stunts you pull."

"I'd do it again. In five seconds."

"Well, just keep your trap shut on that, huh?" We were in
e heart of the city of Wayne now, and the engine had built
a dull, rasping roar. "Sounds as if your latest Coke-can
pair is giving out down there," she noted.

"Yeah, it'll happen. They don't make Coke cans like they

used to." I changed the subject. "All right, suppose we ca
kill this thing at the preliminary hearing. What then?"

"They bind us over for trial in circuit court." She hung
left on Wayne Road. "Let's just hope it doesn't come to tha
I'd give odds they'll come to us with some kind of deal. Ho
would you feel about pleading to reckless endangerment
something?"

"Well, oddly enough, I don't have any convictions, and I
just as soon keep it that way. Tell you what. I'll settle for
commendation for getting that homicidal asshole off the road.

"Get real."

"I don't know," I said wearily. "They offer a deal, I'll look
it then."

We turned right on Sims, parked in front of the polic
station, and went in. Carole presented some paperwork
the desk uniform, who then retrieved a large brown envelop
from the back and dumped its contents on the desk. M
wallet, keys, cigars, matches, change, and last but not leas
my trusty .45 automatic, minus clip. That wasn't the way I
turned it in, but I decided not to make an issue of it. I signe
the form, loaded up my stuff, and walked out with Carole.

My dark blue 1971 Mustang ragtop sat safe and sound
the far end of the parking lot. As we walked toward it, Carol
asked, "Why not come up to the house, have dinner with u
hang around?"

"Sounds pretty good. Thanks."

"I'm sure Will would like to see you. It's been a while."

"School out for him yet?"

"Next week."

When we reached the Mustang, I unlocked it, opened th
door, and peered around. Everything seemed okay. I shut th
door and faced Carole, busying myself by lighting up a sho
cork-tipped cigar. Wonderful.

Carole stood with arms folded, watching me. "Thanks,"
said abruptly. "For bailing me out and everything."

Her padded shoulders rose slightly in a shrug, and sh
smiled. "No problem."

"How'd you come up with the scratch?"

"I signed over a thousand-dollar CD. Part of Will's colleg
fund, so don't go skipping out or anything, huh?"

"Oh, well, okay."

Her smile was even broader now, dark eyes alight. "You know what this means, Ben? I'm your jailer."

"I beg your pardon?"

"I posted your bail. Under the law, that puts you in my custody just as surely as if you were behind prison walls."

"I don't get it," I said, exhaling smoke.

"Any time I want, I can request any Michigan police officer to take you into custody and lock you up. They'd have to do it. No questions asked."

"You got to be kidding. That's incredible."

"So behave yourself," she said, wagging a finger.

"Oh, I will. I got nothing going on, aside from work—"

A sharp whistle sounded inside the Mustang. I opened the door, dropped into the bucket seat, picked up the cellular phone, and answered. The conversation was brief. I hung up and got back out slowly.

Carole's expression was a question. I said, "About tonight, I better take a rain check, okay?"

"Okay," she said, almost too casually.

I gestured absently at the car. "Got to go downtown, Harper Hospital. Friend of mine's got the big C. Pancreas. Doesn't have long before he checks out."

"I'm sorry to hear that."

"Yeah. So, um—well." I stared past her at the grove of tall trees waving in the afternoon breeze, then focused on Carole again. "What's the tariff for your work this time?"

She sighed. "You heard my exhaust system just now."

"Oh, yeah. I heard it."

"I think it's time, don't you? Start to finish. No more Coke cans."

"Yep. You're right."

"Anytime, I expect to hit a chuckhole on the Lodge and see everything fall out from under there."

"Sure. I'll take care of it, next few days or whatever. Have to track down the parts." A challenge all by itself; the Thumper was the product of an unholy mating of Axis powers. This being Detroit, parts for such cars were hard to come by. "I'll let you know."

"Okay. I'll get back to you on the preliminary hearing." Her expression turned hard. "You stay out of trouble in the meantime. I mean it, Ben."

I held up both hands. "Yes, ma'am. I'll be good."

"You better." Her smile was cold and sweet. "Or I'll have you locked up." She clapped her hands once. "Wow!" she said to the world at large. "What power I have!"

"Uh-huh," I said sourly. "You drive careful, now."

"You too." She hesitated, smile fading, then nodded once and walked away without looking back.

I got into the Mustang and fired up the big 302 motor. WABX came on just at the start of the Dead's "Touch of Grey." I jammed the shifter into gear and powered out of the parking lot, listening absently to the snappy beat and somber lyrics.

One thing I'll say for a night in jail. It gives you a renewed appreciation for the better things in life. Like being behind a deep-dish steering wheel, rumbling east on Michigan Avenue toward Detroit, to pay respects to a dying friend.

Not that jail was a new experience for me. My first time was at seventeen, way way back, when I got caught possessing a case of Stroh's long-necks while driving near my home in the far northwest corner of Detroit. The cops threw me in the precinct holding pen, where I spent six endless hours till my daddy strolled in about midnight to spring me.

My relief at being released was short-lived. Daddy's attitude was typically bitter: "Guess you ain't such hot shit now, huh Benjy?" My mother went into her martyr act, telling me at every opportunity that we Perkinses may have been plain, simple folk, but till then none of us had ever, *ever*, been locked up. Which was certainly untrue. I happened to know that a forebear we referred to as Grandpaw Frank, who was something of a family black sheep, had pulled thirty days for punching out a heckler at a Rome, Georgia, political rally in 1904. Which Mother, as usual, conveniently forgot.

My older brother Bill, who had followed family tradition by going to work on the line at Ford's a few years earlier, had treated me as if I'd become an unclean person; while my younger sister Libby greeted me each day by chanting "Jail-bird! Jailbird!"

It's probably no coincidence that shortly after that I took a night job at Ford's, hanging doors, and hardly ever went home again.

My second brush with jail happened maybe three years

ater, when I was locked up with a couple of others after a ate-night brawl behind Miss Penny McNasty's saloon in Dearborn. Like a fool, I'd interrupted a couple of gents who vere in the process of roughing up a stranger in a business uit. I'd been tossed in the can along with the goons and anguished there until the suit, who turned out to be up-and-:oming union boss Emilio Mascara, sprang me. He freed me rom more than jail; he freed me from the assembly line, too.

went to work for him as a "personal assistant"—which meant enforcer—as he muscled his way to the top of the union.

My third prison experience was sort of a bookend to the econd one. After seven years of power and dubious glory, Mascara got nailed on tax evasion, conspiracy, and racketeering :harges. The feds felt I could be useful to them as an nformant, so they immunized me in an attempt to make me estify against Mascara. With the nobility of the young, rrogant, and pigheaded, I refused. That got me a contempt :itation and an open-ended stay in Wayne County Jail, which ended ignominiously a week later when Mascara was convicted. got kicked out of jail, out of the union, out of Ford's—out of ny world.

After that I walked the straight and narrow. Sort of. I became supervisor of maintenance and security for a swanky apartment complex out in Belleville and wandered into pri-vate detective work as well. Those skills came in particularly 1andy when I was locked up the fourth time, after a lady riend was found strangled with a coat hanger in my apart-nent's walk-in closet. I got loose and cleared myself by olving the case and finding the killer, who ended up very lead under my riding mower.

That was, what, five years ago? Five eventful years where it ;eemed everything happened to me but jail. Till now.

As I entered eastbound I-94 at the Dearborn-Detroit line, thought about Carole. My ex-lover, lawyer, and now, to 1ear her tell it, jailer. Though I really didn't expect kudos for vhat I'd done, I was still in a mild state of shock that they'd :harged me, with two felonies yet.

Well, I'd leave it in Carole's hands. It was not her kind of aw—her solo practice focuses on women's issues such as livorces, abused spouses, and sexual harassment. And she loesn't get paid, except in services such as the exhaust-

system job I'd agreed to do. But I knew I could count on her.
She's tough, experienced, and most especially, motivated.
She valued the work I'd done for her, professionally and
personally. She valued my big-brother relationship with her
young son Will. Most especially, I think she felt a sense of
secret glee that I'd gotten nailed. She thinks I play fast and
loose and get away with literally everything but murder; I'd
tripped on my dick for once, and she figured it served me
right.

I swung south on the Lodge Freeway, crossed the Wayne
State University campus, and took the Forest exit over to
Woodward. I'd made good time, for the most part driving
against the rush-hour traffic. The sky remained glum as I
motored south toward the heart of Detroit and the odd drop
of rain spat on my windshield. The light at Selden went
green, and I made a rubber-burning left ahead of a rank of
outbound traffic. The gaunt facade of Harper Hospital rose
ahead of me. I began to look for a parking space. This was
going to be no fun, no fun at all.

I knew Jerry had been sick. I'd gotten together for dinner
with him and Lynne a couple of times since winter, and he
hadn't looked good. I figured that once he landed a new job,
he'd perk up. Instead, he'd begun making the regular trek to
doctors, eating up money that he didn't have. I got no energy,
he'd told them. No appetite. Please help me.

Evidently, from what Lynne had told me on the phone,
they hadn't been able to.

Thank God she'd sounded pretty steady on the phone. I
didn't think I could handle a weepy bedside scene, but that
wasn't what she had in mind. She'd asked me to come down
and talk to them. They had a job for me.

I found a space in an unguarded lot, shut down the motor,
and bent the rearview mirror down for an inspection. My
dark blue eyes were ringed with gray. My heavy black hair
looked shaggy, and I finger-combed it flat. I'd been unable to
brush this morning in jail, so I had a potent case of Russian
Army mouth. And I hadn't shaved either, so my face bristled
black with beard. But that was no big deal; if Don Johnson
can look like a slob, why can't I?

Conscious that I was about to see Lynne, I wished I looked
better and felt better. I also wished I wore clean clothes other
than the day-old blue jeans and red pullover sport shirt. But

there was nothing I could do about that now. I got out of the Mustang, locked it, and hoofed toward the hospital.

I had no idea what Lynne and Jerry wanted me to do. I found myself hoping it was something simple. The detective work had been motoring along nicely since winter. With these felonies staring me in the face, I needed no heavy action. If that's what Jerry had Lynne had in mind, I hoped I'd have the strength to decline.

And even before I hit the doors of Harper Hospital, I knew better.

CHAPTER 2

Harper Hospital is a unit of what is loosely referred to as the Detroit Medical Center. This good-for-what-ails-you complex includes, in addition to Harper, old Grace Hospital, plus Detroit Receiving, Hutzel, and Children's. And it's conveniently located, right where a lot of injury-related crime occurs, in the midst of a strip of squalor flanked by Cass to the west and the Chrysler Freeway to the east, running from Wayne State to the north almost all the way downtown.

I checked in at the visitor desk and was directed to the north wing on the seventh floor. The medicinal atmosphere of the old hospital seemed soaked with a million secrets. Nurses, doctors, and orderlies bustled; gowned patients lay, sat, or walked with painful slowness; visitors strolled aimlessly with resigned faces. I walked the dim green halls and hoped, for the thousandth time, for a quicker, more merciful way out, like a blackening explosion in the chest or a bullet in the head.

The door to room 703N stood ajar. I pushed it open and stepped inside. The near bed was empty and sheetless. The far one stood next to a blinded window. A wall lamp gleamed at the right; a silent TV mounted to the ceiling threw light from the left. Lynne Witkowski sat on a chair at the foot of the bed, in which all I could see was a skinny sheeted lump and the back of a man's head.

She smiled at me and stood as I came in. "Thanks so much for coming, Ben," she said, giving me a quick kiss on the cheek, a warm squeeze of the hand, and a very direct, searching look. Then she turned to the bed. "Honey? Ben's here."

The lump shifted. The head turned. The light fell on an unfamiliar face. Pasty gray, lined, eyes with all the depth of dimes. Jerry Witkowski, or what was left of him.

"Hey, Ben." His voice was soft but distinct. "Bring a twelve-pack along, pal?"

Lynne laughed. "Now, you know better than that, Jer."

Her husband struggled to slide himself up against the headboard. "I don't mean for me. I mean for himself. Visiting a dying man ain't easy."

"Come on, Jerry," I said, "you can whip this thing."

"Bullshit," he replied amiably. Having gotten himself situated, he activated a switch on the bed frame, causing a whining motor to elevate the head of the bed. Now I could see him better. That blocky, muscled laborer's body had been burned away. All that was left was basic body components beneath a head that was still large and square but nearly hairless. "This is a real learning experience, Ben. I've learned it's easier to be a dying man than to visit one."

I looked at Lynne, who had resumed her seat. "Isn't there anything they can do for him?"

"You can talk to me, pal," Jerry said, voice somewhat reproving. "The answer is no. I got a week. Maybe two at the outside."

"I'm sorry," was all I could think of to say.

"I ain't breaking no new ground here," Jerry said softly.

I looked at Lynne again. She wore dark slacks, dark sneakers, and a blue Saint Mary's Parish Athletics T-shirt. Her expression was calm and wise and sympathetic. I sensed that her sympathy was directed at me rather than her husband.

Jesus Christ, I thought.

She said: "We tried to get him into a hospice, but there weren't any openings. We could just go home and wait there, but—"

"I don't want her in my face every minute," Jerry broke in. "She spends too damned much time down here as it is."

"I want to be with you," she said.

"She spends every waking minute either working or sitting around this hellhole."

"I don't mind, Jerry."

"I do." Jerry winced and moved in the bed. "You got to take some time for yourself, too."

"Go ahead, tough guy," she said. "Get out of the bed and throw me out of here."

"I just might," he said, weak voice belying his tough words. They smiled at each other.

I swallowed hard, wishing for a cigar. "They keeping you comfortable, Jerry?"

"Best they can, I expect. They had to start the heavy stuff yesterday. . . ." He closed his eyes and locked his jaw, fists clenching.

Lynne asked, "Coming on again?"

He nodded.

"Should I call the nurse?"

He opened his mouth and exhaled audibly. His eyes opened. "Pretty soon, I guess."

Lynne looked at me. "They'll give him anything he needs, codeine and heroin even. But he wants to stay as alert as he can."

"Besides," Jerry said, smiling faintly with pale lips, "I never so much as touched reefer . . . and now here I am . . . turning into a fucking junkie."

"You take whatever you have to," Lynne shot back, her narrow face pale. "Stopping the pain, that's priority one."

"Hope I'm not doped up when I check out. I want to see what it's like. Ain't going to do it but once, hate to miss it."

"You bullheaded Polack," she said gently.

I felt profoundly uncomfortable, like the time I'd accidentally seen them heavy-necking in the backseat of his old Ford Galaxie parked behind Miss Penny McNasty's, way back in what now seems to have been a gentler, more innocent time. I remembered how the sight had made me hate him so intensely; how, upon their marriage, I'd broken off all contact with them, a twenty-plus-year silence that ended only the previous winter when Lynne tracked me down.

I felt ashamed.

Jerry's faraway eyes were on me. "Got time for a job, Ben?"

I cleared my throat. "Whatever you want. Just name it."

Lynne folded her hands tightly and bowed her head, staring into her lap. Jerry said, "It's about Kevin. He took off a couple months ago. Haven't seen him, haven't heard from him."

He paused, apparently to work his way through another

pasm. Without looking at me, Lynne said, "Kevin doesn't
know his dad's sick. We've tried everything we can think
of—"

Jerry broke in. "I want to see him again."

Lynne looked toward the window.

"Find my son," Jerry said weakly. "Bring him here."

"Okay," I said.

"And hurry."

Lynne suddenly stood and went to her husband. "Real
bad, sweetheart?"

His eyes were closed, his face strained, as he nodded.

"I'll call them," she said. "I'll get them down here."

He opened his eyes and swallowed. "Do that on your way
out."

"I'm not leaving you."

"They're gonna put me under anyhow. Go on. Take Ben
downstairs, fill him in. Then go home."

She threw me a frightened look, but when she answered,
her voice was strong. "All right. Whatever you want."

She bent and kissed him. I went to the bed, took his hand,
and squeezed it. "Hang in there, big guy."

He nodded in dismissal. Lynne turned and walked to the
door, and after one final look at Jerry, I followed her out.

We stopped at the nursing station. As Lynne conferred, I
paced a circle in front of the elevators. I wasn't thinking about
the job—tracking down an errant eighteen-year-old didn't
seem all that tough to me. I was thinking about Jerry back
there.

I was no stranger to the deathbed. You get to my age, your
old folks have pretty much dropped out of the picture. One
by one they'd gone.

My daddy had emphysema, but that wasn't what killed
him. He went in for a "routine" cataract operation and never
revived from the anesthetic. Turned out that wasn't unusual
for an emphysema victim. From what I know about emphysema, I think the old guy got lucky to go out like that. No long,
tortuous, futile days in the hospital.

My mother went without the benefit of a hospital. She was
a volunteer in a Detroit nursing home and had the bad luck
to be on duty one day during the '67 riots when some

funsters firebombed the place. Not particularly pleasant, but relatively quick.

Then there was Uncle Dan. He was eighty-seven and very frail when he went in to have his gall bladder removed. Something else went wrong during the operation; they opened him up a couple more times and were obviously getting nowhere when we had him unplugged and set him free.

That went on for weeks. But unlike Jerry, Uncle Dan lost most of his awareness right at the outset. He knew what was happening, but he kept going delirious and almost incoherent. Several times he thought he was back in the Twenty-seventh Squadron in France, mistook me for Frank Luke.

Unlike those folks, Jerry Witkowski was right on top of it. And he was handling it in his usual no-bullshit way. I thought that Lynne, left to herself, would have succumbed to the human tendency to pretty up the business with euphemisms. Jerry wouldn't let her. It wasn't that he wanted to die. It wasn't even that he wasn't afraid to. He was just a regular working lug who'd taken just about every knock life can give a man, and had each time picked himself up and gone on and done what he had to do. Right now what he had to do was die, and he wasn't going to whine about it or make things tougher for Lynne by being selfish.

All he wanted for himself was to see his son again. As I stood there, arms folded, breathing air that smelled of pharmaceuticals and pain, I knew I'd see to it that that happened. For Jerry's sake, sure. But for Lynne's, too.

Everyone needs one person for whom you'll go to the limit, no questions asked. For me, that person was Lynne Jones Witkowski.

I didn't care what the circumstances were. I didn't care if I had to cross half the country and drag the kid back here by the hair, kicking and screaming. Jerry and Lynne would get what they wanted.

Lynne and I took a table in the center of Harper Hospital's snack bar. The evening was drawing on, visiting hours were about to end. Several uniformed nurse's aides babbled brightly in the nearer corner. A doctor in a surgical gown bright with hardware sat behind us, pensively reading the *Detroit Free Press*, absently spooning cottage cheese into her mouth.

Three civilian types—an old dad, an old mom, and a pretty daughter in her twenties—sat over by the windows, drinking coffee and chatting comfortably. I suspected they had a long-term patient here; visiting the hospital had become part of their routine. On the other hand, the middle-aged couple in the far corner sat silently, holding hands for dear life, staring grimly over each other's shoulder. Probably kin to an accident victim, waiting for word that they feared would be the worst.

Lynne and I had organized ourselves large Styrofoam coffees, mine black, hers light and sweet. She'd paid for both, giving me a dirty look when I protested. I knew a buck was no big deal, but bucks are things the Witkowskis have never had much of. He had been a laborer for Sturgis Industries in Romulus, laid off for long stretches over recent years, put out of work for good when they closed and demolished the plant. Lynne had been working a shift and a half at the Westland K mart snack bar since God knows when. They lived in a low-rent duplex and owned a ramshackle pickup truck, but I still could not figure how they got by. Hell, I probably made more money than they did, between the detective work and the maintenance job; but I had nobody to support and no future to plan for.

Lynne sipped her steaming coffee without pleasure and set the cup down. "Let's get one thing out of the way at the outset. We're paying you for this."

"Like hell."

She leaned forward. "We're making out okay."

"Sure. What's the rent in this place, six hundred a day?"

"Oh, that's no problem. As part of the plant-closing package, Sturgis extended medical coverage for ninety days."

"Damn big of them. Makes me feel warm all over."

"Jerry was diagnosed on the eighty-eighth day, so he's covered a hundred percent."

"Good."

"You're not kidding. Plus, Jerry's got life insurance. Ten thousand. We took it out when Kevin was born, and we've always paid the premiums, no matter how hard things were."

"Uh-huh."

"So I won't be destitute. I'll have money to pay the bills, to pay for Kevin's college, and to pay you."

I fidgeted. Ten large was chump change nowadays; no way

would it cover all that. "More often than not, my clients are well-off people, people I don't know. I give full value, but I take down every nickel I can squeeze. Y'all ain't exactly well-off, plus you're friends. I take your money, I feel like I'm cashing in on—um—"

"Jerry's dying."

"Yeah."

"You can say it out loud," she told me. "It's no secret. He'll be dead very soon, and none of us will ever see him again. I've faced it. I understand it completely. I've accepted it. I've done my grieving, and I won't... There's no way I'll..."

She bent slightly and clasped her forehead with her hand. Her shoulders trembled under her shirt and her long brown ponytail slipped forward over her shoulder and dangled in the air. Her free hand clenched and unclenched, but she made no sound.

I wanted a cigar but felt that lighting up at that moment would be an asshole thing to do. "Two-fifty a day, plus expenses," I said.

Her breathing became audible as it steadied. She sniffed once and looked up at me, blinking. Her all-eyes, somewhat narrow, face was pale, but that mouth that seemed to smile all the time was okay now. "You're twisting my arm," she said, "but okay."

I snorted, picked up my coffee cup, and drank. I'd gotten the last cup from an aged pot, so it was just the way I like it, gritty and grainy and strong enough to chew. I looked at Lynne as she gave her eyes what she thought was a surreptitious wipe. She was older, definitely more experienced, and hopefully wiser. But I could still see the lanky, sexy, cheerful kid that I'd dated and pursued and, in my youthful arrogance, thought I was impressing, only to be set down hard when Jerry Witkowski entered her life and won her over with just a figurative crook of the finger.

A mean little voice inside me said, He's checking out, but you're still here, big guy.

I chased the thought, shook my head grimly, and liberated the long-overdue cigar from my shirt pocket. "So what's the scoop on Kevin?"

CHAPTER 3

LYNNE WRAPPED BOTH HANDS around the coffee cup and averted her eyes, a new pain replacing the other. "Well, he just disappeared a couple of months ago. Didn't come home one night, and we haven't seen him since."

I flared a match and lighted the cigar. "He ever take off before?"

"He's spent the night away from the house. Things like that. He's almost an adult now; we haven't been terribly strict."

"You usually know where he goes?"

"No." She looked at me intently. "Like I said, Ben, he's almost a grown man now. It's not our business to—"

"He's what, eighteen?"

"Almost."

"About to graduate, then."

"Next month." She licked her lips. "He hasn't been at school since leaving home, though. I checked."

"No calls? Letters? Rumors?"

"Not a word." She sat back in her chair and crossed one long leg over the other. "He's always been independent, but—I can't help worrying that he's been kidnapped, or..."

"Odds against." She looked at me. "I've done my share of runaways over the years. There's a lot of press, and you see all the pictures on milk cartons and stuff, but the fact is that close to a hundred percent of these disappearances are one of two things. There's parental kidnapping—behind custody disputes and such. Or the kid just up and says, 'I'm history,' and splits."

"I see," she said slowly. "Well, obviously the parental kidnapping is out."

I drew on my cigar and exhaled blue. Tough territory here. "Leads us to, how're y'all been getting along?"

She smiled crookedly. "Let's just say he's a typical teenager."

"Typical as in what, exactly?"

She shrugged. "You know what they say. Somewhere around twelve or thirteen the child you love disappears and is replaced by a sullen, difficult, emotional little alien."

"That what happened?"

She nodded. "They also say, in the late teens or early twenties, the alien disappears and you get your kid back."

"I guess so. I wouldn't know."

"They never said anything about the kid just vanishing on you."

"Happens, though. And there's usually a reason."

Her eyes hardened. "What are you suggesting? That we've abused him or something?"

"I said no such thing. Steady on, now."

"Well, we haven't. We never let him bully us, but we always took good care of him. We raised him to do right. We've tried to understand him and be there for him. And I mean to tell you, it's cost us."

"In what way?"

She drained her coffee and grimaced. "Jerry always wanted to clamp down. The rock music, the weird hair, the clothes. Kevin got to be real surly and hostile. Jerry's first reaction was always to retaliate. I always tried to placate him. Make him understand. Kevin was trying to find his own way, that's all. We had to be flexible." She spread her hands, palms up. "We did our best."

I thought about the two times I'd seen Kevin. He'd gotten his mother's fine-boned build and his father's heavy head. When I first met him, back in January, he'd worn his brown hair long and greasy, down to the shoulders. The second time, in March, he'd shaved it down to boot-camp length. The hostility in him toward me, toward his parents, toward the world at large, was palpable. He seemed to regard all the rest of us as a revolting species of insect, but his parents hadn't seemed to notice. Maybe they'd gotten used to it.

I tapped ash into the cheap tin ashtray, balanced the

igar on the rim, and fetched out a small spiral pad and
en. "Okay. Who are his friends? Who does he hang out
vith?"

She didn't have to consider. "There were some boys in the
neighborhood he used to pal around with. But they haven't
een him for months, except around school."

"You checked?"

"Of course." She looked down into her empty coffee cup.
Norwayne is a transient neighborhood. A couple of his old
als have moved away. Those still around had nothing to tell
ne."

I made a mental note to touch base with those friends if no
etter lead offered itself. Odds were that my questioning
vould be a little more, shall we say, effective, than hers.

"I walked the streets and pounded doors and got nowhere.
even put up a sign at the convenience store on Venoy.
Nothing."

"So he's still got pals, but you don't know who they
re."

She nodded, watching me.

"Girlfriends? Anybody special?"

"Never discussed it. I presume so. He's a normal, healthy
oy."

"You talk to his teachers and that?"

"I went over there. They weren't any help at all. Just said
hat Kevin hadn't been at school since he quit coming home.
Ie'll probably flunk out, but that's not the important thing
ight this minute."

"Yeah." I picked up my cigar and puffed it back to life.
What kind of stuff is he interested in?"

She smiled wanly. "Rock music. We got him a cheap stereo
nd some records as presents, plus he walked around with
adio headphones plugged into his head most of the time.
Drove Jerry nuts."

The tension was coming off her in waves now. There
vere, clearly, things she was not telling me. Dirty family
ecrets: keep 'em hidden, don't let the neighbors find out,
ot even the friendly local private detective. I wasn't going to
adger her. I'd been through this before. Generally, what
arents view as dirty family secrets turn out to be standard
lements of this run-of-the-mill garbage that we call life. And
ltimately such things proved worthless in this kind of inves-

tigation. I'd find Kevin, but odds were it would not be as a result of any revelation from Lynne. Still, I had to grill her.

"He work?"

"Oh," she said wearily, "he got a job about a year ago, stocking shelves at the Farmer Jack up on Ford Road. His boss wasn't very nice to him, so he quit after a month or so."

More likely mouthed off or played hooky and got canned, but I wasn't going to press it. "How about favorite places? Where does he like to go?"

She stared at me, caught unprepared by the question. "I really don't know. He used to play video games, back when there were arcades all over the place. I know he used to go over to Dynamite Park last summer. Said a lot of his friends hung out over there."

Which said a lot for his friends. Dynamite Park's gotten so ugly with the dope and the booze and the sex and the brawls that Wayne County established a sheriff's substation there and patrols the place with mounted deputies.

Time for the big enchilada. "He ever get arrested?"

She stared at me stonily. "No."

I nodded and squashed out my cigar in the ashtray. My smokes were gone, the coffee had gone cold, it was getting late, and Lynne was tired. And I was running out of questions.

"What about travel?" I asked finally. "There any place away from here that he's been to, that he's interested in, or whatever?"

She looked past me, eyes bleak. "He's never been much of anywhere. We took him to Cedar Point once, a few years ago, when Jerry was still working. Down to Toledo once, for my aunt's funeral. Up north a few times, when a friend of Jerry's let us borrow his cottage in Traverse City." She leaned forward. "We've hardly ever had any money, Ben. We've never been able to just drop everything and go."

"I hear ya, kid. I'm no jet-setter myself." I looked at my pad, at the two words I'd written there: SCHOOL and FRIENDS. Wow, an abundance of leads. I didn't know where I'd find the time to pursue them all.

Lynne toyed with her empty cup. "I've done absolutely everything I could think of to find him. I even ran an ad in the *Free Press* personals for a couple of weeks. The ad said, 'Kevin Witkowski, your dad is dying, please call home.' No reply. That's when we decided to hire you."

"Well, you covered pretty much all the bases." Except for one: the morgues. But I didn't mention that. "I'll have to backtrack over everything, see what pops up."

Lynne began, out of habit, wiping her side of the table with a paper napkin. "Are we about done?"

"Yeah, I reckon. We can finish up on the way out."

We discarded our trash and exited the hospital. The night was warm and redolent of the sounds of the city all around us. Lynne guided us into the east parking lot, and I walked close to her, radar on full alert. In those parts, the best security is your own security.

"What are you going to do?" Lynne asked as we neared their aged gold Ford pickup truck.

"Think I'll breeze over to the school tomorrow and ask around. Wayne Memorial High, right?"

"Right. What then?"

"I'd like to look through his room and his stuff and everything."

She reached into her pocket and out came jingling keys. "I've already done that."

"I'm the professional. I need to cover all the bases."

She preceded me to the driver's-side door of the pickup, unlocked it, and swung the door open on dry hinges. She looked at me, her face invisible in the darkness. "Do you think Kevin's in trouble?"

"Definite possibility."

"He's a good boy."

"Maybe the trouble's not so bad, then. And there may not be any trouble at all. But there's no way to know yet."

She climbed up into the driver's seat. I shut the door. She rolled down the window. Now the dim light was on her face, and it looked old and wan. "I'll be at home till two, if you want to stop by before then."

"I'll do it, after I go to the school."

She fired up the truck. Her exhaust system needed work, too. One job at a time. She gunned the engine, jammed the floor shifter into reverse, and said, "Find him."

"I'll do that."

"Good luck."

"I'll take all of that I can get."

She smiled. I stepped back from the truck, and she swerved

out backward into the lane, ground the gearshift into first, and roared away.

When I was sure that she'd made it onto Selden without being pounced upon by a squad of thugs, I kitty-cornered my way across the lot in the general direction of the Mustang.

Could be a snap. Could be Kevin was shacked up with some willing divorcée somewhere, taking his fill of flesh and food and fun.

Could be I'd find him before the sun went down again.

But I doubted it.

CHAPTER 4

THE ALARM CLOCK HONKED. I sat up, smacked it off, pivoted, and got up. I wasn't in as rotten a mood as I usually am first thing. Any day you don't wake up in jail is bound to be a decent one.

I've found that that first half hour is critical to setting the tone for the rest of the day. The objective is: no surprises. Accordingly, on the night before I'd laid out my clothes, my shaving gear, and my essential personal items such as cigars, matches, wallet, and keys. I'd also prepared the Mr. Coffee machine and set the timer—don't know how in the hell I ever got by without that little gem—so that a full pot of hot black joe would be waiting for me at the precise moment I entered the kitchen, fresh from shaving and dressing. It all went off without a hitch, right down to the day's *Detroit Free Press* flopped in front of the apartment door.

Still pretty much in robot mode, I sat at the small dinette in the kitchen and began to read. The coffee maker was within easy reach to the right, the ashtray and matches ditto to the left, and I drank and smoked and read, getting the old, battered body revved up to take on yet another day in the fast lane of Detroit metropolitan living.

I dealt with the essential items first. Calvin was trying to talk Hobbes, his stuffed tiger, into writing a school paper for him. The Detroit Red Wings had just been eliminated in the play-offs; the Pistons had won their first series but now faced a juggernaut known as the Boston Celtics; and the Detroit Tigers were trying to put some kind of campaign together without the assistance of catcher Lance Parrish. Sparky Anderson was optimistic, but then Sparky always is.

I fired up my second cigar and tackled the first section. Mayor Young made a righteous statement to the effect that the voters should decide the casino gambling issue. Several more nonentities were hinting that they might run for president over two years hence. Elliot Andelson, the Southfield rabbi/activist, announced a series of marches and public rallies and in an editorial was compared favorably to Martin Luther King.

A teenager at Cooley High was shot to death in a spat over a pair of tennis shoes; three junior-high kids were killed by an out-of-control driver on Conner Avenue. I found myself wishing I'd been there; I'd have shot out more than the guy's tires.

Speaking of which, there it was. Right next to an ad for a strip joint. My fifteen minutes of fame: BELLEVILLE MAN CHARGED IN TRUCK SHOOTING. Glumly, I read the two paragraphs of dry text. The reporter made me sound like a cross between Stallone and the Godfather. Marlon Rambo.

I wadded and tossed the paper, reassured that the world was no more fucked up than it usually is, refilled my mug, and carried it and my cigar into the living room. Unfortunately there was nowhere to sit, not without doing some cleaning, and I wasn't in the mood. It occurred to me, and not for the first time, that a guy in the maintenance business could probably do a better job keeping his own place sorted out. Matter of fact, though my furnishings are comfortable, I could also put some time and money into snazzing them up a bit, a fact that has been noted over the years by various female guests.

My defense is that this apartment is strictly temporary. Forget the fact that I've had it some fifteen years now. I requested an apartment facing the lake when I hired on here, and I'm still waiting for it, and till I get it, I won't waste time and dough on this one.

The framed poster above the couch caught my eye. In it a scantily clad blond, holding a glass of champagne, leans on the hood of a Rolls-Royce. The caption says POVERTY SUCKS. I toasted her, said "You got it, babe," drank, and set my mug down on an end table. The word "poverty" reminded me that it was time to stroll on to work, and I started for the door, only to be distracted by the blinking red light on the phone-answering machine.

Ah. I went to it and mashed the "play" button. The

machine whirled and clicked and hissed. Rockabilly sounded tinnily in the background, and Barb Paley's voice said, "Well, hiya, lover. I'm here, but you know what? You aren't. I checked real careful. The men's room, even. So, I... Listen, I'll hang around till Eddie closes up. Maybe I'll see your face in the place yet. Kissy, kissy!"

Oh, Christ, I thought as I erased the message. I *had* made Barb a halfhearted promise that I'd meet her at Under New Management last night. Sorta conveniently forgot about it in the course of my thrills-a-minute visit to Harper Hospital. The message light had, no doubt, been blinking when I got home, but I'd sorta conveniently forgotten to check it then.

Jesus Christ, Barb, what in the world am I going to do about you?

I walked out of the apartment, secured the dead bolt from the outside, and headed for the exit.

My morning commute takes exactly three minutes, and I never go near my Mustang. That's the beauty of living where you work, which in my case is Norwegian Wood, a three-hundred-unit apartment complex on Ford Lake in Belleville.

I'd hired on there, way back when, as purely a temporary thing. I'd just finished eighteen months of drifting after only barely surviving the big union scandal, and the job looked like a pretty good filler till I could line up something that befit the talents of a discreet, tough ex-factory rat who is, shall we say, good with his hands.

Well, fifteen years later Norwegian Wood is beginning to look pretty permanent. The pay's decent, and it includes a free apartment. The work isn't bad, either. Requires some skill with tools, a modicum of diplomacy, management ability, and enough aggressiveness to bust up those late-night noisy parties, deal with intruders trying to crash the security gate, and chase stray dogs off the golf course. Not that it's exciting— take it from me: cleaning out clogged pipes gets old after the fifteenth or twentieth time. But it's survivable, which is about as good as you can expect from a job, and it affords me copious free time to take care of the detective work that comes along.

Like this Kevin Witkowski thing.

I smiled as I sauntered along through the brilliant May

sunshine toward building one. Don't look over your shoulder
kid. Something's gaining on you.

I rounded the corner into the maintenance office to find
the usual tableau: the coffee maker hot and ready, my in-bo
jammed with job slips, Robin Trower's "No Time for Us
rumbling from the boombox courtesy of WABX, and my tw
morning men, Randy and Brian, poised and anxious to get o
with the day's work.

Randy was slouched down in his folding chair, arms folded
head bowed, Detroit Tigers baseball cap slid forward and
concealing his eyes. Brian was on his feet, back to me
playing air guitar energetically. "Morning, troops," I boome
as I entered.

Brian dropped his air guitar and faced me, grinning sheep
ishly. He's twenty-one or so, a tall, muscular fella, blond hai
cropped short except for a tiny ponytail in back. He wor
jeans, a T-shirt—I DON'T HAVE A DRINKING PROBLEM. I DRINK
GET DRUNK, FALL DOWN, NO PROBLEM—plus a tiny littl
earring augered through his right lobe. His long, honest fac
smiled in earnest. "Hey, Ben."

As I filled my mug from the percolator, Randy yawned
stretched, and shoved his ball cap to the back of his head. A
the big three-oh mile mark he's short and wiry with a runner'
build, a hawklike face, collar-length hair, and a tiny dar
mustache. He yawned again, and for a moment I didn't thin
he'd ever exhale. "Oh, man, am I beat."

I carried my mug to my desk, sat down, and fired up
cigar. "Jeez, Randy," I said sharply, "hate to inconvenienc
you with work and shit."

"Not your fault," he said, stretching his corded arms. "
had me some accidental ass last night; didn't roll in till three."

"Accidental ass?" Brian asked, taking the chair next to him.

"Yeah, you know what I mean. I'm walking along in South
land Mall, not even looking for anything, out there buyin
socks or whatever, and this sweet young thing gives me Th
Look. Now I have to be polite and all, so I stop and chat, and
we do some brews, and then I go home with her. Turns ou
she's a gymnast, and man, did *she* have the moves."

Brian was staring at Randy with awe. I was less impressed
"Okay, story hour's over. Let's do some business."

"Doug called in," Brian said.

"Jesus. All right, don't keep me in suspense."

"Said a tree fell across his street and blocked it."

"A tree fell," I repeated.

"He can't get out," Brian continued. "He lives on a dead-nd street; won't be able to come in till the city comes and auls the thing away."

"Which, no doubt, won't be today," I concluded sourly. oug was my afternoon man, at least in theory. "All right, e'll just have to hustle extra hard." I sorted the job slips uickly and divvied up the squeaky hinges, the repaints, the ead circuits, all the mundane jobs we maintenance men are eir to. Then I hit the biggies.

"Brian, today you've got the lawn out in the east end, ehind building three all the way to the perimeter fence. aise the blade a half inch and just mulch it. Check the pool rst thing and again around lunchtime. If I see even the niest cloud in that water I'm going to be very unhappy.)kay?"

"Got it."

"Randy, my friend," I said, smiling broadly, "you've got the ain drain in building two. Congratulations."

His face crumpled in disgust. "Oh son of a bitch, no!"

"Yes, indeedy."

"You want me to snake out that grungy old soil pipe!"

"Certainly. Every drain in the building is running slow. lakes sense; the big pipe's never been cleaned out. I figure ou're just the man for the job, being as you got all that lumbing practice last night and everything."

"Oh, man," he whined, then his eyes went hot. "What bout you, 'boss'?"

"Don't look at me, pal. I done did the one in building five ast month. We go by seniority here; now it's your turn to tink for a week."

"Fair enough," he argued, "but I don't see *you* taking on to jobs today."

"You noticed that, huh?"

"Goddamn right I did. Doug's out screwing off; that leaves ne and Brian holding the bag all day long."

"I got no problem with that," Brian said.

"Rank hath its privileges," I said, giving Randy a hard look.

"I'm working an outside job starting today. I'll be in and out
I'm counting on you two to hold the fort."

Randy shot to his feet, muttering. "Well, I'm going to d
the fucking drain first. Get it fucking over with. The
squeaky hinges can just fucking *wait*." He churned aroun
behind me and into the toolroom with a slam of the door.

I jerked a thumb in his direction. "Emotional," I said.

Brian folded his arms across his T-shirt. "I'll take the drai
instead, if it'll make things easier."

I frowned at him. Nobody, and I mean nobody, is thi
selfless, except possibly Brian. "No way, kid. Fair's fair. Don
worry, you'll get the next one."

Brian nodded and leaned forward. "So, you got a ne
case?"

"Yep," I said, relighting my cigar. "Runaway kid, seventee
years old, his dad's dying and wants to see him one las
time."

"Wow," Brian said slowly. "Sounds pretty important. Som
way I can help?"

Banging and clanging sounded from the toolroom behin
me. I ignored it and looked at Brian, whose face was a
earnest as ever. His offer was more than just native courtesy
in the past few months he'd shown an avid interest in m
detective work, had even ridden along on a surveillance onc
and watched me conduct an employee background investiga
tion. I'd thought that the reality of detective work—ninet
percent boring—would turn him off, but it didn't. He kep
after me about it. He was, in fact, my very own groupie.

"No thanks," I answered him. Clip-clopping sounded ou
in the hallway, and I looked up to see Debra Clark come in

Brian shot to his feet, reddening, as she held out her han
toward him. "You took my keys by accident," she said.

"Oh. Sorry." Brian dug into his pocket. Debra did not loo
at me, which wasn't surprising. Brian handed her the keys
"Going to work?"

"Yes, I'm running late now." She turned her head an
looked at me for the first time. I looked right back. Tall, dar
lady in her mid-twenties, dressed for work in a sleek blu
business suit and high-heeled black pumps. Her fine, ligh
brown hair was parted in the middle and wrapped sleekl
around her delicately featured face. She had the build of
goddess and a face that would have been gorgeous if it eve

smiled. Wound tight, totally controlled, that's our Debbie. Debra, I mean.

She'd lived at Norwegian Wood for a year, and Brian had lived with her for six months, which was handy because he was always around, and uncomfortable because associating with a tenant in such a way was a technical violation of an unwritten rule. But I'd kept my mouth shut, because Brian was obviously gone on her. She said, "Good morning, Ben."

"Ms. Clark," I replied.

I ceased to exist as she turned to Brian. "I hate that shirt," she informed him.

He looked down at it as if he'd never seen it before. "Sorry," he mumbled, "it's all I had clean. I haven't done laundry lately."

The toolroom door bounced open and Randy emerged. He'd put on knee-high rubber boots, elbow-high rubber gloves, and a tool belt, which hung heavily, and carried an electric snake and a huge pipe wrench. "Here goes," he griped.

Debra leaned up and kissed Brian. "See you."

He hastened to her side as she headed for the door. "I'll walk you out," he said, and they disappeared.

Randy hoofed past me. "That Debra may be a cold one, but at least she cured Brian of the dreaded Hawaiian disease."

I stubbed out my cigar. "What's that?"

"Lackanooky," Randy answered, grinning as he clanked out the door.

I laughed, leaned back in my chair, and clasped my hands behind my head. All's under control in this part of the world, I thought. Now to get cracking on the errant Kevin Witkowski.

The guidance and counseling office at Wayne Memorial High School bustled with students, teachers, and other faculty types. I stood along the wall, leaning, arms folded, waiting my turn and watching. I gathered that some sort of end-of-the-year rush was on; there was much talk about graduation requirements and considerable perspiring by some of the students, and not because of the unseasonable heat, either.

When it was my turn, I told the sharply dressed young lady who I was and that I needed information about Kevin Witkowski. When she confirmed that I was neither a parent, guardian, or relative, she asked me to wait and disappeared into one of the adjoining offices. A few minutes later a portly, dark-haired, middle-aged man bustled out ahead of her, as she directed him toward me.

"Chuck Hoops," he said. His fleshy, sunken-eyed face smiled neutrally. "How can we help you?"

"Ben Perkins." I referred to a blank scrap of paper from my notepad. "I've been sent to ask about one of your students. Kevin Witkowski." With bureaucrats, it pays to make it sound like you're following someone's orders. Bureaucrats usually cooperate instinctively at the behest of the all-powerful They.

Not Hoops, though. "What's the problem?"

I referred to the scrap again. "My information is he hasn't been to school lately, and I'm checking up."

The din of conversation in the small room quieted noticeably. Hoops was watching me carefully. "Mrs. Harper says you're not a parent or guardian. What's your capacity, Mr. Perkins?"

Oh, I thought, about a twelve-pack on a good night. "Private detective," I said softly.

Now there was near-total silence. Hoops pressed his lips together and nodded. "Let's talk back here."

I followed him into an office that was not much larger than your average walk-in closet. A piled-high desk crossed nearly the total width at the left. Sun streamed through a narrow window dead ahead. Hoops swung the door shut and went behind the desk. "Have a seat." He gestured at a cheap plastic chair and sat down himself in a low-backed chair behind the desk. The man was apparently all legs; when we were both seated, he was invisible from the top of his shoulders down.

"May I see some credentials?" he asked.

I fished out my wallet, extracted my private-detective license, and handed it to him. He studied it intently through his thick glasses. "Excuse me a minute." He pulled a thick notebook full of computer printouts from one of the piles, opened it, found an entry, and dialed. "This'll take just a second."

After a brief wait, he said, "Mrs. Witkowski? Chuck Hoops over at the school. How are you? . . . Good, thanks. Hate to disturb you, but there's a gentleman here named, uh—" he referred to my license—"Ben Perkins. A private detective out of Belleville. He's asking for some information about Kevin, and I . . . Oh, I see. . . . Well, normally we like to have these things in writing, so maybe . . . Uh-huh . . . Well, I guess it's

all right, as long as you're... Certainly.... Yes, ma'am....
Yes, ma'am.... Thank you, Mrs. Witkowski. Have a nice
day."

Perspiration shone on his broad forehead as he hung up.
Apparently Lynne had been pretty direct with him. He
handed my license back and grinned. "You understand, we
don't release information about students to just anyone."

"Yeah, well, that's good." I put my license and wallet away.
"Here's the bit. Kevin hasn't been to school, far as we know.
Hasn't shown up at home for a couple of months, either.
Parents hired me to track him down."

"I see."

"Thought I'd start here. What can you tell me about
Kevin?"

"Well, let's just see." He picked up his phone, punched
two buttons, and said, "Linda, please bring me the file on
Witkowski, Kevin." He glanced at me "What grade?"

"Senior."

"Senior," he repeated into the phone. "Thanks."

We sat there and stared pleasantly for a few moments.
Hoops seemed relieved to be away from the demands of the
anxious teenagers outside. A woman came in, handed Hoops
a file, and vanished. He opened the folder and squinted at it.
"Mm-hm. Senior. You were right."

I rode tight herd on my impatience. "What can you tell me
about him?"

Hoops squinted, did a double take, read some more.
"Why, he hasn't been to school in over two months!"

"Yeah, we knew that already."

He looked at me, offended. "He certainly can't expect to
graduate with this kind of attendance record!"

"Well, that's not really the—"

Hoops waved the file in the air. "So he can forget graduating and starting college in the fall, too. He'll have to repeat
all his second-semester courses."

"I'll be sure to tell him that. When I find him," I added
meaningfully.

"You tell him to get his butt in here next time you see him."

"Yes! All right!" God, how I wanted a cigar. "Listen. Mr.
Hoops. Can you tell me—"

"Chuck," he corrected, laying the file down on his desk.

"Chuck, then. What can you tell me about Kevin? Friends, activities, and so forth."

Hoops arched dark eyebrows. "Nothing about friends. All I can tell you about him is what's in this file. I've never met him, and we have over a thousand students here."

"All right," I sighed, and pulled out my small pad. "What does the file say?"

That perked him up. "Well, let's see." He opened the folder again and began leafing through the pages one by one, tongue tip edging through his lips. "Mm-hm. Uh-huh. Oh. Mm-hm."

He sounded like a doctor probing a patient's abdomen. I said, "Mind sharing that with me?"

He looked up at me, distracted. "Oh, it's nothing much. Pretty average grades, up till this year; then we show some slippage. No school-sponsored activities, as far as I can tell. Evaluations have been..." He did some more reading, and said, "Same old same old. Doesn't work up to his potential. Big *big* problem here at the school."

Big problem everywhere. "Any disciplinary problems?"

"Well, for that we have to look in the *back* of the file, you see."

"Well, shall we?"

"Certainly! Just one moment." He flipped over a wad of paper, moistened a thumb, and accompanied his leafing with the litany of mm-hum, uh-huh, etc. I edged down in the uncomfortable chair. Jesus, I'd gotten package pickup from Sears faster than this.

Finally he looked up from his poring. "Nothing to report, I'm afraid."

Shit.

"Except, of course, for his suspension last March," Hoops added casually.

CHAPTER 5

LYNNE SURE AS HELL hadn't told me about that. I straightened
in my chair. "Suspended? What for?"

Hoops was studying the document. "Vandalism," he said
vaguely.

"Can I look at that?"

Hoops handed the mimeographed form over. "I can't let
you keep it. Doesn't say much, anyway."

It didn't. Entitled REPORT OF DISCIPLINARY ACTION, the
form, complete in sloppy block printing, simply said that
Kevin Witkowski had received a five-day suspension last
March for vandalism. Beyond that, the form was devoid of
who, what, when, where, why. The signature at the bottom
was illegible. I handed it back over. "I need to get the
lowdown on that, Chuck."

Hoops was still immersed in the file. "You know what?
Kevin never came back to school after his suspension." He
gave me a toothy grin. "How's that for detective work, Mr.
Detective?"

"Outstanding," I said patiently. "How can I get the details
on this?"

Hoops elaborately replaced the form in the file. "Well, I
suppose you could ask Denny Lombardozzi. Our assistant
principal. That's his signature on there."

I started to rise. "Where do I find him?"

Hoops reached for the phone. "Never mind. I'll get him in
here. I'd better be in on this, too." He squinted to me and
added, "Policy."

I receded back into the chair. "Okay."

Hoops dialed, talked, hung up, and entertained himself

leafing through the file. I stared out the window across th
lawn toward Palmer Road. Beyond it the squared-off roofs
the Norwayne neighborhood cut along the sky. Lynne's hou
wasn't far from here, I realized. Kevin probably walked
school every day—till two months ago. God knows wh
happened then.

The door opened and a very tall, lanky man entere
instinctively ducking his head to clear the door frame as h
did so. He was curly-haired and swarthy, his darkish skin pa
tan and part genetics. He wore a crisp cotton shirt, gray si
tie, and dark trousers, and was nattiness itself next to th
rumpled Hoops.

I stood as Hoops introduced us but still had to crane n
neck to look into Lombardozzi's face as we shook hands. Th
man had to be six feet eight or nine. I squinted at his face ar
after a moment placed him. "U of D, power forward, mayb
ten years ago," I said.

His smile was genuinely pleased. "Good memory, M
Perkins."

"Call me Ben, okay? Anyway, hell, you were a fixture
the sports pages. Till you graduated, anyhow."

He answered the unspoken question with no hesitation. '
wanted to pursue my career in education. I believe in th
youth of America, and I wanted to do my part to help then
My ideals were more important to me than the gargantua
sums of money available via an NBA career. Besides,
wrecked my knee while trying out for the Indiana Pacers.'

I laughed, but at the same time I felt instant respect. /
least the man had had the foresight to do more in colleg
than play basketball and bang chicks.

Hoops handed the form over to Lombardozzi, who leane
against the wall by the door as he studied it briefly. "Ol
yeah," he said.

"What's the story?" I asked. I wish I had a deuce for eac
time I've asked that.

Lombardozzi skated the paper back to Hoops. He looke
bored. "Well, seems that young Kevin trashed a car in th
visitor's parking lot. Did a real number on it."

"Really. How'd you catch him?"

"He didn't try to hide it. He stood right there till the gu
came back out of the school." The tall man's face becan
grim. "He'd smeared excrement all over it, inside and ou

us he spray-painted graffiti on the hood and the trunk.
irty Jew,' 'kike bastard,' things like that." His eyebrows
ched. "Also something that said, 'Death to Zog,' whoever
at is."

"Oh yeah, I remember that," Hoops put in. "It was that
l geezer who did the talk on the Holocaust, right?"

Hoops nodded. "Odd thing was that we'd never had trou-
e with Kevin before. Then, bam! Here he was."

"It's also odd that he owned up to it," I said.

"Owned up to it?" Lombardozzi said sharply. "Hell, he was
oud of it. He stood right there at the car waiting for the old
an to come out, then started screaming stuff at him, slogans
d that. Attracted quite a crowd. I was called out, and I
llared him and took him to my office. He strutted along as
he'd scored the winning touchdown."

This squared with nothing that Lynne had told me. It was
o inconsistent with my own brief encounters with Kevin.
e'd never struck me as a talker, let alone a haranguer.
Vhat'd you do?"

The assistant principal's dark face was etched with frustra-
on. "I read him the riot act. All I got back was a long,
coherent lecture about the Zionist conspiracy. I mean, the
d wasn't even in the same room with me; he was in cuckoo
d somewhere."

"What about the victim? He call the cops?"

"I did. Wayne police took a report. But the old man
ouldn't press charges or anything. That left me without a leg
 stand on. I hung tough anyhow, told Kevin if he'd apolo-
ze in writing and make financial restitution, I'd let him off
th a warning. He told me to go screw, so I hit him with the
ax. I suspended him five days."

"Oh wow," I said. "That'll teach him."

"Best I could do."

I got to my feet, stretched, paced, thought. "And he never
me back," I said quietly.

"Just as well," Lombardozzi said.

Hoops roused himself. "Hey, Denny, that's not the attitude."

"I'm not in the counseling business," Lombardozzi shot
ack. "I don't have to pretend that every student problem is
lvable. I know dangerous creeps when I see 'em, and I
n't want them in my face or around my school, thank you."

hough he hadn't raised his voice, his large hands had closed

into fists and his face had flushed darker. I didn't know exact
what Kevin had said to him, but the kid had gotten to him a
right. This troubled me. Denny Lombardozzi was no twinki

Hoops looked disapproving but said nothing.

"You're looking for him?" Lombardozzi asked me abrupt

"Yeah. His dad's dying, wants to see him again."

"Might be better off not. He's one nasty little bastard."

"Not for me to judge." I looked at the tall man. "Th
victim, the old Holocaust survivor. How can I find him?"

"I wouldn't know. Peg Kalus, history department, set u
the lecture. She'd know."

"Why talk to him?" Hoops asked.

"Maybe Kevin's kept after him," I answered.

Lombardozzi sighed. "Come on. Peg's probably in th
lounge taking a load off. I'll walk you."

Lost in thought, I shook hands with Hoops and followe
Lombardozzi as he ducked his way out of the office.

As I'd thought, the Witkowski home was less than a quart
mile from Wayne High. It sat toward the Venoy Road side
Norwayne, a neighborhood of government-built duplexes erecte
during the war to house workers at the area's defense plant
Norwayne is an irony wrapped up in an enigma. Its house
were intended to be temporary, but most are still in us
better than forty years later. The homes are flat-topped, box
and laid out in government-issue rows, yet most of th
neighborhood streets wind and curve just like today's mo
upscale subdivisions. Norwayne is at the very lowest end
the middle-class scale, has a reputation for violence an
crime, and some sections are downright slums; yet som
others, occupied obviously by long-timers, are landscape
meticulously cared for, and attractive.

The Witkowski duplex fell somewhere in the middle of th
range. The two-story clapboard building was resolutely ord
nary, but it had been painted recently. Chain link fenced in
very small yard on the Witkowski end, and someone—n
doubt Lynne—had tilled a tiny plot of earth in preparatio
for Memorial Day planting. Two very large sycamores grew a
the back of the building, providing shade from the late sprin
sun.

I parked the Mustang at the curb behind the coppe

lored Ford pickup, hoofed up to the right-hand door, and
ocked. It squealed back almost immediately and Lynne,
essed in light blue cotton slacks and a white shirt beneath
r orange K Mart smock, smiled out at me. "Come on in.
ffee's on."

I entered. The long, narrow kitchen was brightly lighted
m the sun streaming in through the window over the sink.
e place was sparkling clean and smelled neutral, as if no
oking had been done there for a long time. Maybe Lynne,
th no one else to cook for these days, was bringing discount
ow home from her job at the K Mart snack bar. I didn't ask.
ust trailed her over to the counter and waited as she served
e up a hot mug of the black stuff.

"Find out anything?" she asked as she stirred a cup for
rself.

"Not a whole lot," I answered, "except that Kevin hasn't
own his face around there since pulling his vanishing act."

She nodded and sipped coffee, leaning relaxed on the
unter with her other hand, gray eyes shrewd above the lip
the mug.

"Also," I went on in the same tone, "he kicked off his
scheduled vacation with a five-day suspension, courtesy of
r. Denny Lombardozzi, ex–U of D basketball star, now
ayne High's assistant principal."

She froze, then lowered the cup. "They kicked him out?"

"Uh-huh. I gather you didn't know that."

Her thin face was pale. "Heavens, no." She stepped to the
tchen table at the end of the room and sat down slowly,
es averted. Unwillingly I remembered another occasion,
ring last winter. She'd hired me to track Jerry for a few
ys, suspecting that he'd gone off the reservation fidelity-
se with person or persons unknown. When I'd come here
report that her suspicions seemed to be correct, she'd
ng herself at me, and had I succumbed to hormones
stead of common sense, we could have done *The Postman
ways Rings Twice* right there on the kitchen table. Good
ing I held off. Jerry was, in fact, seeing a woman, but
ings weren't exactly what they seemed.

Still, I felt a fundamental stirring as I looked at her. Christ,
thought, you'd think that after better than twenty years the
esire would have faded. I also felt a tad guilty. I was

supposed to be her friend, but it seemed as though all I eve
brought her was bad news.

She let out a long, audible sigh. "Aren't they supposed t
notify the parents?"

"You'd think so. But I don't know, they've got a lot of kic
and a lot of stuff going on all the time; individuality sorta ge
lost. I mean, *Room 222* it ain't, over there."

She didn't look over at me. "What'd he do?"

"Well, he trashed a guy's car."

"Another kid's?"

No choice but to tell her. I walked to the table, pulled bac
the chair opposite her, and sat. "One of the history teacher
arranged for a lecture by an old Holocaust survivor. Man b
the name of Kraus, lives up in Oak Park somewhere. Whil
he was doing his talk, Kevin apparently smeared shit all ove
his car and spray-painted some pretty nasty stuff, too."

Lynne's mouth was pinched as she looked somewher
beyond me. I saw her knuckles whiten as they gripped th
mug. "What proof do they have that Kevin did it?" she aske
sharply.

"Best proof there is, as in, Kevin didn't deny it. He stoo
right there by the car till Kraus came out and started yellin
stuff at him. Caused quite a ruckus, from the way it sounds.

"That's impossible," Lynne said flatly.

"I'm afraid there's not much question."

"Five *days*? That seems pretty stiff."

"They offered him a slap on the wrist if he'd apologize an
make restitution. He, uh, declined."

"Had to have been a prank, that's all. Kevin would nev
er... No wonder he took off. He was ashamed to tell u
about it. They drove him away, that's what they did."

"I don't think so," I said guardedly, "but what do I know?"

"Those bastards," she said softly.

This was tricky country, and I knew it. Very carefully
said, "Look, the whys we can look at later, at leisure. Rig
now the thing is to find him. Right?"

"Right," she said unwillingly. "Okay. You wanted to look
Kevin's room."

"Yeah, if it's no trouble."

"I can't imagine what there is to find," she said, smilin
crookedly, "but you're the detective. Come on."

CHAPTER 6

SHE LED ME THROUGH the parlor, around a corner, and up
narrow, steep flight of stairs carpeted with a runner whose
attern had long since been walked away. Three doors with
rcelain knobs ringed the landing at the top. The one ahead
as open: the bathroom. The doors to either side were
osed. Lynne opened the right-hand one and stood back.
Help yourself."

"Stick around if you want."

"No, I've got some paperwork to do before I go to work.
e you downstairs."

As Lynne's footsteps creaked away down the staircase, I
tered Kevin's room. It was small, twelve by twelve at most,
th but a single window on the opposite wall looking out to
e west. To the right sat a single-size bed, neatly made.
hat made me doubt that Kevin had made up his bed neatly
e morning he took off for parts unknown? Call it a hunch.
To the left sat a short bookcase and a tall wardrobe chest,
ors above drawers, no doubt put together from a kit. The
okcase held few books and plenty of everything else. On its
p squatted a cheap audiotape player flanked by small speak-
s. Next to it was an inexpensive tan desk phone. Poignant;
spite their poverty Lynne and Jerry had scraped up the
ugh to give Kevin his own phone. I hoped he used it
sely and well.

On the shelves below was a random clutter of paperbacks
d audiotapes. The bottom shelf was packed with maga-
nes, the top one featuring the close-up, contorted face of
avid Lee Roth below the title *Rockin*. Wow. Maybe Lynne
ould let me borrow that one if I asked nicely.

41

The floor was hardwood that had been refinished during life and needed it again badly. The walls were bare except ⌐ a Detroit Tigers pennant above the bed and, above t⌐ bookcase, a full-color poster of two long-haired men in bla⌐ jackets aiming guitars at each other like flamethrowers. T⌐ caption, in large, defiant red Germanic type, was SKREWDRIVE⌐ Legends of rock.

I surveyed the room once more. Nothing had change⌐ The air was stuffy. No way to get cross ventilation up he⌐ without opening Kevin's window and the doors to his and ⌐ parents' bedrooms. I discerned the faint, flat odor of tobac⌐ smoke. Weedin' off, eh Kevin? Shame on you, son.

I fired up a cigar and began the toss. The wardrobe ch⌐ was first and easiest. Nothing in there but bare hangers, ⌐ sleeveless leather vest, a mottled olive-green-and-black ca⌐ ouflage shirt, and a single high-topped sneaker held prison⌐ by dust kitties. Well, I could rule out Kevin being snatche⌐ unless his kidnappers were considerate enough to let hi⌐ come and pack his clothes while they sat out in the getaw⌐ car, engine running.

The audiotapes on the bookshelf represented an eclec⌐ survey of heavy metal, past and present. Prominently rep⌐ sented were Black Sabbath, the Scorpions, Kiss, Van Hale⌐ and Led Zeppelin. There were also artists I'd never heard ⌐ On an impulse I booted the tape transport. It V'd o⌐ revealing another tape. I extracted it. No label. I replaced ⌐ shoved the transport home, and pressed the ON switc⌐ Nothing. The unit was plugged in, but was stone-cold dea⌐ Well, that took care of motive. If my stereo had bellied ⌐ me, I'd have split, too. Only so much a man can take.

The magazines were about equally exciting. Mostly roc⌐ and-roll fanzines in chaotic piles that, judging from t⌐ streaks of dust, and the way the cheap, glossy covers stu⌐ together, and the odor of paper pulp, hadn't been touched ⌐ a long while. I leafed through it all anyway, hoping f⌐ something instructive, such as a handwritten essay entitl⌐ "Why I Took Off and Where I'm At Now." No joy.

As for the paperbacks, roughly half were spy thrillers, a⌐ surprisingly, the other half were tomes about World War ⌐ some of them quite scholarly. *The Gathering Storm. Hitl⌐ Moves East 1941–1943. The Last Battle.* There was also o⌐ called *The Theory and Practice of Hell.* Across its yell⌐

cover was magic-markered the savage word BULLSHIT. Aside
from that, there was no evidence the books had been read; no
notes, no clues tucked neatly among the pages.

Boy oh boy. I'd invested an entire cigar in this search and
come up with zip. Not the way it's supposed to work. I
toured the walls, examining them carefully, looking for secret
doors and such. Nothing. My tour concluded at Kevin's bed.
I knelt and looked underneath. Nothing but a fine layer of
dust. I straightened, froze, then bent and peered underneath
again. Oh-ho!

I stood and lifted the mattress. There, nestled in the center
of the springs, was a hardcover book. I struggled it free, let
the mattress drop, and looked at the cover. *The Turner
Diaries* by Andrew Macdonald. I leafed through, skimming a
sentence here and there. Seemed to be an adventure story of
some kind. I almost decided to put it back where I found it,
then decided to hang on and look it over later. Of all Kevin's
books, this one had been hidden. Had to mean something.

Thus ended my wanderings through the discards of one
Kevin Witkowski. I started out of the room, then turned,
rescued the unlabeled tape from the player, and headed
downstairs.

Lynne sat at the kitchen table, hunched over an open
checkbook. Empty envelopes, bills, a half-filled shoe box,
and a light-powered calculator were scattered around her.
Her expression, as I approached, was guarded. "Any luck?"

"I don't know. Not really." I held out the book. "Ever seen
this before?"

She took it, hefted it, opened it, flipped pages idly. "No.
Kevin's not much of a reader."

"You sure? He must have twenty, thirty books up there.
Some of 'em pretty heavy stuff. That little jewel was stuck in
the box spring under his mattress, which is an odd place to
hide a book that doesn't have any pictures in it."

She handed the book back. "I don't understand."

"Well, I'm gonna skim it later, see if it tells me anything." I
indicated the mess scattered around her on the table. "Bill
time, huh?"

"Yes. I've let it slide the last few weeks. Have to get caught
up as best I can. I'm also going to write you a check for your
retainer, which you conveniently forgot to mention last night.
Two-fifty a day, right?"

"You're making me grumpy, sweetie."

"Two-fifty?" she pressed.

"Yeah, okay. One day'll do. I think this one'll turn pretty quick."

"Really?"

"I'm sure of it," I lied.

Unfooled, she said, "Fine. I'll have it in a minute, if you can stick around."

I tossed the cassette tape in the air and caught it. "I'll be out at the car. Want to give this a listen. Kevin's receiver is busted up there." I started out, then turned with an afterthought. "Maybe you could find me a snapshot of Kevin, too."

"I'll see what we have," she said doubtfully.

I went out the door, down the stoop, across the lawn toward the Mustang. The heat was building fast as the day rushed toward noon. A Delta Airlines DC-9 screamed by overhead as I opened the car door. Add to Norwayne's list of virtues the fact that it sits right below the north-south approach path for the Detroit Metropolitan Airport. I dropped into the bucket seat, switched the ignition to accessory, booted my *Who's Next* tape from the cassette player, inserted Kevin's tape, and hit the rewind button.

While waiting, I fired up a cigar and leaned back in the seat. Something about Lynne had changed since I'd arrived. As sometimes happens in this work, she was torn between needing my help, yet dreading it. This kind of ambivalence inevitably leads to resentment toward your friendly local detective. What's more, there was definitely something furtive about her as she sat at that table. Something she knew that she didn't want to tell. I swear to God, sometimes your client is a bigger pain in the ass than your adversary. Your adversary's aims are simple and manageable: Dodge you, or failing that, rip your face off. Clients like Lynne are wheels within wheels, go figure 'em.

The rewind stopped with a click. I mashed the PLAY button. White noise hissed from the four large speakers. I turned down the volume. Got to clean and demagnetize the heads once in a while, Kevin. The duplex door slammed, and I saw Lynne walking toward me with her lithe, unconsciously sexy gait. As voices sounded scratchily from the speakers, I saw that she carried a brown leather photo album.

"This is 'Free Speech' on KLOE-Detroit, who's this?"

"Kevin from Westland."

"Hi, Kevin, my man. What's on your mind?"

"About that last caller, you know?"

"Go ahead."

"All I got to say is, he just better *wake up*. He don't have *clue* 'bout what's going on."

"Why do you say that, Kevin? He sounded reasonable to e."

"Reasonable? He's nothing but a Z.O.G. whore."

Lynne reached the Mustang and leaned on the ragtop, ending down, listening to the voices, face unreadable.

"Aw, come on, Kevin," jibed the host's voice.

"Lemme tell ya something. You read your history. It all es back to Rosenfeld and Truman and the cover-up of the hristian Holocaust. They sold us out at Yalta and handed er half of Europe, they own the Jewsmedia, they killed cCarthy because he knew too much and told the truth. hey started the Trilateral Commission to hand the power wn. The Trilats have handpicked every president since en. Andelson's run by the Trilats and the Z.O.G. too. That's known fact."

"So what do we do about it, Kevin?"

"We get *involved*, man! We organize loyal Christians to lock the territorial imperative—"

At that instant the tape snapped and flapped crackling side the tape player. I quickly hit the STOP button and ected the tape. No harm to the player, thank God.

Lynne had sat down on the grassy berm and was cross-gged, face pale. I examined the two broken ends of tape d observed, "I can splice this back together at home. But 's probably just more of the same. That was Kevin's voice?"

"I think so," she said softly. "I didn't understand a lot of at. What's a Z.O.G.?"

"Beats me," I said, drawing on my cigar. "'Jewsmedia' isn't rd to figure out, though."

We said nothing for a long, long moment. A plane roared y overhead. Then Lynne cleared her throat. "Here's your eck."

I took it, tossed it on the seat with a mental note to cash it n the first of never.

"And here's our photo album. Recent stuff's at the back. Help yourself."

The first page held black-and-white snaps, lovingly mounted. One showed the much younger Jerry Witkowski holding the infant Kevin clumsily. The rest showed Lynne, nuzzling the hairless, grinning baby. She looked the way I remembered her from Miss Penny McNasty's, but that smile she bestowed on her new son, I'd never seen anything like that before. It made me feel like a peeping tom.

I flipped to the final pages of the book, inspected, then selected a snap. It was a faded instant picture of Kevin and his mother sitting on the front steps. He had his arm around her, holding her possessively, the faintest hint of a smug smile on his face. His quarter-inch hair made him look like a boot-camp survivor. He wore a camouflage shirt, tight black pants, and hiking boots. The aggressive attire was belied by the sunken chest, frail shoulders, pale arms; I'd gotten the feeling before that his idea of exertion was an intense session of video games.

I removed the picture, put it in my pocket, and handed the album back to her. "Thanks."

She cleared her throat again. About to come clean, huh, Lynne? "I've got something here that might help. But you have to promise me not to mention it to Jerry."

She handed me some small folded tissue papers. As I unfolded them, she stood and brushed off her pants seat. The papers were credit-card carbons. Two of them. Amoco.

I looked up at her. She said: "I gave Kevin one of our gas cards last fall. For emergencies, in case the pickup broke down somewhere. I never told Jerry. He was . . . He wanted Kevin kept on a short leash."

I examined the slips. Both were for gas purchases in the past month. Both bore an illegible signature that started with a K. One carried a license-plate number, the other what seemed to be a phone number. Both gas stations were in the metro Detroit area.

Lynne pointed. "That license number isn't ours. Neither is the phone number." She smiled weakly. "I'd have found them a couple of weeks ago if I hadn't gotten behind on my bills. Maybe you can track them down and—"

"Definitely," I said. I felt better now. Leads were what I'd come here for. I hadn't found them myself, but I take them any way I can get them. "Are these the only charges he's made?"

She nodded.

"Interesting," I mused. "He's quit using the gas card, it's got to be because he's found a source of funds." I wondered what it was. "Well, thanks, kid. I'll check 'em out." I stuck the slips in my shirt pocket and my cigar in my teeth and pulled the door shut.

"Quickly?" she asked.

"Later today. Got another visit to make first."

"Where's that?"

"Oak Park." I waved, fired up the big 302 motor, and roared away.

CHAPTER 7

I HEADED UP TO Ford Road, swung east, and put the cellular phone to work. First call was to Pat O'Shay, my Michigan Bell insider. She was "taking a meeting" and would call back. Next call was up to Lansing. Dick Dennehy was just plain not available, an excuse I found refreshing. Unsurprising, too. He happens to be a state police inspector and most likely had better things to do than hang around waiting for me to try to cadge information off him.

So following through on the phone number and the license plate on Kevin's charge slips would have to wait. Meanwhile, I'd mosey on up to Oak Park and confer with Mr. Solomon Kraus.

Peg Kalus, the Wayne High School history teacher I'd spoken with after talking to Hoops and Lombardozzi, had cheerfully given me Kraus's address and phone number. "He's such a nice old man. Surprisingly vigorous despite his age and what happened to him back there in the war."

"Holocaust survivor?" I'd asked.

"Yes. I invited him here to speak as part of our 'Bringing History to Life' program." Her bright enthusiasm had faded somewhat. "The students seemed to enjoy his talk, but I'm not really sure they believed him completely."

Now, as I rumbled east on Ford Road through the Detroit city limits, I wondered if this little excursion was a big waste of time.

Kevin had trashed Kraus's car and boasted about it. Kevin had taped a call he'd made to a low-rent talk show on a dim-watt radio station, during which he'd delivered an enthusiastic anti-Semitic tirade. Kevin apparently had a racist ax to

48

grind. The question was, Was this pertinent to why he'd disappeared and where he'd gone?

Or was he just a restless, troubled kid with some flaky ideas?

I didn't know. I also had no reason to believe that Solomon Kraus would be able to give me any insight. But it could be that Kevin and Kraus had butted heads before the high-school incident.

Or since.

Oak Park is part of the first tier of suburbs just across the Oakland County line from Detroit. It sits just east of Southfield, the granddaddy of suburbs, and just south of Berkley, where Carole Somers lives; and, like most Detroit-area suburbs, is irregularly shaped, with squarish chunks chopped away to make room for Huntington Woods at its northeast frontier.

The northwest hunk of Oak Park, from Lincoln Road north, is known throughout the area for its high density of people of the Jewish persuasion. This ethnicity is relatively low-key, though. It isn't like Hamtramck, where Polish-language signs abound, or Greektown, where cries of *"Opa!"* fill the air, or certain sections of Dearborn, where wailing prayers to Allah can be heard on the streets five times a day. If you look carefully around Oak Park, you'll notice advertising for kosher food, and you'll see quite a few synagogues; but otherwise, the citizens don't seem to wear their heritage on their sleeves.

As I drove, I recalled that the Jewish community did get worked up over the plans to shove the knife of I-696 through the area. The problem, apparently, was that Orthodox Jews believed in walking to temple. The freeway, as originally planned, would have put an end to that. The community, led by that busy and visible activist Mr. Elliot Andelson, raised such a stink about it that the planners made tremendous changes. Now the freeway, if it's ever completed, will run beneath large landscaped ground-level decks at several points, enabling the Orthodox people to continue their walks to temple. Unprecedented for Detroit, where cars usually take priority over people.

I swung east on Lincoln Road, a pleasant boulevard bisected by a well-groomed median, passed some apartment towers, then pulled into the parking lot of Congregation Beth Shalom and parked. From there I could see that this western end of Oak Park consisted of fairly new subdivisions, while the farther east you went, the older the homes became. I got out my handy Oakland County atlas to get a fix on Kraus's address and was surprised to find that his home seemed to be in the newer section. I fired up the Mustang, headed north a couple of blocks, then west, and parked at the curb.

The Kraus home was a frame split-level with white brick facing, white aluminum siding, and black-shingled roof. The lawn was deep green, impeccably trimmed, obviously cared for by people who knew every blade by name. Shrubs began at the attached garage and meandered in a wood-chip island past the porch, around the corner, and along the west side. The garage door was closed, the driveway was vacant, and I'd have thought nobody was home if the front door hadn't been standing open behind the screen.

I hoofed up the driveway and onto the porch. White wicker chairs sat elbow-to-elbow, and a folded *Detroit Free Press* lay by the door. I picked it up, listened to the silence from inside, then knocked.

A sudden stirring, carpeted footsteps, then a short, stocky man appeared. "Yes?"

"Mr. Kraus?"

"I am Solomon Kraus." His midrange voice was rusty, but his English had the precisely sculpted sound of a diligently studied second language. "How may I help you?"

He didn't look all that old. Late sixties, tops. His demeanor was neutral. "Ben Perkins," I said. "I wonder if I can have a few minutes of your time."

He smiled, showing white, even teeth that I suspected were not original equipment, but his blue eyes were watchful, just this side of wary. "What is this about, please?"

I kept casual. "Oh, I was down at Wayne Memorial High School this morning. Peg Kalus told me about the talk you gave a couple months back on the Holocaust."

"Mrs. Kalus is a very fine woman," Kraus observed.

"And I have some questions about the, uh, incident that occurred as you were leaving the school that day."

His smile dimmed a notch. "Are you with the police?" he asked politely.

"Nope. Private." I got out my wallet and held the private-detective license close to the screen. Kraus didn't look at it. I'm working for the boy's parents. He's run away from home. The father is terminally ill and wants to see the boy one more time."

"How unfortunate," Kraus said. "I have a grandson myself. I know how the man feels. Please, come in."

I opened the screen door and followed Kraus into the living room. His gait was stiff, and he held himself ramrod straight as he walked. Sciatica or something, I figured. His dark blue pants and short-sleeve white shirt seemed too big for him, and he wore open-toed sandals on his bare feet. When he turned toward me and the light from the front bay window caught his profile, I was reminded of pictures I'd seen of Russian generals. Short-cropped gray hair; tiny eyes nestled in wrinkles; narrow, lipless mouth.

"May I bring you refreshment, Mr. Perkins?" he asked.

I'd had no lunch and it was nearly one already. "Sure, thanks. Whatever you're having, if it's no—"

"No trouble at all. Please make yourself comfortable." He marched through an archway.

The back wall of the living room, flanking the archway, was solid bookshelves. At one end sat the largest pipe rack I'd ever seen, along with a large glass tobacco humidor. Beyond that, the shelves' contents alternated between well-worn hardcover volumes, pictures, and knickknacks. The books were mostly obscure-sounding medical texts. Perceptive detective that I am, I deduced that Kraus was a doctor. The pictures were all lovingly framed in gold and seemed to march through time, telling a story of their own.

They were mostly family portraits. The most recent were in color and featured Kraus and just two other people, a young man and a young woman. As the pictures got older, the number of people increased and color changed to black-and-white. What appeared to be the oldest picture showed maybe twenty people of all ages, wearing tight dark clothes and no smiles. I could not identify Kraus among them. I wondered what the occasion was.

"My bar mitzvah," Kraus's voice sounded from behind me. I turned and accepted a cup from him. "April eleventh, 1919. Berlin."

I looked at the picture again. "Large family."

"It was then. Most of them died in the camps." He said that plainly, without rancor or self-pity. "Come, shall we sit?"

"Thanks." I carried the cup to the long sofa and sat at the end, sinking down what seemed like a couple of feet. Kraus took an ornate wood rocking chair with its back to the brightly lighted window and arranged himself in it carefully. The room was quiet except for the hard knocking of a clock somewhere. I looked down at the cup. It was a dainty little china thing, its handle so small I couldn't get a finger through it. It was hot enough to melt skin. I took a sip of coffee. Rich and strong. I'd have to go easy or my voice would go up an octave. "Good stuff."

"Thank you."

I looked at him. From somewhere I dredged up the information that Jewish boys had bar mitzvah at thirteen. That meant he was now eighty-three or so. I marveled. I should look that good at eighty-three. Or seventy-three. Or sixty.

I set the cup down on the low mirror-topped coffee table that stood between us and fingered Kevin's picture out of my shirt pocket. I handed it over to Kraus. "This the kid who trashed your car?"

He squinted at it. "That's him."

"Had you ever seen him before?"

"Never." He handed the picture back.

"How about since?"

"I'm afraid not."

Hey, this was working out dandy. I considered, then asked, "Did he physically attack you?"

"No." Kraus's lined face was drawn. "He simply shouted things. Variations on the theme of 'dirty Jew.'"

I leaned back in the sofa. "If you don't mind my saying so, you don't seem all that troubled about it, Mr. Kraus."

His shoulders rose and fell almost imperceptibly under the white shirt. "I've heard it all before. In several languages."

"Yeah, I guess so. Ask you something?" He nodded, expression indistinct from the bright window light shining behind him. "Why didn't you press charges against him?"

Kraus turned his palms up. "If I did that sort of thing," he said mildly, "I'd be in police stations and courtrooms more than anywhere else."

"He damaged your car, for God's sake. He caused a

mbarrassing and humiliating public spectacle. I don't under-
and why you don't—"

"Fight?" he said, smiling. "I do fight, but on my own
rms. I fight by speaking, by doing my part in educating
oung people. Most of all, I fight by not fighting."

I had no answer to that. If you can make that philosophy
ork for you, go for it. I'd never been able to.

I studied the old man, who sat there calmly. "It's really
uzzling," I ventured. "This kid's folks are good people.
ever heard a bigoted word out of either one of them. It's
ard to understand—"

"Of course it is," Kraus said gently. "No one knows the
ause of blind, irrational hatred. If it were something as
mple as parental influence, it would no doubt have been
rased generations ago."

"Only thing I can figure is, this kid's a loony," I said.

He straightened and stared at me. "Oh, but you're quite
rong," he said.

"How's that?"

"It's a dangerous mistake to believe that people with his
pinions are in some sense deranged. They are not. They
now exactly what they are doing."

I watched him and said nothing.

"Such beliefs are what make me go out and speak on the
Holocaust," Kraus said. "The popular notion is that it was an
istorical aberration during which an insane Hitler mesmer-
ed a nation of well-intentioned people and caused them to
ork his evil for him. But it was no aberration. It was a
onsciously designed state action which required the coopera-
on of millions of people who knew exactly what they were
oing. It simply flies in the face of reason to presume that the
ntire nation went—what is the term?—nuts, all at once."

Hoo boy. I'd lucked into a professor type. Odds were he
ould go on in this vein for hours. "All right," I said. "But
ings are different now."

"Another comforting rationalization," Kraus observed. "And
qually false. I suppose you're going to tell me that 'this is
merica, it could never happen here.'"

"Well, of course there are problems and nut cases, but—"

"Someone said once that this country is always three meals
way from a revolution." Kraus sipped some coffee and went
n. "Economics, Mr. Perkins. That was the key in Germany

in 1932, and it's the key today. As long as most people have enough to eat, they stay too busy to act upon their hatred. When they become hungry—when they lose their jobs— when they have nothing better to do, the hatred which is always with them takes charge. I know. I've seen it. This young man you're looking for, he's the type I'm talking about, and I assure you that he is not alone."

CHAPTER 8

I WANTED A CIGAR, but there was no scent of tobacco smoke in the room, so I held off.

The old man suddenly smiled. "But there I go! Preaching and lecturing! My apologies. It's not really my style. When I speak on this subject, I avoid politics. I merely tell what happened to me. What I saw. The conclusions my listeners draw, the politics they wish to infer, those are not my concerns."

I'd never met a Holocaust survivor before, and being nosy, asked, "What happened to you?"

All expression left his face. He cocked his head. "Back in the old days?"

I nodded.

"Very well. The short version. They came for us in 1938," Kraus said, looking toward the window. "We were among the 'NN,' Nacht und Nebel, Night and Fog. We simply vanished. My mother and sisters were separated from us at once. I learned that they went to Ravensbrück. From there I presume they were sent to Auschwitz. I've never been able to determine that. My brothers and father and I were taken to Buchenwald. My father was beaten to death on the march to the camp from Weimar. He was frail and couldn't maintain the pace, and so they dealt wih him. My brothers had both been politically active, and the SS knew that, and so they were hanged, after enduring twenty-five lashes a day for a week."

The cold, professorial recitation was unnerving. My mouth was dry. I drank some coffee, which only increased my cigar hunger. I took one out and held it up. "Do you mind, sir?"

"Not at all," Kraus said, "In fact, I'll join you." He rose stiffly, padded to the shelves, extracted a pipe from the rack, and began to load it from the humidor. "Understand that, at the time, Buchenwald was not an organized death camp in the way that Birkenau at Auschwitz became. Certainly there were many executions at Buchenwald. How well I remember that building, the death-house, 'the Bunker,' they called it. But there were no, as they say, assembly-line killings."

I fired up my cigar. "Is that why you survived?"

Kraus clamped the stem of the large-bowl pipe in his jaw, flared a match, and drew energetically. "I survived," he puffed, "due partly to luck and partly to treachery."

I watched him return to his rocker and sit slowly, leaving a trail of blue smoke across the room. He looked at me. "I was—I am—a veterinarian. The Germans knew this. After a period of indoctrination, they assigned me to work in the falconry and the zoo."

"The what?"

He smiled. "It sounds hard to believe, doesn't it? But the SS built a falconry at Buchenwald as a tribute to Göring. I don't believe he ever saw it. Yet I was assigned there to care for the birds. I was in good company. Blum, the French premier, was quartered there. We also had a zoo. Monkeys, bears, a rhinoceros."

"Not bad duty," I said, "considering."

"For sport, the SS used to feed prisoners to the bears," Kraus said. "I also cared for the dogs, which were used to track and kill escapees."

"Sorry."

He waved his pipe. "No matter. You are partially right. I was spared the purest hell of Buchenwald life. The animals were fed better than the prisoners; consequently, so was I. I never worked in the quarry, I never saw duty as a corpse carrier. I avoided trouble, I tried to stay invisible. Of course, this was not always possible. I was strung up by my hands for a day during the winter and beaten every hour because I was caught reading a piece of newspaper that served as toilet paper. That was one of innumerable occurrences. Yet in a bizarre way the Germans respected me. They rigidly addressed

e as 'Herr Doktor, you filthy Jew.'" He laughed at the
memory.

"Jeez," I said, exhaling a long stream of smoke.

Kraus nodded and his laughter ended abruptly. "In 1944
the falconry and the zoo were closed, and I was assigned to a
labor group. The word came that I was to be sent to the
bunker, the death-house. Fortunately I had a friend who was
an orderly in building fifty, a medical ward. He was indebted
to me because I had smuggled food to him while I worked at
the zoo. He arranged for me to enter building fifty as a
typhus case. Even the SS were terrified of exposure to
typhus. They seldom came into the ward. When they did
come, it was never for me. I waited out the end of the war,
one minute at a time."

"So," I said after a silence, "you made it."

"Ninety-eight pounds," he answered. "With no family or
home. But I did make it. One of the perhaps ten percent of
camp inmates who survived."

A car engine sounded outside as I finished off my coffee.
"This kid I'm looking for. Kevin. Do you run into situations
like that a lot?"

"Not often," he said mildly. "But enough to convince me
that the horror is still there. Waiting to strike again when the
conditions are right."

I heard footsteps on the walk. "I don't know, Mr. Kraus. As
god-awful unbelievable as the Holocaust was, I just don't buy
into it happening again, here especially."

"Not overnight," he said, "but in time it could, and young
men like your Kevin are the breeding ground." The front
door opened and Kraus got to his feet, beaming. "That must
be Michael. My grandson. He has lunch with me every day.
You will stay to lunch, Mr. Perkins, won't you?" He started
for the foyer as a dark young man came in. "Michael! How
was your morning?"

They hugged, the young man towering over the older one,
chattering in a foreign tongue. I hadn't had lunch yet but no
longer felt hungry. I went to my feet as Kraus escorted the
young man in. "Mr. Perkins, this is my grandson, Michael
Kraus. Michael is—well, what are you, Michael?" The old
man beamed at his grandson. "An engineering student at LIT,
holder of a full scholarship. He also drives a taxicab to earn

the money that young men always seem to need." He looke<
at me. "And this, Michael, is Mr. Perkins, a private detective."

The younger Kraus was thin and dark with glasses, a long
angular face, and deep blue eyes that showed no welcome a<
we shook hands. He wore a dark blue pullover shirt and jean<
that were brand-new but looked like they'd been washed t<
death. He looked scholarly as well as ultrasuspicious, and hi<
handshake was cold and tentative, as if he were afraid I'<
steal his hand. He said, "What do you want with my grandfa<
ther, Mr. Perkins?"

"Well, I—"

"Oh," Kraus said, waving a dismissive hand, "he's lookin<
for someone, that high-school kid who wrecked my car dow<
in Wayne that time. It's a long story, Michael."

The young man tipped his head back, watching me fron<
the distance behind his glasses. "Surely you didn't think m<
grandfather would know where that vicious little terrorist is."

"Michael," the old man said. "Please. Be polite. M<
Perkins is a guest."

This grandson was obviously the apple of the doting grand<
father's eye. I chose to shrug off the hostility emanating fron<
Michael. "Just doing my job here, that's all."

"We were talking about the Holocaust," Kraus elder chime<
in. "We were debating whether it could happen again. You'v<
got strong opinions on that, don't you, Michael?" He winke<
at me. "If Michael spent as much time studying at LIT as h<
does reading about the racist movement, he'd have his engi<
neering degree by now." He eyed his grandson, fondnes<
mixed with concern. "Young men like you should be taking ou<
girls to parties instead of collecting files on bigots."

"Old men like you should be gardening and sunbathin<
and playing pinochle," Michael retorted, "instead of lecturin<
kids about ancient history."

"I have my duty," Kraus said.

"So have I." We'd all remained standing. Damned if I'd si<
till someone else made the move. Michael looked at m<
scornfully. "Of course it could happen again. There ar<
national groups in this country dedicated to promoting jus<
that."

"What groups?" I asked. "I remember the American Naz<
party; where are they now? Then there was that business o<
Hitler's birthday. Those biker-Nazis wanted Belle Isle fo<

their celebration, right? Ended up demonstrating in Dearborn somewhere, all twelve of them."

Michael ticked fingers. "The Silent Brotherhood. The Order. Posse Comitatus. The White American Revolutionary Army. The Aryan Resistance Movement. Aryan Nations. The White American Bastion. The Cross, the Sword and the Arm of the Lord. Mr. Perkins," he went on fervently, "they have a convention in Idaho every year, like appliance salesmen. The Aryan World Congress. People bring their families, a festive celebration of hate."

"You've made quite a study of it," I said.

"I believe one should know his enemy."

My cigar had gone stone-cold dead. I slipped it into my shirt pocket, then folded my arms. "Maybe you can explain something to me. What's a Z.O.G.?"

"Stands for Zionist Occupational Government," Michael said. "That's their term for the United States government. They believe we Jews run the world. Not an original idea. Somehow these people hold us responsible for capitalism and communism at the same time. It is the same thesis espoused in the 'Protocols of the Elders of Zion,' back in—"

"Here he goes," Kraus warned. "The only thing that will shut him up now is food. I'll go get it ready. Tomato sandwiches today, Michael, all right?"

"Fine," the grandson said distractedly as Kraus left the room. I looked at the kid to find his stare burning holes in me. "Any other questions, Mr. Perkins?" he asked, voice as sour as his face.

"Two more. First one: a book called *The Turner Diaries*, by somebody named Andrew Macdonald. Ever heard of it?"

Michael's smile was peculiar. "Andrew Macdonald was a pseudonym for William Pierce, an otherwise respected physics professor. I should read *The Turner Diaries* if I were you, Mr. Perkins."

"Okay. I will," I said, matching his snotty tone.

"Second question?"

"Yeah, almost forgot. What's your beef, anyhow?"

"I don't understand."

I held my hands out, palms up. "I come here, I have a chat with your grandfather, and here you are coming on like I tried to kidnap him or something."

The kid folded his arms, staring at me defiantly. "I am not afraid of you, Mr. Perkins."

I rolled my eyes. "If it comes to a grabass, the smart money'll be on me, kid, but who said anything about that? I don't mean your grandfather any harm."

The kid said in a low voice, "He's an old man who's been through hell, and I won't permit anything to happen to him. I don't know who you are. You say you're searching for that little terrorist; how do I know you're not one of them?"

"Aw jeez. Look," I said, walking around him toward the foyer, "nice talking to ya. Give your grandfather my regards, thanks for the coffee and the chat." I slammed out.

Dynamite Park is a long swath of forests and meadows that follows the meandering path of the middle branch of the Rouge River all the way from the suburb of Plymouth, in the far western frontier of Wayne County, eastward to the city of Detroit. Its sylvan tranquillity is as deceptive as its real name, which, officially, is not Dynamite Park at all, but something bureaucratically soothing like Metropolitan Detroit Wayne County River Rouge Nature Preserve, blah blah.

I found a spot in the easternmost section of the park, off Outer Drive within the Detroit city limits, near where the Middle Rouge and the Northern Rouge intersect. I parked the Mustang at the end of a gravel turnoff, overlooking a meadow that bordered on the forested fringe of the river, put some good gritty Marshall Tucker Band on the tape player, and arranged my lunch on the car hood. Two Burger Barn burritos with everything, two icy-cold cans of Stroh's. There was nowhere to sit, so I slid up onto the hood, used the windshield as a backrest and the high-rise manifold shroud as a table. The burritos went down fast, the beer slower, and I lighted a cigar as I cracked the second can and leaned back on the impromptu lounge, thinking.

This Holocaust business had me thrown. I admit I had trouble squaring what old man Kraus had told me with the Kevin Witkowski situation. I mean, all that was nearly a half century ago, in another country, another world. I knew it was real to those, like Kraus, who had endured it. Maybe it was understandable to those who didn't experience it personally but who were around at the time. But all the books and

movies and talk down through the years couldn't make it real
or understandable to me. Scooping people up wholesale,
marching them into camps and killing them by the millionpack—
for no reason other than who and what they were—I didn't
think the greatest philosopher alive could get a handle on
that, let alone a day-at-a-time working lug like me.

On the other hand, I'd learned that there is literally no limit
to what people are capable of doing to each other. I'd seen
that first hand, at the individual level. Why not in groups too?

But that was then. Now, a half century and a couple of
generations later, here was Kevin Witkowski, buying into it.
This had me thrown, too. I cast myself back in time to when I
was seventeen or eighteen. My background had been like
Kevin's: working-class family. But there the resemblance
ended. Sure, we'd had our prejudices: blacks were seen but
not heard, and Jews were up in Southfield or downtown
running the banks; and we had our politics: Eisenhower was
president and would probably hold office forever until we
could get a good Democrat in there. But those were fleeting
thoughts. I'd had no time for prejudice or politics, let alone
both. I'd focused on graduating high school, which I did (just
barely); getting a line job at Ford's, which I did; getting laid,
which I did; moving up in the union, which I did; and
eventually settling down and getting married and raising
kids, which I didn't and probably never would, now.

Kevin was definitely different. I wondered where his political passion started. Why his parents seemed unaware of it.
And I wondered where it had taken him. I got out my pad
and scribbled down as many names as I could remember
from Michael Kraus's list of white-supremacy groups. God
knew, half of them could be single-bigot entrepreneurships.
But from what he'd said, the movement sounded like a
growth industry. Kevin might have hitched up with one of
them. Convention in Idaho, huh? Depressing, the notion of
scurrying all over the country sorting through sweaty groups
of warpoids, looking for a kid whose gears had stripped.

But hopefully it would not come to that. Maybe he was still
in the area somewhere. Maybe that license number and
phone number that Lynne had found would lead me somewhere, and I'd get this sucker done and behind me.

Then all I'd have to sweat out were the two felonies.
Shaping up to be a fun summer.

CHAPTER 9

BEING THE DUTIFUL SORT that I am, I checked in on Brian and Randy when I got back to Norwegian Wood. Big mistake.

Brian was doing all right, but Randy hadn't gotten anywhere with the soil pipe in building two. The cleanout plug was frozen—typical, after so many years—and he'd dinked around with it just enough to strip the shoulders of the nut smooth. I went to work with him and tried the usual things: penetrating oil, filing, hammer and cold chisel, propane torch, brute force. Nothing. Sucker sat there and sneered at us. Finally I got serious. Drilled a series of holes in the plug and then used the heaviest ball-peen hammer I own to knock the son of a bitch clean out of there. That cost me a trip to the hardware store for a replacement plug, but I returned to find Randy cheerfully at work, powering the electric snake deep into the pipe. The stink was already overpowering, and I got the hell out of there and retreated to my apartment.

The answering-machine light was blinking. Three messages. I rewound the tape and found that the percentages were holding up: two of the calls had been hangups. The third was from Pat O'Shay from Michigan Bell, returning my call.

I sprung a Stroh's loose from the fridge, sat down at the kitchen table with cigar, notebook, and pen, and called her back.

"This is Pat," she greeted, perky as ever.

"This is Uncle Ben," I growled, "and before you ask, the rice business is lousy."

She laughed. The joke goes back to the days she was Patty

62

Johnston, youngest daughter of Norris Johnston, a Dearborn private detective with whom I've worked, partied, and occasionally tangled down through the years. In the twinkling of an eye, it seems that my old pals' kids are growing up. What a sobering thought.

It does have its advantages, though. Those kids who aren't dead or in jail are out in the world working. And some of those—like Pat O'Shay—hold positions with access to information not readily available to your everyday slob.

And some of *those* are even willing to lend a hand to their old "Uncle" Ben.

"How much and how fast?" I asked.

"Um . . . well, a pair of John Cougar Mellencamp tickets at Pine Knob."

I scribbled that down. "Okay, I'll touch base with my friendly scalper."

"Lawn seats are fine," she said helpfully. "As to 'how fast,' is immediately okay?"

"You're a sweetheart, and entirely too good for O'Shay, did I ever mention that?"

"As well as too young for you, so back off," she said sweetly. "What are we looking for?"

"Location of a phone number." I sorted an Amoco slip out of my notebook and read off the number. "Can I wait?"

"Sure," she said, distracted. "Computer's actually up and running and everything. Just a sec."

I lighted a cigar, drank some smoke, inhaled some beer, waited.

"Okay, here we go," she said. "It's a pay phone. Forty forty-nine Trenton Avenue, Detroit."

The address rang no bells. Have to break out the old atlas. "Okay, kid, much obliged."

"Happy to help. Mail me the tickets?"

"Sure. Take care now." Another fifty bucks out the door, I thought as I hung up, but in a worthy cause, and it just might pay off. The gas slip was dated only a month ago. Maybe Kevin was still around here somewhere.

I was nursing my beer, considering whether or not to check out the address this late in the afternoon, when the phone rang under my hand. I picked it up. "Perkins's Plumbing for Pleasure, Ben speaking."

"You screamed?" came Dick Dennehy.

"Matter of fact, yeah. Was hoping you'd call back before died."

"You're one to talk about phone manners. Look at the way you answer the damn thing."

"Puckish sense of humor," I said, grinning.

"Uh-huh. Well, let me see now. Odds are, you called because you've gotten prime box seats to the Detroit Tigers versus the pain-in-the-ass Orioles, and your first thought was to invite your faithful old buddy Dick to go with you."

"Sorry."

"Aw shit. Well then, I guess you called because you've had an attack of conscience and want to settle up on our little wager about the Red Wings play-offs."

"Wrong again. I shoulda known better to begin with 'Never bet on men who skate,' my daddy always told me."

"So that means," Dick said deliberately, "you want to bum some information off me."

"Howdja ever guess?"

"Jeez."

You see, only on TV and in books do people like Dick Dennehy, an inspector with the Michigan state police, fall all over themselves to lend the private detective a hand. "Come on, Dick, all I need is a license-number run. And I don't have to bring this business to you, you know. I could just go direct to Motor Vehicles. Cut out the middle man."

"And wait a week or two for the answer," he said.

"I got nothing but time."

"Like hell," he growled. "Well, let's get it over with."

"Much obliged." I read him the number. "How soon?"

"Have to be tomorrow."

"Thanks."

"Working on a hot one?"

"Runaway kid."

"Who wants him back?"

"Parents."

"They want him back," Dick mused. "Miracles never cease. So, is that it? Is that all you want this time?"

"That's it, pal. Oh, wait. One more thing."

"I knew it. I just knew it."

"Come on, this is easy, too. I'd like you to put out a stiff search for, say, three-hundred-mile radius."

"Jesus Christ, Ben! That's got to be a couple hundred morgues!"

"Cut the clowning. You do it by computer, takes you maybe thirty seconds. You told me that once in a loose moment."

"Did, huh?"

"About the seventh rum and Coke, as I recall."

"Me and my big fat fucking mouth. All right, I'm not crushing much crime today, anyhow. Got me one peach of an assignment. Seems some of the people running our halfway houses have gone into business for themselves. Taking bribes from inmates, letting the grimy little recidivists run loose."

"Hey, free enterprise, Dick. It's the American way."

"Guess I'm not much of a patriot then. Let's get on with it. What flavor of alleged corpse we looking for?"

I fingered Kevin's picture out of my pocket and used it to jog my memory. "White Caucasian, eighteen, five ten, one fifty soaking wet with rocks in his pocket—"

"I get the idea. Skinny little rug-rat."

"Pretty much, yeah. Uh, add brown over brown to that, and no scars or marks that I know of. Military haircut."

"He got a name or anything?"

"Glad you asked me that. Witkowski, Kevin."

"Armed and dangerous?"

"More like surly and loud. But only if he's alive."

"Jesus!" Dick said. "Where'd you get this case, off a milk carton?"

"Clients are friends of mine."

"Don'tcha hate it when friends impose on you? Sons of bitches."

"Yeah, people should do for themselves, I always say."

"You're a man of principle. I've always said that." He paused. "Any particular reason why this kid should be dead?"

"None that I can think of. Aside from everyone dies sooner or later, and it occurred to me maybe he picked sooner."

"Sure be convenient if he was," Dick noted. "Save you chasing all over hell and gone."

"Well, it'd be the first time a case of mine got wrapped up that neat. But I hope you come up empty on the stiff search. The parents are good folks, and that's the last thing they need right now."

He must have heard something in my voice, because he said, "Gotcha. I'll get back to you soonest."

* * *

By now it was entirely too late to go check out the address. Pat O'Shay had given me. I decided to bag it till tomorrow and proceeded to the bedroom. Back there I stripped, showered away the faint odor of old drain, and put on my best pub crawl togs: navy blue cords, a white pullover shirt, and low-topped boots.

Then I motored away in the brilliant cool evening, considering my options. I felt unaccountably edgy, wanted to lose myself for a while, and where could I go for that? Carole's was pleasant enough. I could watch some tube with her, throw some ball with Will. But being there brought a tension all its own. The bowling alley was between league seasons. The judge was in Europe so the poker sessions wouldn't return till after the Fourth, and the Detroit Tigers were on a west-coast swing. So Under New Management got the nod and I blasted east on Ecorse Road, anticipating an evening of long brews and loud brags accompanied by thumping country music from the jukebox.

At Hannan Road I swung left, then immediately right into the gravel lot that wrapped around the shabby-looking, signless cinder-block building. Eddie's Corvette was there, alongside Darryl Rockecharlie's mint green Caddy, Jimmy Joe Putnam's latest brand-new secondhand wreck, and a fire-engine red Ford Escort that belonged to Barb Paley.

Damn. She must have gotten off work early.

I jammed the Mustang into second, floored the gas, doughnuted a one-eighty on the flying, dusty gravel, and screeched back out onto Ecorse headed westbound. Come to think of it, I had some paperwork to catch up on in the maintenance office. Duty before pleasure, as my daddy would have said.

The next day found me on Trenton Avenue, which ends almost before it begins. It starts at Dayton Street on Detroit's far southwest side, near the Dearborn line and right in the shadow of the Chrysler Glass Plant, and runs southeast for a while till it ends at the Conrail yards. To the south are Holy Cross and Woodmere cemeteries. To the west is the Ford Road/Michigan Avenue/I-94 entanglement. And to the south

est sprawls Ford's Rouge plant, the largest industrial com-
lex on earth.

Though you can't see the Rouge from Trenton Avenue, you
now it's there. The air, even on a shining spring day, bears
e harsh scents of gritty soot, sulphur, and diesel; below the
g-city din of cars, trucks, trains, and planes there is an extra
sistent level of subliminal noise, the hard, muscular beating
' Detroit's industrial heart. Forget your Renaissance Center,
art Plaza, and Belle Isle; this is the real thing, a Detroit as
miliar and comfortable to me as an old flannel shirt. A little
orn and tattered, and not pretty to look at, but still working.

I followed Trenton south from McGraw, chasing house
umbers. It's narrow and one-way along there, nothing more
an a black strip that's been patched so many times the
riginal surface is indiscernible. Cars of all flavors lined the
ght-hand curb. Densely packed houses sat behind shallow,
raggly lawns. Most were story-and-a-half bungalows, clap-
oard interrupted by the odd brick. The color scheme ranged
om faded white to chipped green, and it looked as though
o painting had been done since Nixon was in. Tall trees
inked the street on both sides, making the neighborhood
ok prettier than it was.

Below Michigan Avenue I began to get close. Woodrow
Wilson Park appeared on my left, a vast, treeless plain with a
ouple of baseball diamonds, meandering dirt bike paths, and
l odd assortment of play equipment. Beyond that I could
e a field packed densely with ranks of semitrailers. Cars
ooradically spotted both curbs along there. Most were older.
ome were melting into the pavement. Apparently the Traffic
Division tow trucks hadn't been through here lately. Saint
ohn Street T'd into Trenton from the east, and there on the
ght was 4049. I wedged the Mustang between a stripped
ickup and a leaning Chevy station wagon, shut off the
ngine, and got out.

It was noon, and already I felt like I'd put in a full day. I'd
leant to get over here first thing, but Randy had hung the
nake up in the soil pipe the night before, and I'd put in a
ouple of sweaty, smelly hours this morning helping him get
: loose. I fervently hoped, as I walked up the tree-shaded
dewalk toward 4049, that Randy would have the job done
y the time I got back. I also hoped that I would find Kevin
Witkowski here, maybe sitting at a kitchen table eating some

lunch. Looking up at me in surprise. Oh hi, Ben. Wh
Dad's sick? Oh, God! Sure, let's go.

The house was larger than most of its neighbors, virtua
filling its lot. It was two-story, chipped white clapboa
beneath a hip roof shingled in gray, banded around with dar
dirty windows and fronted by a wide veranda accessed
steep-pitched cement steps. I hoofed up them to the emp
veranda. The door stood wide open. No sound issued fro
inside. I tapped on the door frame. No one appeared.
leaned inside and called, "Hello?"

I heard a voice, some shuffling, then the slam of a door a
hasty feet. A short, skinny bald man emerged from t
darkness toward the front door. "Yes? Yes? What is it?"
said, voice a sharp, nasal squeak.

"Good morning," I said. "Is this your house?"

"Hell no," he said. He was as misshapen as anyone I'd ev
met: five feet even, but with arms that sent wrists to kn
level, a long torso, and little stick legs. He was so thin t
shoulder, pelvic, and knee bones showed plainly through
red-checkered short-sleeve shirt and dark twill pants. He ha
better than sixty years on him and, judging from the de
lines around his eyes and mouth, he'd spent most of the
drinking and laughing. "I just live here. You wanna live her
you got to talk to Margo, and she don't get here till six
later, and I don't think there's any rooms left anyhow."

"Oh. So this is a rooming house."

"Well, why the hell else would you come here?" He lean
close to me, enveloping me with the aroma of Old Gra
Dad. "Word to the wise. Margo'll tellya no hot plates, but
you keep it out of sight, under the bed or whatever, she wo
bitch about it." He tapped his temple. "Word to the wise
"That's good to know," I said. "Listen, I'm looking f
somebody, and—"

"Well, ain't nobody here," he cackled. "'Side from me a
Carrie, and she's sacked out 'cause she works graveyard, a
I'm here 'cause I'm on the railroad retirement." He slappe
his right leg. "Had a winch come around on me back
sixty-eight. Gave me a good lick. Imagine my surprise whe
they said I was disabled. Hell, I didn't argue—"

"Good, good," I said. "Could I have a minute of your tim
somewhere other than at the front door here?"

He squinted at me. "Listen, sonny, I may be retired, but
m still busy. You want to talk, come on out back."

He turned and loped away. I followed him down a high,
arrow hall that bisected the house. It had, no doubt, been a
ngle-family residence once, brutally partitioned off a long
me ago. Four rooms on the ground floor, one right, three
ft. A majestic, free-standing staircase rose up into dimness.
t the back was another door with a sign that said, helpfully,
ATHROOM, and next to it was an entranceway to a long,
arrow kitchen. The back door led out onto a brick stoop
tered with cheap aluminum lawn chairs and flanked by
ige rhododendrons. The little man skipped down the brick
eps to the lawn, which wasn't really a lawn at all.

Aside from a patch of grass to the left, the whole yard was
nder cultivation, turned, brown earth moist in the sun. He
as just finishing up the last row, to the far right; a spade
uck business-side down in the dirt, and a rake, hoe, mat-
ck, and pitchfork lay scattered around. At the back, protected
y tree shade, were several flats of small plants in peat pots.
mato plants, mostly. Couple dozen of them. The man
eant business.

"You into truck farming or what?" I asked.

He went to the spade, lifted it, stuck it into the soil,
oved it deep with his foot, turned the clump over, and
egan breaking it up meticulously. "No," he squeaked. "Like
eat good, that's all. Vegetables is good for you. All organic,
at's the ticket. No chemicals. Just good soil, peat moss,
anure, mulch, sun, and water. And work, sonny. Lotta
ork. But it's worth it."

"Rushing the season a little, aren't you?"

He waved a bony, dismissive hand. "That Memorial Day
uff is for rookies. Each year is different. This year the time
now. I'll have it all in before the sun goes down." He bent,
ig in the dirt, and rose, extending his hand. An earthworm
estled in his palm. "See there? This good soil or what?"

Right here in the shadow of the Rouge plant, I mused.
ow about that. "Listen, I'm looking for somebody, was told
e lives here. Young kid named Kevin Witkowski."

He looked at me, eyes rheumy, and shook his head almost
once. "Never heard of him." He dropped the earthworm
ito the ground and buried it meticulously. "We're not big on
ames around here," he added.

I got the picture out of my shirt pocket, went down t‖ steps and over to him, and put it in front of his face. "Se‖ him before?"

The man turned over a new spadeful, broke it up, the‖ leaned on the spade handle and squinted at the picture. "O‖ yeah. He was around."

I felt a brief rush. You caught the scent, Ben old son. "H‖ was, huh? Not anymore?"

"Nope. Not for a while."

I put the picture away. "He live here or what?"

"Ya know, I wouldn't know. Hard to tell who's living he‖ for true, and who's just 'staying over' or whatever." He took‖ filthy blue bandanna out of his hip pocket and wiped ‖ damp forehead. His squeaky voice went singsong. "Peop‖ come, people go. This place is sort of—uh—transit? What t‖ hell word am I looking for?"

"Transient?"

"That might be it. I don't pay much attention, long as the‖ leave me and my garden alone." He put the bandanna awa‖ "This some kind of trouble?"

"Nah, just looking for the kid. Any ideas where I should ‖ next?"

"Sorry. People come, people go, where he's at, I wouldn‖ know. Ha!" He lifted the spade preparing a new thrust, the‖ set it back down, looking past me. "Carrie might kno‖ though."

I looked up on the brick stoop. There stood a tall you‖ blond woman. Very tall, very blond, and very very stacke‖ I'm no geneticist, but my assessment was that everythi‖ about her was God-given except for the hair, which was sho‖ close, tightly curled, and glittery brittle. She was barefo‖ and wore tight white shorts and, above an acre of smooth, ta‖ belly, a white shirt whose front tails were bound below h‖ heavy breasts in a knot. A square knot, no doubt; nothi‖ else would have held that much cargo.

When she was sure she had our undivided attention, s‖ silently picked up a folded lounge chair and started down t‖ steps. The gardener winked at me. "Mornin', Care!" ‖ squeaked.

"Good morning, Bert," Carried answered, bored.

The gardener watched her finish her breast-wobbling d‖

scent, winked at me again, and whispered, "I'm fucking that."

I did a double take. "Huh?"

He nodded, rheumy eyes alight. "Every day," he whispered. "G'wan, ask her your questions, then do me a favor and split. She can't wait long. Gotta have it."

I gave him a light, friendly tap on the shoulder that would have knocked him flying had he not been braced on the spade. "I'll make it quick," I assured him, and walked over to the woman as Bert returned to his work.

CHAPTER 10

SHE'D UNFOLDED THE LOUNGE chair, set it up flat on the small patch of grass, and stretched out on it belly down, tawny back glowing in the sun. Its reflection off her blond hair was almost blinding. Her eyes were closed, and though she gave no sign of hearing my approach, she said when I was six feet away, "I suppose Bert told you he's fucking me."

I groped for an answer and came up empty. With lithe grace she rolled over onto her back and opened her eyes, staring toward the back of the lot. "He can have his fantasies," she said. "It's the incessant talk that annoys me. A couple of weeks ago I decided to teach him a lesson. He was working back here, and I was sunning just as I am now, and I called him over here. He stood right where you are and looked down at me. I looked at him and smiled and unsnapped my shorts." She illustrated this in pantomime, her face dead serious. "Then I took a deep, deep breath, pulled my knees back and whispered to him just as huskily as I could, 'Here it is, Bert.'"

I took a deep breath and worked to keep my voice a monotone. "What'd he do?"

Her mouth crept into a smile. "He turned the color of wet cement. His eyes bugged out. He swallowed so hard I thought he'd taken his tongue with it. Then he turned and staggered away. Scrambled up those steps and vanished into the house. Didn't see him again for two days."

At a distance she'd looked to be twenty or so. Up close here it was evident she had thirty backed into a corner. Her looks and her diction didn't square with the neighborhood. I wondered where she was from. I wondered why she was lounging around back here in midday when most folks were working. I wondered a lot of things. But I said, "Fixed him, huh?"

"I thought so. But he's still talking, damn it." She thrust a long, strong hand up at me, shading her eyes with the other one, really giving me the once-over. "Carrie Longstreet. A pleasure."

I shook her hand and dropped it as if it were a live wire. "Ben Perkins. Right back atcha."

"Please sit." I did so, cross-legged on the grass, within lunging distance of her. She began to toy with the knot below her majestic breasts. "Why are you here? Doing research for *Lifestyles of the Rich and Famous*?"

I laughed. "You got it." I wished she'd quit tinkering with that knot. "I'm looking for someone. Young kid named Kevin Witkowski. Bert ID'd his picture, said he was around here a while back. Heard of him?"

She quit tinkering with the knot for an instant, then resumed, digging at it in earnest now. "There was a Kevin here for a while. I never knew his last name." She freed the first half of the square knot and added, "Let me see the picture."

I held it out. She squinted at it. Her eyes were very large, pastel blue, studious. "That's him."

"When'd you see him last?"

She liberated the second half of the knot. As she swiveled her body toward me, her breasts sprang free, only to be obscured once again as she flattened her chest into the lounge. She braced herself on her elbows and looked at her hands, which assumed an attitude of prayer. "Month ago, more or less."

I took out a cigar, flared it, inhaled of it deeply, thinking, easy son, easy easy easy. "Where'd he go?"

Hers was a longish but well-proportioned face, good complexion unaided by makeup. It still showed some youthful innocence, but was well on its way to hardcase. "Are you acting in some official capacity, Ben?" she asked without looking at me.

Her fingers were long and supple, free of callouses and jewelry, nails trimmed neatly short and polished clear, con-

servative to the point of radicalness in this day and age. "Not
official at all. Private detective."

She unconsciously bent her right knee, raising and flexing
her bare foot. Her muscles, from the gluteus group down to
the soleus, were firm and supple. This one didn't make a
living parked on her gluteus, that was for sure. "Is Kevin
in some kind of trouble?" she asked, voice not betraying a
thing.

I was getting a little tired of being cross-examined by every
pain-in-the-ass source I encountered. People just don't know
the rules anymore. When confronted by the private detective, you're supposed to be docile. You're supposed to be
agreeable. You're supposed to spill your guts. I said, a little
abruptly, "No trouble. He's gone missing and I'm trying to
find him. That's all."

She looked at me, smiling faintly. "Are you uptight for
some reason, Ben?"

Not me, no way. I took a deep hit of cigar. "All this is very
pleasant," I said, exhaling smoke as I talked, "but I've got
a job to do here, and I'd appreciate your telling whatever it
is you know about Kevin Witkowski. Immediately, if not
sooner."

"All right." She dropped her right foot and raised her left
one, flexing it this way and that, sending ripples up her long
leg. "I don't know where he went. He left, ah, abruptly."

"Oh yeah?"

Her compelling eyes fixed on me. "He was asked to leave."

"By who?"

"The other residents." Her hands made loose fists. "This
may look like a dump to you, but it's not. It's a good place to
live. I'm from Livonia. I wouldn't move into just any old
flophouse, no matter what my circumstances were."

I'd wondered about her circumstances; she was well-spoken
and had suburb written all over her. But it was no doubt
some tired old story, and I had other issues to focus on, such
as getting the lowdown on Kevin and keeping my eyes off
Carrie's chest. "So what happened?" I asked as I tapped ash
off my cigar.

"He was noisy and disruptive," she said. "He brought
obnoxious friends around. They'd hang around on the porch,
drinking beer and playing this awful music on a boombox.
They'd keep going till midnight or later, no matter who

complained. They'd leave empty cans and cigarette butts everywhere. I mean, it got to be too much."

I nodded.

"What tore it was the squirrel thing," she added.

"I beg your pardon?"

Her face went stony. "One time he and a couple of his goon friends were sitting out front on the steps. One of them had a slingshot. The kind that straps to your wrist, you know?" Sounded more like a catapult to me, but I just nodded. "They had some ball bearings, and they were shooting at the squirrels who play in the trees out front."

"Good, clean fun," I said.

She glanced at me quickly; then, reassured, she said, "They killed two of the poor things. One didn't die right away, lay there flopping in the street, and Kevin walked over to it and did a little dance around it and then put his heel on its head and slowly smashed it."

As the scene played in my mind, my mouth went dry, and not from thirst. I wondered how Lynne would react.

"I was just leaving for work," Carrie went on. "I screamed at those sons of bitches. One of them said, 'Listen, sweetie, we do what we want to dirty fucking yids.'" She looked at me. "I don't understand. What do squirrels have to do with Jews?"

Game of pretend, I thought as a chill crept into my stomach. I deflected her question by saying, "Who knows? Beered up, bored, and broke, you do about anything for sport."

"Not that," she said fervently. "Oh God no. I thought I was going to puke. Just thinking about it makes me feel the same way." She cocked her head. "Funny thing was, up till then I didn't think Kevin was such a bad guy. But these goons he brought here, I mean, they were trash."

"So you all ran him out, huh?"

She shrugged. "Three of the guys cornered him the next day and handed him his stuff and told him he was gone. So he left."

"And you don't know where he went."

"No. Don't care, either."

Dead end. I examined the red-hot end of my cigar, then pulled a toke and said, "What kind of things did he do of an average day? Where'd he work?"

She lowered her left foot and simultaneously raised the right, and continued to alternate like that, very slowly. "Far as I know he didn't work at all. I don't see how he could, his hours were so odd. I do know one thing. He spent a lot of time hanging around the loading zone."

"Loading zone? Where at?"

She smiled. "It's a bar. The Loading Zone." She pointed to her right. "Around the corner, on Southern."

"Loading Zone, huh? Cute." Not much to go on, but it would have to do. "Okay. Anything else you can tell me?"

"Not about Kevin," she said, looking full force at me.

I stood clumsily, dropped my cigar, and pressed it out with my foot. Remembering her comment about cigarette butts, I picked up the stub and put it in my pocket. "Guess I'll check out this Loading Zone place. Thanks, Carrie."

"Any time," she answered. She raised her chest just the slightest bit, arching her back. Both bare feet were in the air now, toying with each other. "Are you alone, Ben?"

I looked down at her. The thought of Barb Paley crossed my mind, along with the inevitable comparison. Night and day. "Yeah, I am, but I gotta run now. How 'bout later if we—"

Carrie was shaking her head, smiling kindly. "No, not that. I meant are you going to the Loading Zone alone."

Okay, so I made an ass of myself, it happens. "Well, yeah, sure. Why?"

The smile went away and she looked older, closer to her own age and maybe beyond. "Be careful. It's a bad place. You look like you can take care of yourself, but . . . be careful, okay?"

"Always and everywhere. Seeya."

I'd reached the porch steps when Carrie said my name. I turned back. She was up on elbows, reknotting her shirttails, and she did not look at me. "You answered a question I didn't ask," she said, "but if I had asked it, I would have replied that I'd like it very much if you'd stop around again sometime."

"Okay."

She completed her work, rolled onto her back, and clasped both hands behind the cap of bright blond hair. "Have to be soon, though," she said, closing her eyes. "I won't be around long. Moving out to Las Vegas."

"Oh yeah?"

Her smile was dreamy. "The streets are clean. The schools are better, the teachers nicer. They have free day care; my daughter will get free hot dogs and all the juice she wants."

I blinked. "This is Vegas we're talking about?"

"Ever been there?"

"No," I admitted.

She nodded sightlessly. "That's the place. Soon as I get the bread together, and not a minute later."

I looked at the long length of her for a moment, then said, "You take care."

She nodded. "Don't forget to come back."

"Count on it." I left.

A mixed bag of black, white, and Hispanic kids were playing pickup baseball on the nearest diamond of Woodrow Wilson Park. When I reached the Mustang, I stopped and watched them for a minute. The gangly black kid on the mound could really pitch. Half-step windup and jerky little sidearm delivery, but he consistently sent them hard and low and right down the middle of where the plate would have been if they'd had one. From the intensity on his face I could tell what he was thinking. This wasn't play. This was the road to the corner of Michigan and Trumbull, baseball's most famous address. After a moment I shook myself loose, mentally wished the kid luck, got into the Mustang, and fired it up.

Believe it or not, I didn't think about Carrie Longstreet. I thought about Kevin Witkowski, and his friends, and the murdered squirrel.

The "yids" part was bothersome enough. But it wasn't any surprise, considering what I'd learned about Kevin's proclivities so far. The squirrel bit was new and unsettling. I mean, it's not as if squirrels are an endangered species in these parts. We've got a blue million of them. And animals get killed all the time, for food and for sport.

But what Kevin had done was not hunting. It was wanton, casual cruelty. He danced around the dying squirrel and then slowly squashed its head on the street. Christ. And now I was supposed to find this kid and bring him to Mommy and

Daddy. A storybook assignment, practically bursting with noble innocence.

Sure, a sour voice answered in my mind, but it happens to be your job at the moment, and though you screw up from time to time, you always manage to get your job done. Gonna change your habits now?

Nope.

I shook my head, shifted into first, and pulled out onto Trenton headed south.

The street ended at Southern Avenue. Across the two-lane road were the Conrail yards, stretching as far as I could see. Gravel embankments ran this way and that in varying levels, some of them parked full of hopper-ore railroad cars. In the distance stood several corrugated iron towers. Twin Conrail engines pushed sluggishly along one line from left to right. A double-bottom gravel hauler dieseled slowly past me, the driver grinding gears upward. "Around the corner," Carrie had told me. Left or right? Left meant getting behind the gravel hauler, so I swung right.

The street was sections of pitted, heaved cement, crossed at intervals by disused railroad tracks. I motored along a couple hundred feet till another residential street appeared on the right, just before a low, square, dingy building bearing a plastic sign that said COCA-COLA/THE LOADING ZONE/ COCA COLA. I pulled into the tiny lot and parked.

The building was pitted with impenetrable barred windows and encased with fake brick siding that had peeled away in places, revealing good old cinder block. Its asphalt roof slanted shedlike from front to back. The lot ran around three sides and backed onto dense trees, beyond which appeared the backyards of several residences. There were no people present and no other cars in the lot. But it wasn't closed or abandoned; the steel front door stood open.

I started to get out of the car, then hesitated. It was two in the afternoon. Where was everyone? Places like The Loading Zone are institutions in hundreds of neighborhoods like this in Detroit. They operate from early morning till well past midnight, and they're there to serve thirsty factory workers of all shifts. Here we were within shouting distance of Ford's

Rouge, Conrail, Chrysler Glass, and zillions of smaller places,
yet The Loading Zone lot was empty aside from me.

Well, I thought, maybe they water their beer or something. Who knows? What I did know was that this was, or had
been, Kevin's haunt. I also knew that I didn't like the looks of
the joint. The way in also seemed to be the only way out.
Weapon or no?

Come on, dummy, I thought. Since when are you afraid of
a bunch of faggy little squirrel killers?

So I left my .45 automatic in the car.

CHAPTER 11

THE LOADING ZONE EXHALED the aroma of beer, sweat, and tobacco smoke as I sauntered through the open door. The dimness required a pause to adjust the eyeballs. Waste of time; there wasn't much to see. The room was wide and shallow. No booths, just wood tables of various sizes and shapes. No bar, just a counter jutting out of the right-hand wall like a peninsula about halfway into the room. No people, either.

Correction: three people. A man behind the counter, leaning against it with his back to me, watching a small TV mounted above the racks of bottles. And two others in the far left-hand corner, where the shadows were deepest. There were no athletic trophies and no Detroit Tiger pennants. But there were decorations, of sorts. One was a banner on the left-handed wall depicting a large Maltese cross in the center of which was a sideways Z pierced vertically by a sword with a crown above its handle. Above that was a large, crudely lettered sign bearing just one word: SKINHEADS!

The other decoration was familiar. A full-color poster of two long-haired men in black jackets. They aimed guitars at each other like flamethrowers. The caption: SKREWDRIVER. I'd seen it before, in Kevin's bedroom.

I was trying in my own clumsy way to puzzle all that out when the man behind the counter turned to face me. He was maybe thirty and prematurely bald; what hair was left was shorn to stubble length. He wore aviator glasses, a white athletic T-shirt, and a frown. "Help you?"

I ambled over and sat on the center stool. My feet looked for a rail and found none. "Draft," I said.

He studied me for a long moment. Then he fetched a tall water glass from beneath the counter and began to fill it from the Budweiser tap. Up to my right the snowy TV was murmuring the most popular game show of the moment, *Million Dollar Wheel of Hollywood Jeopardy* or something like that. The contestant was an animated woman who looked and sounded a lot like Brenda Vaccaro and seemed to be doing well, at least better than I was. The barman, if that's what he was, set the glass down. "Buck," he said.

"Ben," I answered, extending a hand.

Frowning, he ignored it. "One dollar," he reiterated.

I dropped my hand. "Tab?" I asked.

"You said you wanted beer." He took the glass. "All we've got is Coke and Mountain Dew, anyway."

I stared at him as I took the glass back. "So you want the money now?"

He blinked, then nodded. "Pay up, then drink up."

I fetched a faded dollar out of my pocket and flipped it onto the counter. He palmed it and turned back to the TV.

I sipped at the beer. Flat and watered. Called that one right.

I did not look toward the corner where the two others sat.

"Kevin been in today?" I asked.

The barman barely glanced at me. "Kevin?"

"Witkowski."

"What's it to you?"

"We're old pals. I've drained a keg with him here myself."

"You," he answered, "have never been here before, friend."

I laughed. "You been in here so long, your eyesight's gone. Sorta like a mole."

"If you'd ever been here," he retorted mildly, "you'd know better than to ask stupid-assed questions."

Something in his tone made my guts start to ice up. This clown looked takable, but there was absolutely no sound from the corner, and I sensed that the two men were paying close attention. I did not give them the courtesy of a glance.

"Nothing wrong with questions, pal," I said to the barman. "My daddy used to say, 'If you ask a question, you're a dope for a minute. If you don't ask, you're a dope forever.' "

"I think you better split. And take your daddy with you," he said softly.

"I think I'll finish the beer I just got done paying for, if it all the same to you."

"Last chance."

I held up both hands, trembled them violently, and sai "*Ooooooh!*"

He shrugged and folded his arms. I picked up the nea beer. As refreshment it was the pits, but that was okay. I wa making other plans for it as footsteps approached from th corner.

I took a deep breath and turned halfway on the stool. Th men came in a confident swagger and stopped, flanking me blocking the path to the door. Both were in their earl twenties. Both had dark hair so short it looked painted o There the resemblance ended. The geekoid to my left wa jug-eared and gangly with a long neck that was all Adam apple. He wore a leather vest, jeans, and no shirt. From h right hand dangled a sawed-off length of pool cue. H partner was a tall wall of young man, one of those rotund who's lifted weights since he was six. Tiny little slitty eye shone happily between rolls in his face. His gigantic twi pants were cinched to his gut by a length of chrome-plate chain. His T-shirt was inscribed, in colorful gay letterin ADOLF HITLER EUROPEAN TOUR 1939–1945. At its center wa der Führer's frowning, black-and-white face. He carried n weapon. Probably considered himself one.

I looked at him. "History buff, huh? I am too. Differe era, though. War Between the States."

Rotundo's breathing rasped in the still room. "What's yo business here, asshole?" The high tone and Kentucky twan sounded comical, but I was too busy thinking to laugh. mistake here would make things less than enjoyable. It a came down to how Geekoid would use that pool cue, and had a pretty good hunch about that.

I looked at him. "Want a game of eight ball? I'll spot yo three. Where's the table?"

"The man asked you a question, cracker," he growled.

"Take him," the barman whispered.

"Hold it!" I said, raising my left hand, tightening my hol on the beer glass with my right. "Gotta straighten you out o something, son. I'm no cracker. I was born right here i Detroit."

"Sound like a fucking cracker," Rotundo twanged.

He was one to talk, but I kept my tone reasonable. "Yeah, well, my folks were from Georgia, all right, but *north* Georgia. Hill people. Crackers is *south* Georgia. We got that straight now?"

With the last word I flipped my right hand back, splashing the beer squarely into the barman's face. I kept hold of the glass, completed my windup, and flung it with all my strength at Rotundo's head. It smashed him dead center in the face and, as he screamed and staggered back, rebounded to the floor, where it shattered. Geekoid was performing as expected. Instead of lancing me with the pool cue, as he should have, he had raised it over his head, intending to break it over mine.

By the time it came down, I wasn't around. I'd lunged left, past its path, hurling my stool to the floor at the same time. The cue whished through the air and hit nothing but the counter and snapped in two, the force of Geekoid's swing nearly throwing him to the floor. That was convenient. Before he could recover, I kneed him hard in the side of the head, ramming him down sprawling and sliding through the broken beer glass. Rotundo's face was screwed up with fury behind a drapery of gushing blood as he lurched toward me, arms spread, bellowing. I executed a wholly unnecessary feint, screwed my right foot into the floor, and sent the left—the one they never expect—straight up into his crotch, Lou Groza going for the extra point. The blow stopped him, but it didn't drop him. He just bent over about halfway, went pigeon-toed, clasped his gut, and wailed, "Oh, no!"

Geekoid was out of the picture, moaning and squirming on the floor. The barman had apparently appointed himself spectator and hadn't moved from behind the counter. I stepped over to the bent-over Rotundo and, using his neck as a handle, propelled him two stumbling, dropping steps into the counter with a tremendous crash. It splintered, groaned, and fell back, dropping the barman and tearing out a gaping chunk of drywall as it went.

Rotundo lay writhing on what was now the top of the counter. The barman was gasping and struggling against the combined weight, his face white above the edge. "Get him off me," he panted. "Come on, pal."

"I can't lift him," I retorted, then turned and walked out

of The Loading Zone, trying to get my breathing unde
control.

Southern Avenue was remarkably peaceful. As I hoofe
toward the Mustang, which glowed blue in the sun, I felt ju
a little sorry for those guys. They thought that a numerica
advantage, and ruthlessness, could prevail over training an
experience. It wasn't their fault that they did not major in ba
brawls at Miss Penny McNasty's in Dearborn, with postgrac
uate work at, among other places, the Q Room, Bar None i
Taylor, Christmas Cafe in Ann Arbor, and Tattoos, Boots,
Motorcycle Parts in Willow Run. My curriculum vitae, a
Carole would call it.

The adrenaline-charged euphoria wore off as I crossed th
line into Dearborn less than five minutes later. So I'd roughe
up a couple of bruisers—Skinheads, I guess they calle
themselves. Big deal. I was still, from all appearances, a lon
way from finding Kevin Witkowski. Here on my third da
into the case all I had to show for my efforts was a busted-u
saloon.

I slowed as I approached Wyoming and swung right.
Burger Barn appeared on the left, and I turned in there
negotiated a purchase with the unintelligible drive-throug
clerk, then parked between a couple of semis to eat an
think.

I was positive that Carrie Longstreet had not lied. Th
Loading Zone was Kevin's hangout. Lots of fits. The Skinhea
look, the Hitler theme, the Skrewdriver poster.

What puzzled me was the way the men had reacted to m
inquiry about Kevin. All I'd done was to ask if he'd been i
lately. They could have blown me off simply by denying tha
they knew him. But they hadn't done that. Instead, they'
come on all hardcase. Why so touchy at the mere mention o
his name?

One thing for sure. Kevin wasn't living at the roomin
house on Trenton anymore, but The Loading Zone was sti
part of his world. A world that, even in the afterglow of m
win against three-to-one odds, was starting to make me fe
creepier than hell.

I wadded up my Burger Barn litter and started suckin
down the last of my Seven-Up. My handling of the situatio

ack there now took on the appearance of a big, big mistake.
Like a fool, I'd exposed myself. My name and face would now
e instantly recognized if I ever went back to The Loading
one. If, as seemed likely, Kevin still frequented the place,
he way to tag him would have been to go undercover, stay
nconspicuous, and hang around the place, hoping either to
ncounter him directly or to get hold of a lead as to his
whereabouts. I could not do that now, thanks to my perfor-
ance. I consoled myself with the realization—or was it a
ationalization—that going undercover there would probably
ave failed in any event. I haven't been twenty years old for a
ong time, even if I still act like it sometimes.

Big problem. And I wasn't exactly overrun with other leads
t the moment. Dick Dennehy would come up with an
ddress on that license number sometime today, and maybe
hat would give me a fresh angle, but I felt that it would be
nly peripheral, and a waste of time. The Loading Zone was
he place, and I'd just cut that one off the option list.

Shit. I collected my litter, walked it over to a trash barrel,
nd fired up a cigar as I returned to the Mustang. The name
Skinheads" kept replaying in my mind, along with the weird
Maltese cross emblem on The Loading Zone wall, the
krewdriver poster, and the ADOLF HITLER EUROPEAN TOUR
-shirt that Rotundo had worn. This smelled like more than
st a bunch of casual malcontents; it had the trappings of an
rganized group. I'd never heard the Skinheads mentioned in
he bars, on the street, or in the papers. I wondered if they
ad ever received official attention of any sort.

After a moment's thought, I picked up the cellular phone
nd dialed.

The house sat on Ledyard, east of Grand River, south of
he Jeffries projects, and across the Chrysler/Lodge Freeway
nterchange from Tiger Stadium. It presided in considerably
aded two-story splendor over an angle intersection and was
uilt of soot-stained granite block with narrow windows, an
mmense veranda, and a steeply pitched tarnished copper
oof flanked by a pair of honest-to-God turrets. You look at
hat and you see the kind of money that was down here once.
automobile money, shipping money, timber money, meat
money. Old Detroit money, long gone, replaced by a different

kind of money, in quantities just as vast, but considerabl
uglier.

I double-parked across the street, then threaded my wa
through a tangled maze of Detroit police RMP cars, ur
marked sedans, and an EMS wagon whose back doors sprea
wide. Two paramedics were just hoisting a wheeled stretche
up and in, bearing a black zipped-up body bag. They coul
have been loading potatoes for all the animation on the
faces. At the bottom of the ornate stone veranda step
sprawled the body of a very young black man in trousers,
white shirt, and Reeboks. He'd been shot at least four time
and another pair of paramedics were spreading out a bod
bag for him. Up on the veranda, the double doors stoo
wide, and I could see and hear movement and voices inside
The big action was at the far end of the veranda, preside
over by Elvin Dance, Detroit police captain and chief of th
homicide section. He and another plainclothes detective wer
questioning a black teenage girl wearing a pink halter toj
pink hot pants, and hair done up in cornrows. She sat on th
smooth, curved stone rail, skinny legs dangling nervously, th
sunshine bathing her; the policemen stood in shadow, lister
ing intently. When Elvin saw me coming up the steps, h
peeled off and strutted down the veranda toward me, gri
ning. "Well, well. If it ain't Ben Perkins, the white knight
the Detroit freeway system and scourge of rogue trucke
everywhere."

Oh God. He'd heard. "I see my reputation has precede
me," I said.

"Oh *hell* yeah," he drawled. "I been meaning to whist
you up. When you called for me a few minutes ago, I said t
the dispatcher, 'You just send that white boy on over here
because I wanted to shake your hand personally.'" He shove
out a hand. Having no choice, I shook it. "On behalf of th
people of the city of 'Troit, thank you," he intoned. "Han
tight a second, I'll be right with you," he added, and we
back to the other detective.

The black girl sat on the rail, dead-faced, as Elvin and th
other detective conferred. I looked Elvin over. He wa
dressed and groomed as nattily as ever. His three-piece su
was battleship gray run through with faint pinstripes and wa
as crisp as the day it left his tailor's. His silk tie was maroo
and of up-to-the-minute width. The cocoa-colored skin of hi

face was freshly shaved, his curly-tight black hair was cropped close to his skull, and he sparkled with gold from his fingers, cuffs, and collar. Same old Elvin, tough, stocky, and vibrant with cynicism. Yet today I sensed something else, something in the set of his jaw, the lines around his rich brown eyes, and the strung-tight pitch of his voice. I sensed barely contained fury along with profound fatigue. Dangerous mix for a man in his line of work.

CHAPTER 12

H<small>E WALKED BACK TO</small> me. The other detective resumed questioning the black girl. Elvin reached a pack of Kool from the side pocket of his jacket and lighted one with a gold Zippo bearing the Detroit police emblem. "So what is it this time, Perkins?" he asked, gazing through cigarette smoke toward somewhere across the street—maybe farther away than that. "How can the Detroit police serve you?"

His tone annoyed me. I folded my arms. "Small reminder, pal. All I intended today was a little chat on the phone. You were the one who insisted I come over here."

The black girl said, "I told you already. I was giving Phillip a blow job, to work off what I owed today. Then Clarence come in and say, 'You done stole my rock, man.' "

Elvin considered my comment, then said quietly, "Maybe I thought a friendly face would come in handy. Maybe you was the closest thing I could scrounge up at that partickle moment. Ain't that a bitch?"

"Sure is, bro," I retorted. "If I'd have known you were in this bad a way, I'd have whistled up the Detroit Symphony and had 'em send a violin quartet over here pronto."

"They're on strike. Besides, they don't make house calls."

"Your luck really does suck these days, Elvin. I feel for ya."

He grinned and his eyes lighted, if only briefly. "What's the scoop?"

"Phillip he just kept shooting him," the black girl said, "pop-pop, even though Clarence was already dead, bloody lying there. Then he say to me, 'I be coming back for you bitch,' and went out."

88

"Group called Skinheads," I answered Elvin. "Ever heard of them?"

He drew slowly on his cigarette, blew a funnel of smoke. "Nope, I mean, I've heard the term all right. These young jokers running around with their hair shaved most of the way off, heads painted purple and orange and Day-Glo red. That what you mean?"

"Shaved part, yeah. Never seen the color scheme, though. These guys seem to be into the white-supremacy bit. Heil Hitler, kill the kikes, niggers go home, that routine."

He glanced at me and snorted. "There's clumps of racist nuts everywhere. Can't keep track of 'em all."

"This particular one, though, is all I care about. Hang out at a bar on the southwest side."

"I couldn't stand it no more," the black girl said in a dead voice. Her hands were trembling, and her eyes seemed not to reflect light. "Phillip was just flipped out. Shooting everybody and just a-laughing. All I could hear was shooting and screaming from the rooms all around me. I found Clarence's gun and snuck out onto the landing and saw Phillip heading down the stairs toward the door."

Elvin shook his head. "Look, Perkins. Far as I'm concerned, those little groups is nothing. Just a bunch of loud-mouth white-trash suburbanites talkin' big in bars. Best policy is just to ignore 'em. They're nothing. And as long as everybody—including the fucking papers—ignores them, they'll say nothing."

He pinwheeled his half-smoked cigarette out onto the scrubby grass, knotted his fists, and looked away from me, flaring his nostrils a couple of times. I said, "When'd you last take some time off, Elvin?"

He glanced at me, then away again. "Who knows. But in twelve days, four hours, and sixteen minutes, I'm out of here. Taking Mattie and Leavon and bye-bye for seven whole days."

"I thought he was going after my baby," the black girl said. "I couldn't let him get my little baby. I said, 'You leave off my baby,' and he turned, and I shot him and kept on shooting him till he didn't move no more."

"Where y'all headed?" I asked Elvin.

"Disney World."

"Well, good." I gave his rock-hard shoulder a light tap with my fist. "Take it easy till then, hear?"

As I headed down the steps, he hollered, "And next tim
you come into my city, no double-parking, or I'll have you
ass towed. You hear me, white boy?"

I started the car, rounded the corner onto Third, went u
half a block, and parked by a fire hydrant. The crest of th
sunny afternoon had brought smothering humidity, and I wa
perspiring under my clothes. I was tense and jumpy an
wanted out of Detroit just as fast as I could manage it. No
that I don't love the place. I do. But only the parts that
love. Get it?

Just then, nothing seemed better than motoring west b
the straightest route possible all the way to Belleville, wher
I'd check the day's jobs, clean up, do some swimming, som
beer, some video. But my conscience was troubling me.
hadn't talked to Lynne since yesterday. I owed her a progres
report, one which, I suspected, she would not be overl
thrilled to hear.

I picked up the cellular phone and called her house. N
answer. Called the Westland K Mart. After some confusion,
was informed she had called in sick. That left one other place
only a dozen blocks away. I started the Mustang and set
course for Harper Hospital.

Room 703N was laid out pretty much the way it had bee
on my first visit. Nearer bed empty. Lynne in the chair at th
foot of the far bed, doing some sort of needlework. TV hig
up to the left, doing the silent kaleidoscope bit. Jerry lay i
the farther bed, barely visible under a single sheet. The hea
of the bed had been raised about halfway, but his head wa
slumped to the side against the pillow and his eyes wer
closed.

Lynne laid down her needlework and rose swiftly, putting
cautioning finger to her lips as she came to me. She looke
dressier than usual today. She wore a matching dark blu
pants and jacket set over a pullover top striped horizontally i
blue and white. She'd arranged her long brown hair into
tidy bun at the back of her head. "He just went to sleep," sh
whispered as she reached me. "Let's go downstairs."

As we turned to the door, Jerry spoke. "You two sneaking out on me?"

We looked at him. He hadn't moved, but his eyes were open. Lynne said, "I'm sorry, Jer. Did we wake you?"

"Never went to sleep," he replied gruffly. "How about some water? I'm parched."

Lynne went to him. I strolled over and sat uncomfortably on the edge of the unoccupied bed. She fed him some water from a plastic bottle equipped with a straw. He seemed to take many tiny sips and as much water leaked through his lips as went down his throat. She used a napkin to tidy him up. "That enough?"

"Yeah," he answered, and cleared his throat. He looked at me. "Where's Kevin? Find him yet?"

Lynne retreated to her chair. "No," I answered. "Mainly tracked down where he's been." I gave them a brief summary of the Trenton boardinghouse and The Loading Zone bar, omitting the squirrel as well as any mention of my handling of The Loading Zone reception committee. But I couldn't leave out everything, however distasteful and difficult. "I think what Kevin's gotten tangled up in is a group called the Skinheads."

They looked at me blankly.

"Way it looks," I continued, "they're a white-supremacy group. Anti-Jew, antiblack, the whole WASP routine."

Lynne laughed nervously. "That's silly. Kevin's not a WASP, except for the white part."

"So they're flexible. Come on, Lynne, you heard the tape Kevin made of his call to that radio program."

She shook her head violently at me. Jerry said, "What tape?" Lynne rolled her eyes and looked away from us grimly.

Aw jeez. So much for communication in marriage. This was turning out worse than I'd dreaded. I gave Jerry a summary of Kevin's comments to the radio station. I went on to describe the eerie banner hanging in The Loading Zone. I even told about the ADOLF HITLER EUROPEAN TOUR T-shirt. They didn't think it was funny, probably because it wasn't.

Jerry's expression was unreadable. Lynne's, however, was a billboard. Her long, narrow face was drawn tight, her eyes hot. "You expect us to believe that Kevin is some kind of Nazi."

"What I'm saying is two things. One, the Skinheads are

definitely of the white-supremacy persuasion. Two, Kevin ha
been a regular at a Skinhead hangout. You put that togethe
and what he said on the tape, and—"

"But you didn't see him there, did you?"

"No."

"Did the people you talked to at the bar say that Kevi
hung out there?"

"No. I only have the word of the woman at the boarding
house," I said patiently. "But she had no reason to bullsh
me. And as to the men at The Loading Zone, they didn't sa
anything at all when I brought up Kevin's name. In this worl
usually what isn't said is more significant that what is. No
only that, but their reaction was, uh, hostile, shall we say."

"What'd you do, Ben?" Jerry asked. "Thump 'em?"

I shrugged. "We sorted out our differences."

Lynne strode to the window. "This is bullshit. Kevin is
good boy. You've just gone off on some crazy tangent. All w
hired you to do was to find him, not to—"

Jerry spoke. "Come on, babe. Lighten up. Ben has to g
where the thing takes him."

She turned and glared at her husband, all solicitude gone
"Kevin is a good boy."

Jerry sighed and swallowed once. "Better get the nurse,
he said, voice weaker. "It's coming back."

She blinked, her face relaxed, and she started for the doo
"Okay. Come on, Ben."

I stood. "Ben stays," Jerry said.

She glanced at us, her hand on the knob, then frowned an
left.

I sat back down as the door closed. Jerry closed his eyes fo
a long moment, then opened them and looked at me. "I lie
a little. It's there, but I can handle it for a while yet."

"Oh."

"You've never been married, but when you get around t
it, you'll learn that the wife doesn't need to know everythin
all the time."

"That so?"

Long silence. Jerry shifted his feet under the sheet.
glanced up at the TV. One of our interminable afternoon tal
shows was on. The guest was none other than Elliot Andelson
looking young, suave, vibrant, and very earnest in his expen
sive suit. He sat on the dais next to an attractive young blac

woman. He was holding hands with her, and they were chatting nonchalantly with the host. Jeez, I thought. How far we've come. Wouldn't have dared to have done that even twenty years ago.

Jerry interrupted my thoughts. "You still sweet on her?"

I looked at him. His face was peaceful. I suddenly wanted a cigar. "No."

"You were once, though, way back then."

"Right, but that was then. And I backed off graciously."

"Well," Jerry grinned, "you backed off, anyhow. I just want you to know something. Two things. I know you're doing your best on Kevin. Don't worry about it. You just do what you have to do. And get him here, quick."

"You got it," I answered. "On this bigot thing—"

"I don't know anything about that. I don't understand it. And I don't care. It's not important. There's all kinds of things that just aren't important anymore, you know?"

I nodded.

He struggled briefly under the sheet. "Do what you have to do," he rambled, "and don't fret Lynne. She can deal with whatever comes. I've seen it, over and over. She's tough and she's strong. And she's good, too. The best."

"I know."

"If I had to do it all over," he said, "I'd marry her again. That's God's own truth."

At that point I actually envied him, to be able to say a thing like that.

He cleared his throat. "And I just want you to know, if after I'm dead you was to come courting, why, that would be just fine with me."

I went to my feet and paced slowly around the bed toward the window. "Come on, Jerry. You can't just hand her off—"

"I'm not handing her off," he retorted. "It's as much up to her as it is up to you. I'm not making her your responsibility. She can take care of herself, she don't need you. What I'm saying is, if something was to start up, it would piss me off if you were to back off just on account of me. I won't be here. It won't matter."

I looked at him. "Well—"

"Okay?" he asked.

"Okay."

"Good." He winced and paled and fidgeted under the

sheet. "Better go get her back in here. Along with the nurse
I really need it this time."

"Okay. You hang loose now." He gave me a weary thumb
up. I went to the door and stepped into the hallway. Lynn
was charging along toward me, a short Hispanic nurse trot-
ting to keep up, determination printed upon his face. Lynne's
expression went stormy when she saw me. I said, "So, am I
still employed?"

"Yes," she answered, grimly biting off the word, and went
into Jerry's room.

I watched the door close behind the nurse, turned, and
headed up the hall toward the elevator. Remembering what
Jerry had said, I thought, wowee! Romance is busting out all
over.

CHAPTER 13

TOWARD THE SOUTH SIDE of the Norwegian Wood property, alongside the golf course and near the lake, is an area I call the "back forty." It's a couple of acres of gently rolling scrub brush, dotted by the occasional clump of saplings, that is frequented only by duffers in search of their golf balls, my lawn man every couple of weeks, and good old yours truly.

Right in the center of it is an old, small cinder-block building with a shed roof made of tin and a couple of large sliding doors on the lakeside. It was there long before Norwegian Wood; God knows when it was built. It's not the most attractive thing in the world, and a few years back a couple of tenants petitioned Norwegian Wood management to tear it down, complaining that it hurt the "aesthetic beauty" of the grounds. I was able to talk them out of it by agreeing to keep it painted and halfway presentable. They backed off, which was a relief, because I've found the building useful. I store my ultralight, wings folded, in one half; the other half I use as a workshop for construction projects, tool storage, and maintenance work.

As evening began to drop its darkening curtain, I was back there with my Mustang, changing its oil. I do that every fifteen hundred miles. Cheap insurance. The car radio was on WABX, featuring ninety minutes of the smoking-guitar work of Mr. Robin Trower. Five-sixths of a Stroh's pack sat chilled in the cooler. I wore old cutoffs and an old T-shirt and was smoking a cigar, waiting for the oil to finish draining out of the pan, when the cellular phone rang.

I wiped off my hands on a rag, leaned into the car, and

picked up the phone. "Perkins's Grease Monkeys, Ben speaking."

"Where the hell are you?" came Dick Dennehy. "I jus' called your apartment and got that idiot box of yours."

"Dick! What a surprise! I done thought you forgot all abou' me."

"I said tomorrow, remember? Well, today was tomorrow yesterday, and here I am, on schedule."

"Well, good." I leaned inside the car again and turned the radio down, then sorted through the mess on the passenger bucket seat looking for a pen and a scrap of paper. I found them, as well as the copy of *The Turner Diaries* that I'd found in Kevin's room. Still hadn't gotten around to looking through it. I pulled out of the car, put the pen and paper on the roof, and said into the phone, "Got the plate poopy?"

"Here it goes, for what it's worth. Plate belongs to a 1982 Mercury Marquis Brougham, registered to one Justin Catlin, eight thousand County Route Three, Register, Michigan."

As I scribbled the information down, I searched my mental map for Register. Nothing. For sure, it was nowhere around here. "Where the hell is that?"

"Beats me, son. What am I, a travel agent?"

"You're an out-stater, I figured you knew where all these hole-in-the-wall burgs were, that's all."

"Sorry."

"Listen, I appreciate the info. We done missed our Wednesday, didn't we? How 'bout Saturday at Pringle's?"

"Fine with me, as long as you've got the tab. In return for favors received."

"Sure." I grinned. "Least I can do. See ya."

"Hold it a second," he said. "I forgot something. We come up empty on the stiff search. No DOAs of your friend the budding fascist's description. Sorry."

"It doesn't surprise me, but you gotta cover the bases. Listen, one other thing, while I gotcha: Ever heard of the Skinheads?"

"Fuzzy-headed little fuckers with the green-and-orange hair?"

"Not exactly. Shaved-head types with Nazi leanings. I uncovered a nest of 'em in Detroit, seems my little friend has been playing footie with them."

"Nah, sorry," Dick growled. "I try to keep track of all the nut groups, I'll never have time to do police work."

"Yeah, it's hell making the rounds of all the doughnut shops, ain't it, Dick?"

"Fuck you." He hung up.

I put the phone away, grinning, and read the information again. Register, Michigan. Jesus. I tossed the paper and pen onto the driver's seat. Happy voices sounded faintly from outside the shed. I went to the open doorway. Brian and Debra Clark had come out to the fringe of the lawn behind building three, near the small gully where the lawn gives way to the scrub of the back forty, and were tossing an orange Frisbee back and forth with great abandon, running and leaping, shouting and laughing, carrying on like teenagers. Or like teenagers used to before the advent of MTV, cocaine, birth control, and spreadsheets. They were barefoot and wore matching outfits: white T-shirts, white shorts. I hung my cigar in my face, leaned on the cinder-block door frame, and watched them, mind in slow idle, under one thousand RPM.

And then: BING.

I straightened. Took the cigar out and stared curiously at it. It'll work. By God, it will. Holy shit!

I stepped out of the shed and hollered Brian's name. He looked at me, said something to Debra, then leaped the gully and started across the field toward me at a fast trot as Debra, tucking the Frisbee under one arm, headed back for the building.

As I watched Brian approach, I thought through how I'd put it to him. I had the faint notion to let it rest overnight and look at it again, fresh, in the morning. I'll probably always wish I had. But what can I say? At the time it seemed perfect.

"So he agreed to do it, huh?" Bill Scozzafava asked.

I tipped the mug back, drained the beer into my mouth, and swallowed. Bill took the mug before I could set it down and started refilling it. "Agreed to it?" I said. "He leapt at it. Kid's had a puppy-dog hard-on for detective work for months now. I've let him fool around in the fringes, but you know how I am, I don't like working with people, and breaking in a rookie ain't exactly appealing. I mean, it's my ass if he screws up."

Bill set the refilled mug on the bar before me. "But you made an exception this time, I see."

I shrugged. "I toldja, this Skinhead thing seems to be kids. Early twenties. Even if I was to whack off all my hair and adopt the boot-camp look, and even if I hadn't blown my cover at The Loading Zone already, no way could I pass for twenty-two anymore."

"Really?" Bill asked, smiling. "Say it ain't so."

I made a threatening gesture with the beer mug. Bill just stood there smiling, secure in his six feet five and 225 pounds of bench-press-hardened bulk. For all his size and strength, and his reputation as a former member of the Chicago Bears' Gorilla Gang, Bill's about the gentlest person I know. He never raises his voice. He never swears. Nothing seems to get to him. He just puts in his days, raising his nine kids, doing his knitting, running his body shop in Romulus, and tending bar some nights at Under New Management for walking-around money.

Bill served a customer and then drifted back to me, smile gone, eyes narrow on me.

"What's the matter?" I asked.

He sighed. "Brian's a hell of a nice kid, and here you are throwing him into the lion's den."

The bar was mostly empty, typical of a week night. Most of the patrons were immersed in serious drinking and conversation that was inaudible behind the blare of jukebox C & W. The sole exception: Harry Moscone and Norris Johnston, who occupied the nearest booth and were loudly debating a critical issue of our time: What's the greatest country tune ever recorded? I had, without being asked, already offered my personal favorite: "I'm Just Another Roadkill on the Highway of Love." They hadn't taken it seriously, for some reason.

I looked at Bill and snorted. "Lion's den, my ass! Bunch of little half-wit troublemakers is all."

"How do you figure, Ben?" he asked quietly. "All you know about 'em is based on one little grabass in a bar. And you took 'em. Hurray for you. But you don't dare write them all off based on that."

"Hey, I got to go with what I seen."

He was shaking his head. "They're dangerous."

I waved a hand, put a cigar in my face, and lighted up.

"Fanatics are always dangerous," Bill said. "Doesn't matter
that the cause is. You read your history, you find that the
misery of the world has been caused by fanatics. Don't matter
they're Christians, Nazis, Democrats, Republicans, Jews,
whatever—fanaticism is key. Fanaticism is poison. These
white supremacists are in that league. You better not take
them so lightly."

"Just bar talk," I retorted. "That's all they are, a lot of bar
talk. You see it in here all the time. Guys sitting around
drinking nothing, talking a lot of hot air. They oil themselves
up and the tongues go into overdrive. Hell, wasn't so long
ago you and me sat in that booth over there emptying
pitchers and talking Tigers. We're Detroit Tiger fanatics.
Don't make us dangerous."

Elmer Kent slunk to the bar and wordlessly ordered a
refill. Bill took care of it, topping the mug off expertly. Elmer
took it from him and sidled back to a dark corner booth.
Facing him was a younger woman I'd never seen before. So
Elmer was stepping out on his wife again. I wondered idly if
she'd come barreling in here looking for him, as she had
before. Made for some pretty good entertainment.

Bill leaned forward, bracing himself on his forearms, and
spoke without looking at me. "Tigers ain't the same thing and
you know it," he said finally. "Problem with you is, you're
used to dealing with garden-variety crooks. Them that does it
for bucks or kicks. Fanatics are a different breed of animal.
They do what they do because they *believe*. That makes 'em
unpredictable, which means especially dangerous."

I drew deep on my cigar, exhaled, and said nothing.

"What if you find him and he doesn't want to come along?"
Bill asked finally.

"Oh, he'll come along."

"But what if he won't?"

"I said he'll come along."

"Be tough to talk him into—"

"Talk? Who said anything about talk?" I asked, annoyed.
"I'm not from Ann Arbor, I'm from Detroit." I held up my
hands. "I'm bigger than he is and stronger than he is and a
whole lot meaner than he is. He'll come along."

Bill's eyes looked at me silently.

I tapped a chunk of ash into the cheap tin ashtray. "Ki
got no rights, far as I'm concerned," I said. "All he's got a
two folks who did everything in the world for him, and
return he's stomping on their hearts. He'll come along.
never liked him, and what I've heard about him lately mak
me like him even less. He'll come along, all right. It's wha
said I'd do. I was predicting the future, and it will come tru
He's as good as in that hospital room being a comfort to I
daddy, right this very minute."

Bill grunted and straightened to towering height. "Hate
mention a minor detail, but you don't know where he is."

I tapped my temple with a forefinger. "But I know whe
he hangs out. I have a feeling he'll turn up at The Loadi
Zone sooner or later. That's where Brian comes in."

He snapped open his rag and began to wipe the shiny b
with it, looking pensive. "You just tell Brian to watch out

I leaned forward slightly. "Listen, bro. If I thought the
was serious danger for the kid, I'd never send him in ther
But this thing is cake. He's already got the short hair. All I
has to do is cut off that little pigtail, lose the dumb earrin
dress up in some leather and stuff, learn a little lingo, a
he's in business. He just sits around that saloon, watchi
and listening. When he gets a line on Kevin, he's out
there."

Bill nodded slowly, watching me.

"I'd do it myself," I said, "but I can't."

"I know." Bill pointed a gigantic finger at my mug, whi
held just a slosh of beer. " 'Nother one?"

I glanced at the clock behind the bar and translated it fro
bar time. "Shit. Getting on ten. Gotta run." I slid off t
stool. "Tab this one for me?"

"Don't matter to me," Bill answered. "But I suggest y
put some green against your tab sometime soon. Eddie w
bitching again yesterday."

"Eddie always bitches," I answered, stubbing my cigar o
in the ashtray.

Bill was smiling strangely. "He noticed you haven't been
hardly at all, past couple of weeks. Thinks you maybe got
case of the shorts and are trying to stiff him."

"That's bullshit," I said indignantly. "I been coming in he
fourteen years and I've always been good for the tariff, and I
knows it." I waved and started for the door. "Later, Bill."

"Why the sudden all-fired rush?" Bill called, tone mocking. wasn't about to answer him; I'd dallied too long as it was. The door pulled back as I reached toward it, revealing arb Paley, who smiled at me as I stood there, boxed in, eling stupid. She smiled. "Well, hi there, stranger."

"Hey, Barb," I said awkwardly.

She came to me as the door swung shut, leaned up, and ve me a moist, chaste kiss on the cheek. "Come on, hon," e said, stepping past me. "I worked a split today, my ass is agging, and my throat is ten miles of dusty road. Buy me e. Then buy me several."

I looked at her. She's of average height and plentiful build, ith spectacular permed red hair dancing around her milky, eckled face. She wore a white sleeveless, tailless top, with ld spangles, above prewashed jeans hitched up smooth and m a tempting two inches below the hem of her top. Her sinesslike hands sparkled with more rings than fingers and r nails, as usual, were polished a deep, sensual red that atched the color of her lips. I resented the stirring that I lt. The stirring prompted by recent memory, and the even ore recent encounter with about a hundred mostly bare rds of Carrie Longstreet, reclining on her lounge behind e rooming house on Trenton Avenue.

"Sorry, I'm bagging it," I said. "Really whacked out."

She reversed course, oblivious of the fact that the eyes of eryone in the joint, from Harry and Norris over to my left, d Bill behind the bar to my right, were on us. "Well, okay," e said innocently. "You got provisions back at home plate?"

I lowered my voice and said earnestly, "Give me a rain eck. I'm hitting the road tomorrow; I need some sack time st, the serious kind."

She stood very close to me. "Hitting the road? Where?"

"Got a case. Going out of town. Sorry, kid, but—"

"Oh, a case." She nodded intently. "Well, you better take re of that, hon."

"I will. Listen, you take it easy, Barb." I turned and pushed y way through the door. I was crunching across the gravel t toward the Mustang, feeling a mix of relief and guilt, nen I heard the door open. I looked back, hoping to see ll, or Norris, or anybody other than you-know-who.

"You're not mad at me or anything, are you?" Barb's husky ice carried easily in the still night.

"Oh hell no."

"Okay. I just wondered—I called you, but you—"

"Been busy," I said awkwardly. "This case, and—"

She was nodding. "Yeah, I know. Okay," she said cheeri[ly] "watch your back, hon!"

"Yeah," I said, guilty feeling growing, "you too, Barb."

The door swung shut. I dropped into the Mustang, alm[ost] got back out. Cranked it up and powered out onto Ecor[se] Road, almost turned back. Took it up to sixty, hit the dee[p] dish steering wheel just once with my fist, and kept on goin[g.]

I was at the red light at Ecorse and Belleville Roads wher[e I] noticed a bottle green Toyota MR 2 waiting two lanes to n[y] right. I gave it a double take, then shrugged. For a seco[nd] there I thought I'd seen that car behind me earlier that da[y.] But I'd been wrong before.

Seven-ten A.M. The coffee urn in the maintenance offi[ce] was just starting to chug. I ambled around my desk, thre[w] the day's job slips down on the layer of mess, sat dow[n,] picked up the phone, and punched numbers.

"Shine Inn," answered an anonymous voice.

I was relieved; though the car wash was certainly not op[en] yet, I'd hoped someone would be there. "Phil around?"

The voice grunted, silence echoed, then Phil came o[n.] "Yeah, what."

"It's Ben. How the hell are ya?"

"Tired, man. What can I do you for?"

"I'm sending a man over there for one of my cars. Questi[on] is, Which one is most likely to live for a few days?"

"Damn if I know. I just store 'em for ya, for a fee, whi[ch] you just got around to paying, for which I thank you mo[st] humbly, sir."

I scratched my head. "How 'bout that ugly old Cutlas[s?] Worked pretty good last winter that time."

"Forget it. Sitting on a pair of flats."

"Oh."

"You oughtta do some basic maintenance on these beas[ts] now and then. Your typical car needs new tires every hu[n]dred thousand miles or so."

"I don't rush into things, not with those wrecks. Besides, ou can get a hundred miles out of the cords. You know that."

"Apparently not always."

"Yeah. Well, what about the pickup? Let's try that."

"Ben," he said, "you had that one junked, remember? Said was the worst piece of shit ever made, that it had no usiness being on the streets, that if you ever saw it again ou'd personally shoot its tires out, which from what I hear is omething you're experienced at, hee-hee."

I rolled my eyes. "Help me out here."

"There's the Nova," Phil suggested.

"Any problems you know of?"

"Nothing except the bullet hole in the driver's-side window."

"Yeah, a fella offed himself in there, as I recall. So what if it in't the prettiest thing in the world? My man's not choosy." I ghted a cigar. "Have the keys ready for him a little later this norning, okay? Name's Brian. Tall blond kid with practically o hair at all. He'll mention my name, hopefully not in vain."

"All righty."

As I hung up, Debra Clark came charging into the office. he threw something hard down on my desk and hissed, "You on of a bitch."

CHAPTER 14

S HE WAS DRESSED FOR work in a pleated aqua skirt, matching jacket with ruffled, plunging neckline and padde shoulders, over a white blouse that glinted gold from th chains around her neck. She wore matching high-heele pumps, her short dark hair was expertly prepped, and she' gone heavy enough on the makeup to look very feminine an light enough to look conservative. From somewhere I dredge up the fact that she was some kind of paper pusher for th Environmental Protection Agency office in Ann Arbor. Sh obviously had education and more than a couple of dollars t rub together. Since coming to live at Norwegian Wood she' always been one of those invisible tenants, never complaining never causing trouble.

I'd probably never have gotten to know her had Brian no started living with her. Since then our relationship had alway been distant, borderline glacial. I'd never understood that I'd always been nice to her. I'd never bad-mouthed her ca questioned her integrity, tried to jump her bones. I ofte wished Brian hadn't, either. As a rule you shouldn't, as m daddy always said, take your meat where you get your bread But you only learn that lesson the hard way, take it fro me.

I looked into her dark, angry eyes. "Morning, Ms. Clark Something I can help you with today?" I looked down at wha she'd flung onto my desk. *The Turner Diaries.* Uh-oh.

"I want you," she said in a slow, deadly voice, "to tak Brian off this so-called case of yours."

"He told you about that, huh?"

"Told me? It's all he's talked about since you cornered him last night."

I lay my cigar in the overflowing ashtray and headed round the desk toward the coffee maker, which had just given its sigh of completion. "I didn't corner him, Ms. Clark. struck up a conversation with him, explained a situation, sked if he'd be willing to help." I held up an empty mug. Coffee?"

"No."

I filled one for myself with black steam-hot stuff and went round behind my desk. "I ain't holding a gun on him."

"Oh yes you are, and you know it. Brian *admires* you." She made it sound like a swear word.

"Regardless," I said, picking up my cigar, "if he doesn't want to do it, all he has to say is 'thanks anyhow' and he's out f it, no hard feelings."

"You devious bastard. You know he's not going to do hat."

I was getting a little ticked at her attitude. I was ticked urther to find that my cigar had gone out. I relighted it. Apparently not, or you wouldn't be in here hammering at ne. You prob'ly tried to talk him out of it last night and got owhere, so you're—"

"He's just a kid!" she flared.

"What the hell are you, Methuselah? A whole entire wenty-eight years of age?"

"That's beside the point."

"It's exactly the point. He's old enough to call his own hots."

"You're just using his respect for you to get your own ray."

"Which is exactly what you tried to do last night, now ain't t?"

Her face went softer. "I love him."

I shrugged. "He's well above the bottom of my own list."

"I don't want him to get hurt."

"I won't let that happen."

"You won't be there! He's going in alone!"

"It's just a surveillance," I said patiently. "Bar full of oudmouths, is all. Brian'll do fine."

She looked incredulous and jabbed a finger toward the ook. "Haven't you read that?"

I sat down, picked up my mug, tested the coffee. Second degree burn temp. Perfect. I took a big swallow. "Glance through it. Gave it to Brian so he could get a feel for the, uh culture he's getting involved in."

"I read it last night," she said. "Cover to cover."

I was genuinely impressed, as I always am by people who can sit down and read something for hours on end. "So?"

"It's a parable of sorts. About some superpatriots who overthrow the U.S. government. Slaughter thousands of blacks and Jews. Then they nuke Israel, after which comes a Christian paradise." She shuddered. "It scares the *hell* out of me."

I smiled at her. "Come on, Ms. Clark. Aren't you just a tad on the impressionable side?"

"All I know," she retorted, "is that that's what these people believe in, and you're sending Brian in there without a care in the world as to what can happen."

I leaned back in my chair. On the surface her concern was touching. On the other hand, there was selfishness and a desire to manipulate there, too. We had that in common, she and I. Only difference was, I had the upper hand and she knew it. "It'll be a skate. Day or two, maybe three, and he'll be back home, same as before. I guarantee it."

She straightened, face wiped clean of expression, and said, "I despise you."

I took a final drag on my cigar and wedged it dead in a pile of ashes and butts. "Well, I'm sorry to hear that, because any friend of Brian's is a friend of mine."

I watched her high shoulders, long back, and plentiful rump as she walked out. Whatever I'd said, I did understand her feelings. But when a job conflicts with personal feelings, the job's got to win, otherwise nothing gets done.

Randy ducked into the office virtually the instant Deb left. I had the feeling he'd been lurking out in the hallway. "Wow," he said almost reverently, "that's one pissed-off chick, ain't it."

"Not a happy camper," I agreed. "You get the drain taken care of yesterday?"

"All set," Randy said, collapsing into a chair facing my desk. "They can flush away like mad over there without hearing so much as a gurgle."

"Outstanding. Listen up, got a special schedule today." I told him Brian was taking some vacation time—actually, I

e paying him out of my own pocket—to work with me for a
ouple of days, and that Doug would be working days to help
over.

"What about you, boss?"

"I'll be in and out. Making an out-of-town run today, but
ll be back tonight. Chores are light, y'all oughtta have no
roblem."

"Assuming Doug gets here," Randy said. "Assuming no
oulder crashes into his car or something first."

Brian ambled in. I stood. "I'm walking Brian out," I said to
andy. "You go through the slips here, figure out who'll do
hat. Be right back."

I fired up a cigar as I went out the door with Brian in tow.
Ve headed up the steps and out the front door onto the
urved sidewalk by the parking lot. The morning exodus was
 full swing, cars backing out of their semienclosures and
logging up the lane leading to the Norwegian Wood exit. I
d Brian around the corner and along the deserted sidewalk
ward the swimming pool. There we took seats at one of the
ermanent cement picnic tables, well out of earshot of anyone.

"How do I look?" Brian asked.

He'd had his hair shorn even shorter. Its blondness made
im look bald at a distance. The ponytail was gone, ditto the
arring. He wore a black suede vest over a yellow T-shirt,
ark pants, and sneakers. No political slogans anywhere, but
d seen no need to overdo this thing. "Great," I answered.
You got yourself packed?"

"Duffel's in the car. You figure out wheels for me?"

"Yep. Like I toldja, Shine Inn up on Telegraph in Redford.
ee Phil, he'll give you keys. Car's a Nova, pretty good shape
xcept for a problem with the driver's-side window."

"Look," Brian said, "I can use my own car."

"Rather you didn't. You get in a wreck or something, let it
e with one of my old crocks. They're just police-auction
ejects anyhow; I store 'em up there just for situations like
is."

Brian shrugged. "Your call, man. Then I go to the rooming
ouse on Trenton."

"Right. Remember where The Loading Zone is?"

"Southern, west of Trenton a block or so."

"Can't miss it. How do you arrange to meet me?"

He grinned, answered, then added, "Why can't I just c
you and say 'Hey, Ben, we got to get together'?"

"No, no, no. Where you're going, there might be peop
around you all the time," I answered patiently. "You have
maintain your cover, can't let on you ever heard of me. Kev
knows me, don't forget that. Speaking of Kevin, descri
him."

Brian did so perfectly. "S'pose I spot him," he went o
"Why not let me tell him about his dad? Save you making
trip."

"Nope," I said firmly. "I don't want you involved. Your j
is to observe and to report. Period."

"Okay," he said, disappointment on his long, handson
face.

"Now," I said, "as to a meeting place, I've got that figure
out. Here's what we do." I explained at some length. "K
thing is the left-turn indicator. You've got to do that; it'll
night, that's the only way I'll know it's you. Then on your w
back be looking northeast. If you don't see one blink
headlights, keep on going, don't turn in. Do a U at All
Road and go through the whole thing one more time. N
blink of headlights, abort the whole thing and head for t
barn. Okay? Now repeat that."

He did so, twice, the first time with some prompting, t
second time perfectly. Brian wasn't aces in the imaginati
department, but he'd always been meticulous about remem
bering and following directions, which was a major reason I
tapped him for this job. Some goofheads who've worked f
me I couldn't count on to change a roll of toilet paper witho
constant coaching.

His grin was excited as well as apprehensive. "Seems li
an awful lot of cloak and dagger, Ben."

"Playing it safe," I answered. I tapped ash off my cigar a
the morning breeze carried it across the lawn, disintegrati
it. "The priorities are finding Kevin and keeping your ass o
of a sling."

"Which one's more important?"

"Finding Kevin." He nodded. "I really don't think there
any real risk for you. But there's no harm in being careful

"I can handle it."

"I know you can." I stood. "Better put you on the roa
kid."

We walked back toward the parking lot. The morning sun
as strengthening; looked like it would be another hot one. I
ade a mental note to tell Randy to speed up the lawn-
atering schedule. When you think about it, something's out
whack in the way we view lawns. We spend tons of money
water and fertilize them so that they'll grow better, only to
end further tons of money to chop the new growth right off.
o figure it.

Brian's car was an old red Chevy Caprice with aluminum
eels, fat rear tires, and rust along the rocker panels. As we
ached it, he said, "You didn't say anything about Debra
king to you this morning."

"Nothing much to say."

He opened the door and sank down into the bench seat next
his canvas duffel bag. "She's pretty pissed off," he said quietly.

"She wouldn't be, if she didn't like you a little."

He looked up at me, unsmiling. "I know Randy says I'm
ussy-whipped."

"Screw Randy."

He ignored me. "I admit, part of the reason I'm doing this
to show her I'm all grown up now and everything. If I
anted a mom, I'd go back to my own. You know?"

"Yep."

"If I'm going to do this work, maybe I ought to be more
e you. Stay away from the heavy steadies."

"That ain't a bed of roses either, pal," I said, thinking about
arb Paley. I tapped the roof of his car. "Better roll. Watch
ur ass, Brian."

He gave me a thumbs-up. "See ya," he grinned. I stepped
ck as he cranked up the engine, backed out of the stall, and
ared away toward the exit.

As I walked back toward building one, I had a sudden
ack of apprehension. Sort of the feeling you get as the
ller coaster starts cranking and clanking up that first tall
ope. The feeling that all hell's about to break loose and
ere's no getting off.

I shook off the feeling. Brian's going to do his job, I told
yself. Time to go do mine.

According to my well-worn Michigan map, Register was a
lage near the center of the state's Thumb area, a little over

a hundred miles due north of Detroit. The area is about
hilly as a billiard table, and not nearly as exciting. Su
there's a lot of summer tourist and resort action along t
coast from Saginaw Bay around the Thumb's tip down t
Lake Huron shore, but the interior is a lot of dead,
nothing: farms and villages, villages and farms, broken up
the occasional farm and the odd village.

Moreover, you can't get there from Detroit, at least
direct freeways. I ended up taking I-75 north nearly
Saginaw, then went east at the Frankenmuth exit and pick
up a secondary state highway that took me northeast throu
places like Watrousville, Caro, and Cass City. I found Reg
ter at the very northeast corner of Tuscola County, plunk
down for no good reason I could think of between N
Greenleaf and Gagetown.

It was well past noon when I rumbled into Register. T
sign at the village limit gave the town name, its population
2,500, which may have been true fifty years ago—and
somewhat defensive slogan: "We Like It Here."

Now I was on—what else?—Main Street, and the sig
were about what you'd expect. Two churches: Lutheran a
Methodist. A farm bureau, grain elevator, and Ford tract
dealer. A Sears catalog center. A large gray bank faced wi
massive granite pillars. A school, which apparently ran t
gamut from K through twelve. A tiny post office on which t
zip code was painted brighter than the town name. A saloo
which I fully expected to bear a bucolic name like Dew Dr
Inn, but was in fact called BAR. As I cruised slowly into t
center of town, where Main Street broadened to allow diag
nal curb parking, I was conscious of curious looks from t
sidewalk strollers. I'd might as well have been carrying
rooftop sign that said I'M FROM DETROIT.

Register's central intersection was controlled by the tow
only traffic signal, a two-bulb job, green above red. I wait
there obediently, scanning the curb signs. A big one told
that straight ahead was the way to New Greenleaf, Bad Ax
and something called the Sanilac Historic Site. According
another sign, County Route 3 went to the north. Bingo.
swung left.

Register petered out quickly as I went north through
residential area laid out on streets named after presidents a
ideals. A gas station and a party store marked the villa

limit. After that it was pure boons. Lanes leading to farms appeared every half mile or so. Mailboxes leaned where the lanes met the road, some bearing numbers, some not; I spotted 7400 and then 7600 and then knew I'd guessed right back there.

Route 3 took a sharp bend east at a creek bridge, and just past that was a lane with a mailbox that said 8000. That's all. It didn't say CATLIN, it didn't say KEVIN'S HIDING OUT HERE. Though I'd been expecting it, I overshot it, and had to back up fifty feet before I could turn in.

CHAPTER 15

T HE NARROW GRAVEL LANE followed the creek a piece, then meandered left and up a slight rise between two fallow fields. Up ahead was the house, standing on what passed in these parts for a hill. It was a tall, square brick two-story General Grant with a nearly flat roof, ornate molding running around the eaves, narrow windows, long porch. The lane expanded into a parking area of sorts, running from the house to an old silver-gray barn on my right and to a decrepit garage on my left. There were no cars in the parking area, nothing there at all except for the steel tower of a wind pump rising from the center.

I circled the wind pump and parked facing out at the front of the house. I was struck by the silence as I shut down the Mustang motor and climbed out. A lot of people find the country silence peaceful, soul enriching or something. Not me. I'm an urban person; I'm accustomed to the subliminal throb of the city all around me. The country makes me edgy. It smells like cowshit, landfill, and dead skunks. It's no safer than the city; there's just more room to do crimes in, and more places to hide, that's all.

Well, time to go to work. I walked up the wood steps onto the porch and beat on the front door. No answer.

I peered inside through the first window on the right. A living room, apparently. Older furniture, TV set, scatter rugs. No people, alive or otherwise.

I walked around the house, peering through windows at each opportunity. Bedroom, bathroom, kitchen. All empty. For no particular reason I got the feeling that no one had been here for quite a while.

The backyard hadn't been mowed all season. The tall grass ran back to a grove of sycamore trees and ended at a freshly cultivated field. Beyond that a line of steel utility towers marched toward the property and then bore due south, its wires glinting in the sun. Not a soul to be seen, anywhere.

When I'd completed the circuit of the house, I hoofed across the unmowed lawn to the garage. Its wood door was not only closed, it was nailed shut. I walked around the building through tall weeds and, at the back side, saw why it was disused. The rear slope of the roof was caved in. Birds hurtled upward at my approach, screaming all kinds of things.

Then I walked across the gravel parking area to the barn. It had no front doors at all. You could see straight through to the field beyond and the tree-lined creek past that. Someone had been stripping the weathered siding off the southeast side, leaving only the massive hand-hewn beams. There was nothing inside but a lot of old hay and junk. This looked like a farm, but it hadn't been used as a farm in God knows how many years.

I wandered back over toward the Mustang, thinking hard. Justin Catlin, where the hell are you? Why did your plate number appear on one of Kevin's credit-card slips? Was he staying here with you? If so, why? If not, why did he buy you gas?

Or—the thought was discouraging—what if an illiterate gas clerk miscopied the license-plate number, and Justin Catlin had nothing whatsoever to do with Kevin?

I was damned if I'd just turn around and go home. Not without checking the house. If Kevin had been here, there might be some evidence of it inside. If he hadn't—well—I'd deal with that conclusion when it was unavoidable.

I opened the Mustang trunk, sorted through the junk, and selected a stumpy steel pry bar and a pair of pliers. I shoved the latter into my belt and carried the former around to the side of the house. The windows ran low to the ground here, and the tall grass ran right up to the foundation. I looked around nervously, saw no one, then wedged the business end of the pry bar between the sill and the sash and gave it a good hard shove.

With a sound of tearing wood, the latch ripped out and the window rose an inch. I filed the pry bar in my back pocket, raised the window with effort, and climbed inside.

I was in the dim living room, between two unmatched easy
chairs. To my right stood a wood stove—obviously not in use
since the flue pipe was missing. To my left stood an old
sagging sofa, partnered up with a lamp-bearing end table. A
portable TV stood on an aluminum cart, and several straight
chairs were parked against the far wall. Other than that, the
room was empty. No decorations on the walls. No knick
knacks on the end table. The air, vintage 1910, was thick and
smelled sweetish sour.

Not only was the house abandoned, but it looked and felt
more like temporary quarters than a home.

In the far right corner was an archway. To its left, a flight of
stairs led up into darkness. I went through the archway into
the kitchen. It was small, floored in old, soft yellow linoleum
and housed a group of mismatched appliances. The large
stainless-steel sink was dry. I turned on the cold tap and it
sputtered and farted, disgorged syrupy brown water at inter
vals, then finally ran more or less clear after sixty full
seconds. Hadn't been run in a long while.

A second door at the kitchen entrance led into a small
bedroom that ran along the side of the house. There was a
single bed framed in wood, mattress bare. A rickety chest of
drawers proved upon inspection to be empty. Ditto for the
closets. For the hell of it, and because it had worked the last
time, I looked under the bed and lifted the mattress. Found
nothing.

I went back into the kitchen, leaned against the archway
and stared absently around the living room again. I'd felt just
the slightest prickling way down deep in the brain. Like
bubbles from a gigantic fish circling the bottom of a pond.
Could get no handle on it, and time was a-wasting, so I
climbed the flight of squeaky steps.

Nothing in the three rooms up there, nothing but darkness
and dust and bottled-up air. I roamed the rooms in a slow
circuit, looking for something, anything. Nothing, except the
certainty that these rooms hadn't been used in years.

Okay, Justin ole buddy, what's the story? Looks like you've
been and gone. Damned inconsiderate of you. What I'd have
to do now was roll back into Register and ask around about
him, flash Kevin's picture, see if anyone had, and was willing
to share, information about them, what they were doing,
where they might have gone. The larger question niggled at

e. Who was Justin Catlin anyhow? Why had Kevin come
ay the hell out here? Had they known each other before?
hy—

A grinding crunch of gravel sounded faintly from outside
e house.

I walked quickly to a window, stooped, and peered out
om around the frame. Through the dirty glass I saw a black
ep Comanche pull into the parking area, followed by a
ber gray Chrysler New Yorker. The Jeep skidded to a stop
ocking the front end of my Mustang, and the Chrysler
nipped around behind it. Doors were opening before the
hicles had come to a rest, disgorging men in dark, casual
othes. They had a purposeful, disciplined look that I didn't
e at all.

Oh, shit.

I trotted out of the bedroom and thundered down the
airs. All things being equal, I didn't want to be found, but
ere was the problem of the Mustang, now effectively under
eir control. I decided to exit the house the way I'd come in,
ake a break for it, find somewhere to hide outside. I was
ading across the living room when that prickling deep in
e brain crescendoed into a full-fledged message. Despite
y anxiety I looked back toward the kitchen. Sure. Yeah.
rfectly obvious, dummy. But no time to check it out now.
Through the windows I'd gotten the impression that the
sitors were fanning out. I bent, turned, stuck one leg
rough the window followed by the other one, and dropped
t and down into the grass. I turned right and started to jog
ward the rear of the house. I didn't give myself good odds.
ere were woods back there, but first there was a lawn and
field and—

"All right, freeze!"

I skidded to a stop and spread my arms out without
rning. A morning dove hooted from the trees ahead of me.
said, "I'm not armed."

"I am. Go flat on the ground. Now."

I heard footsteps. A backup. I started to turn. "Look—"

The gunshot was deep and throaty and scared hell out of
e indigenous birds. It also scared hell out of me. I dropped
 the ground, dunking my face in the tall grass. More
otsteps, a pair of new sneakers, and my hands were yanked
rd to the small of my back. I heard the oily snick and felt

the pinching embrace as my wrists were cuffed togeth
followed by an expert impersonal frisk that missed no part
my body. My pliers and pry bar were removed and tossed
somewhere. "Up now," the voice grunted.

I stumbled to my feet, aided by a hard, pinching hold
my upper arm. The man was a young, dark-haired toug
shaved and groomed, trousers and sport shirt and an oran
hunting vest, no doubt concealing his hardware. His face v
expressionless, almost bored; a killer face or a cop face
couldn't tell which. He spun me and shoved me toward t
front of the house. "Move."

His backup stood at the corner, sleek automatic point
carefully toward the ground. He was dressed similarly to
captor. So were the four other men who appeared around t
corner at that moment. "This must be the only one," one
them said.

"You covered it top to bottom?" my captor asked.

"All clear."

"Secure it. Let's roll."

Two of them peeled off and trotted to the front of t
house. "What about that clown wagon he's driving?" one
the others asked.

Clown wagon? "That's a 1971 Ford Mustang," I said.

The hard slap to the back of my head nearly knocked
down. "Shut up, ya dumb shit," my escort barked. I sho
my head to clear the stars as he stopped me from falling, d
the keys out of my pocket, and tossed them. "Emerick, y
take it, follow us in." With another shove he propelled
forward. "Let's go."

A few minutes before, I'd been afraid these were co
Now, as we crossed the lawn toward the vehicles, I fou
myself hoping they were.

The room was square and windowless, the tongue-a
groove walls bare except for a gaily colored calendar dat
May of 1962 and advertising a bright red hay baler. A d
fly-speckled bulb shone from the ceiling. I sat on the du
wood-plank floor, leaning against the wall. I had no chai
had no wallet, keys, change, or watch, I'd had no compa
for better than three hours, and I had no idea where in
hell I was.

The men—whoever they were—had loaded me into the
ck seat of the Comanche. I sat bench-center, flanked by
o of them, as we drove away. They'd turned right onto
ute 3, away from Register, and followed a route so circu-
us that I was lost inside of ten minutes. They'd ignored my
estions, gazed off indifferently at my demands, given each
her secretive looks at my threats. Finally I'd shut up,
ving run out of hot air. It does happen.

After thirty minutes we'd rolled into a village. No sign at
e limits; could have been Pigeonshit, Michigan, for all I
uld tell. I could see church steeples and trees, buildings
d houses. Based on the angle of the sun, I knew we'd come
roughly from the east. Beyond that, nothing.

A quarter mile into the village we swung right into a grain-
evator facility. We followed an alley between corrugated
el warehouses all the way to the rear. There we parked
d they took me inside a flat, low, anonymous building and
ked me inside this room.

I'd passed through the stages of feeling angry, foolish, and
ured. Now I was profoundly bored and more than a little
noyed. I'd reflected back on the events and determined for
re that there was something big going on here, something
 wandered into out of left field. If they were cops, they had
 on B & E, but cops have jails and forms and fingerprint
ds and the flash of cameras and the cold slam-bang of
rred doors.

f, on the other hand, they were bad guys, God only knew
at was going on and what their intentions were. All I could
 was wait and—

The door clattered. I pushed myself to my feet. It opened,
d a short, pudgy man stood there, peering at me benignly
m behind rimless glasses. He had large eyes, a small
rsed mouth, large ears, sloping shoulders, little-stick arms,
d legs. He wore a dark business suit, its jacket buttoned
gly around his bowling-ball belly. He looked like the
endly pharmacist who counsels you about your irregularity
oblem. His voice was thin and diffident. "May we have a
rd, Mr. Perkins?"

They knew my name; that proved they could read. "That'd
 a step forward," I growled.

He kept his hand on the knob. "Please stay right where
u are," he cautioned, then came in and closed the door

behind him. He put his hands into the jacket pocke
squinted at me, and asked, "Why did you break into Jus
Catlin's house?"

"Now wait a minute. First of all, I want to know who t
hell you guys are."

"That's not important. Please answer my question."

"Who's this Catlin guy, anyway?" I pressed.

He shook his head wearily. "Bear in mind who is bei
detained by whom, Mr. Perkins."

"Hey, I've had three or four hours to think about that. N
I want some answers. Like, for starters, who are you."

He thought about it. "You may call me Ponder."

"Great. Pleased to meetcha. Who do you work for?"

"That's not important. Why did you break into Jus
Catlin's house?"

Evidently we could go round and round like that for days
switched tacks and decided to spring the thin, go-for-bro
story I'd formulated. "Like I said, who's Catlin? I was tryi
to dig up some poopy on Bill Hopewell."

The eyes behind the lenses flickered. "Hopewell?"

"The guy who lives there."

You could practically hear the brain hum behind Ponde
kindly, ice-cold face. "What is your business with Hopewell

"Well, I'm a private detective."

"We know that."

"What'd you do, run my license with the state?"

"That's not important."

"Thanks for keeping me up to speed on that. Anyhow,'
said, warming to my earnest urban-yutz act, "this Hopewe
ex-wife Annie hired me to track him down; seems he has
been making his support payments lately."

"Annie," Ponder repeated thoughtfully, face betraying nothir

"Anyhow, old Bill's a gun nut, see. Subscribes to all t
magazines. I found out he filed a change of address with o
of them. Route Three, Register, Michigan." I grinned. "
here I am, wherever 'here' is."

Ponder withdrew his plump hands from his pockets, fold
his arms loosely, and stared at his shoes. "The house whe
we found you is not the only one on Route Three, M
Perkins."

"Heck, I know that. I figured on hitting all of them ti
found him. That's all."

He suddenly looked hard at me. I stared back, maintaining what I hoped was a vacuous expression. He said, "You're no doubt aware that breaking into a dwelling is an offense."

"I sure am. And believe me, Mr. Ponder, I'll never do it again. Frankly, I had no idea y'all had such on-the-toes law enforcement out in these parts. You must take stuff seriously, to send a flying squad down on me behind a lousy little B and E."

He looked sour. "It is not wise to annoy me."

"Hey, I'm not trying to be an annoyance. I'm just kinda wondering who you guys are. I know, I know," I added hastily, "it's not important. But what is important is, I got to get back to work. Time is money, like my daddy always said."

He took a deep breath and nodded abruptly. "Very well. I'll have you driven back to your car. You get in that car, and you hit the road, and you go home, Mr. Perkins. And don't come back."

CHAPTER 16

So PONDER WAS RUNNING me out of town, just like a
old wild-West marshal. This would never do. I had busines
to finish at the Catlin house. I looked at the pudgy little man
turning up the earnest/stupid quotient on my face. "But I go
to find—"

He jabbed a finger toward me. "Just tell Mrs. Anni
Hopewell that if she needs money, why, go out and get a job
Wait tables, clean toilets, or peddle her ass. I don't care
Register, Michigan, is off limits to you, Mr. Perkins. I will no
hesitate to make life unpleasant for you if I see your face i
this area again."

"Free country," I grumbled. "Man has a right to do hi
job."

"Except when it conflicts with mine," Ponder said. H
turned and opened the door. "Let's go."

I walked toward the door. "How 'bout if I go home in th
morning instead of tonight?"

"I told you—"

"Look," I rushed on. "I'm in the detective business. If
don't get some kind of answer for my client, I don't get paid.
Not strictly true, but it sounded good. "Let me spend th
night in town. Who knows, maybe Hopewell will show up, i
one of the bars or something. I'll stay right in town, I won
go anywhere near Route Three. Whaddya say?"

"Well—"

"It's getting on for evening anyhow."

"All right," he said abruptly, standing back to let m
precede him. "You stay in town, and you hit the road brigh
and early."

* * *

I felt pretty silly when I found that we'd been in Register
ll along. Wise guys.

One of Ponder's goons drove me in the Comanche into the
enter of the village. My Mustang was angle-parked near the
entral intersection. As I got out, the man said, "You know
he rules. Spend the night, then out of here in the morning.
ot it?"

I was irritable. The agreeable-yutz act has a short shelf life.
ut I managed to grin as I said, "Sure, right, I got the
essage."

The Comanche roared away up the street. I went to the
lustang and got in. Nothing seemed to be missing, most
mportantly my emergency road kit containing cigars and
atches. I fired one up, inhaled gratefully, and sat there
r a few minutes, staring up the sidewalk at the store-
ronts, barely noticing the strolling pedestrians or the red
low of the waning sun reflecting off a hardware-store
indow.

Each question yielded more questions.

Questions within questions.

Where was Kevin? Who was Catlin, and where was he?
Vho was Ponder, and what was he up to? How was I going to
et back out to Catlin's house? I had the feeling that Ponder
vould not take kindly to finding me lurking about the place
gain. Just a hunch, but you sense these things after a few
ears in this business.

Jesus.

I got out of the Mustang. The late-afternoon air was
olding the heat in a grip of humidity. Summer was nearly
pon us. I looked up and down the street. Across the way, a
w doors up, was the saloon called BAR that I'd seen on my
vay in. Across from it was a three-story building labeled
OOMS.

An idea flickered, blinked out, then came to life hot. Sure,
vhy not? Every bar has its Barb Paley.

Some hours later I woke up as if I'd been kicked, and sat
p muscle-locked and staring. The small, shabby room sneered

back at me. Things fell quickly into place. Second-floor room
Dave's Lodgings, Register, Michigan.

The sound of John Cougar Mellencamp wafted intermittent
through the half-open, double-hung window. I got off th
hard, uncomfortable bed and peered outside. Night ha
taken Register over. The street was dark except for th
occasional streetlight, the two-bulb traffic signal, cars
transit, and the front door of BAR, which opened and shut
monotonous rhythm as people churned in and out.

Place was hopping. Perfect. I checked the time. Eleven
thirty. I felt physically refreshed, which was a good thing
because if my idea worked, I was going to be up pretty la
tonight.

I collected my wallet, cigars, matches, and keys, scanne
the room once, and left. In the lobby I almost tossed m
room key on the desk—win or lose, I had no plans to com
back here tonight—but reconsidered and kept it. Someon
might have been watching.

I hit the sidewalk and crossed the broad street, forced
wait while a semi roared past. As I approached BAR's door,
felt nervous, as though Ponder's people were concealed
upper rooms or behind the wheels of parked cars, watchin
me. Well, they probably were. That was all right. I had
plan of sorts.

The barroom was surprisingly large. It stretched wide an
long, practically vanishing amid smoke and dimness towa
the rear. A five-piece guitar, drum, and keyboard band w
playing heavy-footed Mickey Gilley from a stand to the left.
long, ornate oak bar divided the room lengthwise at the righ
It was jammed tight with drinkers sitting on stools an
wedged into the spaces between them. The floor area w
cluttered with tables; the left-hand wall, past the bandstan
was lined with booths. Mostly full. I mean, this place w
hopping; I wondered if it was the only saloon in Registe
Probably.

I grabbed a table just as its pair of occupants rose to leav
A harried barmaid took my order for a Stroh's. It came fa
and went down cold. I ordered another, fired up a ciga
leaned back in the chair, and began taking inventory.

It took me fifteen minutes to spot her.

Funny thing was, she even looked a little like Barb. N
quite as tall, and her hair was long, brown, and straig

stead of a short, red, permed explosion around her head,
it like Barb she was hefty, busty, freckled, dimpled; she
vored lots of loud makeup, dangly earrings, and more
ngs than fingers; like Barb she was a fixture in this place.
he went from table to table, beer mug held sloppily in
ie hand, chatting gaily with the men and ignoring what
w women there were. The big tip-off was the way the
en reacted to her. They were kindly, bemused, tolerant.
he didn't seem to be attached to any one of them. Not
t, anyway.

I was trying to figure out an approach when she took care
the problem for me. She was headed back for the bar with
er empty mug when she suddenly hung a left, cruised up to
iy table, and dropped heavily into the chair across from me.
This seat taken?" she asked, hanging an arm over the back of
ie chair, the action, as she well knew, drawing her open-
ecked checkered shirt tightly against her breasts.

"It is now," I said, grinning. "How are ya, darlin'?"

"Thirsty." She banged her mug on the table and said loudly
 no one in particular, "'Nother round over here, eh?" She
ocked her head and looked at me. I read her as maybe only
alf bombed at this point, skating along on the thin ice of a
eer high. "You're not from around here."

"Nope. Just thumbed my way in."

The barmaid brought a fresh round, picked up our emp-
es, and left. My new friend was staring at me. "Thumbed?
Iow the hell can you thumb your way into a creepy little
own like this?"

I shrugged. "I don't know. I was on my way up to Caseville
hen this grain hauler picked me up on the fifty-three
ighway. Ended up here. I'm not too far off track, am I?"

"Couple miles is all." She stuck out a glittery hand. "I'm
'rudence. They call me Pru for short."

"Ben." We shook. She withdrew her hand and drank the
d off her fresh beer. I asked, "You from here, Pru?"

"Oh hell no." She put her mug down overly hard. Dis-
inces start getting cloudy when you're this far along. "I'm
om Shabbona."

"Where's that?"

"Down the road and over a ways." She smiled. "You think
legister is the capital of nowhere, oughta try Shabbona.
'hat's why I come up here. Shabbona's so small it doesn't

even have a bar." She took a pack of Marlboro out of her shi
pocket, shook a weed out of it, and stuck it in her mouth.
leaned a flaring match over and she lighted up, guiding m
hand with her fingertips. She thanked me with a nod as sh
exhaled smoke. "So," she asked, "what do you do for a livin
Ben?"

We drank, we smoked, we told casual lies as the ban
played on.

Two hours later we were navigating our way out the bac
door of Bar. Prudence was half numb by now, having drun
beer steadily the entire time. I'd fallen behind her pace a
once and stayed there, hoping she wouldn't notice. I neede
my wits if I was going to carry this off.

Things looked good at this point. Though there'd been n
groping and no coarse talk, our conversation had contained
flirtatious subtext. It was pretty obvious what the next ste
was, and Prudence seemed all ready for it, though she woul
have been indignant had I broached the subject openly. Sh
was the type who would insist on maintaining the romanti
fiction. Stranger in the night and all that.

The blackness of the alley was broken only by a singl
security light set up high on a power pole. "I'm over here,
she said, directing us toward a dark blue Chevy Citatio
parked crookedly against the wall of a warehouse. "'Preciat
your walking me out, in case of muggers or whatever," sh
added with a giggle.

"Hey, my pleasure," I answered. She dug keys out of
small handbag and jingled them, searching for the right on
as we drew up to the car. "You okay to drive home?" I asked
hoping she'd say no.

"Oh sure." She looked at me, face almost invisible in th
darkness. "I'd invite you home for a nightcap. Problem is m
husband'll be getting up in a while. He goes to work awfu
early."

"Damn. And I wanted to see Shabbona real bad, Pru. I'
be rolling out in the morning, haven't seen anything of thes
parts."

"I ain't even tired yet," she said petulantly.

"I really like sight-seeing," I said earnestly, giving her a
opening big enough to drive a truck through.

"Tellya what. Want to drive around awhile?"

"Sounds great, kid." Critical question now. "How 'bout if I heel it?"

The keys flew toward me and I caught them, just barely. No speeding tickets, now," she said gaily.

She skipped around the back of the car and got in the passenger side. I got in, adjusted the bench seat, and started up. Prudence slid over to the center of the bench seat till she was against me from knees to shoulders. Her body felt warm and comfortable and inviting. It had been a stretch for the kid, and before I'd even found reverse gear on the tree shifter, I felt the beginnings of arousal. Now stop it, I thought as I backed the car out. Keep your mind on business, idiot.

There was no conversation. The compact had been made. Prudence put her hand on my thigh lightly and began to trail it along, back and forth, seemingly unconsciously. I focused on driving. I got us around to Main Street, made the left on Route 3, and headed north, just as I had this morning. Checked the rearview. Empty.

"We're leaving town," Prudence said drowsily at one point.

"Lot of nice country out here," I said. "Look at that moon."

It was a bright, sharp sliver, silvering down on the sleeping countryside. "Pretty," she said, her thigh massage gaining strength.

I kept an eye on the rearview mirror. Nothing. Looked like I'd eluded them. Odds were they were watching only the Mustang, which sat peaceably back there in town. They hadn't seen me leave the bar. Maybe they hadn't even seen me go into it.

I felt Prudence's head drop onto my shoulder. She took my free hand in hers and sighed. This all took me back to high-school days, and for an instant I relived the fresh anticipation of a new score. The feeling was gone in an instant, at least for me. Prudence obviously still felt it. I felt desire for her, mixed with sympathy and regret.

We crossed the creek and passed Catlin's place. All was quiet and dark up there. I checked the rearview again—nothing—and began watching the road in earnest now. Presently, a dirt road offered itself on the right. I made the turn and powered the car along the uneven grade through a tunnel of trees.

"Where are you taking me, Ben?" Prudence asked innocentl

"Sight seeing, sweetheart."

"I like you. I'm glad that trucker made a wrong turn an
dropped you off in Register."

That wasn't the story I'd given her, but who cared?
squeezed her hand, let it go, and took gentle hold of he
knee. "I'm glad, too," I said.

I felt her moist lips briefly on my neck. "Let's sto
somewhere," she whispered.

Not yet, damn it! "Sounds good to me."

Thankfully, another dirt road appeared. I swung the ca
right. We broke free of the trees and bounced along on th
Chevy's weak shocks at about twenty miles an hour pas
early-season cornfields that glistened in the moonlight. I wa
watching the road ahead now. I didn't want to miss m
landmark.

"Anywhere along here," Prudence murmured, kissing m
again. "It's all right. Nobody ever comes back here at thi
hour."

That's what I'd counted on. I powered the car over th
crest of a hill—slope is a better term, I guess—and, as w
started to coast downward, spotted my landmark at last. Stee
utility towers marched along from northeast to southwest
crossing the road about a hundred yards ahead and entering
massive black forest to my right. I let up on the gas. "Look
pretty good up here."

She looked out, then pushed gently away from me.
glanced at her as I slowed the car, wondering if she'd change
her mind. She hadn't. She was unbuttoning her shirt.

The shoulder dropped away swiftly into a ditch on th
right. Nowhere to pull off just here. As we passed under th
utility wires, I saw a weedy turnoff to the right just ahead
The ditch ran through a culvert under the turnoff, whicl
ended where the forest began. I slowed the car to a crawl an
rolled it right into the turnoff, then ahead about twenty fee
where the lane, if that's what it was, ended at the forest. I cu
off the lights and shut off the motor. Dead silence.

Prudence sighed and melted into me. I took her in my
arms and kissed her, telling myself I was just playing along t
make it look good. She kissed me back fiercely, telling me i
was very much for real. Her free hand was working expertl
at my belt buckle, and mine was off on its own exploration o

er soft, protuberant belly. Her breasts were tightly encased
a half-cut brassiere, and my hand went around back as we
lled tighter together. Fingernails bit into my back, and she
urmured low in her throat as I took hold of the bra's clasp.
ne quick snap, son, and you're on your way.

CHAPTER 17

By now she'd undone my belt and my jeans and w:
headed for home. A petulant voice inside me said, Why th
hell not? It's been a couple of weeks, for chrissake. I:
out-of-town ass, no complications except the good kind. Sur
you're using her, but she's using you, too. You can still follo
the plan, after a brief, tasty intermission. She wants it ba:
wouldn't be gentlemanly to pull the rug on her now. And it
a little late in the day to be going all christer, after wh
you've been doing with Barb Paley.

Prudence's hand had found and freed my penis and w:
giving it eager, gentle, yet urgent exploration. I broke th
kiss and pushed back. She came forward, trying to stay wit
me, but I let go of her. "Hold it, kid. Wait a minute," I sai
hoarsely.

"What's wrong?"

"Call of nature," I answered, mouth dry, heart poundin;

"Oh," she said, releasing my organ. She took a dee
breath. "Okay, you sure got to take care of *that*. Damn beer

I buckled myself up. "Back in a flash."

She was gathering her shirt together over her breasts. "I
be in the back. Lots more room back there. You hurry, now

"Absolutely." I opened the door and got out. I heard th
passenger door of the Citation open, but I did not look bacl
I trotted to the woods and then into it, moving at a fast wall
using the dim moonlight to navigate among the giant tree
Presently I hit a treeless area: a grassy swath within the fore:
that had been cleared away for the line of utility towers.
bore left when I reached that and followed the fringe of th
forest.

128

I wondered how long she'd wait. I wondered if I'd ever
en as horny as I was just then. I felt like a world-class
it—I'd used Prudence, though not as ruthlessly as I might
ve. I searched what I'd done for some sort of heroism, and
und none. All the same, I felt like I'd done the right thing.
works out that way sometimes.

Catlin's farmhouse appeared twenty hard hiking minutes
ter.
I paused for a break where the forest ended. Across the
ng, moonlit field the house, the garage, and the barn
owed mistily. The wind-pump tower reached for the night
y, the sycamores stood in tall, dark guard, rustling in the
ght breeze, and the windows of the house were dark, dead
les. I wondered if Ponder had stationed someone at the
use to keep an eye out. I watched awhile, didn't see any
gn of it, decided I'd have to take the chance.
I'd gathered a second wind by then, and I loped across the
eld in an easy jog till I reached the lawn. Gaining entry to
e house would probably be no problem this time. I didn't
ink Ponder would go to the effort of repairing the broken
indow latch, and I was right. They hadn't even closed the
amned thing.
I stood by the side of the house, tiptoed up, and peeked in.
arkness. Well, if the window was still open, that meant they
adn't detected my earlier intrusion through electronic means.
hey probably were maintaining watch on the farm at a
stance, from the front, waiting for Justin Catlin to return.
hy, I didn't know. But I felt cautiously optimistic that I'd be
le to get into the house, back out, and away without
tracting their attention this time.
I climbed inside and crouched on the floor, listening. The
d musty place felt like a tomb. The blackness was almost
tal; the angle of the moon was such that its rays did not
ach through the lower floor windows. I reached into my
ck left pocket and took out a stubby pencil flashlight. I held
low to the floor and switched it on. The sharp little beam
ached across the floor to the opposite wall. I cupped it with
y hand and crawled clumsily across. Wouldn't do to let the
ght show through the windows.
The opposite wall fronted the staircase, which climbed up

into the second story. I crawled along the wall, using th
flashlight to examine it closely. The old, hard, painted w
plaster was flawless. No cracks, no seams, no suspicio
joints. When I reached the base of the stairs I turned th
flashlight off, stood, and felt my way around the corn
through the archway and into the kitchen. I turned the lig
on again and inspected the wall to my left.

The area under the staircase was dead space. No access
it. At least, someone wanted it to look that way. I'm n
architect, but I've been around long enough to know ho
uncommon it is for such space to be left unutilized. Mayb
some idiot had designed this place. On the other han
maybe there'd once been access to that area and someone ha
walled it off. For some reason.

The wall in question ran about twenty feet from the arch
the floor-to-ceiling cupboards at the far end of the kitche
The dinette table and a couple of chairs stood against it abo
halfway down. Built into the wall were two sets of recesse
wood shelves that went about seven feet up. They we
painted white, and they held plates, vases, and other bric-
brac, and they looked innocent to anyone without my type
suspicious mind.

I went to the nearest one and inspected it closely. Th
shelves and the surrounding molding were built in snugl
painted over thickly, and covered with a fine layer of dust.
took hold of one of the shelves and wiggled it, just to mak
sure; there was no give. Okay, scratch that one.

I pulled the dinette table and chairs away from the wall an
inspected the other shelf set. It, too, was painted and bui
snugly. The wood and the bric-a-brac did not seem to be a
dusty. Or was that just my imagination? I grabbed the midd
shelf and shook. No give. Or maybe just a tiny little bit
give. I shook it again, harder, and heard the faintest rattlin
A cup on the bottom shelf was vibrating. Ah-ha.

I inspected the molding all the way around. I checked eac
shelf. I was looking for levers, switches, soft spots, anythin
and got nowhere. Yet I was convinced that this wasn't really
built-in set of shelves; it was a door, held into the wall b
invisible hinges.

So how do I open the son of a bitch?

I inspected it all over again. I picked up each piece
bric-a-brac and set it down. I squinted closely at all th

oints. I took hold of every surface and wiggled. Nothing
worked. Finally, in frustration, I dropped down to the floor
nd peered under the bottom shelf, where the toestrip met
he yellow linoleum floor. And there it was.

A small strip of steel, about the width and thickness of a
hoehorn, emerged from the molding, just an inch above the
loor and invisible from anywhere but down here. I took hold
f it and wiggled it. It only wanted to go down. I pushed it,
nd the shelf set inched in with a muffled metallic snick,
ausing the bric-a-brac to chime briefly.

I stood and focused the beam of the pencil light straight
head. The shelf set was in fact a door, and it stood invitingly
pen and inward, blackness showing around the edges. I
ushed it. It sighed inward. I stepped forward and directed
he light inward. I got a glimpse of the underside of the
taircase, rising upward to the right. Below it were heavily
oaded plank shelves, a filing cabinet, and a long, shallow
lesk built into the far wall with a personal computer sitting in
ts center, incongruously high tech under its plastic dustcover.

I went inside. A light switch was mounted on the near wall
o my right. Why not? I thought. I pushed the door closed
nd hit the light switch, illuminating the tiny room from two
are bulbs mounted above.

I tucked my flashlight away. Horniness, fatigue, and the
eer high were forgotten; here was a nosy detective's dream.
Now I knew why the rest of the house was so bare; every-
hing Justin Catlin cared about was hidden right here in this
ot, stuffy, airless little room. Now, hopefully, I'd find out
vho he was. And maybe get an idea of where Kevin was.

No time to lollygag; I went straight to the filing cabinet and
pened the top drawer. It was piled nearly to the top with
ewspaper clippings. Most were about a year old and seemed
o be from newspapers all over the country, including *The
Washington Post, The New York Times* and the *Seattle Intelli-
;encer.* I leafed through quickly, then backed up and did
ome skimming, then backed up yet again and began to read.
They pertained to the highly publicized trial of an organiza-
ion called The Order. I'd heard that name already, from
Michael Kraus. The articles confirmed that The Order was
et another white-supremacy group with revolutionary leanings.
Robberies that netted some $4 million . . . the machine-gun
nurder of controversial Denver talk show host Alan Berg . . .

weapons caches including crossbows, plastic explosives, han
grenades, night-vision scopes, automatic rifles...the Ber
murder weapon, a .45 caliber MAC-10 submachine pisto
found in the home of Gary Lee Yarbrough, a former membe
of the Aryan Nations and the White American Bastion...Orde
founder Robert J. Mathews killed during standoff with polic
at his house in Whidbey Island, Washington, when his am
munition cache blew up...

According to the articles, some twenty-three Order mem
bers were charged under the Racketeer Influenced and Cor
rupt Organizations Act. Eleven pleaded guilty and receive
sentences of up to twenty years. The rest were convicte
after a sixteen-week trial and received similar sentences. I
several places it was mentioned that one Order membe
identified as Richard Robertson, was still at large.

These references had been highlighted with a yellow mark
er, followed by a large exclamation point in ballpoint pen.

By now I was sitting cross-legged on the floor, my lap full o
the dusty, yellowing clippings. I stared at the highlighte
markings, thinking hard, as the words stabbed at my eyes
Richard Robertson still at large.

The clippings gave way to a wad of greenbar compute
printouts, which looked and sounded like teletype messages
They were addressed variously to "Richard," "Richard R.,"
and "Dick." They were full of incomprehensible talk abou
meetings at Hayden Lake and people I'd never heard of
interspersed with virulent racist diatribes.

Richard Robertson, federal fugitive. Justin Catlin. Th
names were dissimilar, but that was probably the whole idea

I sorted the papers into an irregular pile, stood, threw
them back into the drawer, and closed it. The middle drawe
was labeled SPECIAL ACTION. I opened it. Nothing excep
for dust and a couple of empty manila folders.

The bottom drawer had no label. I hunkered down and
opened it. It was lined front to back with manila file folders
Each tab had a name, and the names were meticulously
alphabetized. I did the natural thing and went straight to W
Werbe, Wickham, Witkowski.

Deep breath as I pulled the folder out. It was distressingly
thin, and I thought at first that it was empty. But it wasn't
There was a single sheet in there, a newspaper clipping from
the *Detroit Free Press,* dated late April.

Three columns of text, parts of it highlighted, along with a vivid picture.

Though Kevin's name wasn't mentioned even once, I felt my jaw lock up. My heart hardened and quickened as I forced myself to read the article a second time.

I rose slowly to my feet, tucked the article into my pocket, and closed the bottom drawer with a vindictive kick. My feelings were a mix of wonder, disbelief, and anger: you done fucked up my whole summer, kid.

All that was left was the computer, and I wasn't about to tinker around with that. Cars I can do, computers are a black art as far as I'm concerned.

I palmed my penlight and switched it on. I'd planned to inspect the hardware of the secret door—marvelous piece of carpentry, that—but didn't even think of it. Instead, I hit the single-rod latch, turned off the lights, opened the door with my penlight held low, and left the room. I carefully closed the secret door behind me and put the dinette table and chairs back where they were. Fastidious.

False dawn was muddying the sky as I slipped out the open window. Christ, I'd been in there a long time. I felt raggedy, yet hopped up. I had to resist the urge to run. I moved at a good, fast gait across the lawn, across the field, into the woods where the utility towers cut their swath. Morning dew soaked my shoes and my jeans from the knees down, and the old body was putting out advisories about fatigue and hunger and things like that, but I ignored it. I was thinking about Terry in the hospital, and Lynne in her K Mart smock, and the sad little group of baby pictures of Kevin that Lynne had proudly mounted on the first page of her photo album.

The little turnoff by the dirt road was empty. Figures; no woman waits forever, even for me. I stood there in the gathering light, looking both ways on the road, hoping for something as fortuitous as an early-rising farmer chugging along in his pickup, slowing, stopping, opening the door: "Register? Sure, partner, I'll run you right over there. Have some coffee?"

No such luck.

Never had I felt so out of place: a Detroit boy of the automotive persuasion marooned in the country with no set of wheels in sight. Well, I thought, no sense in standing here. Might as well head south, then bear west. Find Register, grab

the Mustang, take the first piece of decent pavement south
go home, grab some sleep...

Evidently, Wolf had an assignment for me. But as usual he
was taking his time getting to it. He paced the living room o
his sumptuous Prinzregentenstrasse apartment, blue eye
flashing as he lectured me about the political situation
especially his meeting with von Hindenburg in a few weeks

I silently waited him out. Politics wasn't my thing; opera
tions was. Suddenly he stopped and folded his arms and faced
me, all animation gone from his face. "It's time to resolve the
Geli question, Ben," he told me.

I instantly knew what he meant. It shocked me. He wa
passionately in love with her. Like other inner-circle mem
bers, I'd assumed he would marry her, niece or not. "Geli?"
echoed, startled.

Wolf nodded. "The decision is irrevocable. I love her, bu
certain liabilities have emerged, as you know."

I didn't know. Not for sure. His relationship with her wa
causing a stink; maybe his motive was to erase that. At the
same time, she'd become angry about his domination of her
She wanted to go to Vienna to continue her singing lessons
and he wouldn't let her. And she did not reciprocate hi
feelings. Her interests were elsewhere, as I knew full well.

Wolf broke into my thoughts. "She must answer for he
dalliance with Emil Maurice."

Ah-ha. So it wasn't politics. It was personal vengeance
That made sense. Emil had preceded me as Wolf's body
guard. He'd found it impossible to resist Geli. So had I, bu
Wolf didn't know that, thank God.

"And you will settle accounts with Emil, as well," Wol
added.

I nodded. The vision of the beautiful, blond, high-spirited
Geli rose in my mind. Killing her would not be easy, but
had my orders. "When?" I asked.

"Tomorrow," Wolf said, resuming his pacing. "I leave fo
Hamburg in the morning. She will be alone here."

"Very well," I said.

Wolf stood by the bookshelves at the far wall, back to me
"Make it look like suicide—"

I snapped awake and focused on the ceiling of my bedroom

the dream pinwheeled away, disintegrating; Geli's scream-
g face, Wolf's burning, hateful stare. I was lying fully
thed atop my mangled sheets. Thundering echoed in the
stance. The light was grayish feeble. Must be early yet, I
ought. Then I realized from the din up above that it was
ning like hell outside. Could be noon, for all I knew. I
rned and looked at bright orange numerals. Eleven-thirty.
The thundering came again from far off. I sat up, blinking
ndpaper lids. Something weird about that sound. It came
ain, and I realized what it was. Hard pounding on my
artment door.

Oh man. Talk about your morning routine being bitched all
hell; I hadn't even prepared the Mr. Coffee. I stood,
ck-walked out of the bedroom, and did my best not to
unce off walls as I navigated up the hall toward the front of
e apartment.

The door was rumbling again as I pulled it open to find
ebra Clark standing there. She looked dark and cute in
me kind of snug, light-colored tennis outfit; a poplin rain-
at was draped over her shoulders. I rubbed my eyes,
ited for the world to quit dancing, and stared at her as I
ned on the edge of the door. "Man, they must have one
eral dress code over there to the EPA, Ms. Clark."

She looked sourly at me. "It's Saturday, Ben. I don't work
turdays. Where in the hell have you been?"

"Munich, I think," I mumbled, "about, what, 1931 or so."

"Knowing you," she retorted, "you were probably sleeping
f a night in a blind pig, or worse. May I come in, or is
mething going on in there that you'd rather I didn't see?"

I stood back, holding the door partly for support and partly
admit her. "Sure, come on. You wouldn't by chance feel
ke putting a pot of coffee on, while I bang my head against
e wall?"

"I don't make coffee for anyone but myself," she said as she
epped in, "and I've already had my cup this morning." She
oked around the living room. "Dear Lord."

"Maid's been off sick."

"I think your maid passed away a decade ago."

"I think you're right. Come on in the kitchen. Set a spell."

Fortunately, automatic pilot kicked in, enabling me to get
e coffee maker going without major mishap. Clark wisely
pt her peace as she shed her raincoat and sat at the dinette,

looking everywhere but at me. When I had the machi~~
grunting and hissing, I searched my pocket for cigars, fou~~
none, and panicked. Good; that was a sign I'd live. There w~~
more good news; I found several preowned weeds in t~~
ashtray on the counter. I selected the largest and began~~
unscrunch it. "So what's up, Ms. Clark?"

She wasn't through chewing me out. "I've been trying~~
reach you all morning. I left three messages on that stup~~
box of yours."

"I was out of town. Didn't get back in here till eight or s~~
Been up all night, besides. Turned off the phone by the be~~
Sorry to've inconvenienced you."

"Brian called me last night," she went on with some hea~~
"Some ungodly hour, two A.M. or something. He tried to c~~
you first and called me when he couldn't reach you."

"Could have broke his cover, the dumb shit," I sai~~
lighting up. Rancid but wonderful. *Ahh.*

"He said he was alone and not to worry about his 'cove~~
He also said he absolutely has to talk to you."

I looked at her. "What, he find Kevin?"

CHAPTER 18

"No," CLARK ANSWERED. "BUT apparently he did spend
the evening at that Loading Zone bar. He's anxious to tell
you about it."

I glanced at the Mr. Coffee. It had produced maybe a
quarter cup of coffee, despite huffing and puffing as if it had
run twelve miles. Time to clean the sucker, I thought. "Take
a letter to Joe DiMaggio," I said to Clark. "Dear Joe: Now, if
you could just—"

"I don't take letters," she shot back. "Haven't you been
listening to me? God, you're impossible!"

"I'm not God. I'm also not awake yet. Give me a break."

She stood. "I've talked to you when you're awake, and
you're impossible then, too."

"Well, you're just worked up."

"I'm worried sick about Brian!"

"You know him. You tell me," I said, then inhaled on the
cigar stub. "Did he sound upset or scared or anything?"

"No. But—"

"Then everything's fine, and not to worry, kid. I'm on top
of it."

She looked around querulously. "That cigar smells like a
moldering mattress. I'm getting out of here. Brian said he'd
try you again at the 'specified time,' whatever that is. You just
be available, you hear me?"

She stomped out of the kitchen and out of the apartment
with a slam. I turned and checked the earnestly burping Mr.
Coffee. Half a cup now, maybe. I rescued a mug from the
dish drainer, went to the coffee maker, slid the carafe to the

side and the mug under the stream without wasting a single
precious drop. Still got the moves, kid.

"Take a letter to Joe DiMaggio," I said to the room at large.
"Dear Joe: Now if you could just send me an IV attachment
for this thing..."

An hour, a shower, a change of clothes, and a quart of
coffee later, I rejoined a considerably brighter world. The
rain had stopped, and a horizon-wide swath of blue sky was
advancing toward us across Ford Lake. I strolled over to the
maintenance office in building one to check on Friday's work.
The elusive Doug has actually made it in, and he and Randy,
from the looks of things, had finished up the assignment
pretty well. I signed their time sheets, tossed them in the out
box for delivery to Marge on Monday morning, then headed
back to the apartment.

As I walked, I opened my mental file on the Witkowski
case and flipped through the facts, such as they were. There
were more questions than answers, and all kinds of holes;
though I was getting an instinctive idea of what might have
happened, I had no proof of anything. No real idea of what
was coming. What I knew consisted chiefly of what I didn't
know: Who was Catlin? Who was Ponder? What was Catlin
up to? Why was Ponder after him? Where was Kevin, and to
what extent was he involved in all this? Why was that
clipping kept in the file labeled WITKOWSKI?

I slammed back into my apartment. I had the sinking
feeling that I was creeping around the periphery of something big and dangerous. More troubling, I may very well
have put Brian right in the center of it. The thing was getting
beyond the simple task of "find Kevin and bring him to dad."
I still had to do that, but the odds were against my being able
to do it clean. I'd end up going feetfirst into the mess. What
was worse, now I was dragging Brian into it with me. Damn
it.

I stood in the kitchen and stared blankly out the window.
There's no turning back, old son, I thought. What you do
now is get yourself some more facts. Then see.

I sat down at the dinette with my pad, pen, and telephone
and punched out Solomon Kraus's number in Oak Park.

"Yes?" he answered after two rings.

"Mr. Kraus? Ben Perkins. Was up to see you a couple of
ys ago."

"Yes, Mr. Perkins. I was hoping you'd call. I wanted to tell
u something."

That was hopeful. "Yes?"

"I'm sorry about Michael's behavior the other day. In many
ays he's just a boy yet. Gets very intense, particularly on
e issue of these racists."

"Yeah, I noticed."

"Often I wish he'd divert that energy elsewhere," Kraus
minated. "He has a girlfriend, and Rachel worships him,
t Michael devotes little time to her. Too wrapped up in
is ... political business. But that's not important. I just felt
d that you felt you had to leave so abruptly. We were
ving a nice conversation, and I wish Michael hadn't spoiled
"

"No problem, sir. Listen, I'm wondering—have you ever
ard of a man named Justin Catlin?"

"No," Kraus answered carefully, after a pause.

"Sure?"

"Positive."

"Lives up in a place called Register, Michigan. On the
humb. Ring any bells?"

"Not one," he said definitely. "I'm sorry."

"Okay." I made a big random X on my pad. "That kid who
ashed your car, the one I'm looking for—he seems to belong
 a group calling themselves the Skinheads. Have you ever
ncountered them?"

"I've seen them on television," Kraus said. "Rock singers
d such. *Entertainment Tonight* featured them. They screw
ieces of metal through their noses and color their hair
reen. Disgusting."

"Well, that's not exactly what I'm after. These Skinheads
e a racist group of some kind. I don't know how big they
e, or—"

"All these things," Kraus said, "are beyond my experience,
m afraid. I wish Michael were here. He keeps up with the
irrent groups and so forth. I don't concern myself. I tell my
ory and let it go at that."

"Yeah. Well." I doodled as I thought about what I'd seen
p there in Catlin's secret room. Not much except for the
ipping in Kevin's file, and I wasn't about to mention that.

Another thought floated to the surface. "How about the ter·
'Special Action'?"

"I'm sorry," Kraus said. "Repeat that?"

"Special Action. That term mean anything to you, asid
from the obvious?"

Silence. "I'm afraid not."

The pause had gone just a beat too long. "Come on, sir,"
said gently, "level with me. I'm really in a quandary here."

"Please, I'm not trying to be evasive, I do want to hel
you. The term has connotations, that's all. But they're s
remote—so long ago—I don't want to seem as though I'·
grasping at straws—"

"Grasp away. May help, may not, who knows?"

He sighed heavily through the phone. "Though the Naz·
believed fervently in the rightness of their cause, they tende
to sanitize their crimes by using euphemisms." He paused fc
breath. " 'Special Action' is a general translation of the ter·
Einsatz."

"What does it mean?"

"Much more than appears on the surface." Kraus took
long breath. "The Special Action Groups—Einsatzgruppen—
were specially picked units of SS and SD men. There wer
four Einsatzgruppen in all, designated A through D. The·
original mission was to follow the German armies into Polan·
in 1939 and herd the non-Aryans into ghettos. Later, i·
forty-one, their mission was expanded."

"To what?"

"Once again," Kraus said evenly, "they followed the Ge·
man armies into Russia. Only this time their mission was t·
exterminate. Specifically Communist officials and Jews, bu
they weren't particular. Their slaughter ran into the hundred·
of thousands. Men, women, children, babies—shot down i·
pits, gassed in vans, unimaginable, Mr. Perkins—"

"Yeah," I said.

"And later, when the Germans were retreating," Krau·
barreled on, in full lecture mode now, "the Einsatzgruppe·
were responsible for covering up evidence of their earlie·
crimes. They were the worst of the worst. Not men. Animals.·

We were silent for a moment. I lighted a cigar. Kraus'
lecture had gotten to me. I wondered if Catlin's use of th·
term 'Special Action' was just a coincidence, or—

"But why do you ask, Mr. Perkins?" Kraus asked.

"Oh," I said carefully, "I picked up the term yesterday
hile doing some research, that's all."

"As you can tell," Kraus said with a shaky laugh, "its
nnotations are quite unpleasant. I don't think any Jew of
y era can hear it, even in translation, without shuddering."

"I can see why. Well, listen, I'll let you go. I appreciate you
king the time—"

"Not at all. You are a pleasant man and a good listener."
And you interrupt a lot, old fella, but I forgive you.
hanks. I don't get accused of that often."

"I only wish Michael were here so you could ask him about
ese Skinhead people. Whatever there is to know about
em, he'd know."

"I can call back, if—"

"He's away," Kraus said regretfully. "Went up to the UP to
ckpack for a week. I won't see him till next weekend."

"Okay. I'll try him then. Take care, sir."

"Good-bye, Mr. Perkins."

I stood and wandered a circle in the kitchen, leaving a trail
cigar smoke behind me in the shaft of sunlight. I tried to
inimize what Kraus had told me, and didn't get far. Special
ction Group. Surround and slaughter. Animals—

The phone rang. I snatched it up. "Perkins's March of Time
roductions, Ben speaking."

"You were s'posed to be here half an hour ago, asshole."

Aw, jeez. "That must be you, Dick. Nobody else addresses
e with such embarrassing reverence."

"I'm two drinks ahead of you already."

"Be there in thirty."

"By then it'll be four drinks. Bring money." He hung up.

Tradition has it that Novi got its name from its status as the
xth stop—NO. VI, the sign supposedly said—on the Detroit-
-Lansing railroad. I don't know if that's true. I do know
at, as recently as ten years ago, Novi was little more than a
llection of cow paths and a cluster of tiny little stores at
rand River and Novi Road.

But one of the many wonderful things I-275 has brought to
e far western suburbs of Detroit is a new, improved Novi,
omplete with cookie-cutter subdivisions, hotels, a regional
all, innumerable strip malls, and office/apartment complexes

carpeting the countryside. It's the latest magnet of an urba
flight that began after the 1943 riots and has proceeded lik
Sherman's march from Detroit through places like Dearborn
Livonia, and Southfield. When they've used up Novi, they
pull up stakes and move even farther west. I don't know wha
they'll do when they bump into the flight proceeding ea
from Battle Creek. They'll discover they've run out of Michi
gan, and God ain't making any more of it.

Pringle's is a remnant of Novi's more bucolic days. It onc
made a fine living serving burgers and beers to bikers an
truckers pulling in off Grand River. It's yupped itself up wit
a new coat of paint, but it still isn't what you'd call flossy. Ju
a long, low, flat-roofed place with booths and tables, a kitche
of sorts, and decent service. The location is convenient, th
prices are low, and the business is boozing.

Dick Dennehy and I have been meeting there once a wee
for God knows how long. We picked Pringle's because it
convenient for him, coming down from Lansing, and for m
running up from Belleville. Theoretically, Wednesday is th
appointed day, but the schedule frequently slips, as it ha
this week.

The Saturday lunch crowd was just clearing out when I g
there. Dick presided over our usual booth, second from th
end, left-hand side. He was nursing a rum and Coke, smok
ing a Lucky straight-end, and reading the *Detroit Free Pres*
when I slid into the booth across from him. "Hoddy," I said
"Sorry I'm late."

"You're forgiven," he grumped. He mashed the pape
together and pushed it over to the side. He's a big guy, a ta
overweight, with short gray-blond hair, a squarish face, an
aviator glasses. His gray suit doesn't fit all that well, but it
cheap. He doesn't try to look like anything but what he is
which is an inspector with the Michigan state police, assigne
to the Office of Special Investigations, whatever that is.

"I'm not as far ahead of you as I thought I'd be," Dick sai
as he signaled Cindy. She nodded and went to the bar. "I gc
caught up in the paper here, story about this Andelso
character. How 'bout him, huh?"

"Didn't see the paper today," I said, firing up a cigar.

"He's announced a march next Tuesday from Grand Circu
Park," Dick said, squinting as he drew on his weed, "down t
Hart Plaza. Gonna have a big rally there. Make a speec

out peace and tolerance for fellow man. Wants to 'defuse
cial and socioeconomic tensions' or some such shit. Fucking
oublemaker."

I grinned. "Have we lost our liberal ideals, Dick?"

"Politics got nothing to do with it. All it is is a police
roblem. Crowd control, traffic control. Stuff like this draws
ooks like pussy draws Marines. Pickpockets, smash-and-
abs. Then there's your loonies. You'll have counterdemon-
rations to deal with, waving their banners and shouting
eir slogans, and yelling 'Hi, Mom' to the Minicams."

I needled him. "Freedom of speech, freedom of assembly—"

"Details," he grunted, leaning back in the booth as Cindy
rought a Stroh's for me and a fresh rum and Coke for him.
/e thanked her, admired her profile as she scooted away,
en took a pull from our drinks and a draw from our smokes.
ike I said, we've been hanging around together for a long
me. "So," he said, "you track down your errant teenager
et?"

"No. And I'll tellya, this thing gets curiouser by the
inute."

He leaned forward. "Confide in Uncle Dick."

CHAPTER 19

I GAVE HIM THE short-form version: Kevin's interest in th
white-supremacy movement, the reception committee at th
Skinhead bar, the secret room at Justin Catlin's house
the references in Catlin's files to the trial of The Order peopl
as well as the highlighted comments about Richard Robertso
the man who got away. My presentation was by no mear
complete. I didn't tell Dick the name of the Skinhead bar, no
did I tell him where Catlin's house was. I also didn't mentio
the clipping I'd found in the file with Kevin's name on it.
didn't even want to think about that.

Dick's face was glacial, his gray eyes remote. "So you thin
Catlin's really this Robertson character?"

"Could be. Gives you pause, don't it?"

"Yeah. Wonder what he's up to."

"I don't know. I'd like to find out. And I'm not the onl
one."

"Whaddya mean?" Dick asked guardedly.

I braced myself and told him about my detention by th
squad of men led by the man who called himself Ponder.

Dick reacted as I'd expected. As he listened, he turne
pale, then flushed. He straightened in the booth and squashe
his cigarette out in the ashtray, turning it into pulp. When
finished, he glared at me and rasped, "So who the fuck ar
these people?"

"No idea." I picked up my beer and leaned back, conten
to let Dick spin along.

"It's not us. No way. And it's not the MBI either. They'r
too pussy; their big thing is computer crime and shit. And n

ay would those nine-to-fivers in AG fuck up their social lives
ith a round-the-clock."

"Golly, Dick," I teased. "The way you talk about the Michigan
ureau of Investigation and the attorney general's office,
ou'd think y'all don't work for the same state government."

He waved me away with a hard hand. "Ya know what it
unds like to me? It sounds like feds."

"That's my take, too."

"Fucking feds," Dick said.

"Which flavor, do you think?"

"It's got feds written all over it," he said, almost in a
ance.

I rapped the table. "Oh, Dick! Last bus leaving for Planet
arth, pal!"

He blinked twice and focused on me. "What was the
uestion?"

I repeated it.

"Oh Christ," he snorted. He picked up his drink, took a
be-clanking swig, and set it down hard. "Who can tell
ymore? They've used up the alphabet twice over. FBI,
ecret Service, CIA, DIA, DEA, ATF, fuck it, I don't know."

I drank some beer and smoked some cigar and kept my
outh shut, for once. The hook was set and I didn't want to
sturb it.

"I'll check around to make sure," Dick said pensively, "but
m about a hundred percent positive that we've had no
ficial word about any fed action like this. Which means," he
lled on, voice hardening, "they've snuck into my state. And
at just ain't kosher. They're s'posed to do us the courtesy of
tting us know. They're even s'posed to inquire first, just to
ake sure they won't trip over something we've got going.
ut that's the feds for you. Arrogant assholes. Think they own
e country."

"What about my theory?"

Dick arched his eyebrows. "About Robertson? Sure. Hits
me good notes. Congratulations, Ben. You might have got
e right for a change."

"Now wait a minute. Give me just one example of when I
ew one."

"Well, that Alex Farr business last winter," Dick said,
ressing out his cigarette. "Your judgment wasn't so swift on
at one."

"Yeah, but it came out all right," I retorted. "What are yo
going to do about this?"

Dick folded his arms and stared with glum anger past m
shoulder. "Not a hell of a lot we *can* do, way it stands nov
What I'd sure like to do is deal the feds out of the actio
somehow and take Catlin down myself. Be a hell of a goo
bust. Assuming Catlin is really Robertson, that is."

"Even if he is, I mean, so what?" Cindy, timing well hone
by years of experience, brought us a fresh round, took th
empties, and left. "Just another one of these right-win
white-supremacy nuts, right?"

Dick wrapped his large hands around his glass. "Th
'Order' outfit is more than that. Sure, they talk politics lor
and loud, but that's just for show, to pretty up their re,
motives, which are pretty boring. Rob banks and get ricl
Take away the political nonsense, and they're just garde
variety assholes."

I drank some beer and thought about "Special Action" an
Einsatzgruppen and wondered if Dick was off-base for once

"How 'bout you?" Dick asked. "What's the next step?"

"Find the kid," I said. "Bring him back to his dad."

"You don't think this Robertson thing changes the comple
ion any?"

"Might complicate things. I'll deal with that if and when
comes."

"But you don't know what he's up to," Dick said softl
"Might be wise to find out."

"That's the cop talking. Private detective is a differe
thing." I took a swallow of beer and looked into Dick's har
skeptical eyes. "In this work, I've learned you got to focu.
Do the job and get out. If you lose focus, you never get don
You move from one situation to the next one, and the job ge
bigger and bigger till you drown in it. You find yourself tryin
to change the world, which is impossible. Or people's mind
which is even harder. I don't have the time, energy, or desir
for any of that."

"Neither do cops. But that's what's expected of us."

"So you done lost the battle before it starts. Ulcer cit
Deal me out. I'll do what I said I'd do, and that's it."

Dick nodded. "What an idealist," he said.

"What do you mean?"

He smiled. "You're sitting there acting like you contro

events." He leaned forward. "But, just suppose—what if it
urns out that events control you?"

"Perkins's Housekeeping Service, Ben speaking."

"Ben? Lynne."

"Hey, kiddo, how're ya doing?"

"Oh, so-so. I hope I'm not interrupting anything, but—"

"Nah. Just trying to do something about this pigpen that I
call my apartment here."

"I tried to reach you earlier, but you must have been out."

"Yeah, had a meeting up in Novi, just got back a while ago.
What can I do you for?"

"Well... the news on Jerry isn't so good. He's declined
quite a bit just since you saw him."

"Oh, Christ. I'm sorry to hear that."

"Well, it's, um—it's what they predicted, so... they're
keeping him knocked out, pretty much."

"How can I help?"

"... Are you getting anywhere finding Kevin?"

"Well, I've got a lead. I had to put a man out undercover to
work it. I'm waiting to hear. Best I can tell you."

"Do you think you'll find him?"

"Guaranteed."

"When?"

"That's the tricky part. I won't lie to you, there's no
predicting. It's full-court press, Lynne. I guarantee that."

"Well, I know you're doing all you can.... There's something you can do for me."

"Name it."

"Forgive me for being such a bitch the other day."

"Nothing to forgive, kid."

"Oh yes there is. I was so nasty to you."

"I been bitched out worse. I had a mom once."

"You're doing so much for us. I'll never be able to thank
you enough. I'm trying to be strong, but this is—so hard. I'm
afraid to be alone. I want my boy back."

"I'll get him for you."

"I know. Thank you. That's the best I can do right
now."

"Hang in there, babe."

"Good-bye."

* * *

"Perkins's Detroit Tigers Fan Club, Ben speaking."

"This is Carole."

"Hey, how's the legal eagle?"

"Aside from being afraid to drive my car with the exhaust system about to fall off, fine. How're you?"

"Tigers eight, Angels four, top of the ninth. Next question?"

"No question. Just an update."

"Shoot."

"Bad news first. Your preliminary hearing is set for two o'clock Friday in Judge Archbold's courtroom. Same place as the arraignment, Twenty-ninth District Court in Wayne. Be there."

"Yeah, okay."

"In your best suit, please."

"Aw shit, I was planning to wear a tank top and cutoffs. Jesus Christ, Carole."

"Well, with you it pays to make sure. Now for the good news. I suspect the worst you're going to get is a good chewing out and a dismissal."

"You work that for me, dear heart, and I'll personally buy you the biggest, juiciest steak dinner in Detroit. Just name the place."

"The Whitney will do nicely. But—"

"I was thinking more on the order of Denny's, frankly, but okay. This is great news, Carole.'

"It's not a hundred percent certain. There've been no official discussions. But I don't think the assistant DA really wants the case. He knows also that there's a good chance it'll be thrown out in circuit court once it's handed up there for trial. All we have to worry about now is Judge Archbold. She may not see it the same way."

"Well, reason with her. Marshal your best legal arguments. Throw a hissy, yank her hair, scratch her eyes out. Whatever."

"Ha ha. You're *such* a riot. Now what about the exhaust system?"

"How about tomorrow evening, barring the unforeseen?"

"Fine. We'll see you then."

"Perkins's Perfect Pizza Parlor, Ben speaking."

"Well hi there, lover."

"Oh, hi, Barb."

"Eating dinner?"

"Just finishing up."

"Are you busy later?"

"Pretty much, yeah."

"That case you're on must be pretty intense."

"Yeah, it is."

"I'm getting sort of lonesome, hon."

"I'm sorry. Can't help it right now."

"What's the matter? You sound down."

"It's not you. I'm just—I'm expecting another call. On the case. I'm getting pretty worried."

"Oh. Well, I'll let you go."

"You take care, Barb."

"'Bye."

"H'lo."

"Aw, *fuck*! Wrong number!" SLAM.

The phone hummed in my ear. I clumsily tossed it back onto the cradle, sat up, kicked off the sheet, and turned on the bedside lamp. The squarish orange numerals of the clock said 12:02. "Aw, fuck" was what Brian had said. Translation: 1:00 A.M. Just enough time to get into position.

I got out of bed and hoofed over to the closet. The old body sent messages to the effect that you didn't get a decent night's sleep the night before, idiot, and here you are cutting this one short. Fuck it, I thought half numbly. Detective's a twenty-four-hour-a-day profession. I dressed quickly in my night operations outfit—black corduroy pants, heavy black work shoes, black long-sleeve turtleneck top. Then I reached my .45 automatic down from the top shelf.

I'd actually cleaned, oiled, and reloaded it today. I stepped into the dim bedroom light and gave it the once-over. Seven rounds in the clip, one under the hammer. Perfect. I tucked it under the waistband of my pants against my spine and untucked my shirt to conceal it. Then I left the apartment and vanished into the soft, dark, deceptively peaceful, summerlike night.

CHAPTER 20

A SMALL SUBDIVISION SITS on the north side of North-line just west of the Allen Road intersection at the Taylor-Southgate border. The first street in goes east about a hundred feet and dead-ends at the Detroit, Toledo, & Ironton Railroad right-of-way. From the cul-de-sac you get a good view of Northline Road traffic for maybe half a mile. But the subdivision houses all face away from it, which means you can sit there virtually unobserved.

I reached the cul-de-sac at 12:45 and parked facing out, the railroad tracks with their weird cement arches at my back. The sky was black and almost starless; the moon was a golden half-pie sitting starkly in the sky, making the landscape look bright once your eyes had become accustomed to it. I leaned back in the Mustang's bucket seat, lighted a cigar, and smoked in the silence, keeping an eye on Northline Road.

It being very early Sunday morning, traffic was light. Wouldn't pick up till very late morning, except possibly for a burst around two A.M., closing time for the bars. I watched a station wagon go by, then a pickup, then a couple of sedans. Finally, after several minutes of nothing, a sedan with the vague outlines of a Chevy Nova went by, headed west. Its left turn indicator was blinking. Bingo.

I watched it disappear into the distance. No other cars came along in its trail. Good, he'd shaken himself loose. Presently it appeared again, coming eastbound. I switched on my headlights, then switched them off. The car swung north into the subdivision, slowed, then came east again toward me. It was the Nova, all right. It pulled in behind the Mustang and shut down.

Footsteps approached as I leaned over and opened the
passenger-side door. Brian slid in about halfway, leaving his
legs and feet dangling outside. The grin on his long, innocent
face looked relieved. "Hey, Ben," he said, "it worked like a
charm, huh?"

"Welcome back to the world, kid. How's it going?"

He yawned and stretched. "Pretty good, I'd say. You know,
this is a hell of a good meeting spot. How'd you find it?"

I gestured vaguely toward the subdivision houses. "Had a
lady friend lived back in there once."

"So," he said, smiling, "you've had late-night meetups here
more'n once. What happened to her?"

"I don't know. You drift apart, you lose track." I reached my
cigar out the window and knocked ash off. "Fill me in. You
found Kevin?"

"Well, I've seen him."

I felt a surge of relief. I'd had the vague, nagging fear that
Kevin was lying dead in a ditch somewhere. "Okay, you talk
to him? You give him the word?"

"Well, I—" He looked at me. "Can I just tell you this in
order, instead of bouncing around?"

"Okay, I'll shut up or something."

He slouched in the bucket seat and stifled a yawn with his
fist. "First I got a room at that place on Trenton. Not as nice
as Norwegian Wood, but what the hell."

"You want to do detective, you gotta sacrifice, kid."

His innocent face made a smile that was not so innocent.
"There's this woman there, Carrie somebody—"

"Carrie Longstreet. Yeah, I met her. She can park her
sandals under my cot anytime."

"Oo. I mean to tell you."

"Careful, now. No dipping your wick on the job."

He laughed nervously. "I wouldn't do that anyway. I got
Debra, remember? Well, anyway, last night I went up to The
Loading Zone, hung around there till they closed."

"Have yourself a festive evening?"

"More like bored shitless. For a while, anyway. And what a
sucking dive that place is. Till around ten or so all that came
in was Joe Sixpacks from the neighborhood."

"Careful now. I'm a Joe Sixpack myself, and proud of it."

"Like hell. Like I said, around ten the place started to fill

up. Skinheads. I got to talking to a couple of them. Prett
nice guys."

"Oh yeah. Sweethearts."

"No, really," Brian said earnestly. "They were real nice t
me, anyhow. Clued me right in on stuff. They got thi
greeting: 'Eight eight.' Stands for the eighth letter of th
alphabet. H-H. Heil Hitler."

"Cute, if not especially clever," I said. "You bring up Kevi
at all?"

"No. I did just like you said. Didn't mention Kevin o
anything else, just told 'em I'd moved into the neighborhoo
and all that. They bought it, no questions asked."

"How about the Nazi stuff? Much talk of that?"

"Oh man, every other word was nigger, kike, Jew-bastard
whatever." Brian looked out the side window. "They have thi
little ceremony they begin meetings with. Read what the
call a Declaration of War written by some guy name o
Mathews. I gather he got killed by the cops or something
He's like some kind of God to them. Hitler, too. One gu
called Hitler a reincarnated prophet from the Bible."

"Uh-huh."

"That made me uncomfortable. Because they said thos
things so casually. One guy was talking about piling up skull
in Hart Plaza. Just real singsong and offhand. And they ha
music playing on the jukebox, called it 'oi' music, Britis
heavy-metal shit. One song was called 'Nigger, Nigger.' An
other one called 'Prisoner of Peace,' about some old krau
named Hess."

"Hm. One of Hitler's last surviving old pals."

"Lots of other songs. I can't remember all the words. Lot o
'em talked about 'mud people' and what was gonna happen t
them." He looked back at me. "You think mud people mean
blacks and Jews and stuff?"

"Nonwhites, I guess. Come on, get to Kevin."

"Didn't see him last night. But I heard a guy ask abou
him, where he was. The bartender said Kevin would b
around tonight probably. So I let it go at that and went home
To the rooming house, I mean."

"Good. You didn't get overanxious."

"I called you to set up a meet, but there was no answer.

"Yeah, I was out." I took a hot final toke on my cigar
opened the door, dropped the butt on the pavement, an

essed it out with my heel. I looked at Kevin, whose long,
ndsome face and close-shaved blond head seemed to gleam
the moonlight. "Want to get out and walk?"

"Yeah. Great. Getting stuffy in here."

"Careful, don't slam the doors."

East of the circular cul-de-sac was a narrow berm coated
ith long grass; then the railroad right-of-way rose to the
acks. I ambled that way and Brian tagged along. "You went
ack to The Loading Zone tonight?" I asked quietly.

"Uh-huh," Brian said, skipping over the curbstone. "Same
eal as last night. Joe Sixpacks till ten, Skinheads after that.
evin turned up at midnight."

"The witching hour," I murmured. We ascended the rail-
ad right-of-way and stopped on the tracks, which glowed
ully in the moonlight. We were on a section of straight track
at shot north toward Detroit and south toward Toledo,
ecorated here with narrow cement arches every thirty feet
: so. The sight was eerie. Sixty-year-old dreams gone wrong—

"What are those arches for?" Brian asked.

I laughed uneasily. "Well, this is the Detroit, Toledo, and
onton Railroad, once owned by old Henry Ford. Back in
e early twenties, Mr. Ford had this idea of converting it to
lectricity. I think his buddy Thomas Edison was in on the
:heme. Didn't work out, I gather. These arches were for
arrying the electrical lines."

Brian stood still, hands on hips, looking one way, then the
ther. "Wow. Spooky, ain't it."

"Tell me about Kevin."

"Okay." He took a deep breath. "I was shootin' shit with a
uple of guys. Trying to keep my ears open and my mouth
aut, which you said is an advanced skill for the private
etective—"

"And takes years to master," I said. "I still haven't managed
completely."

He laughed. "Anyhow, it was just past midnight when I
ealized that Kevin was there. He was over at the bar, talking
the bartender. I mean to tell you, my heart about stopped,
en. I kept thinking, 'Here you are, you son of a bitch.' I
anted to do a flying tackle, like back in high school, and
ke him down."

"So what did you do?"

"Just sat there and watched him. I figured I'd work out

some way to bump into him, strike up a conversation. But
never got the chance."

My heart fell. So close, goddamn it. "He split?"

"Not right then," Brian said, surprised. "He wandered th
room, real slow, looking at everybody. I felt his eyes burnin
through me as he went by. Then he closed the front doo
dropped the security bar across it. Somebody pulled the plu
on the juke and everybody shut up all at once, as if somebod
had hit an off button somewhere."

I folded my arms. Brian picked up a chunk of gravel an
tossed it in his hand.

"Kevin started talking," Brian said. "I couldn't figure out
lot of it, but—"

"Just tell me what he said." I tried to keep the tension ou
of my voice, but failed.

"Okay," Brian said hastily. "He talked about somethin
called the Special Action."

Bingo. I closed my eyes briefly and took a deep breath
"Okay."

"I didn't know what he meant. I still don't know. But h
said it's on for soon. That the Special Action Group is down t
serious training at the Bunker."

"Bunker" rang an eerie bell, too. It was the term Solomo
Kraus had used for the death-house at Buchenwald. I kep
that to myself and asked Brian, "What the hell is that?"

"I don't know! I just don't, Ben. Everybody seemed t
understand. I couldn't raise my hand like in a classroor
and—"

"I know, kid. Don't mean to nag you. Go ahead."

Brian tossed the rock higher in the air and caught it. "H
kept referring to 'Number One.' A person called Numbe
One, the big boss, I guess."

I had the sudden strong certainty that "Number One" wa
Justin Catlin, née Richard Robertson, federal fugitive. He'
been preparing the Special Action up in Register. Now h
was in Detroit.

"Kevin told us time was getting short. If any of us wante
in, to strike a blow for the oppressed Aryans, we knew wha
we had to do to qualify." He threw the rock up the right-of
way. It became invisible and landed with a faint clatter.

"So how do you qualify?" I asked quietly. "Do you know?"

"I didn't then," Brian said without looking at me. "But ter Kevin left, I asked one of the guys."

"What did he say?"

Brian turned slowly and faced me. "To join the Special ction Group, you have to kill a nigger or a Jew."

This didn't surprise me. In fact, it was the first thing Brian ad said that seemed to fit. I said, "Not choosy, huh?"

"Jesus!" He walked toward me. "They're talking *killing* eople, Ben."

"I know, I know." I gestured toward the cars and we kittered down the embankment, which gave me time to link through the options. "What you do now is, go home."

"Okay," Brian said at once. "I rented the room for a week, —"

"Not the rooming house," I said. "I mean home. Norwegian Vood. Right now."

We reached the Mustang. Brian stopped stock-still at the ack end and folded his arms, back arched, glaring at me. Why the hell should I do that? The job isn't done yet. We on't know where Kevin is."

"Sure we do. He's at some place called the Bunker, cook- ag up mischief that I don't want you involved in, kid."

"I'm no fucking kid," he spat.

"Tone it down. Don't want to attract attention." I went to ne driver's-side door, reached in for a cigar, and came out rith match flaring. "This is bad shit going down, Brian," I aid, puffing the cigar to life. "You walk. That's final."

"I'm real surprised at you, Ben." His young voice was more ngry than disappointed. "I never seen you turn tail before."

"I'm not turning tail. I'm pressing on. It's you that's istory. Thanks awfully, and all that."

"Fuck you. If you're still in, I'm still in."

"Oh yeah?" I asked, voice dripping with sarcasm. "So hat's your plan, Mr. Marlowe?"

He missed the reference. "Well, I'll keep hanging around nere evenings, try to talk to Kevin, find out where this unker is. Whatever they're doing, we got to stop it."

"Oh yeah?" I shot back. "What are you going to do, whack black or a Jew so you can get in?"

"Well, no."

"This is too dangerous." I knocked ash off my cigar and

stepped toward him, menace in my gait. "I don't want yo
hurt."

"I'm no different from you," he retorted. "I took this jo
and I'm staying with it. Period."

I hung my cigar in my teeth and leaned on the Mustang
ragtop, watching him.

"So what about it?" he demanded, finally.

I felt slightly ill. Reverse psychology is effective, but
didn't like using it on Brian. "All right. Here's what we'll do
First, you will kill no blacks, and no Jews either."

"Boy, am I relieved."

"During the day, I want you to stay out of sight. Tomorro
night, go back to The Loading Zone and do like you bee
doing. Get a line on where we can find Kevin."

"He's at the Bunker," Brian said. "How am I going to fin
the Bunker without joining this Special Action Group? An
how'm I going to do that without killing—"

"You let me do the thinking. That's what I get paid for."

"Okay." He seemed to study me in the near darkness. "
don't get this. Don't you want to stop these guys, whateve
they're doing?"

"Number one, with what?" I shot back. "You and me
We're good, but we ain't that good, and I don't see recruit
lining up at my door. Number two, we don't know what thes
jokers are really up to. Number three, we got our hands fu
just getting done what we been hired to do; I ain't biting o
more. Number four, the city of Detroit has a pretty big polic
department. They can handle whatever trouble these clown
are planning."

After a long silence, Brian growled, "Oh, you are such
bullshit artist. You can't kid me, I've known you too long. Yo
wanna take 'em, mister. And all by yourself, if you ca
manage it."

"No way, kid. I dropped the avenging angel act long ago."

"Fuckin' bullshit artist."

I dropped my cigar to the pavement and squashed it dead
"Get going," I said. "And stay in touch. You know the drill."

Brian sauntered to the door of his Nova. "I just want to sa
one thing."

"Fire away."

He pulled the door open and leaned on its top, his fac

uminated in the moonlight. "However this comes out, I've
?ver in my life felt so good about what I'm doing."

I tried to keep my feeling of profound uneasiness out of my
?ice. "Well, good. Take care now. Watch your back."

He dropped into the car, shut the door, fired up the
?gine, and rolled away. I got into the Mustang and watched
s taillights disappear east on Northline Road, bound for
?etroit. When he was gone, I started the motor, rolled over
? Northline Road, and sat at the intersection for a moment.

I felt guilty about the way I'd manipulated him. I felt I
?ould be the one going east, into unknown trouble, and he
?ould be headed west, toward home. I thought through the
?vents leading up to this moment and decided that there
?ally was no other way, no other way at all.

I swung out onto Northline Road, headed west, toward
?me.

The reasoning should have made me feel better, but some-
?w it didn't.

CHAPTER 21

Though I slept in till eight, I woke up tired and grumpy. Even my trusty old morning routine failed to energize me. I gulped steadily at a pot of coffee, smoked cigars, read indifferently through the Sunday *Free Press*. Nothing soothed the itch, dulled the edge.

I went out onto the small wood deck and leaned on the rail. Lighted a fresh cigar. Existed there in the early Sunday morning silence, vaguely feeling the sunshine and the balmy breeze, and sorted through the jumble of facts, rumors, and feelings that roamed my mind like nervous little men.

Presently, I confronted the essential problem. And it wasn't pretty. I'd been kidding myself thus far. I was not content with a little piece of the action. I wanted the whole enchilada, and I wanted it for myself.

Okay, I admit it was stupid. Ego and vanity had taken precedence over a cold assessment of facts and capabilities. Even worse, I was clearly exceeding my area of responsibility.

Once again I fought the feeble fight. Now listen here, Benjy old son, you stupid son of a bitch: you're a private detective. That's all that you are. You're not a center-stage man. You work the dirty little corners, just in from the wings. You pop onstage for a fleeting moment and do your five-word line, or your minor piece of business, and then you're gone again. In this you're no different from 98 percent of the population. And you're certainly no better. You don't star in the plays, let alone write them. It's nothing to be ashamed of.

By accident, you've wandered into a scene from which the star is absent. That doesn't mean you have to take the lead. You can hand it off. You'd be an idiot not to.

But I was so goddamned angry. That made it personal. And
e anger would always be there if I didn't act upon the
ea that had come to me on the drive home from meeting
ian, that had interrupted my sleep repeatedly during the
ght, that sat on the front ledge of my mind right now.

I mentally fondled the idea for long minutes, stared at it in
mb amazement, then trudged back inside to the telephone.

Setting up the meet was like trying to arrange a cozy
nner between Shimon Peres and Yasser Arafat. But much to
y surprise, I got agreement after maybe six phone calls.

Next I pulled together some household supplies and food
gredients and played Julia Child for a while, mixing, blend-
g, experimenting, till I had formulated an old jelly jar full of
juid that was just dense enough and red enough to pass
spection.

Then I went to my closet, elected one of my white dress
irts to make the ultimate sacrifice, and ripped and tore at it
l it looked just right.

By now the morning was running out on me. I packed the
uff, not forgetting my .45 automatic, and left my apartment
a fast trot.

The ramp from eastbound Michigan Avenue to northbound
elegraph Road was backed up bumper to bumper. I pounded
e steering wheel and cursed. This was Sunday afternoon,
iouldn't be this kind of traffic. Then we stopped entirely,
id I sighed explosively and leaned back in the seat. Gonna
e late, goddamn it, and that could blow the whole thing.

Then for no particular reason I glanced at the rearview
iirror and saw a motorcyclist hard on my bumper. I looked
head, then back into the mirror. Hm. I'd seen him before.

He drove a black Kawasaki, one of the bigger ones. He
ore jeans and a sleeveless denim jacket. His helmet was
ietallic red and equipped with a black wraparound visor that
ompletely hid his face. His hand twisted the throttle grip
ervously as we sat there, gunning the engine: *yin-yin*-YIN!

Could be I was dreaming, but I could have sworn I'd seen him
ull out behind me on Belleville Road, fifteen minutes earlier.

The traffic started to move, and we finished the curve
umping us onto Telegraph Road. I passed the reason for the
elay—a young woman in hot pants and tank top changing
ne tire of a red Chrysler Laser convertible—and powered up

into fourth gear, flinging the Mustang into the left-hand la
of the six-lane boulevard. The Kow shot past me to the rig
and ahead of me a ways, then slowed to pace me. I watche
him as we came up on the Cherry Hill intersection. If he w
in fact tailing me, he was either extra cute or extra stupi
trying to do it from ahead.

I decided to waste a few minutes on a test. I sudden
stood on the brakes, downshifted, and slid hard to the le
swinging into a U-turn lane that crossed the median over
the southbound side. My timing was good and the sout
bound traffic was light, and I was able to power out the
without stopping. I took the center southbound lane an
slowed to the speed limit, watching the mirror. Nothing.

I was passing the Dearborn Heights Golf and Count
Club, nearing the Michigan Avenue intersection again ar
scolding myself for my paranoia, when I picked up the Ko
in the rearview mirror, slaloming between cars and coming
me like a bullet. He slowed abruptly as he reached me, we
past, and fell into sync with me again, about fifty feet ahea
as we went beneath the Michigan Avenue underpass.

No license plate. Well, if that wasn't a tip-off, what was

Fine, then. I'd be late for the meeting, but the guys'd ju
have to wait, something they ought to be used to. I was goir
to run this creep to ground and find out what gave. I turne
off the radio, smashed out my cigar, tightened my seat bel

Then I jammed the shifter into third, floored the gas, ar
shrieked the Mustang into the center lane, charging tl
Kow's tail.

He must have been watching me in one of the tw
rearview mirrors, because he goosed the bike as soon as l
saw me coming. I stepped the Mustang up to 75 and ke]
pace with him, wondering what the Kow's top end was. Mir
was 140 and change all day long, so speed, comparative
speaking, was no factor. The factors were maneuverability,
which he had plenty more than me, and guts, which remaine
to be tested.

Telegraph's three southbound lanes were lightly sprinkle
with Sunday traffic, mostly oldsters pedaling four-wheele
sedately home from church. The Kow zipped adroitly amor
them, waggling his tail as he lane-changed. I kept up wit
him pretty well, charging his tail whenever I had a clear sho
as we crossed the southern frontier of Dearborn and entere

arborn Heights. I sat loose and comfortable in the bucket
, hands at ten-to-two on the wheel, right foot working the
, left planted on the floorboard an inch from the clutch
lal, eyes glued to the biker, waiting for him to screw up or
unlucky. I wasn't choosy. I'd cream him from behind,
wd him from the side, anything to break up his rhythm
l force him down. He had maneuverability on his side, but
ad the Mustang. I couldn't be brought down by a grease
·k, an errant bird, a bee flying into my shirt.

Telegraph's traffic lights are synchronized, meaning you
. take them green if you stick close to the speed limit. We
ren't, and the first traffic light into Dearborn Heights was
ning red as we approached it. The Kow saw his chance,
:d the left-turn-only lane to dodge a car waiting at the
.pe, and shot across the intersection just ahead of an
vancing row of vehicles. I had no prayer of doing the same
ng, and the center and right lanes were ganged up with a
iting dump truck and a line of cars waiting to turn right. I
erved left, downshifted, jumped the curb onto the grassy
·dian, floorboarded it, and hurled the car into the intersec-
n, my eyes taking microscopic pictures, my mind calculat-
; angles and inches.

And I'd have made it clean except that one of the crossing
·s took more time than he should have clearing the inter-
:tion. Stupid slowpoke sumbitch. No time to discuss it with
n now. I swerved right to miss him and damned near lost
The Mustang hurtled at an angle toward a filling station on
· far right-hand corner. If I'd hit the brakes, I'd have locked
r up, and that would have been all. Instead, I punched gas,
;ained some semblance of control, and hurled the car
aight toward the corner, seeking the gap between a light
le and a guy wire. Instinctively I ducked as the Mustang
nped the curb and plowed airborne through an assortment
freestanding signs advertising gas prices, a tire sale, and
·e car wash with an eight-gallon fill-up. Metal exploded as
:ns shot into the air on all sides. I landed and jinked left,
ir wheels spinning and smoking, and dived back onto
legraph ahead of an angrily honking pickup truck, thinking,
od. World can always use a little less sign clutter.

The Kow was a quarter mile down in the center lane, still
.uling ass. I felt moist under my shirt now as I slungshot the
ustang up to sixty and grabbed fourth, dodging vehicles by

inches as I edged the deep-dish wheel left and right
expected the Kow to pour on gas, which he did. I a
expected him to take the right lane, but he didn't. Inste
he swerved over into the left lane directly into my path
didn't let up. I was going to power him right onto the med
if I could. I had a vision of how it would be: bike and bil
becoming separate cartwheels in the sunshine—he was box
in ahead of me, passing a double-bottom UPS truck, j
inches away from impact now—

He swerved hard left and roared onto the median whe
the curbstone had worn away. Without hesitating I did
same. He cleared the gentle crown of the median and plung
down the other side toward the oncoming traffic, jumped t
curb, and crossed to the center lane. I kept the median til
car had gone by and then clattered onto the left lane, head
south on the northbound side. There were no more nor
bound cars; the I-94 interchange was coming up, and I cou
see a lineup of grilles waiting like football players at a r
light just beyond the overpass. Deciding to give the Ko
something to think about, I powered forward, aimed at
angle toward the motorcycle, intending to finish it rig
there. He lunged forward, as I careened left, and swerv
right, missing me by inches. I corrected to take him from t
left and just missed him again. We roared under the I-
overpass just as the light ahead turned green. Several ca
advanced toward us. The Kow swung right just past t
bridge and reentered the southbound lanes. I did the san
hot on his tail, as we chased through the intersection
green.

The Kow didn't hesitate for a second. He took the fi
left-turn lane and banked hard, booted leg out for balanc
and shot straight across northbound Telegraph. Now
downshifted and stomped the brakes, locking them ha
feeding enough wheel to put me into a semicontrolled broa
side skid with the front end turning to the left. At the rig
instant I floored the gas to break the skid and with two ha
moves of the wheel corrected and straightened. My mo
wasn't quite as slick as his. I got into the turn all right, but I
the curb and careened over the last small patch of medi
into the northbound lanes. The Kow was beelining into
bank driveway as a northbound car squealed and shrieked
my appearance, veering to my right with a bouncing hop on

he median. I beat the rest of the cars across Telegraph and
not into the bank driveway as the Kow disappeared around
he side of the building.

Thank God it was Sunday; bank was closed. I roared
round the bank, going through the auto-teller lanes the
wrong way. The Kow had circled the bank and dived onto
northbound Telegraph. I did the same, cutting in front of a
anker truck and playing dodge 'em with a gang of weekend
bikers who trailed the procession of a 1957 Chevy club.

As I broke free of the procession, I saw the Kow beating
gears northbound in the left-hand lane. It was clean and
green between me and him and I ate up the distance quickly,
hunched over the wheel now with every muscle and tendon
locked like a vise. What now, asshole? Show me your best
moves, we ain't done nothing yet. A station wagon pulling a
rickety trailer was hogging the center lane, and the Kow
zipped past him and then slalomed right, crossing all lanes
and plummeting up the entrance ramp to eastbound I-94. I
braked briefly, banked the Mustang right, and nipped the
green indicator sign as I just barely made the ramp, too. Not
bad.

But this, I thought as I powered up to seventy, is your big
mistake, mister. Taking the freeway was playing to my strength,
not to his. I forced myself to loosen up as I left the entrance
ramp chute and poured out onto the expressway. The Kow
was a hundred yards ahead in the right lane, and I drew up
toward him, feeling the big 302 motor rumble hungrily,
begging for more. Stay with it, old gal, we got him now.

Orange signs warned of construction as I advanced on the
Southfield Freeway interchange. The right lane was pinched
off by an angling line of orange cones. The Kow obediently
merged left, and I followed suit. I knew that the Southfield
Freeway interchange was closed, having been under recon-
struction since the dawn of time. There were no more exits
till Oakwood Boulevard, two miles ahead. Plenty of time, I
had him boxed in; the freeway was walled by high cement
New Jersey-type barricades on both sides. He couldn't get
off, he couldn't turn back, and I'd match his mph with my
mph any time.

I closed the distance steadily. The Kow beelined along in
the right lane and I kept the left, intending to flank him and
then edge him right, right, right, till his choice was either to

stop or be smeared into spaghetti fixings on the cement wall
The orange cones gave way to black-and-white sawhorse
topped with blinking orange lights as we hit the construction
zone. I knew what he was going to do the instant he did it
He jumped right with perfect timing between two of th
sawhorses and whipped onto the new ramp headed toward
the northbound Southfield, beneath a sign that said EXIT
CLOSED.

My response wasn't nearly as pretty. I crushed three of th
sawhorses, sending wood and metal and yellow light fixture
scattering across the roadway and doing God knew what to
my front end. But I made the ramp, hanging fifty feet bacl
on the Kow's tail. The new cement beneath us was white and
clean and still a bit rough as we curved to the left, the ramp
ascending to cross over I-94, cement walls rising on both
sides of us. The Kow plunged over the crown of the ramp.

As I did the same, I saw at last why the state highwa
department seemed to prefer that no one use this exit ramp
just yet.

CHAPTER 22

THE PAVEMENT ENDED A hundred yards ahead. Just flat-out ended. Beyond that, the roadbed, if you want to call it that, consisted of loose gravel topped by a dense crisscross grid of heavy iron bars. Gigantic yellow paving machines stood around idle. There seemed to be a drop-off where the pavement and its flanking barricades ended, and nowhere to go on either side, nowhere suitable for a 1971 Mustang, anyway. The Kow didn't have that problem. He shot through the gap between the barricade and the drop-off and rolled down the embankment out of sight.

I was too busy to care. The instant I saw the drop-off I hit the brakes as hard as I dared and downshifted into third. The Mustang engine bellowed and screamed as its RPM redlined, and the seat belt squeezed my midsection like a toothpaste tube as the car shimmied and skewed and smoked, threatening at any instant to break loose and spin and ricochet off the New Jersey barricades like a pinball in a chute. Somehow I kept the wheels from locking up completely and the car slid half sideways, slowing but still at frightening speed, closer closer closer to the drop-off, and then KA-CHUNK the left front wheel dropped off the edge as the car came to rest and the engine choked dead.

My hands were trembling as I opened the door and stepped out on weak legs. I'd hoped the Kow had bought the farm at the bottom of the embankment—a street bike like that is worthless in such situations—but no such luck. He'd made the bottom of the embankment all right and was bouncing along the hard, grassy ground between piles of construction supplies toward the shoulder of westbound I-94.

When he reached pavement, he kicked her ahead, merge
into traffic, and waved the single-digit salute at me by way o
farewell.

Well, shit. I still didn't know who he was or why he ha
followed me. All I knew was that he'd outsmarted me. Thi
time, anyway.

I walked around the Mustang. The grille and the nose o
the hood showed nicks and dings from their encounters wit
ad signs and sawhorses. Something had caught the leadin
edge of the ragtop on the passenger side and ripped a six-inc
gash in it. I'd also lost the right sealed beam. Otherwise, n
problems. I inspected the front end, which leaned dow
slaunchways. The left front wheel hung free over the edge o
the two-foot drop-off; the car was resting on the axle. I hope
to hell I hadn't torn up the front end too bad.

I got in the car and fired it up. The engine's rumbl
seemed disgruntled. Pilot error, old gal; sorry. I put her i
reverse, turned the wheel so the tire was perpendicular t
the drop-off, and babied her back. A slight grinding sound
and then the front end popped up, and I was on all four
again. I turned and looked out the rear window as I backe
the car slowly up the ramp, around and down toward th
eastbound side of the freeway.

As I got onto the freeway headed eastbound, I realized th
entire chase had taken less than fifteen minutes. Gawd
Perkins, I thought, you can sure pack a lot of fun into lif
when you try. Too bad it came to nothing. I looped off th
freeway at Oakwood and got back on I-94 westbound
headed for Telegraph again, wondering if I'd be late for th
meeting.

I wasn't. The Denny's restaurant at Eight Mile and Fiv
Points looked pretty deserted; the Sunday lunch crowd mus
have just checked out. I pulled into the lot and stopped i
the center on the Eight Mile side, surveying the parked cars
There, that one at the end: a newer gray Plymouth sedan
Might as well have had one of those pizza-delivery signs o
the roof that said UNMARKED COP. So Elvin was here, waitin
inside, most likely getting impatient. Tough shit. I had thing
to do just yet.

I scanned the lot, sizing up my options, then wheeled th

Mustang around and back along the Five Points side to where three brown Dumpsters overflowed God knows what onto the weedy gravel. Beyond there was some open space next to an outlet onto Five Points. I parked the Mustang facing the street, primed for an instant getaway, which, if everything went right, I'd definitely need.

Before getting out I checked my .45, verified that it was loaded, tucked it into the waistband of my pants against my spine, and pulled my shirttail down to conceal it. Then I got out, deliberately left the Mustang unlocked, retrieved the small sack out of the trunk, and strolled along the parking lot to the gray Plymouth. Its windows were open; trusting soul. I tossed the sack onto the floorboard on the passenger side, stood back to size up the situation again, then went into the restaurant.

Elvin Dance sat as animated as a Buddha in a corner booth, gazing dully out the window toward Eight Mile Road. Today he wore a three-piece chalk white suit over a luminous blue regimental tie. His gold-glinting cocoa hands were folded around a full coffee cup, and a carafe stood waiting off to the side next to an ashtray that held a Kool cigarette smoldering alongside three crushed-out mates. Elvin's round, lined, glowering dark face remained frozen, and his eyes hardly flickered as I approached him. "You're late, man."

"Well, nice to see you, too, Elvin," I replied, sliding into the booth across from him.

Gold twinkled as he grinned for no reason and took a heavy hit off his cigarette. "This better be good, I got no time to frig around."

I took a cigar out of my shirt pocket. "Don't worry, it's important." A waitress swept to the table, took my order for coffee, and disappeared. I fired up the cigar with a wood match flared on my thumbnail. "Sunday duty must be a bitch."

The Detroit police captain grimaced. "I don't hardly notice it anymore. Been pulling Sunday duty for two years." His voice went harder, louder. "Where the hell's that pal of yours?"

"He'll be here," I answered patiently. My coffee arrived and I took a sip. "He might be having trouble finding this place. Not exactly convenient for him, coming down from Lansing."

"Tough shit. Them glamor boys is on their own, far as I'm concerned."

This didn't bode well, but I let it pass. "Why'd you insist on this place, anyhow? Would have been a lot easier for everybody out west farther, like Farmington or Novi or—"

Elvin's eyes burned like the end of his cigarette. "Look out that window, Perkins. Look around you. What do you see?"

I looked out. "Nothing special."

He poked a finger toward the window. "That's Eight Mile Road. The boundary between the city of 'Troit and Southfield." He pointed in my direction. "Over there is Five Points. The boundary between city of 'Troit and Redford."

I was beginning to get the point. "Aw, jeez."

He looked away from me. "I don't leave the city of 'Troit anytime 'cept in an emergency. This don't qualify as no emergency. You said you wanted to meet at a place convenient both to me and to your buddy, who's coming down from Lansing. I was happy to oblige. This here corner is as far north and as far west as you can get without leaving the city of 'Troit. Fair enough?"

"Hey, you bent over backwards, Elvin. Thanks."

He flicked fingers at me. "You fuckin' suburbanites and out-staters, what do you know?" He made that inappropriate grin again and did an excellent imitation of an announcer voice. "But anyway, welcome to Detroit, Mr. Perkins; we're glad to have you!"

"Thanks." I studied him through cigar smoke. Hard to believe, but Elvin Dance seemed to be going squirrel. I felt sorry for him. I also had the distasteful, yet appealing, thought that I could use it. This thought was disrupted by a hard poke in my back.

I looked up to see Dick Dennehy towering over me. "Hi, guys," he said jauntily, then looked over at Elvin, who hadn't stood, hadn't even changed expression. "So you're the DPD flatfoot, huh?"

The men stared at each other. I was struck by the contrast. On the one hand you had Dick Dennehy: tall, out of shape, cheaply dressed Caucasian out-stater. On the other you had Elvin Dance: squat, heavily muscled, expertly tailored black Detroiter. They had only two things in common: They were both police detectives and they both knew me. I knew that neither fact guaranteed instant friendship, nor even a spirit of cooperation. I'd settle for the latter, if by some miracle I could get it.

Elvin's eyes were hooded as he growled at Dick: "My name's Dance. Detroit police homicide."

"Dennehy. State police OSI." Dick's gray eyes gave Elvin a razor-sharp appraisal. "Mind if I sit, or what?"

"Free country." Elvin leaned back in the booth as Dick slid in next to me, and put his hands to work lighting up a fresh Kool. "So," Elvin said, waving out his match, "you a big friend of this here hillbilly, or what?"

Dick's face went puzzled. "Friend? Friend? Let's not get carried away here, all right? Old Ben here is a loose cannon, and I just keep him on the deck, that's all. How 'bout you, Captain? You two must be pals, being fellow Detroiters and all."

Elvin's lip curled. "Sheeit. Perkins's a Detroiter like I'm from Grosse Pointe."

"Hey," I said, "Grand River/Lahser area, man. Redford High School."

"Way back when," Elvin retorted. "You been out in Belleville since before I've known ya. Makes you an out-stater, practically. Nah," he said to Dick, "we ain't friends. He pops up now and then, workin' one of his pain-in-the-ass cases, shuckin' and jivin', grinnin' and stinking up the environment with them putrid dead-cat-shit cigars of his. He always comes on open and helpful, but always ends up wanting to mooch information off me."

"That's Ben all right," Dick answered. "I'm ashamed to admit this, but I'm the one got him his private-detective license. Weak moment; what can I say? I keep waiting for a chance to lift it. Or maybe even bust him behind something."

"I busted him once," Elvin said, a small smile cracking his face. "Brought him in for questioning behind a knifing downtown a few years back. Couldn't make anything stick, though."

"Could we dispense with the seminar," I asked, "and—"

"That case is still open," Elvin said darkly. "Got anything to add to your previous statement, Perkins?"

"No. You guys had enough fun now?"

"Be nice to find out what this is all about," Dick said. "I'll have you know, I postponed a haircut to make this meeting."

"You got the floor, Ben," Elvin grunted.

"Much obliged." Well, in one sense I'd put the two cops on common ground. Terrific. "Both of you guys have heard pieces of this thing from me. I'm gonna lay it all out now, and—"

"And then make your pitch," Elvin cut in.

"Me? Make a pitch?"

"Who, me?" Dick mimicked. "You can't bullshit us, Ben. Go ahead. Tell us the story, make your pitch, we'll tellya to go screw, then we can all go home."

"Gentlemen," I said, "I am indeed dazzled by the display of cooperation. Here goes."

I related the events of the Witkowski case pretty much in sequence. I told about Kevin's altercation with Solomon Kraus, other evidence of his racist leanings, my "interview" with the Skinheads at the bar, my discovery of Justin Catlin's secret room, evidence of his "kinship" with Richard Robertson, my brief apprehension by Ponder and his gang, Brian's undercover activities and the things he'd learned in two nights at the bar.

The policemen smoked in silence throughout my recitation. They changed expression only once. When I told them what the criteria were for joining the Special Action Group, Elvin's heavy brows went up for just a second, and Dick turned and gave me a hard look.

As the waitress brought us fresh carafes of coffee, I summarized. "So here's what we've got, guys. Number one: These Skinhead characters probably started out as a more or less social group with racist leanings. That was till Justin Catlin came on to them. Catlin may or may not be Richard Robertson, the fugitive; I guarantee you, though, he's a big shot in the national white-supremacy movement. He's organized these guys into something called the Special Action Group at a place called the Bunker. Kevin Witkowski's recruiting for him. Looks like he's more than just a goofy admirer; he's an executive. Probably Catlin's second in command." A fact that I dreaded relating to Lynne and Jerry.

The policemen were silent for a minute. Then Elvin asked guardedly, "What do you s'pose this 'Special Action' is?"

"One strong possibility?" I answered. "Who's the most visible liberal activist on the Detroit scene right now?"

"Elliot Andelson," Dick said.

"He's perpetrating that rally on Tuesday," Elvin said. "Maybe these clowns plan to bust it up or something."

"Or something," I answered.

"So the fuck what?" Dick said acidly. "So they pull some pain-in-the-ass counterdemonstration. Your boys can handle that, right, Elvin?"

I held up a hand. "It's easy to dismiss 'em. I was doing that myself when I got into this. Till I read those clippings about the other groups, people like The Order. These guys were operators. Heavily financed and armed to the teeth with the latest stuff. If Catlin's got these Skinheads on the same tack, we're in for more than Howdy Doody time."

Dick had been smoking his cigarette and looking away from us. Now he turned back, eyes narrow. "There's a couple of things you weren't exactly clear on, Ben."

"Bullshit. I gave you a very clear, lucid presentation of the facts at hand."

"Oh, no," Dick countered. He ticked nicotine-stained fingers. "Number one, What's the name and location of this bar where the Skinheads hang out?"

"Number two," Elvin chimed in. "Where's Justin Catlin's house located?"

"Number three," Dick added. "How do you know Kevin Witkowski is Catlin's Number Two?"

I took a final hot pull on my cigar and crushed it out in the remnants of Elvin's cigarette butts. Teaser time. "Call it a good guess?"

"Uh-uh," Elvin grunted. "You got more, now give."

I extracted my wallet from my back pocket and dealt a folded scrap of torn newspaper onto the table. I let Dick unfold it because I didn't want to look at it. Nor did I have to; what it depicted was branded on my brain. A headline that said SIX CHILDREN DEAD IN SCHOOL-BUS BOMBING. Some text. And a picture of the smoking, burned-out hulk, surrounded by cops and medics and screaming, crying black women.

Dick skimmed it, slid it over to Elvin, and exhaled loudly. Elvin gave it a one-second glance; then every muscle in his body seemed to seize as he looked at me. "East side, last spring," he whispered. "It's still open. We never got lead one."

Dick's head was bowed as he played with a fresh pack of Luckies on the table. "What's the tie-in, Ben?"

"That was in a file in Catlin's office. A file with Kevin Witkowski's name on it."

Neither policeman spoke.

"Brian was told that to join the Special Action Group you had to kill a black or a Jew." I tapped the clipping. "That little caper was Kevin's ticket to the big time."

CHAPTER 23

'I DON'T KNOW 'BOUT big time," Elvin said. "Lots of time, maybe. There's physical evidence and eyewitnesses. All we need is a suspect. Oh, man. I *like* this one."

I wished I could share Elvin's enthusiasm. All I could think 'bout was having to tell Lynne and Jerry, sometime soon, what Kevin had evidently done. And I grated at the obligation of having to do anything on behalf of the little son of a bitch. As my daddy would have said, this business offered no pluses. None except the debatable satisfaction of getting done what I said I'd do.

Elvin was coming along nicely, so far. Dick was another matter. He was a little faster than Elvin, and he smelled a rat. That takes care of question three," he growled. "What about questions one and two, Ben?"

I feigned bewilderment.

"Where the Skinhead bar is," he said impatiently. "And the location of Catlin's farm. Spill."

"Yeah," Elvin chimed in. "Here's how we'll handle this. You state people take the farm, and we work the bar. Sooner or later we're bound to find this Witkowski creep, and he'll take us straight to the Bunker." His dark eyes found me. "So come on, Ben. You done right good so far. Now give over."

I looked down, shook my head slightly, and sighed.

"Oh Gawd," Dick said.

"Cat gotcha tongue?" Elvin asked sharply. "I ax you a question, Perkins."

I refilled my coffee cup. I really wanted a beer, but this was Denny's. Just my luck. "I know how y'all want to handle this, but it just won't fly. Sorry."

"Who you talkin' to, boy?" Elvin asked.

"I have a job to do," I said. "I hired on to find Kevin an bring him to his daddy." I shrugged. "Let's face it, if I let yo handle this your way, Kevin and his daddy'll get lost in th shuffle. There's not much time."

"Screw Kevin and his daddy," Dick mimicked. "What w got here, buddy boy, is a multiple-murder suspect, and ever indication is that him and his pals aren't through yet."

"I have a job to do."

"We also got some nice jails to lock you up in," Elvi noted. "Well, not so nice, I guess."

"I also have a plan," I said.

"Ah-ha!" Dick boomed. "A plan. Ben has a plan. Do w want to hear his plan, Captain?"

Elvin rolled his eyes, shrugged, then leaned forward, dar fingers interlocked on the table. "Okay. Turn me on."

Fifteen minutes later, Elvin and Dick looked at each othe without expression, then went to work lighting up fresl cigarettes. I drained my coffee cup and sat back in the booth I was wired from the caffeine and tense about the outcome I'd given it my best shot; now we'd just have to see.

The initial reaction was not promising.

Elvin exhaled smoke and smothered a giggle. "That th biggest crock of horseshit I ever heard."

Dick was shaking his head. "Jesus, Ben, whaddya thinl this is, *The Godfather*?"

"Don't rush to judgment," I said. "Take your time. Think i over."

"Ain't nothing *to* think over," Elvin said. His face had gon thunderous. "You've had your fun. Now you're out of it. Yo ain't nothing but a pain-in-the-ass private *de*-tective. You place in the order of things is somewhere lower'n whaleshit. don't care what the books say, I don't care what the movie say. This here's the real world, the city of 'Troit, and I am police officer for the city of 'Troit, and I will do the polic work in this city. Not you. You read me?"

I beckoned with fingertips. "Don't hold back, Elvin. Giv it to me straight."

Elvin's eyes were smoldering, the tendons standing out o his bull-like neck. "I will give you Wayne County fuckin' *Jail*

what I'll give you. Now, you tell us where that Skinhead
son is, and where Catlin's farm is, and then get your white
out of my city."

Dick was silent and watchful. I unwrapped my last cigar
I lighted it. "Okay. Here's the information. Ready?"

Elvin settled back.

"Number one," I said, "I got a man working undercover
ready. He's just one step from being inside completely.
mber two, my way is a better shot at bagging the whole
w. If you guys go barging in, you might only pinch off a
dful. Most of all, you want Catlin. Number three—"

Elvin shook his head as if waking from a dream. "What am
earing?" he asked Dick. "I don't believe I'm hearing what
ant to hear from this man."

"Doesn't sound like it," Dick grunted.

"Number three," I repeated, "this way, I'm taking all the
k. If it goes bad, the egg won't be on you. Number four,
way's more secure. You guys plan a grandstand play and
re's a leak, the opposition'll just melt away and leave you
h squat."

Elvin's face lighted up. "You're hard of hearing! That's what
s. You gettin' older, Perkins, your brain cells is dying off by
truckload. A beer-truckload."

"Number five," I said, "I won't do it your way. You either
it my way, or you get fuck-all from me, Elvin. Sorry."

I waited. It all came down to this.

Dick was smoking and fidgeting, not even part of the
bate. Elvin's face wiped clean. He cocked his head. "Do
u have any idea what I can do to you for withholding
ormation?"

"Sure I do. Chapter and verse. And you know me, from
y back. You know how flexible I am except when it comes
getting my job done."

Elvin's stare shifted to Dick. "What about this honky?"

Dick shifted. "As it happens, I'm a fellow honky. But I'm
o a police officer. And in my judgment, Ben's right."

I took a pull of cigar smoke and exhaled, silently patting
yself on the back. Technically, I didn't need the state police
this caper, but I knew that, left to himself, Elvin was
out as movable as the Detroit/Windsor Tunnel. All I could
pe was that Dick would come in on my side, and that the

peer pressure might turn the tide with Elvin. I was part
the way there now.

Elvin's expression faded to nothing. Dick said, "Ther
one aspect to this that Ben didn't mention. This flying squ
that pounced on him at Catlin's house—this guy Ponder
whoever. I think they're feds. I think they're running so
action that they've cut us out of." He squashed his cigare
out with one savage thrust into the ashtray. "I want the
making no collars in my state," he said, voice almost a hiss.
want to take care of the business here. I want Ponder and
crew to slink away with nothing, then eat shit and die slowl

Elvin looked out the window.

"Now, Captain," Dick said. "You're Detroit and I'm sta
but we're both Michigan. You may not like old Ben he
banging around in your backfield, but how do you feel abo
these east-coast assholes coming in here?"

Elvin was obviously torn between his feelings for me a
for the east-coast assholes. "Like you," he murmured final

"Ben's way strikes me as our best chance to take this wh
thing down quick, clean, quiet, and total. Right out fr
under Ponder's nose. I say we go for it."

Elvin looked at us wearily. "Easy for you. *I'm* the one
to walk out that door and—"

"You don't trust me?" I asked, astounded.

Elvin jerked a thumb at me and asked Dick, "Would y
trust him?"

"Oo, man, I don't know."

"Come on, Elvin," I said, genuinely pissed now. "I wa
this deal done right worse'n you. I'll be careful."

"You're not the one on the receiving end," he noted with
scowl.

"Trust me, okay?"

Elvin abruptly shoved his way out of the booth, mutteri
something about a phone call. When he was out of earshot
looked at Dick. "Think he'll go for it?"

The state police inspector arched his brows. "Better th
even chance at this point, I'd say."

My cigar had burned itself to a two-inch ash, then died
tapped it clean and relighted it. "Appreciate your backup, c
son."

"Were you surprised?" he asked.

Elvin had taken an open-air booth in the corner and w

ing against the instrument, listening to the receiver, face
n. "Yes," I lied.

Ha!" Dick said. "Well, don't get too swell-headed about
r persuasive powers. I'm just a sucker for gonzo opera-
s, is part of it. But that's not the biggest reason."

lvin was talking urgently now, his tones audible but
ntelligible over the faint din of the nearly empty restau-
t. "What's that?" I asked.

Headlines," Dick said, square face smug with satisfaction.
tate and City Cops Bust Federal Fugitive, Smash Local
rorist Ring.' Nothing helps your career as much as making
 department look good. I'm surprised you didn't use that
ument on the captain."

I was saving it," I said. Actually, this wasn't true. The
h was that the argument hadn't occurred to me. I'd been
absorbed with the problem of Kevin and the Skinheads,
ried about Brian and Lynne and Jerry, anxious about the
b Paley problem, and my preliminary hearing coming up
t week, not to mention that anonymous biker that had
ed me—a man can't stay on top of everything.

Any holes in the plan that you can see?" I asked.

Nah," Dick said. Elvin slammed the phone down and
mped back toward us. "Except for one minor detail."

What's that?"

You could get yourself killed," Dick said casually.

lvin shunted himself into the booth, fury coming off him
nearly visible waves. "No sale," he said.

What?" Dick asked.

I had our people touch base with Andelson's," the captain
l, shakily knocking a cigarette loose from his pack. "They
n't buy in."

 was confused. "What do they have to buy into? The plan
sn't—"

lvin flicked his Zippo and said across the flame, "They
n't cancel the rally. I argued with 'em, but they said no."

 moved in for the kill. "So we're go?"

lvin closed his eyes, sighed smoke, and opened them
in. "We're go. God help me."

All right," I said calmly. "Let's get it on."

lvin reached a thick billfold out of his coat pocket. He
lt some dollars onto the table, hesitated, then reached

something across to me. I took it and tucked it away. "T care of it," Elvin whispered.

"Not to worry. See you around, man."

Elvin laughed sourly, gave us both a hard look, then out of the booth and walked away.

Dick and I settled the bill and went to the foyer. glanced outside, nodded, looked back at me. "Wish I co stay for the fun," he said, "but something tells me—"

"Wouldn't be fittin'," I agreed.

"Yeah. I might get the sudden urge to arrest some Would that be a gas, or what?" He pursed his lips. "Ask something?"

"If I said no, would it stop you?"

"Never has before. Ever occur to you to just bag this on

"No. Of course not."

He stepped closer to me, lowering his voice as a coupl patrons walked out. "This Kevin character, he's one st asshole. Now you didn't know that going in, but you kno now. Why sweat it? Write it off. Back out clean. Who'd bl ya?"

I looked into Dick's tough, seen-it-all eyes. "This ain't him. It's for his mom."

"Special lady?"

"Sort of. Way back. Different turn here, happensta there, my whole life might've been different."

Dick's eyes widened for an instant; then he grinn "Might have known a broad was back of this. Why don't just do things for money, like us grown-ups?"

"She's paying me, don't worry."

"Oh, yeah. Sure she is. Remind me to bring a shovel n time we get together, all right?"

First Brian had called me a bullshit artist; now Dick doing it. "You better split, man. And just make sure move quick when the call comes, okay?"

"We'll be ready." He pushed the front door open. "Bet give me a few minutes' head start."

"No problem. I'm going out the back way, anyhow."

Dick gave me one final look, shook his head, and left strolled back across the restaurant and down a hall past kitchen and rest rooms to the rear. There I found a fire that was unlocked, thank God. I pushed my way outsi closed the door behind me, and breathed deeply.

Here a gravel alley separated the restaurant building from
a high chain-link fence. Beyond that sprawled a vacant warehouse building and a vacant parking lot. I looked left and
right and saw no one. Perfect. It had been nearly ten
minutes; time to go.

I hesitated, though. My heart was sending shock waves
from head to boots. My hands were slick to the point where
wiping them did little good. When you dream up a bit like
this, it sings in your head. You picture it going down, with
everything coming out all right in the end, as the credits
crawl.

But as Elvin had said, this wasn't the books or the movies.
This was 'Troit.

CHAPTER 24

THE BOLT HEAD GLOWED red. I shut off the propane torch, laid it on the cement, then clumsily reached my socket wrench up to the bolt, shoved it home, and turned. The bolt head gave easily—too easily. It tore right off. The crossover pipe fell from the engine and landed right on the tip of my knee. I shuddered and swore, my eyes fogging up and obscuring my view of the rusted, oily underside of Carole's car. "Oh, goddamn you, you bastard," I gasped. When the pain had subsided, I shoved rusted pipes out of the way, pushed my tools and torch to the side, and rolled myself out from under the car, the creeper's wheels squeaking on the hard cement.

Will Somers, Carole's seven-year-old son, sat on a folding chair against the wall of the one-and-a-half-car garage. He's a blocky chunk of strong-built boy with his mother's large brown eyes and blond hair cut short in preparation for summer. He wore red shorts, a red T-shirt, and red high-topped sneakers, and he held a Stroh's beer in his lap.

I squinted at him. "Hope you brought a beer for me."

He laughed and handed the can to me. I cracked the top, bent my head back, and guzzled. I came up for air and surveyed the garage, hoping the view had improved. It hadn't. Carole's blue Thumper station wagon sat up high on safety stands. Rusted and torn bits of exhaust system lay scattered on the cement. A gleaming pile of new parts—pipes, muffler, resonator, and hangers—lay by the open roll-up door. My toolbox sat open next to Carole's big portable radio, which murmured WABX's Sunday-night all-request show. Full darkness had taken over outside, and I was

owhere near done yet, but past the point of no return.
reat.

"You about done yet?" Will asked for the third time.

I drank some more beer. "No. Just got the old stuff off,
hat's all."

"Well, you're halfway," Will said hopefully.

"Not quite. Getting the old stuff off is the easy part.
Vhere's your mom?"

"Up in her office." The boy added innocently, "She said
he wouldn't come out here till you were on your third
eer."

I grinned. "Smart lady." I poured the rest of the beer down
nd held the empty out to him. "Better go get me that third
ne, kid."

"Okay." He trotted out of the garage toward the back door
f their tall, gaunt Cape Cod. I picked up the new crossover
ipe from the pile, carried it to the Thumper, then lay on my
ack on the creeper and squeaked myself underneath the car.
Might as well get the hardest one over with first.

I'd just gotten the pipe lined up on the manifolds and
egun to thread in the new bolts when WABX began a
ews-brief segment. I stopped work and listened to the
eadoff story. "A Detroit police captain was shot to death this
fternoon in what police spokesmen are calling an ambush-
tyle slaying. Elvin Dance, who led the department's homi-
ide section, was a twenty-six-year veteran of the force.
olice have questioned several eyewitnesses but do not at
his point have a motive or solid leads, and no suspects are in
ustody. . . . In an address to the Baptist ministers' convention
t Cobo Hall, Mayor Coleman Young called for a return
o . . ."

I thought about Elvin at Denny's, Elvin at the murder
cene last week, Elvin slowly going street-happy, doing his
ob and dreaming about Disney World. I thought about
Kevin, Brian, the Special Action, and the Bunker, and won-
lered if any of us would get out of this in one piece. I'd just
ompleted loose attachment of the new crossover pipe when I
eard two sets of footsteps on the cement. "Refill time!" came
Will's voice.

"Perfect." I rolled myself out from under the car and got
lumsily to my feet. Will handed me a fresh cold one. "Done
et?" he asked.

"See that pile of parts yonder? When that's gone, I'n done."

Carole stood next to her son, hands on hips, surveying th car. She wore a snug white tank top over pink shorts, an sandals with laces that snaked up her ankles. Though he blond Lady Diana hair was perfect as usual, she was othe wise at-home casual. No makeup, no jewelry, no brassier even. I looked her over, struck as I always am by the size an the vividness of her. No wonder she does so well in th courtroom. You can't take your eyes off her.

She looked at me with no lack of sympathy. "Quite a job eh?"

"Aw, it's not so bad," I lied. "I'll have you rolling again i an hour or two."

WABX began a Pink Floyd set, starting with some of thei really old stuff. I cracked the fresh beer and gurgled som down. Carole said, "I really appreciate this, you know."

"Hey, kid, you do for me, I do for you, right?" She smile dutifully as I sat in the folding chair and stretched my legs Any job under a car is the pits. You get cramped up, cut up greased up, and bruised; the underbody rains rust and greas down on you, and there's hardly any room to breathe. It's n place for a claustrophobic or for any other human being, fo that matter.

A shrill whistle sounded from my Mustang out on th driveway. I was in no mood to get up. "Get that for me, wil you, Will?"

"Sure!" He scampered joyfully out to the car and got in We heard nothing for a moment; then Will got out of the ca and came back slowly. "Wrong number, I guess," he reported

"Oh." Then I straightened and looked at the boy. "Wron number?" I asked carefully. "You sure?"

"Guess so," Will shrugged. "He said a bad word and hun up."

I looked at him intently. "Tell me what he said. Exactly."

Will looked up at his mother uncertainly. "I'm not allowe to say it."

I gave Carole a glance. "This once it's okay."

Will tried to keep a straight face. "He said, 'Aw, shit.'"

On the one hand, I was relieved that Brian had touche base. On the other hand, he'd given the code word for thre A.M. Another long night for old Ben.

Carole was watching me closely, her expression troubled. "Will, it's past nine, you go take your bath now," she said, voice distracted.

"Aw, Mom, can't I—"

"No. Drag it along now."

"Okay." He left the garage dejectedly. I got to my feet and stretched. "Back to it, I guess," I said with heartiness I did not feel.

"What was that about?" Carole asked.

"What, the phone call? Nothing. Wrong number, I guess." I wore my best dumb face; fools 'em every time.

"There's that dumb face again," Carole observed. "Who're you trying to kid, anyway?"

"Nobody! There's nothing going on, okay?"

She stood her ground, tall and close to me. "You haven't been right since you got here. Something's really bugging you. You want to talk about it, I'm right here."

I sighed, regretting my sharp words. "That's right kind of you, but everything's cool." I drank some more beer, set the can down, fetched some more pipes, and dragged them over to the Thumper. "Better keep going if I'm going to finish up this month." I lay down on the creeper and inched myself under the car.

Carole's voice came, somewhat muffled by the car between us. "Mind if I stick around?"

"Hey, help yourself. 'Preciate the company."

I heard the folding chair creak as she sat. Past the left front tire I could see her sandled feet, her ankles and thighs. Great wheels, I thought, and not for the first time. Next on the agenda came a hanger, and I tried to eyeball the problem by the light of my trouble lamp, but found I could not concentrate. I looked out again at Carole's legs. "Can I bounce a situation off you?" I asked.

"Sure," she answered.

I plunged on. "This lady friend of mine. Name's Barb. She hangs out at Under New Management. . . . been there forever, like me, you know?"

"I know."

"It's nothing heavy. Laughs, and that's pretty much it. At least from my end. But she's—she's gotten intent. Way into my face. More than I want or need."

"Perils of singlehood," Carole said. "Happens to me all the time."

"Does it really?"

"No. Proceed."

"Thing is, I like her. She's no mental giant, but she's sweet. Got a heart as big as all outdoors. I've never heard the woman say an unkind word about anyone."

"Sounds to me like an ideal situation," she observed.

"Well, it's not. The thing is, we're just drinking buddies, that's as far as it can ever go."

"I suppose you're trying to tell me you're not screwing her?"

Surprised by her harshness, I fumbled for an answer. "Come on, get real."

"I am being 'real,' as you put it. What's the problem? You can't bring yourself to break it off with her?"

"That's right." It was suddenly getting hot and close under that miserable car.

"I suppose that's because you don't have a new one lined up yet?"

"That's pretty nasty, Carole."

"Truth hurts sometimes. More than sometimes. Whatever became of good old Ben, master of love 'em and leave 'em?"

I began to wish I hadn't started this. "I've never been like that."

"Tell me about it. What's so special about this Barb person that you can't just push her off the pier? You had no trouble doing that to me, after dragging my heart around for a while."

"Carole. Come on. Let's just drop it."

She stood, and I watched her feet pace from one end of the Thumper to the other. Her tone was quite controlled, her words as well chosen as if she had written them out beforehand. Damn lawyers. "I don't want to drop it. I find this fascinating. Tell me what it is about her, Ben, that entitles her to so much of your otherwise well-hidden sensitivity. Or contrarily, tell me what it was about me that caused you to withhold it. Is she a better drinking buddy than I am? Was my crime the fact that I made it past high school? Is she more submissive in bed? Was I not sufficiently enthusiastic about the Detroit Tigers? What was it?"

"It was mutual, that's what it was," I shot back. "And I had

10 idea you felt so bitter. We've stayed friends, which I never
expected to happen, and—"

"Friends? Well, I will concede that we can't seem to
disengage completely. Beyond that, I don't know. I wonder
about it a lot."

"Friends talk about stuff, help each other out. Friends
don't dig up old personal shit and throw it around. I was
hoping we could have a simple conversation about a problem
I'm having, and—"

Her feet stopped. "You want a simple conversation, come
out from under there so I can see you."

"I'm staying right here. I got work to do."

"You just don't want to face me. I *dare* you to come
out."

"If you dare, you're square."

She exhaled explosively. "This is getting petty, and I'm
getting tired. See you in court. And wear a tie." She walked
out, her sandals clattering on the cement.

When I was sure she'd left, I squeaked myself out from
beneath the Thumper and stood. I needed another stretch
break and a few minutes to clear my mind. Sometimes I'm
not so swift in the mouth department. I start to walk across
what looks like a peaceful plowed field only to find it salted
with mines. Ain't it just like a woman anyhow: Let three
years go by and then POUNCE!

It was 3:02 A.M. by my dashboard clock as Brian wheeled
his Nova into the Northline Road subdivision. Welcome to
Monday.

It had started raining just as I finished up Carole's exhaust
system, and it built into a full-force thunderstorm on my
drive back to Norwegian Wood. Now it had settled down to a
steady torrent that promised to continue for most of the
night.

I stifled a jaw-cracking yawn as Brian shut down the Nova
behind me, trotted to the Mustang, and fell inside, bringing a
gallon of water inside with him. I hadn't been to bed at all.
I'd given my .45 automatic a good, thorough cleaning and
spent the rest of my time working on the plan, dotting every
I and crossing every T that I could think of.

"Whoa!" Brian said, grinning. "Really dumping, huh?"

"Frog-strangler," I agreed.

He wore boots, dark slacks, and a pale T-shirt under his leather vest. All this was indistinct in the near-total darkness, and I couldn't read his face at all. He sounded enthused, though. "Have I got news for you, big guy."

"Good, bad, or indifferent?"

"Good. I had a little talk with Kevin."

"Oh. He showed up at the bar?"

"Like clockwork, man. Toward the end there he went to the can, and I followed him in. He was in a real rush, but I wasn't letting him slip by me this time."

"Hold it. Tell me exactly what you said to him."

"Well, I said I had some news for him, important stuff. He tried to blow me off, but—"

"Did you say who you were?"

"I told him my name. Why not?"

"Did you mention me?"

"No. You said not to. For chrissake, Ben."

"Okay, good. You told him you had news for him. What then?"

"He said he had to leave, he was running late. He said we could talk tomorrow. Uh, today, or whatever. He's going to meet up with me this afternoon. Isn't that great?"

"Yeah," I said guardedly. "Where are you going to meet him?"

"The rooming house on Trenton. I told him I was living there. I didn't say anything about knowing that he lived there a while back. Pretty slick, huh?"

"Good thinking. So what happened then?"

"He left."

"Is there anything else that he said, or that you said, that you haven't told me?"

"No. It was like twenty seconds we talked. He was in one hell of a rush. How about this? I stayed with it long enough to set up a meet, but I didn't tip him off to anything."

I let out a long, long breath. "Okay. You done good."

"Thanks," he said, pride sounding loud and clear.

"There's just one slight hang-up."

"Hang-up? Like what? I figured what you do is come down to the rooming house this afternoon and wait with me. When Kevin shows up, you tell him about his dad. Take him to the

ospital, right on the spot. And then the job's done, man! We
lid it!"

I felt like a shitheel for what I was about to do, but there
vas no choice. "Things've been moving. We got to make
ome technical adjustments to the plan."

CHAPTER 25

"WELL, OKAY," BRIAN SAID uncertainly. "What do yo
want me to do?"

I reached the newspaper off the floorboard, flicked on th
dome light, and tossed the paper onto Brian's lap. It was th
state edition of this morning's *Detroit Free Press*, reeking (
ink. The double-check headline took up half the width unde
the masthead. POLICE CAPTAIN DEAD IN WEST-SIDE SHOOTING

Brian read it, then looked at me. "I don't get it."

I withdrew a soft, well-worn wallet from my hip pocket an
handed it to him. He opened it. The gold badge shown dull
in the light, its engraving rubbed nearly smooth. It wa
nothing fancy, but heavy and substantial; obviously the rea
thing. Brian's intake of breath was sharp. I shut off the dom
light. Brian's voice was tight. "This the cop's? Where'd yo
get it?"

"It's his, all right. I'm a friend of the family. It's on loan
Don't lose it."

"Jesus Christ, Ben!" he said.

"How does it feel to be a cop killer?"

"Oh man, oh man," he breathed.

"You know what this means."

"But . . . the rules are, blacks and Jews—"

"Dance was black. His picture's on the jump."

I heard the paper fall to the floorboard as Brian leane
back in the bucket seat. Only his outline was visible in th
near darkness. "A police captain. Holy shit. A *black* police
captain. Goddamn, Ben, how the hell did you work this?"

"Took advantage of a situation," I answered, voice rougher
than I expected. "Elvin went down, I touched base with hi

people, arranged a little loan there. We got lucky. Now you can get all the way inside."

The troubled silence that followed was broken only by the steady din of rain on the ragtop. A bolt of lightning cracked in the west, sending a finger of fire earthward. Seconds later thunder rumbled. Another wave of thunderstorm fury was coming, probably closing in on Norwegian Wood now, some fifteen miles to the west. I fired up a cigar and cracked the side window to keep from gassing us to death. I resisted the urge to babble, to lay some big sell job on the kid. He had to stand up on his own.

Finally he said, "It's not like we have to do this now. I'm seeing Kevin tomorrow; we can do it the way I planned it, dodge the Special Action entirely."

"I'm not so sure about that," I said. "Kevin's up to his rump in whatever they're planning. He might just tell us to go screw. Then we've got diddly. We've got to get him to the hospital, remember; that's the job."

"I know. It's just that—this thing is getting by-god scary. These boys aren't farting around. They mean to hurt people. I been figuring, well, we can move around that, still get the job done. That's how you've been talking. Guess you changed your mind?"

"I'm not forcing you," I said. "You want to pinch it off here, just say the word, we'll do it some other way. I just thought, after the way you talked the last time—"

"I'm still in, Ben," he said evenly.

"You sure, now."

"All the way."

"You know what you're up against." I swallowed hard, at once euphoric and depressed. "You know what you gotta do."

"I whacked that nigger good," Brian said. "I blew his fucking head off, sent him to jig heaven."

"That's the line you lay on Kevin this afternoon," I said.

"He'll buy it," Brian said. "Hell, I got the badge to show for it. No way can they deny it, 'less the cops turn up the shooter beforehand."

"I wouldn't fret that if I were you."

"It's solid, then."

"Yep." I inhaled deep on the cigar. "Tell Kevin you want in on the Special Action. That'll get you to the Bunker. Once

you know where it is, you whistle me up, I drop by and put
stop to all this nonsense before it gets any uglier."

"Yeah!" Brian said exuberantly. "Right on! Just one question.

"What's that, son?"

"How do I whistle you up? You thought that through?"

"Uh-huh." I laid it out for him; he sat still and silent, taking
it all in. "And then, after you've put that on the air, I want
you to do just one more thing. And I fucking mean this
Brian."

"What's that?"

"I want you to get yourself away from there any way you
have to. Get moving and keep moving till you're clear.
mean, all the way out of Detroit."

Thunder rumbled again, closer. Brian was looking at me
"Aw shit, Ben! You're cutting me out just when the fun's about
to start!"

"No other way. I see your face on or near the premises,
will take time out to break both your fucking arms for ya."

"Just isn't fair. I'm in the hot seat, doin' all this ground
work, and just when payoff time comes, you're sending me
home to my mommy."

"Not only will I break your arms, but I'll see to it that you
do nothing but snake out soil pipes and do wiring checks up
in the attics all summer. Mind me, now."

"All right! Okay!"

"Thought you'd see it my way." I opened my window a tad
more, shot a chunk of cigar ash outside, and rolled the
window back up. "Now, you got that line memorized?"

"Oh sure. I remember it from typing class anyhow. Imagine that, me at a frigging typewriter. You sure you can
translate that bullshit into a location?"

"Yeah. I got the contacts. Only simple way to do it,
actually."

"That's assuming I get through in the first place. Might be
tough; those programs get jammed up sometimes."

"You just keep trying. I'll be listening, I promise you that."

The new storm wave reached us in a full fury of lightning
and thunder. The din on the Mustang ragtop became a
clatter, accompanied by metallic drumming on the hood as
gravel-sized hail fell briefly. Then rain resumed as the front
sped past us toward Detroit. The smoke inside the Mustang
was getting thick enough to cut into bricks. Pretty soon I

ouldn't need the cigar; all I had to do was sit there and
reathe. I admired Brian's ability to sit there without puking.
Kid had guts.

"Anything else?" he asked finally.

"Nope. I think we've covered it. You take care of your end
nd do just like I say, and we'll be fine."

He chuckled. "I guess none of this surprises me. You and
our talk about 'we're gonna do our job and that's it.' You
vere bullshitting, just like I figured."

"No, I wasn't," I said lazily. "This is one of the subtleties
bout private-detective work. You focus on the job at hand,
ut if other problems get in the way, there's nothing wrong
vith fixing them, too, while you happen to be around. Get
t?"

"Uh-huh. Whatever you say." He picked up the newspaper,
hen punched my shoulder lightly. "Put it there, Ben."

I shook hands with him, hard. "Get clear, afterward," I
aid. "Don't disappoint me."

"I won't. You just be sure to cover your end."

"Not to worry." The next words came hard. "Get going."

He opened the door, jumped out into the rain, slammed
he door, and disappeared into oblivion. I waited till the Nova
aillights had vanished eastbound on Northline Road, then
tarted the Mustang and began to roll.

Though my exhaustion was damned near terminal, I felt
opped up, strung tight. I drove as fast as I dared through
he storm, telling myself I'd be able to sleep when I got
ome. I was wrong.

I rapped on the aluminum door and waited. Lynne appeared
ehind the screen and arched her brows when she recognized me. "Find Kevin?"

"Close, kid. Real close. 'Nother day or two."

She pushed the door open, and I entered. The thunder-
torms the night before had cleaned the air and the sky, and
brilliant early-summer sunshine beamed through the kitchen
window. The table was practically covered by an opened
section of the morning *Detroit Free Press*, along with a
half-filled mug of coffee. No sign of food anywhere. Figured.

Lynne wore a pretty blue skirt and a white sleeveless
pullover top. Fancy-duds clothes for K Mart work. I had a

feeling she wasn't putting in many hours these days. "Wha
in the bags?" she asked.

"Eats." I set them down on the table, opened them up, a
began laying out the contents. "Courtesy of our friendly loo
Burger Barn. We have fried-egg sandwiches with cheddar, v
have your prepackaged orange juice, plus a couple of goo
Danish. Fill up that stomach for another action-packed day.'
looked at her. "You haven't had breakfast yet, right?"

She'd braided her long brown hair and pinned it back in
a bun. She hugged herself as she looked at me witho
expression. "No. I'm not eating much these days."

She looked it, too. Her eyes were bigger in her face; t
bones were more prominent in her hands. I'd have swo
she'd dropped ten pounds in the past week. "Well, here. D
in."

She hugged herself tighter. "It's sweet of you. But I do
think—"

"I know it's slop," I grinned, "but it's here and it's hot,
let's go."

"Thank you," she said faintly. "I'll just save it for later."

"Lynne," I said sharply. "Put the food in the face, the
chew and swallow. Or I'll have to get ugly."

She gave me a plaintive look, then dragged herself to t
table and sat. I unwrapped the sandwich and ripped t
sticker off the top of the juice. She picked up the sandwic
examined it as if she'd never seen such a thing before, the
took a bite. I unwrapped my own, took a big chomp out of
and chewed heartily. Ordinarily I shun breakfast like th
plague, but these weren't ordinary days. Besides, I had a
example to set here. I'd seen this before and I meant to hea
it off. Lynne would not commit suicide through starvation if
could help it.

"You look tired," she said, after conquering her first bite

"Pretty busy lately." I'd come off my no-sleep night and h
the maintenance office only to have Doug call in on me
Don't feel well. Seeya tomorrow, Ben. Asshole. I'd put Rand
on the crisis work and told him I'd be back later to take car
of the scheduled lawn jobs. He didn't ask me about Brian. H
was getting pissed off, and I didn't blame him.

"Tell me what's happened."

I gestured. "Take another bite first."

She frowned, then did as I asked. I set my own sandwic

own. I did not relish what I had come here to do. Lynne's
reaction to my previous news about Kevin was fresh on my
mind. But I at least had to prep her. Get her ready for the
inevitable fact that things change and there's no going back.
As if she didn't have enough of that to deal with already.

"This Skinhead thing is bigger than I thought," I began.

She chewed slowly, steadily, eyes dull on me.

"It takes on the shape of a terrorist group."

She bowed her head, closed her eyes, swallowed. Took a
deep breath and looked at me. "Is Kevin involved?"

"I'm satisfied that that's the case."

She froze in her chair, eyes glassy. "Where is he?"

I gestured. "Eat."

She bit off a morsel and chewed.

"Somewhere in Detroit," I answered. "Place called the
Bunker. My man's on the move now, ought to have a line on
where it's at pretty quick." I hoped.

She swallowed and licked her lips. Her hands, which held
the sandwich, trembled slightly. "Terrorist group," she
murmured, as if the term had just registered. "Do you know
what they're up to?"

I leaned back and looked at her expectantly. After a moment she grimaced and bit off some more sandwich. "Not
sure, but I don't believe they're setting up a patty-cake
tournament."

She did not smile. "You really don't know very much, do
you?" she said around her mouthful.

"Legal proof ain't my bag," I answered. "I know what I
know, and what I know is, the honcho heading up this bunch
is bad news. Federal fugitive. I know the group at this
Bunker is nothing but flat-out hardcases. I know that whatever they're planning ain't particularly pleasant. And I know—"

"Kevin's involved," she said, and swallowed.

"Up to his rump."

She let her sandwich drop to the table. Though she hadn't
taken enough to sustain your average sparrow, I'd strong-
armed her about as far as I cared to. Besides, I'd left my .45
automatic out in the car. She balled her fists, rubbed her
eyes, then cupped her face in her palms. "I've thought about
this, about what you told us before," she said.

I unpeeled my orange-juice carton and drank down the

contents without taking a breath. It wasn't beer, but it'd ha
to do for now. "Yeah," I said, to fill in the dead space.

"We're not bigots," she said softly. "I mean, I won't say t
word 'nigger' hasn't passed our lips once or twice. We gre
up with that, it was what we heard; how could we help i
You grew up the same way I did, you know what I mean. B
it wasn't in our hearts. Ever."

"Uh-huh."

She brought her hands down and drew herself straight, h
expression faraway. "Now, my father—you remember him?

"Oh, sure." Not strictly true. I vaguely recollected a ta
angular, balding man, all grins and fussy energy and a phot
graphic memory for sports statistics.

"He hated Protestants," Lynne said. "Remember, once I
asked you what your religion was, and you said Souther
Baptist?"

I didn't remember that at all.

Lynne's smile was wan. "Oh, my father went into a I
around the house. Lectured me. 'Don't tangle with tho
Holy Roller creeps.' Stuff like that. It was so senseless. H
acted like I was pregnant by you or something. Pretty sill
huh?"

"Silly, all right."

She cleared her throat. "But that's not me. Or Jerry eithe
Never has been. Protestants, and blacks, and Jews, and .
We've just been—we've always been too busy. We've nev
had time to hate people."

I nodded.

Her eyes went to me slowly. "I don't believe it," she sai
"I don't believe a thing you're telling me." Her voice bega
to crack around the edges, but she went on determinedl
"There. I promised Jerry I wouldn't blow up at you agai
And I told you I was sorry I was so mean." Her stare was h
and defiant. "I do not believe what you're telling me abo
my son."

My mouth was dry. "I don't doubt you gave him a goo
raising. But sometimes that isn't enough. Him goin' ba
doesn't make you bad. It's not your fault."

She ignored that. "I think you'd better go now."

I stood. She did likewise and began packing the breakfa
remnants away into a bag with harsh motions. I made to hel

her but retreated at her angry glance. "You working?" I asked.

"No. I'm going to the hospital. I'm taking leave from the store. Jerry would be furious, but he's so out of it he's lost all track of time. So I'm doing what I want." She completed the cleanup and threw the trash into a wastebasket under the sink. She looked out the window for a long minute, then at me. "Thank you for bringing me breakfast."

"No strain. I'll be in touch."

She hesitated. I had the feeling she was torn between hitting me and hugging me. I could think of no more to say, so I left.

CHAPTER 26

I ROLLED UP TO the security booth at the Norwegian Wood entrance. The gate was down and Mel, my day man, was slumped in his seat, head back, snoring toward the ceiling. I hit the horn and he jumped, squinted at me, then hit the button to raise the gate. "Hey Ben, how are ya?" he asked nervously.

I scowled at the fat little guy. "The Third Army could have paraded past here while you were catching your Zs, pal."

"Just resting my eyes, man. Your eyes get tired, sitting here keeping a sharp lookout."

"Occupational hazard. Don't let it happen again. I'm talking to you, now."

"I wasn't sleeping," he whined.

"You heard me. Now listen up. You see a bottle green Toyota MR 2 skulking around out here, you whistle me up, hear?"

"MR 2. Is that a car?"

"No. It's an elephant. For godsake, Mel, it's a racy-looking little two-seater, kind of chunky and squared-off looking. You see it, you call me. Simple. Got it?"

His vigorous nodding made his chins dance. "Okay. I'll be on the lookout."

"Knew I could count on ya." I popped the clutch and roared up the curve of the driveway and down the slope to the big parking lot in the center of the Norwegian Wood complex. The MR 2 had picked me up as I was leaving Lynne's place and hung stubbornly in my rearview mirror. I'd taken him for a little excursion through the city of Wayne, trying to think up a way to nail him. I didn't lose him, but I didn't catch him; I never even got close. Finally he'd dropped me off at the intersection of Belleville Road and Michigan Avenue. Probably because he knew I was headed home.

I got out of the Mustang and stomped toward building three. First I'd had the Kawasaki tailing me the other day. Now the MR 2. I'd seen that before, too. Could be the same guy. Could be different guys working for the same outfit. The questions were who, and why. Was it the cops? Was it the Skinheads? Was it Ponder's crew? The questions were making me cranky. This Monday was bad enough already.

Thank God Randy was on the job and squeezing off the chores like clockwork. He'd taken care of the crisis jobs and was just finishing the routine stuff in building three. His answers to my questions were sullen and distant. That figured. Nobody was happy with me today, not even my client.

I did my daily walk-around. Everything was peaceful. Then I had lunch—cold pizza and cold beer—and carried a fistful of cold ones with me out to the maintenance shed. I changed the oil on the John Deere riding mower, then fired it up and chugged it over to the back forty, which was starting to look like a hay field from all the rain.

I seldom do the mowing anymore—I'm an executive, you understand—but it is in fact one of my guilty pleasures. Probably because it's predictable, and unlike most things in life, you can see where you've been. I powered along the broad field, round and round, eating up a giant swath of grass that spewed in a stream of damp, aromatic clippings from the side of the mower. Swigged beer and smoked a cigar and reviewed the questions as they rotated through my mind as if on a merry-go-round.

I wondered if Brian would be able to carry off his story about Elvin's death.

I worried about the amount of faith I was putting in the Detroit police and the state people. Be just my luck to have to tackle this thing all alone.

I fretted about the showdown that I knew was coming. What if I couldn't get Kevin clear of it?

I remembered the list of weapons I'd read about in Catlin's clipping file, remembering also what it's like to get shot.

I steamed at the memory of the Kawasaki and the MR 2. Whoever those guys were, they were too good behind the

wheel to be civilians. Or cops, even. They were almost a
good as me, hard as that was to admit.

Round and round I went on the mower. Round and round
the questions went in my mind. No answers. And nothing
would happen till I heard from Brian.

When the mowing was done, I put the mower away and
closed up the maintenance shed. I was hoofing back toward
the complex when I noticed Debra Clark sitting alone on her
deck behind building four. I waved; she did not respond. I
changed course and headed over there.

She sat in a heavily upholstered deck chair, one leg crossed
over the other. She wore a blue business suit but had kicked
off her black pumps. She wasn't drinking, reading, or anything else; she just sat there, staring out at the field.

I had one unopened beer left. I held it up. "Buy you one?"
She shrugged, dark eyes averted, mouth a neutral line.

I popped it and held it out. She did not take it. I set it
down on the deck at her feet. "Got off early today, huh?"

She blinked. "I'm not feeling well."

I looked her up and down. What the hell could I say? "I
saw him last night; he's okay."

She said nothing.

"We're closing in on the finish," I said. "Another day is all,
probably. Then it's back to normal." I hoped I didn't sound as
false as I felt.

An errant breeze blew a strand of brown hair onto her face.
She brushed it back reflexively.

"Believe me, I don't like this behind-the-lines shit," I said.
"I'm no general. I'm a trench grunt. I wanna be in the thick
of it. Having him out there is as hard on me as it is on you."

Her eyes flickered, and her fingers began to drum on the
arm of the deck chair.

"All I can say is, hang on tight, kiddo. With just the tiniest
bit of luck, he'll be handing it off to me before the going gets
rough. And you know the first thing he'll do is come back to
you."

She uncrossed her legs, bent, and picked up the beer can.
She examined it briefly, then raised it some more. I thought
she would drink, but she cocked her arm awkwardly and
hurled the can at me. It missed by a mile, but I jumped
anyway.

She was on her feet, face fierce. "I'll do much better than

at," she said coldly, "if anything whatsoever happens to
rian." She wheeled toward the sliding door to her apartment, then reversed course hurriedly, picked up her pumps,
nd disappeared inside.

I inhaled and exhaled a long breath. The beer can had
olled almost to the fringe of the lawn and had gurgled itself
mpty. I picked it up and squeezed it into a small, tight
luminum wad as I walked away.

Sparky Anderson had just skipped over the foul line, on his
ay to the mound to take the ball from Hernandez, when
nocking sounded on my door.

I hoisted myself up from the couch and walked over there
uickly, soundlessly repeating Brian's name as I opened the
oor. Barb Paley.

She had a grocery bag in her hands and an uncertain smile
n her freckled face. "You alone?"

I realized then that I'd forgotten to take her name off my
uthorized-visitors list at the front gate. A shrink would
robably call that a significant oversight. But hell, you can't
eep track of everything.

"Yeah, hi there," I said as I stepped back. Here's your
hance, big guy, I thought as she came in. Time for the
and-shaker; let's get it over with.

She set the bag down on the coffee table with a muffled,
eavy clank of beer cans and turned to me. She wore tight,
ow-slung white corduroy pants, flip-flops, and a navy blue
University of Detroit athletic T-shirt that had been chopped
ff just above the latitude of her navel. The shirt was stretched
o tight across her breasts that I could not fail to note the
rominence of her nipples. Her fiery hair was moussed down
nd back in a reddish avalanche, and her face wasn't as
ainted as it usually is, just a little lipstick and a little some-
hing around her blue eyes, which mirrored my look of
peculative hunger.

"*It'll be Kirby Puckett to face Mike Henneman here in the
ottom of the ninth with two on and nobody out,*" George
Kell said from the TV.

"Brought some beer along, huh?" I asked lamely.

She smiled and cocked her head. "That's just a decoy," she

said. "I think we've got some other business to take care
first."

"Such as what?"

"Such as fucking each other's brains out."

Dry-mouthed and rigid, I said nothing as she took her shi
by its torn hem and pulled it up and off, casually tossing
across the living room. Her heavy white breasts wobble
slightly with her intensified breathing as she looked at m
mouth partly open and eyes bright. I started for her the
with but one thought in mind, but she stopped me with
cautioning finger and a saucy smile. "Uh-uh. No cloth
allowed."

As I stripped, she stepped out of her flip-flops, peeled he
pants down to her feet and kicked them away. I advance
toward her and she retreated to the couch and fell back on
it, strong legs spread, eyes locked on my waist as I reache
her, adjusted her, and entered with a drive that brought
unison gasp from us as we reached home.

She hung her heavy legs over my shoulders, put a stror
hand behind my head and kissed me just once as we rocke
to the beat. I was there with her and yet far away, with ju
one conscious thought: it's okay, it's all right, it's what sh
wants and what I need. . . .

Mrs. Janusevicius's garbage disposal had gone fritz—agair
She's one of Norwegian Wood's original tenants, and this ha
to be about the hundredth time in the sixteen years she"
lived there that her disposal had up and quit. Problem is, sh
has a bad habit of throwing used twist-ties into the sink
which then get sucked into the disposal and bind it up
Goddamn twist-ties anyhow; seems like behind every plumb
ing problem there's a twist-tie somewhere.

Since she was spending the day at her daughter's, I ha
her unit to myself. I shut off the power to the disposa
reached down the drain, and probed. No foreign matter. N
twist-ties. Hm. I restored power, hit the reset switch, an
tried the disposal again. Nothing.

Well, well. Looked like the thing had given up the ghost.
went to the maintenance office-supply room, got a new
disposal, and hauled it back to the apartment. This ought t
keep me busy for awhile.

It was one o'clock, time for the "Free Speech" call-in show on KLOE. I turned on my portable radio and half listened to the talk as I worked. Hoping to hear a familiar voice.

The night's events were a troubling memory that I touched now and then, gingerly. Not that anything had gone overtly wrong. On Perkins's scale of fun romps in the sack, that one was a good, strong nine. I'd let myself sail away on an escapade featuring plenty of beer, laughs, talk, and sex. Tomorrow would take care of itself.

But now was tomorrow, and looking back on the night I felt guilty. Barb had given it her all. She'd been sweet, funny, and endlessly rapacious. Once, as we were knotted on the bed in the midst of a slow sweaty one building to yet another climax, she'd raised herself over me and, half smiling, with what I was sure were tears in her eyes, said she loved me. In response I had kissed her. I'd held her close as she finally drifted off to sleep. I'd been unable to sleep, myself.

I got the old disposal loose from its collar-rings and dragged it out from under the sink. Good job, ya jerk, I thought. Instead of resting up so you're fresh when (if??) Brian calls, you spend the night socking it to a lady who, for all her travels, is still possessed of a peculiar kind of sweetness and vulnerability—a lady you know you're gonna have to punt. You just know it.

Oh yeah, I knew it. The problem was getting up the guts. Or was it? Maybe the problem, as Carole had suggested with her usual piercing logic, was that Barb was handy inventory on a shelf that was otherwise empty.

Maybe I felt that using Barb was okay as long as I felt guilty about it.

Maybe Carole was right that I wasn't such a nice guy sometimes.

The talk show gave way to a commercial break. Then it resumed with a caller who told the host about a place called Teddy Kennedy's Salt-Water Car Wash. Boffo, man. I was tightening up the seals on the new disposal when the host took another call. "Brian from Detroit, how are you?"

"Yeah, man," came the distant voice, wobbly as hell. "This is Brian from Detroit, you know, man?"

"Yeah, Brian, what's on your mind, pal?" said the host.

I sat up straight and leaned toward the radio.

"That other caller, he was talking about the Supreme Cour and all?"

"They ought to retire those old farts *right now*," the hos said. "That's *my* opinion. Use the Green Berets to retire them, if we have to."

"Yeah? Well, here we go. Is to men, now time all men."

I scrambled for my toolbox, found a pen, scribbled furiously on the flap of the disposal box.

"What was that?" the host asked. "I didn't get that."

"Here we go again!" Brian said. "Is to men now time, *al* men." He laughed. "That's my opinion. What's yours?"

The host chuckled uneasily. "Brian from Detroit, thanks fo sharing your thoughts here with us on KLOE. I guess.... Mark from your car, you're on KLOE. Hi, Mark."

"This demonstration those Andelson people are pulling, got a sure-fire way for controlling that. The fifty-caliber machine gun. That'll take care of 'em—"

I shut off the radio, ripped the flap loose, and stuffed it into my pocket. Looked at the disposal. Not done yet, but some things had to wait. I bounded out of the apartment and across the sunbathed parking lot toward building one. Randy was just coming out, and he stopped and stared as I pounded up to him. "Where's the fire, Ben?"

"No fire," I panted. "Listen, I got to run. Go finish up the disposal in Mrs. Janusevicius's place, willya? Only take you a couple of minutes."

"Okay, keep your shirt on," Randy grumbled. "You gonna be back today?"

"Yeah. Maybe. I doubt it, though. Hang in there."

"You, too, Ben," I heard Randy say as I set off on a fast trot for my apartment.

Thirty minutes later I was screaming eastbound on I-94, bound for Detroit. I guided with one hand and held up my street atlas with the other, plotting my course. Not too bad. ETA twenty minutes, tops.

The problem had stumped me for a while. In order to find out the location of the Bunker, Brian had to convince Kevin and the other Skinheads that he had whacked Elvin. That part wasn't too tough. The problem was that, once he'd been taken to the Bunker to join the Special Action Group, he

ght not be able to get the location to me without giving
mself away. I mean, he couldn't just pick up a phone: "Uh,
.n? Hi, it's Brian. Listen, these maniacs are holed up at
ven-oh-six Eleventh Street, few blocks north of the river.
.n't miss it, son. Call in the troops."

But I knew, from the tape that Kevin had made, that the
.inheads were fans of this "Free Speech" call-in show. They
.obably listened to it all the time. I figured Brian's new
.ddies wouldn't give a second thought if he called the show
mself. The problem now was, how could he put out a
cation? He couldn't just announce an address on the air.
.other means of pinpointing the spot would be a phone
.mber, but he couldn't just up and announce that either, not
.thout raising suspicions.

The answer was a code, and it was like everything else I
eate: crude, not pretty, but workable. I chopped off an old
.ping test line, "Now is the time for all good men to come,"
.d let each word represent a number. "Now" through "to"
.ood for one through nine, and "come" was zero. Brian's
ceuliar commentary "Is to men now time all men" had
.zzled the "Free Speech" host, but to me it meant the
.one number 298-1468. Simple.

I'd called Pat O'Shay at Michigan Bell, and she looked up
e number's location. It was a pay phone in an Eleventh
.reet bar. I doubted very much that the bar was the Bunker;
.ust be awful close, though.

I hit the Dearborn city limits and hugged the left lane,
.uring on all the gas I could manage. I considered calling in
.e troops right now but decided to hold off for a bit. I might
.ve to do some snooping around down there before I got a
.x on the Bunker's actual location. Then I could sent out the
.oller and move in for the kill—

An alarm bell binged in the back of my mind. I looked at
.e rearview mirror. I-94 was lightly traveled at this midafter-
.oon hour, and I could see each car clearly. One of them,
.bout ten car-lengths back, was a bottle green Toyota MR 2.

Identical to the one I'd seen this morning, as well as five
.ays ago, last Thursday.

Now, this would *never* do.

CHAPTER 27

I STILL WANTED TO know who the son of a bitch was. I w
still rather childishly angry at the way he'd outwitted me a
eluded me. But the most vital thing now was, I didn't wa
him in my face while I was doing business.

Fortunately I had a plan this time. A plan that should wo
as long as I played dumb.

I drifted over to the right lane of I-94 and rolled up t
Michigan Avenue exit ramp. The MR 2 followed.

Good. Come to papa.

As I looped around to bear westbound, I picked up the
phone, squeezed a number out of deep memory, and punch
numbers. Sammy D. was on the job and willing to lend
hand, since business was light at that moment, and I pro
ised him a hundred for doing nothing more than hitting
button at the right time.

Now, as I cruised west, I slowed to old-granny mode
didn't want to lose the MR 2. I wanted him fat and happy a
riding me as close as possible. Within a couple of blocks h
come up to within twenty feet or so. I did my best to prete
he wasn't there. Made a sedate right on Greenfield a
motored north without a care in the world. The MR 2 stay
with me.

Presently, I swung right into an older residential neighbo
hood. Ford Road was only a couple of blocks north now, and
dredged my memory for its geography, thinking through h
it had to work. I'd been to Sammy D.'s only a week before,
the layout was still pretty clear in my mind. When I reach
Kendal Street I turned north again, the MR 2 in tow.

God, I wished I could have worked this on Sunday, wh

at biker asshole gave me the slip. I'd thought of it, but
ammy D. wasn't open Sundays. But today was Tuesday,
ee-hee.

Sammy's place showed up on the left, at the southwest
orner of Kendal and Ford Road. It was an old brick machine
op converted to that most handy of auto-age establish-
ents: a drive-through beer store. You entered through a
arage door on Kendal, and exited through an identical one
cing Ford Road. A car was just going in as I approached.
ill okay. Sammy knew what he had to do, and so did I.

I signaled a left and slowed. The MR 2 slowed also.
robably thought I was going west on Ford Road. I swung
to the driveway and bumped up the uneven slope and
rough Sammy D.'s entrance. I didn't look around; I kept a
eather eye on the rearview mirror as I pulled up behind the
receding car and stopped. The MR 2 stopped abruptly on
e street behind me. Trying to figure out what to do. He
ally didn't have much choice. Ford Road is a big, busy,
ultilaned road, and there was nowhere convenient for him
 wait out there. While he sat there, a pickup truck wheeled
 a tight, tire-hissing U-turn off Ford and bounced up the
riveway into Sammy D.'s, just barely stopping behind me in
me. Still the MR 2 sat, but the intrusion of the pickup must
ave given him some reassurance. He spun his wheel and
ulled into the building behind the pickup.

I stuck my head out the window and peered forward. The
riveway was flanked by wire racks hanging dense with bags
 chips, peanuts, and other snacks. Past them were the
ming coolers packed with gaily colored six-, eight- and
 e-packs of everything wonderful. The driveway I sat on
as just barely wide enough for one car; there was nowhere
 go except ahead or back.

Sammy D. himself, a rotund, bearded man with a bald
ate and greasy black side-hair hanging down to his shoul-
ers, had just delivered a couple quarts of Bud to the car
head of me. He took money from the driver, then waddled
ackward toward the cash register, scanning the narrow drive-
ay toward the open entrance door. He winked at me, looked
own toward the MR 2, then winked at me again and went
ehind his counter.

Come on, Sammy, do it.

I heard the MR 2 gun his engine. Getting impatient. I

didn't dare look back; didn't want to give myself away. J
when I thought Sammy D. had forgotten what to do, I hea
a motorized grinding sound from behind me. A beauti
sound. The sound of the rolling garage door on its way dow

I picked up my .45 off the passenger seat, stuck it in r
waistband, and opened the door. The garage door was bett
than halfway down now. I don't think the guy in the MR
realized what was happening for a moment. When he did,
jammed the car into reverse and tried to back out. Unfortunate
he popped the clutch a little too fast, and the engine died
walked past the pickup, grinning, as the garage door hit t
floor with a metallic crash. I was squinting at the MR 2 to t
to get a make on the driver—

He'd dropped down in his seat and, like lightning, t
business end of what looked like a small automatic point
toward me out the open window of the MR 2.

I froze for a precious instant, then dived down and to t
right, taking a snack rack with me to the cement as a fusilla
of shots rang out, flat snaps followed by bursting glass behi
me as the bullets blasted six-packs, quarts, and jugs. A y
came from my left, and I cocked my .45 and squirm
forward along the cement to the dubious shelter of the ne
snack rack. I was banking that the shooter would expect n
to retreat, and the next volley proved me right as he raked
area well behind me with another cluster. *Jesus,* I thougl
this guy's a fucking maniac. No choice but to put him dow

Dead silence for an instant. Then wailing began again fro
my left. Must have been the driver of the pickup truck.
edged myself up slowly, squinting through a gap in the ch
bags. I could see the front left quarter-panel of the MR 2, t
open driver's-side door, and a booted leg below its botto
edge. Good enough.

I braced myself, then rose suddenly and shoved the sna
rack to the floor with one hand and aimed the .45 with t
other. I was jumpy as hell, so my single shot turned into tv
that came so fast they blurred together. I dropped to the flo
again and looked.

One slug—must have been the second—had taken a pal
sized hole out of the heavily starred windshield. The oth
had gone more or less where intended: right through t
driver's-side door. That foot I'd seen before wasn't the
anymore.

I rose slowly as a moan sounded from the MR 2, climbing
a wail. Keeping the .45 carefully aimed, I stepped over the
ack litter, heading toward the car, slowly slowly, alert for a
ick, ready to pop him. Something was dripping out the
oor. Blood.

I reached the car, pulled the door the rest of the way open,
d jammed the .45 inside. A body lay crossways on the seat,
male body, tall and slightly built, sport shirt and jeans and
ts of blood issuing from his left leg. A Colt .32 automatic lay
n the floorboard by the gas pedal. I picked it up and threw it
ack behind me, then grabbed the shooter's shoulder and
visted him so I could see his face.

Michael Kraus.

"Oh," I said softly, "ya son of a bitch, ya." I stepped back
om the car, shoved the .45 into my waistband. "Why the
ick you do this, huh?"

I heard an engine roar as the car ahead of mine squealed out
f the drive-through onto Ford Road. The intrepid Sammy D.
ame loping through the devastation toward me, literally
aving his arms, stomachs aquiver. "Jesus to Jesus, Ben, you
idn't say nothing about shooting!"

"This asshole here started it. What do you want from me?"

"Look at this mess. Jesus fucking Christ."

"Gimme your belt," I sighed.

"Huh?"

"Your belt, fat-ass! We got to get a tourniquet on this kid
efore he bleeds to death here." I glared Sammy into submis-
on, took the thin black belt, and cinched it high on Kraus's
ght thigh as best I could, getting myself all bloody in the
rocess. He was moaning, in shock, twitching there on the
at and in no mood to engage in discourse with me as to why
e'd followed me and then tried to blow my head off.

Sammy's swarthy face was pasty white at the sight. "I gotta
ll the medics," he said, as if it was an original thought. "And
e cops, too."

"Hey!" the driver of the pickup hollered, "somebody move
is piece of shit Mustang so I can get out of here, huh?"

"Keep your shirt on, creep!" I shouted. "I'm going."

"No, you ain't," Sammy said. "You're staying right here.
ou got a lot of questions to answer. I ain't takin' no heat for
ou; I'm just a simple merchant, I don't know nothing. Jesus,
wish I'd never gone along with this."

"Can't hang around, sorry." I sauntered around him tow: the Mustang. "Got an appointment downtown."

"I ain't covering for you," Sammy warned. "I can cover a lot, but not for this, no sir."

I dropped into the car. "Fine. Don't cover. Give 'em name, anything you want, Sammy. And hey, thanks for t help here, huh?"

I fired up the big 302 motor, jammed it into gear, a wheeled out and onto eastbound Ford Road as fast as I coul

Out there, on the wide-open road, I felt the shakes co over me, but good. Generally, when I shoot someone, I kn who it is and why. I knew who Kraus was. I remembered was a cab driver, and that might explain his abilities behi the wheel. He might even have been the Kawasaki driv What I didn't know was why he followed me, why he want me dead.

Unpleasant thoughts. Made even less pleasant by a ne flash that came over the radio as I sat waiting at the I-interchange.

Elliot Andelson and his wife had been kidnaped by "unkno armed men" as they parked their car near Kennedy Square preparation for their march and rally. Four people had be shot during the action; two were dead. The kidnappers, a their victims, had vanished.

Sounded like the Special Action was well under way—a I was headed straight into the middle of it.

Eleventh Street is more alley than anything else. I do think more than a half-dozen blocks of it exist. A couple them run just west of Tiger Stadium, whacked off at t Fisher Freeway. The other three pick up just south of the cutting through a no-man's-land of abandoned semiindustr blight between Porter and Lafayette, ending again almost sight of the Detroit River.

I rolled down the heaved, uneven pavement all the way the end, U-turned, and came back. The street was solid wi sooted brick multistory factories and warehouses. Dirty gla windows reflected the light dully. The facades, conceived a built in a more optimistic time, were ornate beneath tl neglect, with elaborate granite moldings and long-forgott company names engraved deep. Most of these were board

er with signs whose messages were dreamy to the point of
ing ridiculous. AVAILABLE NOW. 30,000 SQUARE FEET. PRIME
ACE FOR LEASE. CALL TODAY.

I saw no squads of terrorists lurking about. Hell, they
uld have done a precision march up the street if they'd
anted to, for there was no traffic to speak of and no
edestrians, either. I looked for signs of recent habitation and
w none. If Brian had been right, one of these buildings was
obably the Bunker. But which one?

At the corner of Eleventh and Porter sat a bar. No name,
d it didn't need one. That stretch of Porter was like so
any others around those parts: boarded up, boarded up,
arded up, BAR. I looked for a street number and saw none.
ould be this was the one with the pay-phone number Brian
d broadcast to me. I had to make sure before doing any
rther snooping.

I found a parking spot a few doors east on Porter, locked up
e Mustang, secured the .45 automatic against my spine
ader my waistband and shirt, and hoofed back. An older
ack man leaned listlessly in the bar's entranceway. A couple
others stood at the corner, watching the traffic with rheumy
es. The bar occupied the corner ground floor of a taller
uilding whose upper windows looked out at the city like
ead eyes. Dim neon advertised Stroh's and Bud behind
sted steel security grates. A bright orange-and-yellow one
id LOTTO. I peered around the corner up Eleventh Street
gain. Nothing had changed. I shrugged and sauntered to the
r's entrance. As I passed the old black man he chanted,
"assuh, yassuh."

The inside was thick, smoky, and virtually silent. Men sat
bow to elbow at the bar on the left. Tables sat scattered
ensely in the darker space to the right. Toward the rear a
uple of windows looked out onto Eleventh. Just past them
as an old-fashioned phone, the kind where you could actual-
close yourself in and make your call in privacy. I was
arprised the Michigan Bell demolition crew hadn't caught
p with it yet.

Nobody looked at me as I walked down to the booth. The
oor was accordioned open. I stepped half inside, bent, and
quinted at the label in the center of the rotary dial. 298-1468.
ingo.

This was the place. Or the area, anyway. Probably the best

Brian could do. I pictured him on his way west, away fr
this. Go, kid, go.

But what do I do now?

I could scout Eleventh Street, ask around, see if I co
get a line on the Bunker. The notion wasn't attractive. O
guy in these acres of abandoned factories—forget it. The
nail me long before I'd spot them.

What the hell, I'm no hero anyhow. Time to whistle up
troops.

I picked up the receiver, fed the slot, and began to dial.
gotten halfway through when I stopped.

Through the double glass of the booth and bar windows
saw a face glaring in from the sidewalk. Kevin Witkowski

Hole lee shit.

I stayed expressionless and turned half away, completi
the dialing. As the other end of the line buzzed, I peer
back toward the rear of the bar. City code required
accessible back entrance to places like this. I wondered if a
inspectors had been here since about 1953. I figured I co
give the word and just break like hell for the back, hopi
there was a way out. As the ringing quit and a voice grunt
"H'lo," my bright idea went down the toilet. Two hus
young, shaved-head characters appeared back there and sto
negligently, watching me.

Toward the front of the bar there was a noisy commotion
Kevin shoved his way in, followed by another Skinhead.

The rank of black men at the bar hardly looked up.

I reached a cigar out of my shirt pocket, snapped off
one-inch chunk, and dropped the rest. I squeezed the chu
as tight as I could and began to wedge it tightly into the g
between the cradle and the casing of the pay phone. T
voice in my ear said again, "H'lo? Who's there?"

"Your old pal Ben," I said, "and this is the place."

I hung up the phone and turned as Kevin and his sideki
reached me.

Even in his fearsome black leather boots and vest, Kev
still looked pale and scrawny and harmless. What made t
difference was his thin, bony face stamped onto his fathe
large head. It burned with barely contained joyful rage, t
face of a young man who had gone off the reservation
good.

I said, "Well, well, if it ain't Kevin W. Fancy seeing a friendly face way the hell down here."

His two friends from the back joined him. Now there were four against one, and there I was, penned in a phone booth. Kevin deliberately pulled his open vest aside. Beneath it, hanging from a strap over his shoulder, was an ugly black blunt-ended machine pistol. "You come quiet," he said.

"Thanks, no, Kev. I got chores to run back home." I started toward them. Kevin stepped back, but the three others pushed me hard into the booth. Their faces were smug and almost indifferent. They had the numbers and they knew it. One of them said, "Who is this clown, Kevin?"

"Friend of my mother's," Kevin sneered. "Private eye or something. Dumb cunt probably hired him to find me. How'dja get this close, Perkins?"

I looked toward the bar. No one had turned. It was that kind of place. "Look, I just stopped off in here for a beer, you know?"

"Yeah. Sure. You come all the way down here to nigger town for a beer. Now you listen." He reached under his vest, no doubt getting a grip on his machine pistol. "You come along, or we'll splatter you right here. Don't think of them niggers over there as witnesses, 'cause they'll be as dead as you. I really don't care. It's up to you. What'll it be?"

I sighed. "Well, long as you ask so nicely, sure."

I stepped out of the booth. Two of the goons flanked me as we walked toward the front. Kevin had fallen behind, and abruptly I felt my shirttail move as he took my .45. "Ha," came his voice as we reached the door. "What were you gonna do, Perkins, shoot me with this?"

We went through the door onto the sidewalk. The old black man was still there, leaning against the wall. "Yassuh, yassuh," he said agreeably as we trooped past and turned left down the Eleventh Street sidewalk.

CHAPTER 28

IT WAS AN AWFULLY long walk on that short street. Halfway down we crossed to the west side and continued along the sidewalk. The street was populated only by litter, dancing along in the errant breezes. At that moment I felt more stupid than scared. After all the planning, all the cunning, all the warnings to Brian, here I was, the old pro, the alleged smart one, snatched. Jesus.

"So you've got the street under surveillance," I guessed.

"Sure do," Kevin said. "Spotted you the minute you showed up."

"What's the plan?" I asked, doing my best to sound indifferent.

"That's up to Number One. Come on, this way."

We bent off to the right across a wide apron paved with bricks. It led to a truck bay recessed into a gigantic brick building topped by a squat water tower. At the back of the truck bay was a loading dock. We mounted it via a set of small cement steps. The loading-dock doors were all rolled down and padlocked. We went to the end. Kevin had his machine pistol out now and leveled at my midsection. "Hold it, Perkins."

One of his men tapped on a steel man-door, listened, then pulled it open. Two other Skinheads peered out at us, weapons ready. Kevin shoved me. "Inside."

We walked in. The door slammed behind me. We walked up a dim hallway past several offices that were long out of use. Dust hung heavy in the thick, bottled-up air, mixed with the old petroleum-based scent of heavy manufacturing. In the distance I heard echoey male voices and the sounds of movement. Presently the hallway turned left, and we went through an open set of double doors and stopped.

I blinked to adjust my eyes to the piercing brightness of klieg lights that beamed down on a rough-hewn wood platform built in the center of the cavernous room. Two people stood on the platform. I guess dangled is a better word; their wrists were bound and raised high in the air by ropes that led up into the darkness; their feet barely touched the platform. One was Elliot Andelson, wearing white shirt, red tie, gray vest, and pants. The other was an attractive black woman with long, straight black hair, wearing a shimmering blue outfit and matching pumps. She looked terrified; he looked resigned and defiant.

Ranged around the platform, in the fringe of the light, were perhaps a dozen Skinheads. Several were armed, the weapon of choice being the same kind of chunky machine pistol Kevin carried. Their posture was a casual at-ease, and their faces were indifferent as they looked at us.

The one at the far end was Brian.

It was all I could do to keep my mouth shut. You son of a *bitch*, I raged inside. Why didn't you take off while you had the chance—

"So, Kevin," came a jovial male voice, "who do we have here?"

The man sat on a second small platform just past the first one, up high on some kind of stool. I could not make out his face clearly. I could see that he was dressed casually, wore a close-cropped dark beard and glasses. I said, "Mr. Robertson, I presume?"

Before my voice had echoed away into the vast blackness, something jabbed me hard in the kidneys. "You address him as Number One," Kevin hissed.

I gasped, fighting the pain, and straightened. "Or is it Mr. Catlin? What name do you go by down here?"

"Number One will suffice," the man said, annoyance evident in his low voice. "Give me some light, Dennis."

A switch snapped somewhere and another klieg came on, lighting up Number One. He was much slighter than I expected, a very fit, small-boned man in his fifties. He wore a navy blue turtleneck shirt over prewashed jeans and shiny black pointy-toed boots. His brown hair was long, curling smoothly down to his collar. He had more hair than anyone in

the room except for me and the female prisoner on th
platform. His lipless mouth was a straight, angry line as h
looked me over. "Kevin? What's the story?"

Kevin stepped forward and straightened almost to atten
tion. "This is Perkins," he said in monotone. "Friend of m
mother's. A private detective, Number One."

Number One nodded slowly. Without moving I tried t
scope out the room. Even the brighter light failed to pene
trate to the walls or the ceiling. But now I could make ou
coils of electrical wire snaking around on the stained cemen
floor and a gigantic video camera mounted on a tripod to m
right, aimed at the larger platform. Whatever these clown
were planning, it didn't look good for Mr. Andelson and hi
lady.

"How did you find us, Perkins?" Number One intoned.

"Well, these teenagers of yours kind of grabbed me an
forced me in here at gunpoint."

"How did you *find us*?" he shrieked.

I stayed silent. Stalling.

Number One leaned forward on his stool, trying to bur
holes into me with his eyes. "You're a detective. Did Kevin'
mother hire you? To find him? Is that it?"

I shook my head. Dead silence again, eyes on me from
everywhere. Then my companions edged away from me
"Let's off him, Number One," Kevin said.

A dim roaring sounded in my ears from maximum adrena
line powering into me. I was ready to move, and I'd take
three or four of these guys with me if—

No signal, no nothing, just an explosion in my head and
then I was kissing cement, dazed and moaning. Heavy blows
thudded my stomach and legs, felt like boots, a rain of boots,
a good old-fashioned stomping. I curled into a ball and then
lashed out with both feet and someone screamed and fell.
Then, just as suddenly as it had started, it stopped.

I opened my eyes and looked up. Hard, pitiless faces
stared down at me, ready. They'd hardly raised a sweat. I
heard Number One's voice. "Take him out. Lock him up. If
he resists, kill him instantly."

"Let's do him now, Number One," came Kevin's urgent
voice.

"No. I must know how he tracked us down," Number One

toned. "First we have to take care of the trial. That's why
e're here, Kevin. Now do as I say."

Hands gripped me and raised me. My guts felt all rearranged,
id I thought I'd puke any minute. I wheezed with the pain,
linking as the world did a boogaloo around my head. Num-
er One said, "Camera ready?"

"Yessir," came the answer.

"Let's get on with it. We'll need time to dub the tapes
terward. I want copies at all four major stations in time for
ie eleven o'clock newscasts. You see, men? Even the Jewsmedia
in be put to good purpose."

The Skinheads started to drag me away. I looked around,
ying to find Brian. Couldn't see him. Couldn't see much of
nything at that point.

A new, yet familiar, voice rang out behind us. "You have no
ithority to try us," said Elliot Andelson.

"This is the People's Court!" Number One thundered. "You
re charged with being a meddling Jew who has conspired
rith the Zionist Occupational Government to thwart the
ightful, God-given aims of Christian America, as represented
y these fine young lions here."

"I plead guilty!" Andelson shouted defiantly.

"You plead innocent," Number One countered. "It is we
rho will find you guilty and impose penalty."

We were getting farther and farther away into the black-
ess. One of the men turned on a flashlight. Off in the
istance was a wall, a door. The voices behind me became
choes. I thought about making a move, but at that point
eeded all my strength to remain upright. Besides, as my
addy always said, save your strength for the fights you can
in.

"I demand that you let my wife go," Andelson said. "She
as no part in this."

"The nigger whore will stand trial first," Number One said.
The charge is miscegenation. With which you shall also be
harged, Jew. . . . Roll tape, Dennis. Let us begin."

We reached the door, went through, and from that point on
he only sound I heard was my own pained breathing and the
ffortful grunts of my captors as they half carried and half
narched me along.

* * *

I guess maybe twenty minutes passed. My head cleare
gradually. I straightened from a fetal position, testing myse
and then sat up. The absolute pitch blackness of the roo
made me feel dizzy on top of the pain. I'd never been in su
total darkness before. For a brief moment panic made a ru
at me, but I squelched it. Knock it off, man. There's work
do. Size it up.

The Skinheads had tossed me into some kind of roor
frisked me, then argued over who was going to stand guar
They'd finally sorted that out, and a door had slamme
leaving me in darkness. All I knew was that I was behind
very solid-sounding door, lying on a concrete floor, with
armed man standing outside. I knew that the Skinhead
under the direction of Number One, were about to do som
very unpleasant things to Elliot Andelson and his wife, tapin
the festivities for posterity. I knew that Brian was out ther
contrary to my explicit orders.

As for me, I was unarmed, penned up, with an armed goo
standing guard outside the door. The stomping had bee
agony, and I knew the worst of that was yet to come; but
seemed as though nothing was broken, and I wasn't coughi
up blood or anything. I almost giggled. Shit, you been
worse spots than this, man! These guys really are duml
They didn't hardly hurt you at all.

Okay, let's see if I can stand up.

I did so, weaving in the blackness. Least they could hav
done was left a night-light in here or something. I'd notice
during our stroll back here that there were no lights any
where in this part of the building. It was abandoned, and th
Skinheads hadn't tried to reestablish the electric account. A
they'd done was run lines in from somewhere to give the
just enough power and light for their "trial."

Well, let there be light. I fished a kitchen match out of m
pocket and flared it on my thumbnail. The flame pushed th
darkness back about two feet and made me squint. I raised
high and looked around. An empty room. Brick walls. Ceilin
out of sight in the darkness. No weapons, of course. N
nothing. Just a room.

The match burned down to my fingers and I dropped i
That pain made me forget the generalized pain for a momer
or two. I fired up another match and decided to inspect th
walls. I found the door first. Solid steel built flush into a ste

asement. I could get through that easy, with a stick of
ynamite.

I started to follow the wall: to one corner, turn right, walk
long, *ouch!* as the goddam match burned me. I lighted
nother one and continued my stroll. To another corner, then
ight. Maybe six full steps between corners. Fifteen feet or
o. I'd gone about three steps when a reflection showed up on
ne wall. A window.

Well, what have we here? I went close to the wall, holding
p the flickering match. It was a window, all right, palm-sized
lass panes set in a steel grid. Child's play to bust out of.
xcept for the fact that the window had been bricked over
om the outside. The glass itself could be a weapon of sorts,
' nothing better turned up. *Oh shit* as the match burned me
nd went out, throwing me into darkness.

I went into my pocket again. One more match. I fired it up
nd continued my walk around the walls, ending back at the
oor. Nothing useful. Absolutely nothing.

I raised the match as high as I could. The light died away
s it reached the ceiling about fifteen feet up. Below it ran a
air of two-inch iron pipes. A notion came to me. They could
e old. Could be brittle. Could make for a handy weapon, if I
ould get one loose.

They looked to be two feet below the ceiling, about twelve
eet off the floor. Could I jump twelve feet? Nothing for it but
o give it the old college try—*christ* and the match singed
ny fingers and died as I flicked it to the floor.

Total darkness again. But now I had a plan. Not much of a
lan, but better than nothing. I stood and breathed deeply,
ucking in all the oxygen and courage I could get, feeling my
ruised ribs complain under the stress. In my mind's eye I
ictured those pipes and drew imaginary coordinates as to
vhere they were. I pictured myself back in high-school days,
racticing my slam dunk on the old iron hoop mounted above
he garage door at the house on Bennet Street. This wasn't
nuch tougher than that. I was only about a hundred thou-
and years older, that's all.

I backed up till I reached the wall, keeping my attention
ocused on a segment of blackness where those pipes were,
hen took a couple of half-running steps and leapt for the sky,
ny right hand up as high as I could stretch it.

And came right back down to the cement with a roll and
tumble that lit up the dashboard with warning lights.

I panted and swallowed and got back to my feet slowl
Listened for a minute, straining for any suspicious soun
from the outside. Nothing. The sentry hadn't heard anythin
Thank God for small favors.

I thought I still had a fix on where those pipes were, but
this darkness it was hard to tell. Panic made a fresh mov
but I fought it back. Just start all over, son.

I backed up till I reached a wall. Felt along it till I found
corner. Went the other way till I found a corner. No door.

I rounded the corner and moved along and *here* it is, *here*
the fucking door. We're okay now. Sort of. I leaned my bac
against the wall, taking those deep breaths again. Those pip
should be . . . right about *there*. I counted breaths till I'd don
ten big ones, thinking about Isiah Thomas of the Detro
Pistons, short for a pro, only an inch or so taller than me—*I*
could sure manage this, no sweat. I pictured him doing it.
pictured me doing it. Then I tensed, ran, and sprang.

A pipe brushed my knuckles roughly, and I almost didn
make it, but somehow I got my hand twisted right and caugh
hold, then swung there like a monkey, almost slipped awa
got my other hand up and around the other pipe, an
dangled, feeling my weight trying to stretch me into
Gumby doll. Exhilaration gave way to bitterness as I jounce
myself on the pipes as hard as I could. They rattled, b
there was no give, no break. They'd stay up here, useless a
weapons or as anything else.

I almost let go, but froze just in time. Another idea, Benj
old son; as long as you're up here . . .

I reached my feet forward as far as they would go. Nothing
Okay. That's all right. Lots of strength yet. Clumsily I hand
over-handed myself along, maybe six inches per stroke, checkin
out in front of me with my feet. Presently my steel-toe
shoes brushed the wall. Okay, fine. That meant the windo
was a couple of feet to the right. Perfect.

I grinned savagely in the darkness, thinking about how
might go. I knew this would work. It had to, because it wa
all I had left.

I raised both feet up, straining mightily with my arms, an
kicked forward and to the right. Glass shattered and crashe
to the cement floor, making an unholy racket. I kicked agai

nd again, raking the window with my steel-toed shoes,
ending glass and steel everywhere. The strain in my arms
nd shoulders turned to pain, headed for numbness, but this
was no time to crap out. I pulled my feet up, up, up, using
every ounce of strength that I had, till they reached the pipes
just this side of the wall. There I linked them around the
pipes and felt blessed relief as my legs and feet took some of
my weight off my arms and hands.

I hung there like a trussed hog. And I waited and listened.

A muffled voice from outside hollered, "What the hell you
doing in there?"

Just hanging around, I thought.

The door opened with a squeal. A pool of light shone on
the floor. A voice muttered: "What the fuck?"

The light circled the cement floor, reached gleaming shards
of glass. "Jesus Christ!" Flicked to the window, lighting up
the shattered window and the solidly cemented brick.

Now.

CHAPTER 29

I UNHOOKED MY FEET and let them swing down, gaining momentum as they arced around, pressing them together
into a blunt weapon, swinging hard and back and *there,* at
the point of maximum force, I felt impact, a wet thud like a
sodden pillow dropped on a dock. I heard the man hit the
wall and clatter to the floor as his flashlight spun away and
shattered on the cement, throwing everything into darkness.

When I'd swung back to vertical I let go of the pipes and
dropped heavily to the floor. My arms felt about twelve feet
long. I turned and stepped forward cautiously. My shoe
brushed something, a foot, a leg. I kicked the leg hard. No
sound. No breathing, even.

Grand slam, Ben old son. Mary Lou Retton couldn't have
done it prettier.

I could hear very faint noises in the extreme distance. But
no sign of alarm. The room was far from the action, and I'd
taken out the only sentry. Now for a weapon, and then I'd
take a little stroll and see what was what.

I bent to the body and felt of it. Rag-doll limp, loose-
boned, wobbly. It made me feel a little queasy, but this was
only a physical reaction. Emotionally, I was charged up and
ready to go. No remorse at all. Killing was their tool of
choice; they'd each killed someone to become a member of
the Special Action Group. Now, some number of them would
find out what it's like to be on the receiving end. They'd
learn that hell's only half full.

Footsteps outside. Advancing light, faint.

I'd found no weapon yet, and it was suddenly too late to
look further. I stepped to the left of the door and froze against

he wall. I heard the door squeal open, and the light shone
down on the bloody, blasted head. I kicked the hairy wrist as
hard as I could, knocking the flashlight away, then grabbed
the arm and hurled the man artlessly into the room and down
onto the floor. I wasn't going to play with him. I jumped on
him with both knees and slammed my forearm down across
his throat. In the dim light of the discarded flashlight I saw
the squarish face of the Skinhead stretch tight, eyes panicky.
He scrambled and fought beneath me, but I held him,
squeezing tighter on his throat. Suddenly he froze and forced
out a word that sounded like a cough.

I eased up suddenly on his throat. "What did you say?" I
growled.

"Ponder! Ponder!" he said, voice a rusted wheeze. "Lemme
go, Perkins!"

He wasn't Ponder, that was for sure. Way too young, way
too well built. "Where'd you get that word, asshole?"

"It's a name. My boss. I work for him. I came back here to
spring you, you fuckin' goon. Lemme go."

Suddenly I believed him. I didn't feel much like engaging
in a love feast, though. "Well, you got back here in the nick
of time," I growled, easing off him. "That corpse over there
had just about gotten the best of me."

I stood. He sat up, shaking his head. I picked up the
flashlight and checked the door. No action outside. The man
got to his feet slowly. Taller than me, then, very young.
Leather and denim and chains and no hair. Fit the part.

"So what outfit you work for?" I asked.

"That's not important."

Now I knew for sure he belonged to Ponder. "Swell. You
got a name, at least?"

"Stewart, Jim Stewart."

"Charmed."

"Think we can take 'em?" he asked.

"Prob'ly liven things up out there. What's happening?"

He reached under his vest, pulled out a handgun, and
handed it to me butt first. My .45 automatic. Hi there, old
pal. I put the flashlight in my armpit and jacked out the clip.
Six left. I rammed it home and worked the action once, then
stuck the gun in my waistband. Stewart had drifted to the
door and seemed to be listening. Then he looked at me.

"When I slipped away, they were just finishing up the tria
of Mrs. Andelson," he said.

"Uh-huh. Do I need to ask what the verdict was?"

"They're going to stone her to death," he said.

Oh man. *Christ*. "We got to move," I said. "You carrying?"

"All I got's a thirty-eight," he said. "Big problem is I'm
down to five rounds and that's all."

"I thought all you guys carried squirt guns."

"Only the senior guys. The rest of us, it's catch as catch can."

"Huh." I shined the flashlight down at the sentry's body
"Check the dead there, see what he's got."

He looked down. "Uh . . . well, I'd rather not."

Aw, *come* on. I bent and frisked the corpse by the light o
the flash. He had a knife, which I tucked, sheath and all, in
my back pocket. He also had what looked like a .32 revolver
I checked the cylinder, snapped it shut, and tossed the piece
to Stewart. "Here's eight more. That gives you thirteen
Make 'em count, when the time comes."

"I'll try," he said, putting the weapon away.

"Swell." I tried to think up a plan that would guarantee
results beyond our both getting killed. Nothing felt good
Stewart waited patiently. Real driving force, this guy. I guessed
I could give him points for coming back to help me, but i
didn't look like he was going to be much help from here on.

"Now listen up," I said. "I've got a man out there. Undercover. Tall blond kid named Brian."

"Brian?" he snorted. "Brian's yours?"

"He's a civilian. You got that? When things start poppin',
I'm making Brian your personal responsibility. You use those
thirteen rounds to keep him out of harm's way. That's your
job, you follow?"

"Hey, pal," Stewart said, "you don't give me orders."

"Yeah, I do. Or I blow your fucking head off. Your choice."

He glared at me, then put up both hands briefly. "Okay."

"That's nice." I listened at the door again. Nothing. "Let's
drift out there and look around," I said finally. "Real quiet.
Real careful."

Stewart carried the flashlight, shining it at the floor, as we
moved at a quick walk up a long, dark hallway. At the double
doors we waited and listened; then I turned the knob slowly,

ushed the door open partway, and peered through. The
enter of the action was about one hundred feet away and
partially blocked by a freestanding wall, which jutted out
rom the left. I could see Skinheads, Number One on his
tool, part of the platform. I could not see the camera, or
either of the Andelsons. Voices engaged in some kind of loud
dialogue, rendered unintelligible by the echoing in the gigan-
ic factory building.

Stewart stood there beside me, waiting for orders like a
good little soldier. Nice guy, I thought grimly. Gets in here
undercover and just stands around watching. Big help. I
wondered when the cavalry would arrive. I began to wonder
f it would. But no way could I sit around on my hands.
Things were about to get ugly for the Andelsons. I had to find
a way to keep the Skinheads busy.

I pulled the door partway shut and whispered to Stewart,
"How many men?"

"Uh . . . sixteen, including me and your man. Not including
Number One."

"Guards at the entrance?"

"Two there. Oh, and one in civvies up at the corner. That's
how they spotted you."

"So in the room there we've got an even dozen unfriendlies,
not counting the big cheese. Weapons?"

"All armed. Some with machine pistols. The rest with
handguns. Tons of ammo. I mean, this goddam place is a
fortress. There's only two of us, Perkins—"

"Yeah, but we're inside already."

"With two lousy pistols apiece."

"And we've got the element of surprise."

"They'll kill us as soon as look at us. It'll be a bloodbath."
Naked fear was evident in Stewart's whisper.

I grinned. "Plus, we're on the side of the angels."

"Look," he said, "my assignment was to penetrate and
report. I'm not an action guy. Undercover's my thing."

"Well, welcome to the wonderful world of operations.
Cause we're going out there, you and me, and put the brakes
on this thing before Andelson and his wife get killed."

"Oh yeah?" he shot back. "And how in the hell are we
going to do that?"

"See there, you're getting hung up on details. Don't worry,
I'll tell you in a second."

I pushed the door open again and studied the layout. Th
light out there was brighter now. Seemed like they'd turne
on some more kliegs; must be getting ready to resume tapi
or something. I tried to figure how to get the drop on the
guys. And I remembered the solution I'd stumbled upd
back there in that room.

The high ground.

Amateur operators think only about the plane they're o
They don't look down, or up. Owning the high ground
worth an extra three or four men, if you work it right.

I looked up. Now, with the light somewhat brighter, I sa
that the ceiling was crowded with hardware and apparatu
massive electrical conduits, hanging fluorescent fixtures, co
veyor belts and tracks, heating ducts, and pipes of all size
some as thick as a man. It brought to mind my years on th
line at Ford's Rouge, and I knew that something else had
be up there, and after a moment's search I spotted it.
network of catwalks.

"Yes indeed, I like it," I breathed. I pulled the door sh
again, huddled with Stewart, and spent a few minutes mot
vating him.

When I was done, he said nervously, "This is crazy."

"Oh sure," I said jauntily, "but it'll work as long as neith
of us fucks up. I won't fuck up. And if you do, you'll be dea
Nothing personal, just a fair warning. Got it?"

"All right."

"Okay. Good hunting, pal. And remember Brian. I want n
harm to come to a hair on his head."

I pushed the door open. All clear. Beaming the flashlig
down, I slipped out and headed right, across the vacar
factory floor toward the far wall. With one glance back I sa
that Stewart was sauntering straight ahead, toward the actio
I didn't have a whole lot of faith in him. What I was hoping
in my heart of hearts, was that help would arrive before th
shit hit the fan. Sort of even up the odds a little.

Presently I reached the far wall. It was solid brick from
floor to ceiling, broken occasionally by solid-steel doors tha
were undoubtedly locked. I turned right and walked along
shining the light ahead, and came to a steel ladder, bolted t
the wall and going straight up into oblivion.

Beautiful. I tested the ladder with a tug, found it secure
turned off the flashlight, stuck it in my waistband, and began t

imb. The floor fell away as I rose, ten, fifteen, twenty feet or
≀tter. The air was hotter up here, thick and textured. The
⸱twalk meandered away in two directions, winding drunkenly
ꞥong the pipes and machinery that sat silent and obsolete, no
⸱ubt home to spiders and birds and God knew what else.

I turned left and started along the catwalk, walking stooped
 keep from scraping my head on pipes and ceiling struts
ᴉat reached down from above. I had to go slow. The catwalk
ᴠisted and turned, stepped up and down here and there,
ᴉd was not designed for excursions in the dark. It had
ꜟandrails, but only intermittently, and for all I knew, it could
ꜟd at any point without warning. Plus, I had to be quiet.
ⅈdn't want anyone down below to hear the *clonk clonk clonk*
f my big feet.

As I navigated my way toward the Skinhead conclave, the
ꞥices gained and became intelligible. It was Number One
ꞥlking. Orating, more like.

". . . And by the power vested in me as the supreme justice
f this People's Court, I find you, Melissa Chase Andelson,
ꞥrrupt Negress, whore to the Jews, and conspirator against
ꞥhite Christian America, *guilty* of all charges and specifications."

I heard her sobbing and pleading. Andelson shouted some-
ᴉing I could not make out.

"And," Number One went on implacably, "I sentence you
 death by stoning. Sentence to be carried out forthwith.
ꞧen?"

I bent lower and moved faster, the sound of my feet
ꞥdible on the heavy steel catwalk. A corner came and I
ꞥade a left. Almost there now, almost atop them. The light
ꞥas brilliant down there, the platform clear, as was Number
꜠ne on his stool, the prisoners trussed with their hands
ꞩtretched high, the Skinheads arrayed around the periphery
ꞧith the monstrous video camera squatting among them. The
ꞥew reminded me of the overhead shots of the June Taylor
꜠ancers.

"This is nothing but murder, you bastard," came Andelson's
ꞥard, angry voice.

"We'll get to you, Jew," Number One said. "Just relax and
ꞥatch."

At last I was over the platform. I eased to my knees and
ᴉen flattened out on my stomach on the steel mesh catwalk.
ꞥy view of the action was partially obstructed by a huge,

thick pipe that ended abruptly right next to me. The rop
binding the Andelsons were looped around it and knotted
my side. That was a break, anyhow. As for the rest...

I adjusted myself and looked, trying to figure the best w
to do this. The Skinheads were busily emptying gunnysa
onto the cement floor. Busted bricks, chunks of cinder blo
rocks and stones of various sizes. A low, feral male murm
rose to me.

There were so *many* of them.

I got out the .45 automatic and lay it next to me. Then
knife, which I unsheathed. Eight-inch blade, not overly sha
and pretty worthless up here.

Number One's voice: "Ready, men?"

Each Skinhead held a rock. The eager buzzing was rising
volume. I saw Brian at the rear. He held a rock, too, but I g
the feeling he was thinking of bolting for the exit. I didn't s
Stewart anywhere.

Melissa Andelson's terrified wailing rose as she twist
from the rope, trying to get away. The rawest, ugliest kind
anger was rising in me, making logical thought difficult.
wished I had one of those squirt guns up here. I'd have ac
'em en masse and to hell with Stewart and even Brian.
picked up the .45 and aimed down—who do I take first—

"Now!" Number One boomed.

A hail of rocks and bricks and other missiles showered t
platform in a narrow, deadly fusillade. Dull, moist sounds
impact and then wooden thundering as the missiles rebound
to the platform. Melissa Andelson screamed like an anim
with pure pain, pure terror. I tried to shut out the noise a
aimed the .45 with trembling hands. That one right ther
the fat slob with the big grin, he's first—

The pipe. Something about that big pipe.

The odds were suicidal, but not entirely hopeless. I was
high, some distance away, and the lights would be in the
eyes. The steel grid of the catwalk provided some protectio
There was the element of surprise. If I had just one mo
thing—that damn pipe—

It made a slight elbow curve and ended abruptly, pointe
downward, with a heavy flange. Had apparently been co
nected to something else that was long gone. At the elbo
was affixed a large steel wheel, probably a butterfly valve.

The Skinheads were rearming themselves. I heard the

xcited voices, the woman's screams and moans, intelligible
ow, oh God God God. Number One intoned something
bout the children of Satan, the mating of Eve with the
erpent, but I was looking at the valve and thinking about the
ater tower I'd seen above the building. What a long shot...
ut if it was true, what a diversion... a diversion that could
rove to be distracting to the fellas down there.

I set the .45 down, reached out from the catwalk, and
rabbed the wheel. Tried to turn it left and got nowhere.
rozen. Maybe rusted. Jesus. I adjusted myself forward and
ied again, putting all my strength into it till my muscles and
ints ached. Nothing.

"Ready with the second volley," Number One commanded.

I twisted myself almost crossways on the catwalk and
nked my legs around a post on the opposite side. Got a fresh
rip on the wheel at ten-till-five. Locked myself like a vise
nd applied strength again, starting easy, building force gradually,
arder and harder till my eyes felt like they were about to
op out of my face, my jaw clenched tight, my arms quivering
lightly, as if I was arm wrestling with the Ambassador
ridge.

I did not feel it start to give. But abruptly it did as the
wheel moved left about ten degrees, emitting a high, pierc-
ng, metallic shriek, then locked tight again. As syrupy brown
iquid began to stream thinly out the mouth of the pipe,
eaded downward, the noise from below shut off abruptly.

"What the fuck," a male voice said.

I'd reapplied full force to the wheel, and it gave finally, this
ime for real. As I cranked it left, hand over hand, the stream
uilt and cleared, and then water thundered out the mouth of
he pipe with a sound like an explosion, shooting out and
own under the tons of pressure from the water tower above.

Shouts from below. I sensed commotion bordering on
anic, but I had things to do. I stood up, retrieving the .45
nd the knife as I went. Reached the knife to the ropes
round the pipe and hacked and sawed at each in turn till
hey severed and dropped away. I heard a burst of automatic
gunfire from somewhere, and the ricochet of bullets off metal
o my right. I didn't care. I danced to my left, looking for a
clear field of fire, looking for something to shoot.

CHAPTER 30

THE ANDELSONS WERE ALMOST invisible under the explosio
of water. I saw that he had taken his wife in his arms and w
dragging her toward the back of the platform, away from th
Skinheads, who had fallen back from the water in confusio
looking up toward the ceiling, some with weapons read
some cowering. Number One had left his stool and darte
toward the darkness to the left. He wasn't armed as far as
could tell, but he was yelling: "Shoot them all! Shoot the
all!"

I fired at him and missed by a mile. I'm no marksma
anyhow, and the .45 is no precision weapon, and shootin
downward from such an angle is tough. Five shots left no
Jesus. I dropped to the catwalk as several men returned fir
bullets careening crazily off pipes and struts around m
giving off sparks. I saw the fat slob just on the other side
the abandoned video camera; he was aiming his squirt gun
my direction. I aimed for his head and squeezed off one th
took him just above the sternum, blowing him down an
away.

Several Skinheads went down on their haunches and opene
fire at me, muzzle flashes obscuring them. I huddled into
tight ball, praying like mad as the slugs whanged around m
with a horrid metallic racket. I aimed and fired two more
counting more on luck than skill. Burst a head, just winge
another one who went down and would probably stay there

Movement below and to the right. It was Brian, arme
with a revolver, and he had the Andelsons behind him, th
husband dragging the wife, herding them back into th
blackness. The enemy saw that at the same time I did. Bria

red several wild shots in their direction. They started to hoot back, but I saw one go down with a drilled head and another take two in the belly and flop forward into the spreading lake of water that was still cascading down from above. Must be Stewart, somewhere. We had them triangulated.

I took out another one as he was trying to reload. There were fewer targets now; I wondered if some were deserting. Probably. It's easy to be tough when no one fights back. Number One had emerged from the darkness by the far wall and was moving at a fast crouch behind his men toward the exit. I shot at him again and only got return fire for my trouble. Then the double glass doors at the exit hurled open, driven by two retreating Skinheads who fell, knocking Number One down.

I stood up straight as I glimpsed a helmeted man behind the doors. The remaining Skinheads had started to run. A boom, a flash of light, and one of the punks, who'd found his feet and was trying to retreat past the stage, leapt into the air and bellysmacked still in the water. The man came through the door, shotgun braced on his hip, its ugly snout moving back and forth, looking for a fresh target. Two other men joined him and fanned out along the wall, weapons ready. They were all in uniform. Detroit police.

Weapons clattered to the water and hands shot into the air. Just two Skinheads still on their feet, and they had hands up, screaming their surrender. One of them was Kevin. I wondered where he'd been all this time.

Several more cops came into the room. The gush of water was losing force rapidly. I looked at my .45 and saw that it had locked open—empty. I stuck it in my waistband, trotted to the wall, and clonked down a ladder to the floor. I heard men moaning and the sharp barks of the police officers as they fanned out around the room, collecting weapons into a rough pile by the platform. I walked toward them, dodging bloodied bodies, looking around for Brian and Stewart and the Andelsons, my hands high in the air.

I felt dazed. Aside from the stomping, I was totally unhurt after the worst fight of my life. I couldn't believe it.

"Perkins," I called. "Friendly."

"Says you, asshole," barked a familiar voice from the hall. A bulky male figure in a business suit stormed through the

door into the room. Elvin Dance, face stormy, .38 special
one hand. "Where's the Andelsons?" he growled.

"Back here," called Brian from the darkness to my righ
The greatest sound I'd ever heard. "They're hurt."

Several cops ran back that way as I reached Elvin. "Ba
among the living?" I grinned. He just put his hands on h
hips and glared. "Took you long enough," I needled.
thought I'd fixed that pay phone so the line would stay ope
long enough for you to trace it."

"Takes time," he grunted. "I could bitch about you ar
your stinky fake-blood recipe. Like to've puked. And th
ugly old ripped-up shirt you give me to wear didn't hard
fit." Good old Elvin was back. He'd been going squirrel
before, but now action and success had revived him. I w
glad.

Someone called my name over the racket in the room.
looked around and saw Brian approaching. No damage, far i
I could tell. Thank God. "I oughta kick your ass up betwee
your ears," I said.

His long, honest face looked sweaty and wan and olde
"Yeah," he said, "you told me to run and I didn't. But wh
about you? You told me this cop was dead. Looks plenty aliv
to me. You conned me."

"Figured it'd be easier for you to be convincing if yc
didn't know the truth," I said. "Sue me." I tried to look angr
but I couldn't manage it. Mostly I felt relieved, and ver
very tired. To Elvin I said, "This is my undercover man."

"We won't lock him up, then," Elvin said. Some paramed
ics charged through the door, led by a policeman, and sloshe
back through the lake of water toward the darkness. "W
caught five of 'em outside," he said, "sorta strolling u
Eleventh Street, whistling, hands in their pockets. What
the count in here?"

Kevin and the other unharmed prisoner were braced again
the wall to my right, being frisked. As I surveyed the bodie
on the floor, Stewart appeared from behind and stood next t
me. "Nice work, Ben," he said.

"Hey, same to you, pal," I said pleasantly. "This fella lent
hand, too," I said to Elvin. The police captain nodded
"Looks like we got two unharmed, and eight dead or injure
in here." A thought occurred to me. "Excuse me a minute."
turned to Stewart, grinned, then hammered him up side c

is head with fists clenched together. He collapsed to the
eck, out cold instantly. "Make that nine dead or injured," I
aid to Elvin.

The police captain had not changed expression. "What was
hat for?"

"He's one of Ponder's boys. I figure, lock him up with the
est till he can document who he is. That way, Ponder won't
e able to take any credit for this collar. Besides, he needs a
ttle lesson in manners. Just hung around these clowns,
idn't lift a finger to stop them till I came along."

"Nice," Elvin said. The paramedics pushed past us, carry-
ıg a stretcher that bore Melissa Andelson. She was bloody
nd unconscious, but alive. Her husband trailed the proces-
ion, head down. Looked like they'd be all right.

Aside from drips, no more water issued from the pipe.
'olicemen were everywhere in the smoky room, along with
nedics, checking out the dead and injured. Elvin Dance
hook his head. "Hell of a mess. Least it's all wrapped up."

Kevin and the other survivor had been handcuffed. I said
o Elvin, "You're forgetting one thing, bro."

Elvin's quizzical look turned to shock. I heard a scream
ehind me, and spun. A cop was down, blood jetting from his
eg around a knife jammed into his thigh up to the hilt.
Jumber One was up on his knees, the policeman's revolver
n both hands, pointed at us. "Traitor," he snarled, and fired.

A smack, a grunt, a thud as a body hit the floor. Number
One flung his weapon away and rose to his feet, hands up. "I
urrender," he said, smiling coldly.

I glanced behind me and my heart stopped. Brian lay on
is back, knees drawn up to his belly, which pumped messy
ed. His eyes were open, and his handsome face looked alien
n its agony. I rushed to him, bent over him, touched him
vith helpless hands. "Oh shit, oh God no." He croaked
something. "Not now," I said, "it was all done. Finished. Oh,
Christ." I looked around frantically, saw a pair of paramedics
by the platform, staring numbly at me. "Get over here, for
godsake, do something."

They came to life and scrambled in my direction. I rose to
ny feet as Elvin walked toward Number One, who stood
there, frozen, hands in the air. Elvin had his revolver in his
hand.

"You're under arrest," Elvin said to him, voice tight.

"I want a lawyer," Number One said. "I have nothing say till I've spoken to my lawyer. I know my rights."

Elvin stopped about a man's length from him. "Oh yeah the police captain said. "You got rights. You got all kin rights." He cocked his head. "You know who I am?"

"I know who you are," Number One said. "Nigger."

"Yep," Elvin said. "I'm a nigger, all right." His voice w different now. Higher. Strained. I couldn't move. Neith could anyone else in the room. Elvin's voice was perfect audible in the gigantic, smoky place. "I'm the nigger y thought was dead. Gunned down in a car on the west sid I'm Elvin Dance. Captain, Detroit police."

"Nigger," Number One said with an indifferent shrug.

The shot blew apart Number One's left kneecap, and I fell with a scream to the floor. He twisted and writhed in tot silence, face chalky behind the close-trimmed beard an glasses. Elvin held up his .38 and looked at it as it he'd nev seen it before.

"Captain!" one of the cops said. "No!"

I was barely conscious of the medics loading Brian gentl onto a stretcher, muttering to each other. Two others ha appeared and rushed to the knifed officer. I watched numb as Elvin walked to Number One, whose teeth were gritte eyes defiant. Elvin stood over the terrorist and pinned h chest with a well-polished shoe. "You thought I was dead, Elvin said to him.

"Nigger," the man grunted.

"No, Elvin," I said.

"Sweet dreams," Elvin said, and shot Number One be tween the eyes, puddling his head.

Nobody moved, said a word, or breathed.

After an eternity, Elvin took his shoe off Number One chest. He looked around at us, face vacant, then to the floc as he held up his revolver. "Zindlar," he grunted.

Another plainclothes officer, over by the wall, stirred "Yessir, Captain."

"Place me under arrest," Elvin said.

Zindlar stepped forward, then stopped. All was still agai for a moment. Elvin looked at him. "You heard me," he said

Zindlar's blocky, honest Polish face twisted with emotion The paramedics hustled out of the room, bearing Brian o the stretcher between them. No one else moved.

"Do it," Elvin said.

I thought about the murders that Number One had ordered. I thought about the pain and terror he'd inflicted on he Andelsons. He'd just knifed a cop and shot Brian, no doubt hoping to kill both. I recalled that Michigan has no death penalty—perhaps this had occurred to Elvin too—and could not convince myself that society would be any better served with Number One, or Justin Catlin, or whoever he was, in jail instead of dead.

Most of all, I thought about Elvin, his years of honorable service in one of the world's worst jobs; his selflessness, his courage. He'd been going squirrelly the past few weeks. Hopefully a good lawyer could use that to help him cop a plea, or get him off entirely. If there was any justice at all, no jury in the world would convict him. But his career, his very life, would be destroyed.

In the dead silence I said, "He went down in the firefight."

Elvin's vacant eyes slowly found me, uncomprehending.

"This man went down in the firefight," I said, looking around the vast room at the other men, one by one. "Elvin took him out, all right, at the very end there. Right, guys?"

One cop nodded, then another, then the rest, Zindlar most emphatically of all, and voices murmured in assent.

"Can't do that," Elvin said shakily. "No way."

I went to him, took his .38, put a hand on his shoulder, spoke down at him as gently as I could. "It's what happened, Elvin. Don't you remember?"

He shook his head violently, wiped his eyes roughly, looked at me and away.

"Disney World," I said softly. "You, and Mattie, and Leavon, out of this hellhole for a while. You deserve that, Elvin."

Zindlar came toward us. "Ain't nobody gonna rat you out," he growled. "You can't make us, Captain. We take care of our own. Them medics and everybody, they'll get the word."

Kevin Witkowski, still handcuffed and standing by the wall, said, "Oh yeah? Well, I'll tell. You murdered him."

"You're one to talk," I shot back. "Nobody on God's green earth'll buy your story, shithead. Not against all of us." I looked back at Elvin. "Okay, Captain? You all right?"

He nodded finally. I gave him his weapon and he holstered it. "Let's wrap this up," he said softly.

The other officers went back to work. I walked Elvin over

toward the door, where Kevin stood, bristly and hostile. "
got to roll," I said. "I got to get to the hospital, see abou
Brian." The thought made me feel dead inside. "I'm takin
this prick with me. Just like we agreed. Right?"

Elvin squinted. "Letting him walk like this, it just don'
seem right."

"We made a deal," I said.

Elvin nodded. At his gesture, a uniform uncuffed Kevin
"Where are we going?" he asked warily as I took him by th
arm and marched him toward the door.

"To see your dad," I answered.

Jerry Witkowski died peacefully just two hours later i
room 703N of Harper Hospital, with Lynne and Kevin at hi
side. Though I was in the room for a while, I wasn't ther
when the end came. I felt uncomfortable there in the roon
full of unshared secrets. And it just didn't seem fitting for m
to hang around. Jerry was my friend, but I've noticed tha
plenty of friends have managed to die without any help from
me.

Besides, I had people to check on, phone calls to make
arrangements to complete.

I went back in to find Lynne sitting in the chair by the
bed, head bowed, hands folded. Kevin leaned against the
wall by the window, staring down at the bed, face blank. He
was quite an anomaly with his shaved head, his leather vest
dark jeans, and boots. Jerry lay on the bed under a sheet with
that inertness peculiar to the dead, his shrunken, lined face
wan, yet somehow knowing. The man who had lived there
had gone on ahead. And for us he was becoming part of the
past.

Lynne did not look up at me or react as I put my hand on
her shoulder and squeezed it gently. I stood over Jerry and
looked at him for a while. Then I walked around the foot of
the bed to Kevin. "Word with you outside," I whispered.

He nodded and followed me out. I had the feeling he'd
been looking for an excuse to leave the room. We stopped in
the quiet hallway, about halfway between the brightly lit
nurses' station and a set of double doors at the other end.
There was no traffic; visiting hours were over, and the staff

as maintaining a discreet, respectful distance from room
03N.

Kevin's expression was faraway but not particularly somber.
Gimme a weed," he said.

"Fresh out of 'em. Can't smoke out here, anyway." I leaned
gainst the wall across from him and folded my arms. I
oticed that he would not meet my eyes. "Condolences on
our dad, Kevin," I said.

His head bobbed once in a nod. "Well, he was real sick and
verything." He looked back and forth. "Look, how long are
e going to have to hang around here? I want to get Mom
ome."

"I wouldn't worry about your mother if I were you. She'll
et home fine, I promise."

Kevin stared at me, then nodded, face hard. "Oh yeah, I
et it. You think now that Dad's gone you can just take over. I
now you got the hots for her. You think you're gonna start
icking her, you can just forget it."

"That's not what I had in mind," I said mildly. With
eripheral vision I saw two men in business suits appear in
he hallway by the nurses' station. They didn't look much like
octors. "And let me ask you this. Just what makes you think
ou'd be in any position to stand in the way?"

"My father's dead," he shot back. "I'm the man of the
amily now." The double doors down the hall to my right
pened and flapped shut. Three men, also in business suits,
tood there in the distance, arms folded, watching us. One of
hem was Dick Dennehy. Kevin saw them, turned and spot-
ed the others by the nurses' station, then glared at me with
urning eyes, face trembling. "What is this?" he whispered.

I held up both my hands palms out, watching Dick, who
odded. I dropped my hands and looked at Kevin. "Time to
ettle some accounts, kid."

CHAPTER 31

"**Y**OU FUCKING BASTARD!" KEVIN said incredulously. "Yo can't do this. You got me clear, that's what they paid you do, wasn't it?"

"Well, not exactly."

The door to 703N opened and Lynne came out. When sh saw us, she froze there by the closed door, watching. W ignored her. "You got nothing on me," Kevin said harshly.

"Hm. Let's see. There's a couple of kidnapping charge behind the Andelson thing. Remember that? Attempted mu der if you threw so much as a pebble at Mrs. Andelso Weapons charges, I would think. Plus, there's the sma matter of the school bus that you firebombed. Six kids dea as I recall."

That threw him. He blinked rapidly and blurted, "B deal, just a bunch of niggers."

Tired though I was, it was all I could do to keep my hand off him, to stay calm. "You have to answer for it." I raised m hands and made a beckoning gesture, and the state polic detectives started toward us from both ends.

"You got no proof!" Kevin said shrilly.

"The cops have evidence. And I got your admission jus now. Smart move, Kevin."

"Your word against mine!"

"Your mom heard it, too. Didn't you, Lynne?"

She looked fearful and dumbstruck. Kevin said, "She won rat me. I'm all she's got left."

"Six kids dead," I said roughly. "You'll go away for it."

The cops reached us from both sides, Dick in the lead. H

ave Lynne a pleasant nod. "Good evening," he said to me.
Has our perpetrator been frisked?"

"He's clean," I said.

"For God's sake, don't do this, Ben," Lynne said.

One of the cops snapped a cuff on Kevin's wrist. He just
tood there and took it, looking defiant. "Don't worry, Mom,"
e said. "It's an honor to be a prisoner of war."

"Yeah, well, whatever, you're under arrest," Dick advised
im. "You have the right to, and all that sort of thing. Fuck it,
e'll Mirandize you in the car. Just shut your face meanwhile."

Lynne stepped forward and took her son's arm. "I won't
estify!" she cried, eyes wild. "I didn't hear anything!"

"You will if you have to, Lynne," I said.

She fixed me with a stare that could kill. "He's my *son*,"
he hissed.

"Let's go," Dick said.

Kevin ripped himself loose from the cop's grip and turned
o me, smiling. "You think you've won? Well, think again.
his is only a skirmish. The war is yet to come."

"You'll have lots of time to think about it in the slammer," I
nswered.

"There's plenty more like me," Kevin shot back.

"But not enough," I said. "Nowhere near enough."

Kevin glanced around at the policemen. "You Zogs think
ou've got the people? You've got the guns, and you've
mprisoned their bodies. But we own their hearts."

I stayed still as the procession started up the hall toward
he elevators. Lynne trailed along behind her son. At one
oint she glanced back at me, face full of pleading. She knew
hat, for me, she was the one for whom I'd do anything, no
questions asked. But I was drawing the line here, and I shook
ny head. Her expression turned to hatred, she turned away
nd took her son's arm, and I realized that the Lynne
Witkowski I'd once known was gone for good.

I took the door handle, braced myself, and went in. The
oom was a single, located at Detroit Receiving Hospital, just
short walk from Harper. It looked new, and much more
heerful in decor than Jerry's had been. Solomon Kraus and a
oung, dark-haired woman sat in a pair of chairs facing the

high single bed. Under a thin blanket lay Michael Kraus, fac
toward the wall.

He did not move at my entrance, but Kraus, anxiety pla
on his old, lipless Russian general's face, rose unsteadil
"Mr. Perkins. Here you are at last. Rachel and I came as soc
as we could after your call."

"How is he?"

Kraus wore a dark, full-cut business suit over white shi
and tie. His gnarly hands knotted together nervously as h
spoke. "They say he will recover fully, in time. He'll requir
some therapy, but—" He glanced down at Rachel, who w.
looking at the inert Michael with dark, mournful eyes. "Ther
were policemen here," Kraus went on in a rush. "They tol
us it was you who shot Michael. But they have witnesses wh
said Michael fired upon you first. I do not understand any o
this. And Michael refuses to speak to us, to explain."

I looked at the bed. Michael had not moved. Kraus looke
that way, too, and said, acidly, "Oh, don't let him fool you
He's awake all right. He simply doesn't want to talk to hi
own family."

I said to the inert form, "So do you want me to tell it, o
are you going to?"

Michael did not move, so I faced the others and recited th
facts as dispassionately as I could. The tailing, the chases, m
trick that cornered him in Sammy D.'s, the circumstance
under which I shot him.

Kraus looked horror-stricken as I finished, and Rache
looked like she was about to cry. "He ambushed you?" th
old man whispered.

"Yeah. I didn't even know who he was till after it was ove
And it wouldn't have made any difference if I had known. H
fired on me from under cover, and he meant business. No
only was I defending myself, but there were other people i
that store, too. Innocent people could have gotten hurt."

Kraus shook his head, muttering foreign words under hi
breath. "But why?" he said after a moment. "This makes n
sense at all." He walked to the bed and drew himself straight
"Tell me, Michael," he commanded.

The young man did not move.

Kraus stamped a foot and roared, "I demand an answer!"

Michael turned to us. His face was pale, his lips dry, bu
his eyes burned with the same kind of defiance I'd seen o

vin's just twenty minutes before. "I made a mistake," he
l. His voice was slurred and weak—probably mildly doped—
its coldness came through loud and clear.

Explain!"

I thought he was one of them. One of the supremacists.
came to your house, Grandfather, asking questions about
m. I thought it was very strange. I did not like his looks,
way he talked. I thought he might harm you."

So you got a gun," the old man said tightly, "and tried to
him. Is that it?"

I thought he must have a group!" Michael cut in. "I
owed him and watched him, hoping to find them."

And if you had, what would you have done?" Kraus asked.

Strike back," the kid whispered.

What?"

Strike back!" Michael said loudly. He moved under the
nket, wincing with pain.

Oh, Michael," Rachel wailed.

When we sit by idly," the young man said in a rapid
notone, "we encourage them. We condone them. We
ust act! We must strike back! An eye for an eye, Grandfa-
er. Surely, with your past, you see the need for this."

I see nothing," old man Kraus snarled. "Nothing except a
rorist, of my own blood yet. God in heaven, whatever led
u to this?" He shot out a hand, pointing at me. "Why this
n? What has he done?"

He is not a Jew," Michael said dully.

That does not make him our enemy! What I believe,
ichael, is that you read too much, and think too much. You
llow in the miseries of the past. And you have now created
sery in the present, for yourself and for others."

Talk! All you are is talk! Someone has to hit back!"

For what? For what happened in 1944? Where were you
en? Who appointed you avenger?"

We are still surrounded by enemies."

Certainly. But by adopting their tactics you have legiti-
ized them. You have lent them the credibility of our good
me and what we stand for. You have shamed us."

Michael closed his eyes tightly and turned his head again.
chel, weeping, turned and fled the room. I stood there
ent and uncomfortable. The old man's face was flushed beet
d beneath his short white hair, and he was shaking visibly. I

thought he might strike his injured grandson or have a h‍
attack.

"Come on," I said softly, "take it easy."

He glanced at me. "You have our deepest apologies,‍
Perkins."

"Well, nobody else got hurt. Believe me, I took no p‍
sure in hurting him."

Kraus faced me fully and gave one abrupt nod. The e‍
tion seemed to have added years to him. "I know that.‍
are a good man. Tell me, did you find the young man‍
were looking for?"

"Oh yeah, no problem."

"And he has been to see his father?"

"Just a few minutes ago."

A faint smile appeared. "That's very good. I hope he‍
some help," he said, giving his grandson a meaningful l‍
"Young men have too much to live for to get so wrapped u‍
hatred."

"Well, he'll be getting all kinds of attention, where‍
going."

"Good." Kraus put out a hand. "I wish you well."

I shook with him. "Take care, sir."

The door to room 8 in Detroit Receiving's surgical intens‍
care unit stood ajar. I pushed it open and entered. It w‍
small place, brightly lighted and all business. A big unit v‍
various LED readouts stood to the right of the bed, an‍
ventilator huffed and puffed to the left. A cluster of IV bot‍
hung from a chrome tree, their tubes snaking down to‍
body on the bed. Brian seemed small and helpless and‍
dead as Jerry, lying there. I felt a dull ache inside. Num‍
One was dead, the Skinheads were smashed, the Andels‍
were free, and Jerry had seen his son one last time, but th‍
could be no satisfaction, let alone gloating. At that mom‍
I'd have traded it all for the sight of Brian unplugging th‍
tubes and walking out of the room with me. Slapping bac‍
trading quips, celebrating victory. The way it's supposed‍
be.

Debra Clark stood close to the bed. She wore a gr‍
surgical smock, a paper cap over her hair, and paper slipp‍
over her shoes. I was dressed the same way, under orders‍

supervising physician, who'd also said that if I wasn't out
here in five minutes, she'd personally kick my ass down
stairs.

he room seemed full with the hum of electronics, punctu-
d by the rhythmic pumping of the ventilator. Debra's face
, dry-eyed, pale, and determined as she looked at me. "I
, wondering when you'd slink in here."

I've been around, taking care of loose ends. I kept checking
him. He was in surgery a long time."

Not a scratch on you," she observed.

Dumb luck, is all. Look, Debra," I said, walking toward
bed, "don't waste your breath. There's no way you can
ke me feel worse than I do already."

Oh. I see. You'd prefer that I sing you a chorus of 'Hail to
Conquering Hero'?"

pointed down at Brian. "He's the hero. Not me."

My father was a hero, too. Everyone said so." She looked
ay from me and talked to the wall in a small, bitter voice.
remember that so well, at the wake, at the funeral. They
ded my mother the folded American flag, and fired vol-
s of shots, and even flew the 'missing man' formation over
· grave, and people kept bending down and squeezing me
l saying 'Your dad is a hero. A hero. A hero.'" She took a
·p breath. "I guess I'm just out of step, but I'd rather have
ive, whole coward than a dead hero."

'Brian's going to make it," I said.

'No thanks to you."

I could have told her that Brian had stayed at the Bunker
ectly contrary to my orders, but I held my tongue. Debra
eded a target for her anger, and I was as handy a target as
y. She needed to let go, get it all out. She hadn't done that
t.

I looked down at Brian. His eyes were closed, his mouth
scured by the ventilator mouthpiece. "Hey. Kid."

"Shut up," Debra snapped. "He can't hear you, anyway.
ey said he'll be out till morning, probably."

I ignored her. To the inert body I said, "I suppose this
·ans you'll be taking a sick day or two."

Debra muttered something I couldn't make out. I was
·tching Brian's face closely, and I saw his eyelids quiver just
ghtly. "You know," I said, "you laying out like this poses

one hell of a problem. I'm not sure I can get Doug to s
up for work every day. Hell of a load for Randy and me

Debra turned and pushed at me, face enraged. "Get c

"Wait. Look."

She turned back. Brian's eyelids moved and raised j
notch. The corners of his mouth pulled back just slig
around the mouthpiece. Might have been a smile; I w
sure.

Debra bent and took his left hand in both of hers. '
Brian, sweetheart. You're going to be all right."

I watched as she bent down farther and kissed him.
room door banged open and the supervising physician st
in, dark face angry. "All right, people, that's it," she bark

I held up a hand. "Just a minute, doc."

Debra was kissing Brian and whispering to him, hol
his left hand. I saw the other one rise and open, palm
Debra straightened, watching Brian's face intently. I took
offered hand. "I'm still here, kid."

With barely perceptible pressure, Brian guided my l
over to his other one and pressed it against Debra's.
smile was still discernible around the ventilator mouthpi
Debra and I stared down at him, then looked at each ot

"Out!" the doctor commanded.

We ignored her. Gigantic tears abruptly welled u
Debra's eyes. She snuffled once, then buried her face in l
hands and began to weep. I let go of Brian and took Deb
my arms, and she huddled there crying like a little lost ch

CHAPTER 32

TUESDAY NIGHTS ARE DESOLATE at Under New Management, but there I sat anyhow, at the end of the bar by the service hallway that ran back to the bathrooms. I'd come by to talk to Bill Scozzafava. I wanted to tell him the whole story, just dump it all out. Then I wanted him to come up with one good reason why I shouldn't feel heartsick.

But Bill had called in, and the bar's owner, Eddie Cabla, was working the stick tonight. He served me without argument, but kept giving me beady little looks.

I knew he was working up a head of steam and would, any minute, swoop over and rag me about my tab. I sat there waiting, nursing a beer, smoking a cigar, listening to the good, gritty sound of Creedence's "Midnight Special" coming from the juke, as Harry and Darryl, the bar's only other patrons, abused the old Foosball machine in the corner.

At ten-thirty the big door swung open and Barb Paley churned in. "Evenin', boys," she called to the saloon at large, then motored over to me, eyes dancing, smiling brightly with her pink mouth. "Well, hi there," she said, sliding her tightly jeaned rump up on the stool next to me.

"Hey, Barb, what's shaking, kiddo?" I asked, trying not to sound lifeless.

"*Oo*," she said, peering at me. "You sound like ten miles of bad road, hon."

"Things happen, some days," I said, "and you just got to deal with 'em. Best I can figure, but there it is."

"I know exactly what you mean," she replied, waggling a finger toward Eddie.

I drank some beer. One more unhappy thing to do, and

243

now was the time. I didn't want to manipulate anyo
anymore. I'd done it to Brian, in what I figured was a go
cause, and look where he was tonight—while I sat here
Under New Management, unhurt, at least physically.

"Fact is," I said, "I'm calling it quits, babe."

"Oh," she said. "Oh, wow. You been there forever, too.

I looked into her eyes. "Not the job." I pointed at her,
myself, then back at her.

Eddie delivered her beer, then hovered within earsho
elaborately wiping at the bar. I caught his eye and gave him
poisonous look. He shrugged and slunk away farther.

Barb was watching me, eyes wide, mouth open. Sh
swallowed, cleared her throat, picked up her beer. "Ho
come?" she asked, voice small.

"I'll do the best I can here," I said. "Your feelings for me,
know how intense they are. And I'm grateful. I mean tha
Fact is, though, I don't feel the same going back your way

"You don't have to," she murmured. "I never expected—

"But it just don't seem fair or right, going on this wa
These things got to be out in the open."

She drank, then set the mug down clumsily. "I understan
I'm not even all that surprised. The other night, that had th
feel of good-bye to it."

I took her free hand and held it, looking at her intentl
"It's tough not to have hard feelings," I said. "If you do, I
understand."

"It does hurt," she admitted. "But hard feelings?" Sh
paused. "I really don't think so. No."

"Well, that's good, Barb. That means a lot to me."

There was just the slightest shininess to her bright blu
eyes as she looked at me, then past me. "Sooner or later
won't love you anymore." She let go of my hand. "But I
always like you."

"Me, too, kid."

She smiled. "See? We'll always have that." She turne
toward Eddie. "Barkeep! Another round for my pal ove
here."

"Uh-uh," Eddie said. "Not till Perkins clears his tab."

"I'm buying," Barb said.

Eddie, resigned, shook his head and reached for a mug.

"Make it a pitcher," I added.

CHAPTER 33

ARTICLE FROM THE *Detroit Free Press*, November 6, 1986:

SURPRISE WITNESS SHOCKS BUS-BOMBING TRIAL

Till yesterday, it seemed possible that Kevin Witkowski, the 18-year-old defendant in the firebombing murder last spring of six schoolchildren, might be acquitted of the most serious charges against him.

All that changed when Witkowski's mother testified in Judge Hathaway's Wayne County Circuit courtroom.

In ten minutes of dramatic, tearful testimony, Lynne J. Witkowski, a 42-year-old Westland homemaker, corroborated the testimony of another witness who heard her son admit that he firebombed the school bus.

Kevin Witkowski is a self-professed white supremacist who faces additional charges in the June kidnapping and attempted murder of activist Elliot Andelson and his wife. If convicted of the firebombing, he faces a mandatory sentence of life in prison without parole. . . .

About the Author

Rob Kantner is the author of *The Harder They Hit, The Back-Door Man*, winner of the Private Eye Writers of America Shamus Award for Best Paperback of 1986, and *Dirty Work*. His Ben Perkins short story, "Fly Away Home," also won a Shamus Award for Best Short Story of 1986. His short stories, many of them featuring Ben Perkins, appear regularly in *Alfred Hitchcock's Mystery Magazine*. Kantner lives in Detroit with his wife and three children. He is at work on the fifth Ben Perkins mystery, *Made in Detroit*.

DON'T MISS
THESE CURRENT
Bantam Bestsellers